PENGUIN BOOKS

COUSIN ROSAMUND

Dame Rebecca West was born Cicily Isabel Fairfield in London in 1892. She began to appear in print as a journalist and political writer as early as 1911 and was soon active in the causes of feminism and social reform. Her first book, *Henry James*, was published in 1916. Her classic study *The New Meaning of Treason* and three novels, *The Fountain Overflows*, *The Thinking Reed*, and *This Real Night* are all available from Penguin. A towering and brilliant figure in English letters for more than seventy years, she was a powerful and distinguished essayist, biographer, journalist, and novelist. Rebecca West was made Dame Commander of the British Empire in 1959; she died in March 1983 at the age of ninety.

COUSIN ROSAMUND

Rebecca West

With an Afterword by
Victoria Glendinning

PENGUIN BOOKS

PENGUIN BOOKS
Viking Penguin Inc., 40 West 23rd Street,
New York, New York 10010, U.S.A.
Penguin Books Ltd, Harmondsworth,
Middlesex, England
Penguin Books Australia Ltd, Ringwood,
Victoria, Australia
Penguin Books Canada Limited, 2801 John Street,
Markham, Ontario, Canada L3R 1B4
Penguin Books (N.Z.) Ltd, 182–190 Wairau Road,
Auckland 10, New Zealand

First published in Great Britain by Macmillan London Limited 1985
First published in the United States of America by
Viking Penguin Inc. 1986
Published in Penguin Books 1987

LIBRARY OF CONGRESS CATALOGING IN PUBLICATION DATA
West, Rebecca, Dame, 1892–1983
Cousin Rosamund.
I. Title.
[PR6045.E8C68 1987]   823'.912   86-25349
ISBN 0 14 01.0130 6

Printed in the United States of America by
R. R. Donnelley & Sons Company, Harrisonburg, Virginia
Set in Palatino

Publisher's Note

Cousin Rosamund consists of chapters of an unfinished novel by Rebecca West, in the sequence begun by *The Fountain Overflows* (published in 1957) and continued in *This Real Night* (1984). Rebecca West gave no title to the novel of which these chapters would have formed part, but it was felt appropriate to use part of the title she had given the series – *Cousin Rosamund: A Saga of the Century*. It was originally intended as a trilogy, but evidence has recently come to light that suggests the work might have been extended as a quatrain. Rebecca West's synopsis of the entire narrative is included in Victoria Glendinning's Afterword.

Cousin Rosamund

I

NOTHING was ever so interesting again after Mamma and Richard Quin died. I cannot think that any two human beings have ever been more continuously amused and delighted than Mary and I had been after Cordelia had married and we were left alone with our mother and brother and Kate. But though it was worse than hunger and thirst to miss the warmth and surprise and laughter we were excused the most cruel components of grief. We had not to ask ourselves where our dead had gone and to admit that their destination might be no further than rottenness, and to abhor the criminal waste. Our dead were like the constellations; we could not touch them but we could not doubt their existence. We knew them to be magnificently engaged, and though we could have wished an end of effort for them, we knew that their destiny was as native to them as music was to us. But we had to leave Lovegrove. Our house could have seduced us into the practice of magic; we might have re-created the past and inhumed ourselves in it.

So we let Alexandra Lodge to a composer and his violinist wife, who were glad of the music-rooms, and Mr Morpurgo found us a house in St John's Wood. Rosamund was still working in a Paddington hospital and would always have to be near Harley Street and the nursing-homes, and had taken a flat with her mother near Baker Street, and we chose that particular district because of all North London it is most like South London. There is the same repressed woodland against which the masonry just holds its own, and at night the shadows of the branches lie in as undisturbed a pattern on the quiet pavements, and the street-lamps shine with the same soft yellow submissiveness under the weight of the quiet night, and the

1

houses with their lit windows look like fortresses withstanding that night. We liked the long classical church that stands in a grove at the corner opposite Lord's, with a girl kneeling on a monument among the trees, her long hair falling over her humble shoulders, her face upturned in the ambition of prayer. If we were driving home together at night we often stopped the car just there and looked through the railings at her and walked the rest of the way home.

The house Mr Morpurgo had found for us was a union of two houses of the same period as our Lovegrove cottage, with the two coach-houses on each side enlarged into music-rooms. It was so large that Kate became a cook-housekeeper and had another servant and a charwoman under her, and often wore a black silk dress with a huge cameo brooch at her throat which made her look like the housekeeper in a Brontë novel. This delighted Mr Morpurgo, who approved our habit of wearing Empire dress in the evenings and had filled our rooms with exquisite Empire furniture and had chosen for us Empire stuffs for curtains and upholstery. Because our dresses were like stage dresses, and because the home he made for us was like a stage setting, we were in some danger of becoming more like objects than people. But indeed we had no choice about the clothes. When we first grew up clothes were quite beautiful, though they were nearly always too bulky, and they had a feature which helped all women to look elegant. Sleeves were then very elaborately made, by seamstresses who never touched any other part of the dress. They were cut in several long strips, which were designed to lend every arm favourable proportions. But as we grew through the late twenties, there rose the star of Chanel, who imposed on women the most hideous uniform that they have ever worn. The gravest of us had to go about by day in straight skirts up to our knees, with wide belts round our hips, and our heads buried in flower-pot hats that covered our foreheads, and by night in dresses that were as short and even more ridiculous in form. They were cut with square necks and plain shoulder-straps, so that at a dinner-party the women might have been sitting round the table in bathing-dresses; and they were often embroidered all over with heavy beads, so that the hem formed a sagging frill above the calves. But there was an alternative for the evening in the *robes de style* which Lanvin had just invented for Yvonne Printemps, and though these were eighteenth-century dresses

2

their acceptance gave us permission to wear our Empire dresses. These were indeed beautiful, and old photographs show that they gave Mary's swan-like beauty its full opportunity; and though I cannot look at my photograph and see it any more than I can look at my own image in a looking-glass, I can see that in those dresses I was an interesting spectacle. But to be that, and only that, often seemed a misfortune which continually threatened Mary and myself, though we were always rescued from it by a certain force.

I remember very well a certain autumn day which illustrated our plight. I had gone to Paris for a most interesting concert at the Salle Gaveu. I had taken the opportunity to play some solos by the Russian composers, but the main purpose of the evening was the first performance of a concerto by Louis Besricke, who was still working in the Debussy and Fauré tradition though he indulged in greater technical complexities. Everything was paid for by a Jewish millionaire and we had more than the usual number of rehearsals, as many as even the composer wanted. On the first day it appeared that the interpretation of the concerto which I had evolved while working on it in London was not correct, and the bearded composer stopped me and said, smiling, '*Mais, mademoiselle, vous êtes trop mâle pour mon frêle œuvre.*' The orchestra looked at me with that tender and gracious amusement which a group of men can feel for one woman, though it is rarely felt by one man for one woman, and never by a group of men for a group of women. After that it was all a laughing and sentimental adventure, the rehearsals all seemed to last no more than ten minutes. But not only the rehearsals, the whole of each day was lovely. I used to leave my hotel early before anybody could telephone and walk along the rue de Rivoli, with the first tarnished chestnut leaves blowing over from the Tuileries Gardens, and along the Avenue Gabriel, past the Jockey Club and its tamarisk hedge, always looking through the trees at the Théâtre Marigny and wishing I could have been an actress as well as a pianist, just for the sake of playing at that theatre, and going up to the Arc de Triomphe by the Champs Elysées, then still noble and intact, with not a shop to be seen. There was even still standing that countryish house on the right, where great dogs were always softly belling behind the high garden walls; it had the air of a place where people were living out the long consequences of some violent action. I would go to my

3

practising and my rehearsal inspired by this local excellence; and when I had done with music for the day the city refreshed me again, though not so much as in my lonely mornings, for my French contemporaries alarmed me. After the First World War it had become fashionable in Paris to be silly, and an appalling measure of French intelligence and spirit, and even some of its classical spirit, was devoted to establishing silliness as a way of life. Men loved men and women loved women, not because there was a real confusion in their flesh, such as Mary and I often noted in those with whom we worked, but because a homosexual relationship must be nonsense in one way, since there can be no children, and it can be made more nonsensical still. Where there can be no question of marriage there is no reason against choosing the most perversely unsuitable partner; and often we met gifted Frenchmen who took about with them puzzled little waiters or postmen or sailors, flattered and spoiled but never acclimatised. But it was much more frightening that people of talent injected silliness into their whole structures by taking drugs; for Mary and I, like most artists, knew that drink and drugs were our natural enemies. It was hateful, too, that many of the people who were most heartless in their loves, who took up these young men and gave them luxury and loneliness and a disinclination for their own natural habits, and who smoked opium or took morphine or cocaine and became walking nightmares of malice and fear, often became Roman Catholics, and made no effort to purify themselves, though that effort would not have cost them much. From our childhood we had known the nature of darkness, we had seen Papa abducted by ruin, and we knew that all these people could have stopped what they were doing at any moment, had they chosen. These people thought we were held back from them because we knew less than they did, though of this we knew more, but they were friendly, and they liked our playing, so they asked us to their parties, and these were beautiful. They lived in huge white empty rooms, often with great windows opening on the night sky and the spread lights of the city. I went to two such parties on that visit; but I took greater pleasure in my visits to the villa by the Parc Monceau where the parents of the composer of my concerto lived.

Monsieur and Madame Besricke were like a thousand other people in Paris, and they were apparently undesirable. They were superbly handsome but deformed by pretensions. The

4

old man, who had inherited a moderate textile fortune and had been a poet and critic of some note, wore a Rembrandt beret and disarranged his classical features by an expression intended to convey that he was wise, witty, sceptical, tolerant, kindly and sensual; and his thin wife dyed her hair mahogany red, and wound scarves about her, and sometimes cooed and sometimes tapped her words on her teeth, to show that she possessed an immense range of emotions. It was as if Anatole France and Sarah Bernhardt had gone on living after the essence of them had died, growing old and dusty in the practice of their personal tricks. But running parallel with this stale affectation was a brilliant current of joy and honesty. They saw justly what was beautiful in their son's music and character, and what had been beautiful in their other two sons who had been killed in the war. They saw what was beautiful in my work, and if I went there in a new dress they would make me stand in the light and told me what it did for my looks. They gave me the use of their memories, and through them I know what it was like to listen to the lectures of Ernest Renan at the Collège de France, hurrying to get there as if it were a theatre, and I went to many parties given long before I was born. And they constantly cried out to each other the names of places in France which it was imperative I should visit. The hours I spent with them were somehow like those evenings at home when we sat round the fire and ate chestnuts after we had washed our hair. It was warm and happy in these rooms which were crammed with the litter always collected by nineteenth-century French celebrities, that porridge of Genoese velvets and chips off Gothic cathedrals and Persian rugs and Renaissance bronzes and Limoges enamels and wild-beast pelts and North African silverwork and Greek marbles. Though most of these objects lost their quality and meaning in this hugger-mugger, the Renaissance bronzes and the Greek marbles remained themselves. The old people loved to see me taking pleasure in them; but did not know that for me they held an ironic significance. These bronzes and marbles were made in the likeness of the gods and goddesses, whom the ancients allowed to exist on condition that they understood everything men do and enjoyed everything. Now such images of tolerance adorned only the homes of the innocent aged; and in the white rooms of contemporaries, where the most bizarre transactions were carried on, the only permitted ornaments were those neutral objects, cacti and seashells.

The concert was a success. I was not too *mâle* for my composer, and the next morning it was settled that I would play the concerto during the following year in London and Berlin and Vienna and New York and Boston. The composer had not been sure about it till the performance; he owned with a smile that he had not till then fully understood what he meant by it. The conductor and I smiled back at him, and then exchanged a secret smile, for neither of us had greatly liked the concerto till suddenly, as the music we made was heard by us and the audience, the truth was manifest in the hall. Then we had a lovely lunch at Voisin's, with all sorts of rich things like foie gras that I would not have dared to eat before the concert, and then I took a lot of chrysanthemums to Monsieur and Madame Besricke, and we drank cherry brandy in little coloured glasses and they said that I was to come back soon, and then I took all the flowers I had been given at my concert to an old pianist who was dying in a house in Passy. Then I went to the hotel and put on an evening dress, so that I could go straight from Croydon to a concert where Mary was playing the Emperor Concerto. Then I was driven to the airport, too fast, for it was late, and people gave me more flowers and waved goodbye. As the plane mounted and the earth swung round us like a billowing skirt, I was filled with thirst for the sight and sound of my mother and my brother, and nothing that had happened to me in Paris retained any value. The one interesting phrase in a *concertante* by a worthless German composer ran through my head again and again, until we crossed the Channel, so quiet in that soft and sleepy blue that is the sea's autumn wear, and it pierced my breastbone that I was travelling along a low passage of uninteresting air between the earth where my mother's body lay and the outer space where I felt her to continue. But I could not feel my brother's presence anywhere, then or when the bus took our plane-load from Croydon through South London, which was darkening, and we would have been going downstairs to see if we could help Kate with the supper, had our lives not perished.

The concert at the Queen's Hall was not good, except for Mary's playing. The conductor was bad, someone of whom it had always to be recalled that he was English and that England was having a musical renaissance and he had bored the orchestra. But Mary was superb. She was not strong enough to play the Emperor Concerto by strength; no woman except Teresa Carreño ever was. But she had a substitute for strength in her absolute justice. She had the timelessness of the great player, she played every note with the thought of every other note she and the orchestra were going to play strong in her mind. When she played it was with deep regard for that which went before and for that which went afterwards, though the logical connection would be hard to state in words. Both she and I had more than once had a mystical apprehension of how a musical composition would sound if time were annulled and the notes were heard neither in succession nor simultaneously; but the experience, which was quite incommunicable, was hard to remember when it was most needed, because the conscious intellect got in the way, and she was better at remembering it than I was. She had also to perfection that kind of accuracy, of slavery to the text, which is the sublimest liberty. When Beethoven wrote two slurred notes, she played them and was free as he was in his exercise of his choice to write those notes slurred instead of staccato, and she did not fall into the trap of altering them to something that pleased her own ear better. Her integrity of attention to the composer and the taste which governed the application of her technique made her the nonpareil of our generation. In the hot and draughty assembly of this world, she was the candle which did not gutter.

She played better than I had played in Paris, and without any of the adventitious aid which came from a composer saying, 'Mais, mademoiselle, vous êtes trop mâle pour mon frêle œuvre,' and making the orchestra smile. Her single source of power was her musical genius. She derived no encouragement from the contacts with people which her art involved, and the fact that some of her audience took pleasure in her beauty annoyed her. She felt that she was obliged to appear physically in public in order to play, but that they had no right to take advantage of that necessity to pass a judgment on her for which she had not asked. It did not matter that the judgment was favourable, she still felt it a violation of her privacy. But she knew that her admirers meant no harm, so she was polite and even charming to them when they waited for her after concerts. When I got to the artists' room I found her already white with strain, there were so many people there, and when I got rid of them by telling them that we had to go on to a party and had been asked not to be late, there were other people out in the street with autograph albums, two or three of whom were tiresomely talkative. I could have managed them by thinking vaguely of them and of something else at the same time, but Mary disliked these contacts so much and so feared to show it that she had to give her whole mind to them.

In the car I squeezed her round the waist, and said, 'Cheer up. You played magnificently. And certainly the only good part of a concert is what goes on inside the hall.'

She said, 'I do not like it even inside the hall. I hate the people clapping.'

I was upset by the passion in her voice. I said, 'Well, we would both feel quite awful if we gave a concert and people did not clap.'

Mary answered, 'I know that. But I would much rather nobody was there.'

'Don't be an ass,' I said. 'Think of all the poor little people who save up to give concerts at the Wigmore and the Steinway halls, and get very much what you are asking for, and don't like it at all.' She said nothing, and I repeated to the darkness of the car, 'Don't be an ass.'

She still did not answer and I was suddenly afflicted with the suspicion that she was extremely unhappy. I said, 'Don't you feel like going on to this party? I don't mind going straight home.'

'No, we are nearly there, we may as well try what it will be like,' she said. 'Though, of course, it will be like any other party.'

And so it was. A great house in Prince's Gate had been filled with light and flowers and handsome and favoured people, wearing beautiful jewels and clothes, and we were welcomed to it, with the warm but conditional welcome that is given to guests who are invited because they are celebrities but who were born outside the clan. Usually we were safe, but we had learned, ever since we first met rich people through Mr Morpurgo, how bitterly some of their women resented the introduction into their world of women who could do all they did and could do other things as well and were praised for them. Their bitterness was strange, for it was such as Mary and I might justifiably have felt against them because their child-hoods had been compact of comfort and security and ours had been poor and dangerous. But it was pleasant when all went well. Such parties were suffused with a soft and golden light, which accorded with the champagne we drank, or rather held in our glasses, for though it was pretty, we never thought champagne very nice. There were wonderful jewels to be seen, and this always delighted us, for Mamma had taught us to appreciate them from our earliest childhood, her long keen flight of eye had found whatever was precious in such jewellers' shops as were in Lovegrove, and we had pressed our noses against the dingy shop-windows to see an emerald, a ruby, a diamond, and note its real fire; and as this was a very grand party the men were wearing their orders, those superb inventions, which truly look like the marks glory leaves when it lays a hand on its own. There were mounds and walls of flowers, and a chirrup of talk, like a wood at dawn, which suddenly stopped and gave place to a silence threaded with music. Our hosts were elderly, so we had the pure felicity of hearing the mindless and gymnastic voices of great opera singers bearing aloft without effort arias that performed the true operatic function of transforming crisis into enjoyment. At this time one was likely to come off worse at parties given by middle-aged or young hosts, for they were apt to entertain their guests with German *Lieder*, which seemed to us to have taken a wrong turn ever since the days of Brahms. Too often the solemn continuance of the accompaniment after the voice has ended might be the awed whimper of a bloodhound to whom a larger bloodhound has just described one of its deeper experiences. But that night we had a great tenor and a great soprano who showed us love and despair magically made brilliant and innocent as fountains and fireworks by Verdi and Rossini.

Everybody was nice to us. First we met an old man with a beautiful blue ribbon across his shirt front who took a liking to us and asked us questions about ourselves, where we lived and what we did with ourselves, with a kind and worried smile as if he would like to buy some people like us to keep as pets, but thought he would never be able to cope with the problems of management. Suddenly he told us how he had gone to the opera in Vienna when he was a very young man and had seen the beautiful Empress Elizabeth, and then a duchess called him away. It was like talking with a court card. Then we met people whom we knew well, a young peer and his wife who lived in a long grey colonnaded house set naked in a park under the wild skyline of the Wiltshire downs, the ordained setting for a tragic drama, and were framed to act tragic parts, each having wide eyes and parted lips that seemed to have been forced open by the sight of disaster, but who were in fact happy people who found satisfaction in little exercises of taste and simple skill, in dyeing feather boas found in an old trunk and using them to garland the less remarkable of their family portraits, or in spraying the leaves of the shrubs round their house with gold and silver paint when they gave a party. Among these pastimes they included the giving of chamber music concerts, which is perhaps not so surprising as it seems, for though chamber music insists more often than any other kind of music on the tragic interpretation of life, it has for the most part been composed and performed under the patronage of persons who were seeking only to be amused. But this couple's conception of amusement was of such a nursery kind that it was surprising to find that it embraced Beethoven's later quartets, and to find oneself, when one had taken part in them, regarded as if one had discovered some clever trick like a way of painting a modern chimneypiece so that it looked like a Victorian Gothic organ. They were with some friends of theirs: a photographer who made all his sitters look like fairy princesses, a fat old lady who wrote fairy tales, a painter who was a famous cultivator of dwarf daffodils, a young man who made copies of famous doll's houses, and a physicist and his wife who bred a very small kind of pony. One of them told us about a very funny house he had found in a Spanish sea-port, built by the schoolmaster, which was even funnier than the famous house in the South of France built by a postman.

We were having quite a nice time when we were approached by two of those young men, to be found at all parties in that decade, who had got very drunk because they felt they were going to be killed in the next war. They were wrong, of course, for when the next war came they were too old to fight, but their error was strong enough to force them to actions which now makes it surprising that they were not killed in peace. Their flushed faces were cleft by wide grins showing their well-cared-for teeth, and we knew that they were going to be horrid. One was the nephew of the host so it was difficult. Their method of averting the holocaust they saw before them was to lean over the fat old lady who wrote fairy stories, and say, in unison that must have been rehearsed, 'Ah, Aunt Fanny! Still sleeping with that handsome jobbing gardener? Such fun behind the raspberry canes on those warm drowsy afternoons. . . .'

As we hurried into the next room we were faced by Cordelia. She was looking very pretty, she was indeed one of the prettiest women at the party. She raised her eyebrows in surprise and said, 'Oh, we did not expect to see you here! Are you all right, do you know anybody here? How nice your dresses are! Alan must see you, but he is talking to his chief now. See, I am wearing the necklace you gave me last Christmas, doesn't it look nice?'

We were too slow in answering her, for the sight of her had chilled us for a minute. We forgot that she had been exorcised of her demon, we feared that she would look at us with that white stare, which asserted that we were doing something disgraceful.

Hurt, she put up her lovely little hand and raised the necklace from her skin. 'Am I not wearing it the right way?' she asked, her eyes going from one to another of us.

'Of course you are,' I said, 'we just didn't speak for a minute because you are so perfect.'

'You look as well as anybody here,' said Mary, 'and better.'

'Ah,' breathed Cordelia, happily, and she added, with solemn zest, 'We dined with the Possingworths first.'

We said warmly that that must have been wonderful, but a flash of shrewdness passed over Cordelia's face. She recognised that we had either never known or had forgotten who the Possingworths were, and that we were making an effort to please her in which there was no grain of spontaneity. We saw her swallow and gaze about her, frowning slightly, at the marble pillars, the mirrors and gilt plasterwork. It was her ambitious look, that we knew so well from our childhood. She was saying, 'My sisters may be horrid to me, still I was poor and I am here in this great house, just as they are.' But her lip trembled.

Mary said, 'Forgive us if we are hardly here, we are shattered. Something horrid has happened,' and she told Cordelia how the two young men had insulted the fat old lady, and Cordelia was mollified. But I was not quite sure that she really trusted us. She knew too well Mary's resourcefulness. Alan came up to us and was agreeable, but Cordelia fell silent, and I could see her remembering all the occasions when she had gone out to meet us with affection and we had stepped back coldly. She was suffering. But I could think of no way to comfort her, for I was wondering why she was suffering, whether it was because she loved us and needed our love, or because she was angry at our refusal to admire her perfection. I found myself in a desert. Why should she love us if I were capable of that doubt?

A colleague of Alan's brought up his wife to be introduced to Cordelia, a peeress who was an amateur of music. She said, 'Oh, my dears, so wonderful, that third movement,' and, though our group need not have dissolved, Mary and I passed on through the golden humming glow of the party in another room. There we saw Lady Tredinnick, who had taken us to that horrible first party and had made it up to us so often by letting us see her flowers in her Cornwall garden. She was standing alone, looking up at a picture, and we hurried to her quickly and happily. But when she turned round she was not like herself. Always before, although she was now elderly, evening had been able to annul that masculinity to which her earlier life in the desert had tanned her spare body, and she had put on full femininity with her jewels and her grand clothes. Tonight she looked like a man dressed up as a woman. But she had hardly given the evening its chance. She was less elegant than we had ever seen her, her hair was carelessly pinned up, and one or two of the fasteners under her arms were undone; and when we spoke her name and she turned round her face was not varnished with the imperturbability which a woman of her kind normally assumes at a party. She looked wretched; and she did not look less wretched when she saw us, but slowly said something approving about us, as if she were telling us not to misunderstand her inability to be as we had known her. Then she paused and became wooden. To break the silence, we spoke of the picture at which she had been staring. 'Is it a Poussin?' asked Mary. 'We heard they had a Poussin.'

'Is it a landscape?' asked Lady Tredinnick. She turned round and looked at it as if she had never seen it before. 'Yes. That is their Poussin. There is one very like it at Chatsworth, but that is far finer.' Again she ceased to speak, and under her tiara, between her ear-rings, over her necklace, the face of an ageing proconsul brooded in despairing meditation, in which we could have no part. At that moment a young man came up to her and said, 'Do you remember me, Lady Tredinnick? I know your sons very well,' and we were made still more aware that our old friend had changed. She greeted him politely, but what she was saying could hardly be heard, and she looked like an angry and important old man, offended by the violation of some principle he had defended in Parliament and tested by huge administrative practice. For a second or two we stood suspended, while she inaudibly followed a gracious routine from which her face dissented. Then her voice entirely failed her. She tried to force some sound through her lips, and when it would not come she made a disclaiming gesture and strode away.

I said to the young man, 'Lady Tredinnick must be ill,' and was astonished to find that he was not merely disconcerted, he was so horrified that the sweat was standing on his brow.

Mary said, 'If we go downstairs, could you get us a drink?' He took the chance to recover, and as we stood at the buffet he told us in a pleasant and even tone, though his eyes searched our faces in incomprehensible anxiety, of a journey he had recently made in Italy. It was time for us to go home, and he saw us politely to our car, but as he turned away in the darkness we saw him take out his handkerchief and draw it across his brow.

'What do you think was the matter with her?' I asked.

'She was not ill,' said Mary, 'she was full of vigour. She was unhappy.' We were silent for a moment, then Mary cried out, 'But where was Nancy? She should have been at the concert. She told me she was in London. She always loves to hear me playing the Emperor Concerto, but she did not come and see me afterwards. She always comes and sees me afterwards.'

I said, 'I hope she was not too upset when she went to see her mother with Mr Morpurgo last week.'

'Oh, poor Nancy,' murmured Mary, and, a few minutes later, she said, 'Look, we are nearly at the church, let us stop the car and walk home. I know it is late, but I cannot bear being in the car.'

After the chauffeur put us down at the corner opposite Lord's we stood for a time looking through the railings at the Grecian church, the dark tilted tombstones under the trees, and the girl kneeling in prayer on the monument. Mary said, 'We are so helpless without Mamma. Nancy was safe while Mamma lived, and Aunt Lily too, and Queenie. And Mamma would have known what was the matter with Lady Tredinnick. But we can do nothing for them.' She pressed her forehead against the cold iron and was silent for a while, then burst out, 'What good are we?'

'We are quite good pianists,' I said.

'And what good is that?' she asked. 'What good is that to Nancy? Or to Aunt Lily? Or to Queenie?'

'Don't be an ass,' I said. 'Mamma wanted us to be pianists, so it must be some good.'

'She may have wanted that just out of pity,' she said, 'to keep us busy because we were not able to do what she and Richard Quin were doing. But no. Of course I am being foolish. Everything in real music has something to do with Mamma and Richard Quin, and almost nothing outside it has anything to do with them. By making us play she lifted us up into their world.'

For a time I was caught up in the memory of certain passages of music, and when my attention went back to her she was saying, 'I love those people we knew with Mamma and Richard, I cannot care about anybody else very much. Can you?'

'Yes, of course I do,' I said. 'I like lots of people. Don't you really like anybody at all?'

'Yes, but not much,' she said, and pointed at the praying girl on the monument. 'Not more than I like her. Not as much.'

'Oh, I like people a great deal more than that,' I said. 'And I think, I think, I could like them much more still, if they would ever let us get near to them.'

'I do not want them closer to me,' said Mary. Again we were silent and then she said, 'What a pity it is that all of the people who want to marry us do so in such an unfriendly spirit.'

It was true that our suitors fell in love with us very quickly, before we could get to know them, and proposed to us angrily, as if we had stolen something from them and this was the only way they could get it back, and were so infuriated by our refusals that they never spoke to us again and glared at us across parties. We sometimes thought that we would not mind marrying musicians, but we could not have married anybody of our own grade as concert performers, we would never have seen them, and the people below us always thought of us as stars and were tiresomely respectful. Really we had long known that we need not think of marriage.

'I wish we could have Rosamund to live with us,' I said. 'It would have been lovely if she could have lived with us and been our secretary instead of Miss Lupton, though she's all right.'

'I have thought of that so often lately,' said Mary. 'But of

14

course it is impossible. Her nursing is as important as our playing.'

'Anything she does must be more important than anything we do,' I said. 'I know quite well she should not come down from her level to ours. But one can't help wishing it would happen.'

'There is nothing really lovely left for us to wish for except that,' said Mary. 'Nothing as lovely as it all was when Mamma and Richard Quin were alive.'

There was no point in looking any longer on the churchyard and its trees and tombstones, its kneeling stone girl. We went on our way along the empty streets, between the dark houses, from yellow street-lamp to yellow street-lamp. I said 'Oh, Mary, tell me this. Something worried me in the plane this evening when I was flying from Paris. Richard Quin was called Richard Quin after his uncle who was called by his first and second names to distinguish him from another Richard in the family. But who was that other Richard?'

'Papa told me,' said Mary, 'but I was quite little, I do not remember.'

'Cordelia might know,' I said.

'No, she will have forgotten entirely. She wants to forget everything to do with our family. She will get flushed and look stubborn and say that she never heard that there was any reason for calling him by both names, and that she always thought it was a great pity, it must have struck people as so odd.'

'Well, it does not matter,' I said. 'But it makes one angry that so many things happen and drift away and we cannot lay hands on them again.'

We had turned the corner of the street in which we lived, and went along between the dark houses, kicking at the chestnut leaves that had fallen thick during the day. 'How bright and cold the stars look,' said Mary, 'though it is only autumn. And how queer it is that if you or I were coming home, and the other of us were playing, the music would sound sad as we heard it in the street. Whatever the composer might have meant it to be, whatever we might feel as we were playing, it would sound sad. Do you suppose that the ultimate meaning of music is sadness? But, of course, you do not know the answer to that better than I do.'

The closing of the door made a loud noise in the sleeping

15

house. There were many letters on the hall table, but we did not like letters. None of the people we loved wrote letters if they could possibly help it. We knew that Kate would have left in the drawing-room milk in an electric saucepan and some sandwiches so we went in there, just to make going to bed less bleak. As soon as we turned on the light we cried out in pleasure and hushed ourselves as quickly. Rosamund was lying asleep on the sofa.

'Shall we wake her?' I whispered.

'No, no,' said Mary.

She was lying as Richard Quin had lain that day, years ago now, when he had fallen asleep while Cordelia had gone out of his attic to speak to Nancy and then come back to go on scolding him about going to Oxford. She had as suddenly withdrawn from the waking world, without time to arrange herself. Half of her long corn-gold hair was still held by its pins, half of it streamed in its tight corkscrew curls over the wine and silver satin stripes of the sofa, and her dark green dress was rucked up round her tall and splendid body. Her face was calm, as his had been, but there was the same sense that she was running and winning a race in some co-existent world where dimensions are otherwise, and it is possible to win something like a race without moving from the same spot. It had not seemed right to watch Richard Quin as he slept, and it seemed wrong to watch Rosamund now. A word might have escaped her parted lips which would have taken us so far from our world that we would not know how to comport ourselves. It was strange to have those closest to us so enmeshed in distance.

We shut the door and debated. 'She came early. Kate gave her supper on a tray, I saw the tray on the hearth-rug. Do you suppose she meant to stay the night? Probably not. But she must stay now. It is too late for her to go home. We must see if the spare room is ready. And we must find her a lovely nightgown. Oh, if we had not stayed so long at that silly party.'

But the bed in the spare room was turned down, and one of the fine lawn nightdresses that Constance worked for her was spread on it, and the ivory brushes and combs we had given her as a Christmas present the first year we had made real money were lying on the dressing-table. There was nothing for us to do except choose the better of the two vases of late roses that were in our rooms and put them by her bed.

'Oh, how I want to wake her up,' said Mary. 'But we must not.'

16

'Still, we can sit beside her,' I said.

But she woke of her own accord as soon as we went into the room again. She opened her eyes and looked about her with a look of voluptuous pleasure, and rubbed her cheek against the satin cushion, and put up a finger to stroke it. Then she saw us and said sleepily, 'What is it, that wonderful scent?'

'Lanvin's *Pétales Froissées*,' I said. 'I brought some home this afternoon but we have lots, you shall have this bottle I brought.'

'I should love it,' she said, and her heavy lids fell again. 'The wards don't smell of anything from Lanvin,' she murmured, and drowsed again. 'Where have you been?' she asked, with her eyes shut. 'Was it a nice house and were the people lovely and were the jewels and the dresses beautiful?' We told her, and she murmured, 'It must have been heaven.'

'You must come with us to a party again,' said Mary.

'Yes, there is one next week given by some people we know well enough to ask if we can bring someone else,' I said. 'A good party, too, Carlton House Terrace, a view over St James's Park.'

'You darlings, I will try to come,' she sighed. 'It is the staircases I love, they look as if they went up and there was floor upon floor, and something gorgeous on each. How I would like to be a duchess.' She seemed to sleep again, then started up. 'Mary, Rose, I must wake up and tell you why I am here. It is about Nancy.' She began to laugh, taking out the pins that were left in her hair, and letting her curls fall about her shoulders. 'Oh, you will not believe it.'

'She is all right then?' said Mary. 'I was so worried because she did not come to my concert.'

'But she did,' said Rosamund, 'you need not be worried about her at all.'

'Of course it is all right now you have come,' I said. 'Here is a box of marrons glacés, eat them all, you are worth it.'

'These are the best marrons,' said Rosamund, 'the ones that have just a touch of ginger in the syrup. I probably will eat them all. But about Nancy. You cannot think how happy she is. You know that look she has always had, as if one were seeing her through water, as if she were floating an inch or two below the surface of a river? It has all gone, she is like anybody else.'

Mary and I cried out together, 'She is going to be married.'

'Yes, to the one man whom it is possible for her to marry,' said Rosamund. 'She came to tell me tonight, after she had been to your concert.'

'But why did she not come to tell me?' asked Mary. But she added meekly, 'It is natural that she didn't. Lots of people seem to feel that they cannot tell us things.'

'You know, Nancy has been far more unhappy than any of us guessed,' said Rosamund. She was speaking smoothly without a trace of her stammer. It was not often so. 'She has always wanted to be married, of course. She should be married, too. She would be better at it than any of us. She will know as we will not what to do when her husband is out all day, she will do small things about the house that he will like when he comes home. And she has all that dammed-up affection which she has given to us, and which it is hardly fair for us to take, since to us she has, of course, been only an afterthought.'

She said it lightly and put another marron glacé in her mouth. Mary exclaimed, 'Oh, no.' We both wished Rosamund had not said it, but we knew she was right when she said, 'Compared to what your Mamma gave her, we have all given her only our afterthoughts. But that is not quite the point. What has made her life in Nottingham so difficult is that Uncle Mat and Aunt Clara have given her so much of their attention. They have tried so hard to be good to her, and all in the wrong way. It appears that in Nottingham many families are not so well off as they once were. They used to make all that window-curtain lace and now the people who liked it buy cretonne and chintz instead. But Uncle Mat is very well off, and he is the managing director of a big engineering firm, and controls a department store that has branches in several Midland towns, and Nancy, you know, has quite a lot of money. She is not rich-rich, like the people who give the parties you go to, but she and her brother will each have nearly a thousand a year. They got all their father's money, though he left most of it to Queenie. She could not benefit by his death. There is a law which sees to that. How terrible for her to marry a man for his money and to kill him in order to get her freedom, and get neither her freedom nor his money.' She meditated for a while, stroking her golden head and looking into the distance, then went on with her story. 'Everybody in Nottingham knew who Nancy was. Or she thinks they did, which is the same thing. And indeed Uncle Mat and Aunt Clara thought so too, and dealt with the matter in their own way. Nancy is quite sure, from something that happened, something so horrid that she would not tell me what it was, that Uncle Mat told people in Nottingham about Nancy's money, and let it be understood that any young man who married her would not only get a well-to-do wife but would probably get a good job either in Uncle Mat's engineering firm or in the department store.'

Mary covered her face. I said, 'I remember Papa saying, when Uncle Mat would not ask Aunt Lily to come with Nancy to Nottingham, "You might as well expect a bull to be kind to a horse." This is how a bull, poor thing, might try to be kind to a heifer.'

'Nancy saw that,' said Rosamund. 'She is very fair, very forgiving. But it was even worse for her than it appears. For she understands herself much better than you might think, and she knows quite well that if someone said he loved her she would want to believe him so much that she would not be able to disbelieve him, she would not be able to stop herself from marrying him. Oh, Mary, Rose, this part of her story is horrid because she was ashamed to tell me that. Mamma was in bed, so she was alone with me, and we were just two stupids together, but even so she could bring herself to own that to me. How hateful it is that it is thought disgraceful for women to want to be loved, which only means they want to love.'

Mary said, 'That proves how evil human beings are,' and knelt down by the electric fire and spread out her shivering fingers to the glow.

'Poor Nancy, she sees it all so clearly, not only the general thing, the disadvantage at which any of us might find ourselves. And of course that is not the worst that could happen,' she interjected suddenly. 'Give me another marron glacé, how I love that wheaty sweetness, and that gentle tang of ginger. But to get back to Nancy. She knows just what it would be like to make the kind of marriage Uncle Mat had tried to contrive. She has seen herself and her husband together, in a new house where they might have been happy, had it not been for what her mother had done. She has felt him take her in his arms, and then suddenly shudder and freeze, so that he draws her no closer and she is there, stuck there. And she has heard herself saying, "What is the matter, dear?" and has heard him answer, "Only someone walking over my grave." Poor Nancy stood in my room and said, "Wouldn't that have been awful if that happened? And I used to feel as if it was happening all the time, as if it happened again and again, as if it were the only thing that could ever happen to me, and indeed ought to happen to me." So you see, any marriage she could have made in Nottingham would have been impossible, particularly as Queenie will be released next year. That she had foreseen with the deadliest particularity. She has imagined a husband who would welcome Queenie, but only for that thousand a year, that job in the engineering firm or the department store; and that would have been blasphemy. And of course we could do nothing. We could not have helped. What could we have done,' she asked us, turning on us her huge, bright eyes, and smiling almost as if our common plight amused her, 'now Mamma and Richard Quin have gone?'

'Nothing,' we admitted.

'But now we need not worry any more,' said Rosamund. 'It has all come right. It is the river which has done it really. And of course Aunt Lily and Uncle Len and Aunt Milly, who are getting more like the river the longer they live by it, they just flow on. You know Nancy has been down at the Dog and Duck a great deal this year. Uncle Mat and Aunt Clara have their son and his family back from the East and mercifully there is not really enough room in the house to put all the children and the two amahs unless Nancy goes away. So she has been down on the river nearly all the summer, and she has got quite good at handling a boat, and one evening Uncle Len asked her to take somebody over on the ferry, and when she got back she dropped an oar into the water, and then, you know what she is, she lost all confidence, she felt she had done something very stupid and would never get it back. So she called out for help, but nobody heard, and then a man who was just going into the pub ran down the lawn and turned the boat round and picked up the oar. So she told him how sorry she was to have troubled him, but she had thought that the oar might sink, and then he sat down in the boat and explained the scientific principles which make an oar apt to float instead of sink. He is the science master at that big secondary school about five miles off, and he has taken lodging for the summer with that old Mrs Crump, the widow who has that nice red-brick house with an apricot tree all over it. They sat in the boat until it got quite dark. Then Aunt Lily got anxious and came out and called for Nancy.

'I bet she said, "Alice, where art thou?"' and Mary suggested, 'And "Has anybody here seen Kelly?"'

'That's just what she did,' said Rosamund, 'and the man asked her what the words of "Alice, where art thou?" were. He likes to know everything. They went into the house together and he had a pint but left most of it, and went off home and then came the next evening, and the next, and every evening, and it was always for Nancy, and she liked him very much. He tells her things like why oars float, and she finds it lovely. Then she got terribly upset, because she thought he did not know about her mother and he would go away if he knew. So she shut herself up in her room and cried, but of course Aunt Lily knew why. It is quite dreadful how Aunt Lily understands everything about women who want to get married.'

'The poor, poor darling,' murmured Mary.

'So she went to Mr Morpurgo, who happened to come down there just at that time, if, of course, she did not send for him. But you know how often he goes there.' Of late years Mr Morpurgo had become a familiar of the Dog and Duck. His wife had died, and he was suffering the peculiar resentful unhappiness of a widower who is left alone, too old to remarry, after a long marriage during which he has always felt lonely; and his children greatly offended him. They were in full retreat from his Judaism and would have none of it, even to his love of art; and he did not understand that when he turned the glazed eye of his connoisseurship on them they became aware just how much they would fetch in the open market, and could not forgive him. Something had gone wrong a long time before, and he could not go back and put it right, though he had often asked Mamma how he could do it. So quite often he drove down to the Dog and Duck in his splendid Rolls-Royce, and he and his chauffeur, who was getting old too, would take out their rods and go into the meadow next the garden, so as to get away from the ferry, and take their stand on the bank and watch the sliding black glass of the tree-shadowed river, till the evening came up on them, and they went up to the pub and listened to what the people in the bar were saying, and then had supper, and drove back to Belgrave Square. 'So Mr Morpurgo,' Rosamund went on, 'called at Mrs Crump's and waited till the science master came home, his name is Oswald Bates, and then he told him all about Queenie. And, do you know, the science master had known about it all the time? Mrs Crump had told him. Not horridly, sympathetically. And it seems, just think of it, that there is a reason for that. The village says that if Mrs Crump is a widow she has only herself to thank for it. It is funny,' said Rosamund, with a flash of that ruthlessness I had sometimes noticed in my

21

mother, 'what odd things sometimes turn out to be useful in the end.

'Well, then Mr Morpurgo and Oswald went for a long walk by the river, and you know how that water flowing by makes one talk, Oswald told Mr Morpurgo all sorts of things about himself, and it seems that Nancy has a special value to him because of Queenie. He belongs to a very respectable family. His father was an ironmonger who kept things for farms in a market town, is quite well off and retired and is a preacher for a religious sect called the Heavenly Hostages, it is a sect that if you repent of your sins you become a child of heaven and then you are a hostage and God will treat the world better because you are there, and he has two aunts who are deaconesses, but his mother was dreadful and drank, and he has always been terribly ashamed of her. She was once actually arrested by the police and his father had to go to court and pay a fine, and everybody in the district knew, and it was hateful for him at school.'

'Surely there isn't much hope for humanity,' I said. 'It is always hateful for people at school when they need kindness.'

'But there will be much more happiness for Nancy and him because of school,' said Rosamund. 'Listen to what he told Mr Morpurgo. They moved several times to make a fresh start, in villages outside the market town, but then that meant that the father was away for long hours and sometimes the boy was alone with his mother when he saw that she was going to start drinking. He and his father lived through the whole thing again and again, always with the same end, and he felt dreadfully degraded and he was very much afraid that when he grew up he would be a drunkard too, and be a misery to everybody and perhaps to his own little boy. So he took up science at school because he heard somewhere that science proved that heredity was nothing and that environment was everything, but by the time the poor boy had committed himself to being a scientist he found that if science has a definite opinion on the subject it is that heredity is much more important than environment, so he was very much upset.'

'You ought to know about science since you are a nurse,' said Mary, 'but isn't that very silly? How can they tell? How can they tell whether heredity or environment matters most unless they get people who had only heredity and others who had only environment?'

'The only reason one believes in it at all is that sometimes it works,' said Rosamund. 'Anaesthetics do send people to sleep so that surgeons can operate on them, X-ray photographs really show what is happening inside people. But I am not thinking what I am saying. It is quite easy to take X-ray photographs, but very few people can read them.'

She looked away from us at an empty corner of the room, and her profile was cold, condemning. 'Oh, a lot of it is nonsense,' she said, even with disgust. Then went on, 'But anyway, science did not comfort Oswald as he had hoped, and even though his mother is dead now he doesn't like mixing with people and that is why he always takes lodgings far from the school. Then one late afternoon – and you will see, it is all right, he is not just making use of Nancy, there is real love in it, the choice, the choice that is made by something deep down in one which will not be satisfied by anything else. He saw her down by the landing-stage, and he thought how lovely her fair hair was, and he went near her to see if she was pretty and he thought she looked like an angel, and he wondered how he could get to know her, and he felt it was no good, she would not want to know him. But two days later he came down to the bar for some cigarettes, and he saw her standing beside Aunt Milly and he realised that this girl who looked like an angel was the daughter of Queenie, who was a murderess and far worse than his own mother. And then two days later he came down to the bar for some more cigarettes, really to see Nancy, and it was then that she was down in the ferry-boat and lost her oar and called for help. So you see it was all perfect.'

'Oh, yes,' we breathed, 'it is perfect.'

'And after that Mr Morpurgo managed everything almost too beautifully,' Rosamund went on. 'He told Oswald that he was right about Nancy being an angel, and also how wonderful Aunt Lily was, and he found out that Uncle Len and Aunt Milly never served anybody who had too much, and they went on and on talking, and Mr Morpurgo told him how he had known lots and lots of people whose parents drank and none of them ever did. Then he warned Oswald that Queenie would be coming out next year, and he said he knew that, Mrs Crump had told him, and he would like to help Nancy over that too. So they walked right on to the next lock and had to telephone for the Rolls, and they came back great friends, and it was all settled. But then they went and sat in the garden and went on talking about how lovely it was all going to be, and they forgot all about Nancy, until Aunt Lily who was watching them through the bar window could bear it no longer, and sent down the chauffeur to tell Mr Morpurgo that there was a telephone call from London. When she heard it was all right she scolded him, and kept him with her, and shouted to Nancy through the door, and told her that she was wanted to fetch somebody on the ferry, and of course when Nancy was crossing the lawn Oswald went to her, and it was all right. They will be married at the end of this school term, so that they can have the Christmas holidays for the honeymoon.'

She dropped her head back on the cushion, she closed her eyes and lay loose-jointed among her golden hair, smiling.

We had never in all our lives heard her talk so long without stammering. Like the Thames her story had flowed on, reflecting in its fluency the images, fusing and easy and on their way to the sea, of the people we had previously seen as isolated and static. We longed to chatter about it and discuss what we would give Nancy as wedding-presents, but we leaned over her and asked if she would like to go to bed. She shook her head. 'I am just thinking of it all,' she said, 'I will go when you do.' She had another marron glacé, and we heated up the milk and drank it, and I said, 'But you haven't told us when you heard all this.'

'Because Nancy told me tonight,' said Rosamund. 'Oh, I am stupid, I leave out what is important. There is still a great deal to be done. Listen. She took Oswald to the concert tonight. She has talked to him perpetually about you and Richard Quin and your Mamma and your Papa. You are the glories of her life. So she took him to the concert tonight, and brought him on to see me afterwards.'

'And not to me,' said Mary, desperately, only because she could not keep the words back.

It was strange. Though she seemed colder than me, she minded more than I did this invisible fence round us, through which people did not trouble to break.

'There is a reason,' said Rosamund. 'Nancy is still terribly afraid. She really sees no reason, since her mother murdered her father, why anybody should not murder her. She knows that your family chose not to be murderous, that you were kind to her mother and to Aunt Lily and to her. But that Uncle Mat and Aunt Clara were kind to her, but murderous about her mother and her aunt, and even murderously unkind to her too,

24

when they planned her marriage, makes her feel that all kindness may break down. She is now quite afraid that your kindness may break down over Oswald.'

'But why?' I asked. 'She must know we will be happy because she is happy.'

'It is not what is called a good marriage,' said Rosamund. She repeated it, smiling, tracing the lines of her lips with her forefinger, 'A good marriage. Well, that is confusing her. She is not very clever. She is not even as clever as I am. Uncle Mat and Aunt Clara will be angry. Oswald's father has enough money, but he was only a country shopkeeper. Nancy knows that you have become very prosperous and she is afraid that prosperous people are all of the same sort.'

'So they are,' I said. 'But we watch ourselves all the time.'

'You see, she has some sense on her side,' said Rosamund. 'You do see? She has perceived that riches corrupt, she is taking note of something that is true, and since she could not have protected herself from that corruption, and knows herself, she does not see how you can keep clean. But she is not judging you unkindly for this failure to understand which she takes for granted, she simply sees you as having fallen victim to an occupational hazard. But there is something more painful to her than that. She knows that you all have beautiful taste, that some things are in your eyes right and others wrong. And she is afraid that you will think Oswald awful.'

'But why? How could we?' we asked.

'Because he is,' said Rosamund. 'Quite awful. It is not only that he looks awful, which he does. His ears stick out and he wears spectacles in a hostile sort of way, as if he had put them on all the better to eat you with, and Nancy says that she is going to try to get him to wear bicycle clips only when he is going to ride a bicycle. It is that he is awful, he has no manners, he contradicts everybody as soon as he sees them, the minute he meets you he will tell you there is nothing in music, and he will start explaining something to you. But he loves Nancy and Nancy loves him. To her he is never awful, and of course he is all right inside, it is only that he is frightened and ashamed. Also there is much of his father and mother in him, if he were not an atheist he would be a preacher of the Heavenly Hostages, and there is something abandoned about him, it is easy to think of him shutting his eyes and throwing himself down a high place, his mother threw herself down into drink,

25

he has thrown himself down into hatred of drink and shame at his mother and love of Nancy. Oh, it will be all right.'

'It does not seem quite as right as it did at first,' murmured Mary.

'You make him sound dreadful,' I said.

'But it is all right, as things go,' answered Rosamund coolly, 'and that is just what Nancy guessed, that you would judge him dreadful. She did not talk all this out plainly, of course. But she brought him to our flat, and he told me that I was wasting my life in nursing, he would bet anything I liked that I spent fifty per cent of my time looking after wretched creatures who never would have come into the world if only there was a sound system of eugenics. And he thought Mary was hand-some but all that orchestral music was nonsense, he would rather hear a simple folk-song straight from the heart of the people. Nothing nice till he had been with me for quite a long time. Then he went away to spend the night with a college friend at Acton, and Nancy very timidly said that she was not sure how you would like him, because he had such very different tastes, and it turned out that she has worried a lot about it. Indeed,' cried Rosamund, 'she is afraid that she must choose between you and him. And of course she has chosen him. And that is right.' She looked at us suddenly with her blind look. 'She must go with her husband. That is more important for her than going with you.' Her voice sounded almost harsh. 'But she feels it terribly that she may have to lose you. She was so distressed about it that I gave her a sleeping-pill and put her in my bed and came along to see you tonight.'

'But if he is going to be nice to her, we will do anything to please him,' said Mary. 'Though I wonder how we can do it. I do wish there were only the people one can talk to and the other people that one just has to make signs at and offer curries to. It is the cases in between which are difficult.'

'Well, think of the only peaceful moments we have with the men who want to marry us,' I said. 'They happen when we talk to them about what they do. We will buy little books about science and find out what we can ask him to explain to us.'

'I knew you would not let her go,' said Rosamund, 'and she will still need you. She will always need you.' As soon as the words were out of her mouth she fell asleep.

Again I thought of how Richard Quin had suddenly slept, that afternoon long ago, so short a time before he had gone to war, and my heart contracted. Mary's anxiety took another form. She asked incredulously, 'Can she have gone to sleep as quickly as all that?' and stood up to have a better look at her. But Rosamund's breast rose and fell steadily and Mary said, 'But of course she is not ill, she is so strong, she should outlive us all. It is just that she has had a long day. When is it that they get them up? Some frightful hour like half past six. And she has worked all day, and then goes home for her twenty-four hours leave, and she comes along to tell us this.'

'And it is a good thing she did. We might have been awful to the little man if we had just met him with Nancy and he had been silly about music.'

'Yes, if we had not known about his mother we might have thought Nancy would be better off without him and shown it,' said Mary.

'But how good it is,' I said, 'to think of Nancy, who has always been on the margin of things, not because she deserved to be but because she just was, having a page to herself. Having a husband, a house of her own, children. Though perhaps she won't. People often don't nowadays. I'm sure Cordelia would if she could.'

'None of us will have children,' said Mary. 'Our bodies will be pulled down into the earth and the thing will go on in a different way.'

A distant church clock struck the hour, and a minute later it was struck again by the Empire clock on the chimneypiece. Afterwards its tick-tock sounded loud and slow in the quiet room. When Rosamund sighed in her sleep and murmured, 'No, oh, no,' we heard her clearly, and moved softly to the windows and closed and bolted them, looking up at the stars, which now seemed solemn but not sad. The constellations had slid across the sky since we came back to the house; it had been Orion that was above us as we walked, now Canis Minor was overhead. I thought what a long day I too had had, in my easier mode, and I found that I now could think with pleasure of all I had done in Paris. It was always so when Rosamund was with us, she found whatever we had for the moment lost.

27

II

THE DOG AND DUCK was at all times suffused with a sober and realistic contentment. The three people living there would not have claimed that life always went well for everyone, but they were conscious that for them it had gone much better than might have been expected. Uncle Len felt great satisfaction because the local police sergeant was his best friend, and Aunt Milly and Aunt Lily were extremely pitiful to any draggled and rejected old woman who came their way. But when we went down that Saturday we found the little pub bathed in a rosier contentment. It would have been impossible to paint it justly without recourse to such symbolic devices as court painters used in celebrating royal weddings, without representing cupids supporting garlands above the thatched roof and Hera and her nymphs giving epithalamic blessings from a barge on the river. It was a very warm day, warmer than any we had had in the summer months, and we sat with Uncle Len and Aunt Milly and Aunt Lily and drank tea at a rustic table on the lawn, while the river, full-bodied with autumn, bore past white limbs of driftwood and foundered tapestries of gold and scarlet leaves. Time had made Uncle Len red and impassive, a blood-houndish, meat-eating Buddha, and Aunt Milly had silver hair which made her feel she was like a French court lady in the coloured pictures given away with the Christmas numbers of illustrated magazines, and she too had grown solid to her base. Their gratification was stately; but Aunt Lily was still bony and fair, her ugliness continued to make its tactless allusion to the prettiness of a golden and slender young girl, and her joy was shrill and chattering.

'It's no use,' she told us, 'hoping that the lovebirds will be

28

back soon. They're looking at nests near the school and, bless them, they'll take their time about it, billing and cooing,' she added, in fidelity to her style. 'Oh, I couldn't be more pleased. Just because Queenie was unlucky when she tried it, there's no reason why our family shouldn't get married like other people. There, I've let it out.'

'Hush yourself,' said Uncle Len, heavily, 'hush yourself.' And Aunt Milly said, 'Yes, indeed, you aren't even sure. How do you know your pa and your ma weren't married?'

'Well, we looked everywhere when the house was sold up, and we never found no lines, we didn't find any lines,' said Aunt Lily, 'and Pa was supposed to be away a lot because he was a railway worker, but I never saw him wearing a peaked cap. And there were lots of things. But I wasn't lying, you two kiddies, when I used to tell your papa and mamma that we were brought up particular, because we were.'

'You were brought up right, and your mam deserves great credit for it and we'll leave it at that, if you please,' said Uncle Len.

'If things are bad it doesn't make them any worse to go over them sometimes,' said Aunt Lily. 'Mercy of God! What's that down in the water just by the landing-stage?'

'Wood,' said Uncle Len. 'A log of wood.'

'I wouldn't be too sure,' said Aunt Lily darkly, rising to her feet and rushing down to the water's edge.

'You can count on Lil seeing a dead body afloat once every twenty-four hours until the river goes down next spring,' said Uncle Len.

'Well, she loves a bit of life,' said Aunt Milly.

'Hark at that, girls,' said Uncle Len. 'She loves a bit of life so she's always looking out for dead bodies. I live with a couple of queer ducks, I do.'

'It's nothing,' Aunt Lily shrieked from the landing-stage.

'Look at her running back as if she were a slip of a girl,' said Aunt Milly.

'They're healthy enough, my two queer ducks,' said Uncle Len complacently, drawing on his pipe.

'It was a bit of furniture, actually,' said Aunt Lily, throwing herself down in her chair. 'Looked like the back of quite a nice bedstead, funny what gets into the river.' She lifted her hand to arrange her hair with an exact copy of the gesture which a beautiful woman, whose hair and hands were her particular beauties, might have permitted herself, when she felt the need of a compliment. Uncle Len surveyed her over his pipe with tender horror. In all the years that they had lived under the same roof he had never forgiven providence for having made her as she was. 'Like a camel,' his eyes compassionately said, 'like a camel.' She continued, 'Mind you, girls, there's to be no church wedding. Oswald doesn't hold with it.'

'Silly, I call it,' said Aunt Milly, jerking her thumb at the church-tower above the tree-tops. 'When there it is just next door, couldn't be handier.'

'It's hard on the child not to have a white veil and a train and all that,' said Aunt Lily.

'Give over,' said Uncle Len. 'If there'd been a church wedding Uncle Mat and Aunt Clara would have snaffled it, and then you'd all have had to go up to Nottingham and you'd have been as happy as if you'd been locked in the fridge.'

'Oh, I know it's all for the best really,' agreed Aunt Lily, smiling into the drowsy autumn sunlight, 'but you must let me have my little grumble.'

So the morning passed by, as pleasantly as could be. We learned that Nancy and Oswald were so much in love they could not see out of their eyes, that with what she had and they earned they ought to be very comfortable indeed, and that he was bound to get on, he was ever so clever, as well as being a thoroughly decent young fellow; that for our mid-day dinner we were going to have boiled silverside and dumplings followed by quince and apple tart; that nobody could rightly say what the love-birds would like for a wedding-present, it depended on the nest they picked; and that it was going to be all right about Queenie, Oswald was willing to let Nancy have her at their home for part of the year. 'For the rest of the time,' said Uncle Len, his jowls hanging heavy, 'or all the time, if need be, we'll be glad to have Queenie here.' Through sudden tears Aunt Lily called on us to marvel at his goodness. 'He might be a brother to me and Queenie, the way he's always been determined to make things right for us,' she said, and she went on to explain that it would really be all right, for though Queenie had lost nearly all her remission time for tantrums, she was a changed creature, and there would be no difficulty about her doing a bit of sharing the nest with the young people. But of course it was to be hoped that they would have a family. 'First a girl and then a boy,' she recited. Then, just after we had stopped drinking tea and had begun to drink sherry, Nancy and Oswald came down from the house. They were both indeterminate in appearance, but their joy made bright vapours of them, for they were smiling at everything, as if they were a little drunk.

We ran to the happy phantoms and kissed Nancy, who looked a little frightened. Were we so awful, then, to people we did not like that she had reason for her fear that we would be horrid to Oswald? She said, 'Oh dear, I wish we had known you were coming this morning, it's dreadful that we weren't here!' But Oswald spoke up firmly, 'Well, first things first, my dear. We couldn't have stayed in even if we'd known. What we got to do is to find a house.'

'Yes, Oswald, but this is Mary and Rose,' said Nancy, laughing gently.

'I guessed that. I know Mary, I recognised her from the concert. Music means nothing to me, so I had to look at you,' he said, meaning it quite nicely.

'We think you're very lucky,' said Mary. 'We've a special reason for knowing what Nancy is worth, for we were friends when we were children, then she went to Nottingham, and we did not see her for years, and we missed her all the time.'

'It was the most wonderful day when you came back,' I said. 'Do you remember how Cordelia and I looked down the stairs at you?'

'Yes, and your Mamma was so nice to me,' said Nancy. 'Oh, Oswald, I do wish you had known their Mamma, it is a shame she died.'

Oswald showed no sign of sharing her regret that he had not known Mamma, and no sign either of wanting to know us, but since Rosamund had given us the key to his character he had engaged our hearts. He was no more than Nancy's height, and though he was in his thirties he had the round head and snub nose of a small boy, and the stance and restless eyes of a small boy surrounded by grown-ups whom he did not quite trust. He was what was called in our family a Haowseholder; he did not drop his h's or his g's, but to him a house was a *haowse* and a mouse was a *maowse*. It is an endearing form of the Home Counties accent, and in him it was made specially endearing by the childish ring in his voice. At once he knew that it mattered very little that he did not make the expected polite remark or made an impolite one. He would learn. The less important kinds of knowledge would come to him, for he already possessed the others that were more important. When we parted from them to take up our hats and coats to Aunt Lily's bedroom, we heard Nancy say to him, 'Aren't they wonderful?' and he answered, not mechanically and not in doting, but with grave appreciation of all she was, 'Not wonderful like you.' Their house would be like our house in Lovegrove.

Of course he would be a bore at times. His way of boring was strangely like Aunt Lily's, though the terms of reference were different. Just as she could not ask where anybody was without adding, 'Alice, where art thou?' and 'Has anybody here seen Kelly?' so he could not refuse a second helping of silverside without saying, 'No, had my protein, thank you,' or eat salad without muttering through the lettuce leaves, 'Ascorbic acid and vitamin C,' nor take a plateful of quince and apple tart without defining it as 'enough carbohydrates to carry me through till next Friday'. He had, moreover, too urgent a need for periodic defiances. The elders at our table were conceiving this day as golden within, sunshine without, and warmed from within by rather too rich and filling foods, and glorified for ever in the heart by immersion with their beloved young in a river of affection and laughter. Aunt Milly and Aunt Lily would have liked to say afterwards that they couldn't have hoped to have a nicer lot of kiddies round them, and that one or other of us had been such a scream that they had nearly died. It was unfortunate that when Oswald and Nancy were asked whether they had found a house they liked he could not have answered simply that they had. But he felt it to be time he washed his mental face with a good lather of denunciation. So he began to speak angrily about the pictures which the present owner of the house had hung on its walls. He said he didn't see the sense of pictures anyway and these were those modern things that weren't like the things they claimed to be and wouldn't be serving any purpose if they had. In the drawing-room there had been that great glaring yellow thing that was everywhere nowadays, it was in the art room at his school. Van Gogh's Sunflowers, he harshly defined it, looking very hard at Mary and me. It was evident that he hoped to embarrass us. Making sounds on a piano seemed to him unnecessary, and putting colours on canvas also seemed to him unnecessary, and he thought that people who persuaded the community to reward them for these nonsensical activities would all band together and feel indignation if any one of their number were threatened with exposure. We tried to look as uncomfortable as we could, but that was not enough.

'Van Gogh's Sunflowers,' repeated Oswald.

'Have a bit of Stilton,' said Uncle Len.

Oswald shook his head and repeated, 'Van Gogh's Sunflowers.'

We had a bit of Stilton; we could always have no supper when we went home, Kate knew we never ate much when we had been to the Dog and Duck. Uncle Len remarked that he had hung on the walls of this very room pictures of Fred Archer and Morny Cannon and Danny Maher and young Steve Donoghue, and Sceptre and Pretty Polly, those being the two loveliest horses he had ever seen, and if he'd had the great hulking originals hanging up instead of the pictures poor old Fred Archer and Morny Cannon and Sceptre and Pretty Polly would be smelling something shocking by now. At this Oswald crinkled up his eyelids as a child does when it is suddenly confronted by the deliciously ridiculous, and he laughed as loud as any of us. But Aunt Lily, who was in so sentimental a state that she could spare no time for laughter, shot out her long and bony neck and asked him whether, though he was going to have the original Nancy by him till death did them part, he wouldn't love to hang on his walls a portrait of her, showing her just as she was that afternoon. 'Oh, that,' he smiled, turning to refresh his eyes by another sight of Nancy, 'that would be something different.' That settled part of our problem. 'Our wedding-present!' cried Mary and I. 'A portrait of Nancy.'

It took a minute for them to understand we meant it. 'Do you mean that just anybody can have their portrait painted?' asked Aunt Milly cautiously. 'Well, what's the Royal Academy for?' asked Aunt Lily stoutly, and Nancy said with a dogged sadness, 'No, not me, it's absurd,' and Oswald said judicially, 'It's not a bad idea, but none of your modern artists, please,' and Uncle Len, looking critically at Nancy, 'It's a damned good idea.' Then Aunt Milly and Aunt Lily squealed simultaneously, 'In your wed—' and silenced themselves, but not before Nancy had heard them. Something stony and remote came into her eyes; Mary and I found afterwards that both of us had concluded that she was reminding herself always to do what pleased Oswald.

The afternoon went quickly. Because it was fine there might be some teas, though it was so late in autumn, and Aunt Milly baked some scones, while Uncle Len sat in an armchair, brooding over the intellectual treat which made all his winter weekends happy, a weekly journal consisting solely of arithmetical and mathematical puzzles. It made his summer week-ends an agony of baulked desire; it was published on Saturdays and often the bar and the meals and the boats kept him so busy that it was not till Monday that he had leisure to consider how many schoolboys there must have been if in some improbable circumstances the eldest got three and threepence more than the youngest. Aunt Lily took us up to her room and showed us what she called 'quite a nice letter, really,' from Uncle Mat, by which she meant that it was really not a nice letter at all. It avoided crude statement, using the phrase 'under the circumstances' several times to achieve the same end; and in effect it said, 'We have done everything for Nancy, and she has chosen to go off and stay with you, whose sister murdered her father, and find a husband under your roof. But because she is her father's daughter, we hope she will be happy, and we will give her a handsome present and come to the wedding, and will accept her husband as one of the family.' Jealousy howled round the paper on which the graceless letter was written. But Aunt Lily said, 'Harry being such a simple soul, it must all have been hard to forgive.' There was horror in her eyes. We knew our father and mother had respected her. She had retained her horror of the deed her sister had done, though her love for her must have importuned her honesty to forget it. 'Not,' she added as she folded the letter and put it back in its envelope, 'that the silly sod has made much of a try at forgiving it, I should say.' At that moment we heard the low bay of Mr Morpurgo's huge car, and we hung from the window to greet him, and then ran downstairs and told him of our idea for our wedding-present and asked him to find a portrait-painter. His eyes rolled in their pouches and he said with an air of abnegation, 'Someone whose work they will like. I will try.'

Nancy and Oswald came out of the pub while we were talking and they were having a mild quarrel. He was saying, 'If you make me take off my bicycle clips as soon as I get into the house, of course I put them down and of course someone moves them, and then I'm told I've lost them.' But a casement window opened, Aunt Milly's plump hand held out the clips, her voice said, 'Just where you left them,' and the window snapped shut, but it opened again, and Aunt Milly advanced her bust and said, 'Glad we found them, sonny,' and closed the window gently. The incident was passed over as if it had not occurred, and he rode off to his lodgings, to bring back his bank book, Nancy told us, as she took us up to her room. There we all three lay down on the wide Victorian mahogany bed, Nancy in the middle, and she told us in her flat voice all about Oswald and his drunken mother, and he had no fear at all of marrying her, and how unselfish he was, and how specially nice he was when they were alone. As she talked we raised ourselves on our elbows and looked down on her as she lay in the trough of our shadows, twisting a lock of her long hair round a finger and covering her mouth with it, smiling at us dreamily and secretively; and we were aware she was different, really different. For us who knew her well she had always had a particular charm which was delicate and faintly tart, like the taste of raspberries; it was as delicate as it had always been but more manifest. She was like a woman who, born poor, has always worn her good clothes only on Sundays, but suddenly realises that she is rich and wears them every day. But presently she fell silent and we saw that tears were standing in her eyes. We did not know what to say. Not having been in her situation, we could not be sure that she might not now want to laugh and cry for reasons outside our understanding. But she drew back to what we understood very well, for she smiled brilliantly and began to talk of that first summer of the war, when she had stayed with us on the Norfolk coast. 'Though Richard Quin was so slender he grew quite tall,' she remembered, and, looking round her, said, 'He would be too tall for this low room if he were here. Oh, how Oswald and he would have liked each other.' It was true. We were pierced by a sense of our loss, of our inferiority. He would have rifled the little man's nature with the skill of a burglar, and would have fingered and enjoyed the goodness and talent which we only knew to be there. Our talk rambled on, and because the house in Norfolk had a pretty staircase we fell into a discussion about stair-carpets, which went on until we heard the whirr of Oswald's bicycle bell, and he called up to her window, and she instantly forgot us and ran out of the room and down-stairs. We liked that very much. A short phrase in the middle of the keyboard, repeated three times, with half a bar's rest between each repetition, followed by a descending scale in triplets.

Wondering if we might write an opera when we were older and there was less to do, we went out into the garden, and brought a man and his wife over in the ferry, and then got into the rowing-boat and took it upstream for half a mile or so, leaning back and cleaving the strong autumn water and wishing we could live in the country, and then we suddenly became panic-stricken about our hands, and turned the boat and drifted downstream till we were at home again. We went indoors, because it had started to rain quite heavily, and found Uncle Len and Mr Morpurgo very grave over a puzzle, silent and immobile, yet not inert. It could be felt that inside the pendant bulk of each a small but active spirit of calculation was running round and round, unable to find egress in a solution. All of us tried to help, even to the two people whom we had brought over on the ferry, but it was far too hard. Then Nancy and Oswald were with us again, each with an arm about the other's shoulder, and at the sight of them Uncle Len and Mr Morpurgo pushed the puzzle magazine off the table into the shadows, and smiled at them with a guilty benevolence. But indeed, though Oswald was so nice, it would have been unbearable to see him work out a puzzle one could not solve oneself. But anyway Nancy and Oswald did not notice, they announced that they had been working it out and they thought that they could afford the house they had liked so much that morning. There was a long discussion, and the man we had brought over on the ferry, who was by now having tea with his wife in the next room, put his head in at the door and announced that he couldn't help overhearing, and he wondered if he could be of any assistance, as he was a local surveyor. Then we heard how much less than the agent's price the owner would probably take, and what was wrong with the house and what was right, and there was some joyful affectation of embarrassment when he told us that there was an easement in the garden which sometimes gave trouble, and Aunt Milly asked, 'What, a public one?' in a tone of horror which revealed her misunderstanding of the term. We sat entranced by this professional store which disclosed that a house had its intense and eventful personal life being loved or unloved, cherished or neglected, the subject of both courtship and panderous mis-representation, the victim of aggressions which left such

36

wounds as a troublesome easement, and periodically rejuvenated by espousal to such young couples as Nancy and Oswald. But suddenly Aunt Lily looked out of the window and cried that the storm was over and there was a marvellous rainbow, and we all went out into the garden. Over the scarlet and gold tree-tops to the east a pale green light pretended that this was the end of the world; and on this light was painted the huge childish toy which said that it was no such thing. With exultation we bade each other note that there was a double arc, for everybody believes that two rainbows are better than one, and we were delighted by the scene's abandonment of the ordinary, for the river was now bottle-green and its foam was white as snow, and the driftwood shone with iridescent lambency. Aunt Lily was saying something about the suitability of a rainbow to an occasion when a family, and a family it really was, though few of us were related by blood, but then blood was no thicker than water, there never was a sillier saying, had gathered together to celebrate a most hopeful occasion, when we became conscious that we had an odd visitor.

A tall old man was striding down the lawn towards us. He was wearing a long black overcoat, almost as long as a dressing-gown, his silver hair was bare, and he carried a staff that might have come out of an allegory; as he drew nearer his appearance became more and more of a public performance. His black eyes flashed under prodigious silver eyebrows which it was to be supposed he would take off after the show, and his nostrils were dilated as if to store breath enough for a long passage in blank verse. 'Len, have you anything on you if he wants a subscription?' murmured Aunt Milly. We all saw him, except Nancy and Oswald, who were sealed in contemplation of the rainbow, and we gave him the indifferent and amiable greeting which people in an inn give to a newcomer, telling him that his body has a right to be there and he can do as he likes about asking company for his mind. That welcome was one of the reasons why we liked being at the Dog and Duck, but it seemed as if the old man were disappointed at the way we were taking him.

Oswald turned to me, saying, 'See what I mean? Granted I can't see a rainbow all the time. But I can see it often enough, as often as I can reasonably want to see a rainbow. So what do I want with the picture of a rainbow?' His eyes went past me to the stranger, and vacillated. Then he said, pluckily enough, 'Hello, Dad.'

All of us, even the surveyor and his wife, expressed happy surprise. Aunt Lily cried in ecstasy. 'Now a family we really are.' The old man answered politely; but though his face was impassive it suggested strong disapproval, as the blank sun intimates its power to burn. As he had crossed the grass he had suggested some sort of performer below the level of actual performance, like the buskers who entertain theatre queues. Now he seemed more elevated and more alarming. I recognised in Oswald the perpetual childishness of a child who has grown up in the shadow of a parent made formidable by an exceptional destiny. I had often recognised it in Mary and myself. If we had not been able to play as well as we did, our mother's art, a fiery ball in the sky, would have consumed the marrow in our bones.

Oswald said, 'Oh, Dad, I wish we had known you were coming,' very much as Nancy would have said the same thing to us. There was the same primary and sincere expression of goodwill, 'We wish we had been able to prepare a welcome for you,' and the same secondary and even more passionately sincere expression of fear, 'We wish we had more time to build defences round our delicate happiness and protect it from your excessive and inconsiderate force.'

The fear was reasonable. Mr Bates said ominously that he feared he was intruding. Uncle Len answered serenely and comprehensively, 'That you aren't. Any relation of young Os here is welcome, and the house is full of cold meat,' but Mr Bates was not appeased, and looking very hard from Nancy to Mary and from Mary to me, asked coldly, 'Son, which is your young lady?'

'Why, Dad, I would have thought you could have guessed,' said Oswald happily. 'This is Nancy, of course.'

Mr Bates said sadly, dipping deep into the bass, that he would have liked to embrace Nancy as a daughter, but there was an obstacle.

For a minute we were all quite still. We sweated with terror, for there was manifest in this man the indecency of the prophet. We knew that there was nothing he would not say, in words which could not be forgotten. Mary and I moved towards Nancy, and stood behind her. Oswald's arm was close round her waist. The surveyor and his wife began to walk away, but Mr Bates arrested them with a gesture and a splendid, still deeper note. 'Stay,' he bade them. 'I want all the kith and kin of these young people to understand my views.'

'But this gentleman is not a relative,' said Mr Morpurgo. 'He is a surveyor who has very kindly been giving the young people disinterested advice about a house they are proposing to buy. Good evening, sir, we are very grateful to you and your wife.'

'And who are you?' said Mr Bates.

'My name is Morpurgo. I am a close friend of Nancy's mother, a remarkable woman.'

'And so she is,' said Uncle Len.

'You'd throw anybody in the river who said she wasn't, wouldn't you, Len?' said Aunt Milly, using her hand as a lens in an effort to see the last traces of the vanishing rainbow.

'I would,' said Uncle Len placidly.

'I would throw anybody into the river,' Mr Bates remarked ferociously, 'who said that any woman was not a remarkable woman, and any man not a remarkable man, for God made every one of them and Jesus Christ gave His life for every one of them, and the Holy Ghost is within every one of them.'

'Well, you can't say fairer than that,' said Uncle Len.

'So I will not approve my son's union with Miss Nancy unless he consents to have it blessed by God the Father and God the Son and the Holy Ghost in the true spirit,' Mr Bates continued. 'So let us have no nonsense about a registry office. The Foundation Chapel of the Heavenly Hostages, Ilfriston, Essex, it is going to be, December 14, eleven thirty sharp, Brother Clerkenwell and me officiating.'

Oswald took a step forward. 'No, Dad.'

'Yes, son,' said Mr Bates firmly. 'Marriage is not a sacrament, I grant you. Nowhere in the gospels is it ordained as such, and only the false churches still under the yoke of Rome, though they are ashamed to own it, keep up this pretence out of hatred for the pure gospel. There are but two sacraments named as such by Jesus Christ, baptism and the eucharist. Let us abide by His word, nor let us use Christian marriage as an excuse for fine garments and feasting. But let it be Christian marriage, let a man and a woman made by God ask His blessing when they join together the lives they received from Him. So the Foundation Chapel of the Heavenly Hostages, Ilfriston, Essex, December 14, eleven thirty sharp, as I just said, it is going to be.'

'No,' said Nancy, 'it is not.'

'A young girl like you cannot be joined together to a strange man like the beasts,' said Mr Bates.

'This is our marriage, not yours,' said Nancy, faintly smiling, 'and if you want Oswald to alter the arrangements it was for you to ask him, not to come here and tell us. But even if you had asked Oswald he would have had to refuse on account of me. I have nothing to do with the Heavenly Hostages, and Oswald is going to marry me in that church over there, you can see the tower over the tree-tops. I was brought up in the Church of England, wasn't I, Aunt Lily? We always went to church in Lovegrove, didn't we?'

Aunt Lily said, 'Yes, indeed, dear old St Jude's,' and made a gesture as if she were waving a little flag from a charabanc.

'And all the time I lived with Uncle Mat and my Aunt Clara in Nottingham she was a communicant at St James's,' Nancy went on. 'Why should I suddenly leave my church and go to the Heavenly Hostages, about whom I know nothing? All these people standing here have done a very great deal for me. I could not begin to tell you what I owe them. But not one would ask me to take such as you, the very first time I have ever seen you, have demanded of me. If Oswald should tell me we must obey you I would not marry him, though I do love him. I would think him weak and silly and not able to stand up for himself even about things that really matter. So we will be married in that church, and we will be very sad if you do not come.'

'That's our last word, Dad,' said Oswald.

Mr Bates made a vaguely apocalyptic gesture and looked up at the place where the rainbow had been as if he might have asked it for guidance had it still been there, down at the river as if he might yet be driven to walk on it. Magnificently he declaimed, 'Well said, my daughter. Go on the way you have chosen for the Lord will bring you to salvation. In the end. And very gratefully will I attend your marriage.'

'Thank you,' said Nancy. She wavered for a minute and then made the bobbing curtsy which, years ago, in our dancing class at Lovegrove, we had been taught to make to our elders; and Mr Bates bowed to her over his staff and held out his hand. 'Let us walk together in the garden for a moment,' he said, and they moved away from us, and stood talking beside the sliding and leaf-strewn waters.

Oswald said proudly, 'She understood him at sight, saw that

the only thing to do with him is to stand up to him.' But his face clouded. 'How on earth,' he asked, 'did she come to forget that I'm against any religious ceremony at all?'

'She was excited,' said Aunt Lily.

'It would startle any girl, him coming in like that,' said Uncle Len.

'We were all startled,' said Mr Morpurgo.

'Does it matter?' said Mary.

'Well, a lot of people know my opinions,' said Oswald doubtfully.

'But your dad did promise to come to the wedding,' said Aunt Milly, 'and that was nice of him.'

'I shouldn't discourage him now that he's climbed down,' said Mr Morpurgo. 'I take it that it doesn't happen often.'

'It was Nancy's little victory,' said Aunt Lily.

'I don't see how you can open up the whole thing again,' said Uncle Len.

'Put that way,' said Oswald, 'I suppose it's better to leave things as they are. Give and take. It's a good principle.' His father called to him from the water's edge. He had his arm round Nancy's shoulder and her face was moved and bright, he could not be entirely a humbug, perhaps he was not a humbug at all. 'They're getting on well together,' said Oswald cheerfully, and hurried off to them.

'I wonder how she'll manage to get the kids christened,' said Uncle Len softly.

'Hush, he's no idea,' said Aunt Lily.

'Just think of Nancy going after what she wants,' marvelled Aunt Lily. 'There's more of Queenie in her than you'd think.'

The three at the water's edge were close together. Nancy raised her lips to the old man's cheek, and then drew herself away, and came to us. Her face wet with tears, she told us, 'He is nice really. He understands how hard everything has been for Oswald. I am happy, so very happy.' She lost her power to speak, and walked away from us towards the house, but turned back. 'About the church,' she said, 'it wasn't just for the portrait and the wedding-dress.'

'We knew that,' said Mary.

She had to turn back a second time. 'But it was partly that. That did come into it.'

Both Mary and I were so constituted that we needed a life of this character to run parallel with our lives. It was not only that

41

we loved these people and loved them more year by year. It was that they were candid, and we were their familiars, and we could see how they worked on their circumstances, and how their circumstances worked on them, and how they were imposing form on the chaos that had been given them. Their achievement had great relevance to all that we had unquestionably of our own, which was our musical life. Musicians, by their own talents and their acceptance of tradition, impose meaning on the meaningless world of sound. It would take vanity of a sort incompatible with real music, incompatible with the self-criticism of Beethoven and Mozart, to suppose that musicians are the only servants of meaning, and that the process of art has no analogue in life. Mary and I were supremely happy in our work at that time. I had found a special happiness in having acquired a power, mastered by Mary a long time before, of putting myself in a bland and trance-like state of mind before I played, so that my hands and arms were controlled by my intellectual conception of what I was playing, without giving a chance of intervention to that treacherous element in the soul which hates the will and incites the muscles to frustrate it. Also we were both playing a great deal of Russian music, which had the charm for us that it represented a kind of music misunderstood by Beethoven and Mozart for a reason which cast a bright light on their greatness. For their Turkish marches showed that they had heard Asiatic music (as how should they not, since the Turks had been encamped outside Vienna less than a century before they were born, and had left the countryside encumbered with their camp-followers?), and that they had made not so much of it as we can, simply because they had not listened to their own music as much as we had, and were therefore not sufficiently aware of the definitive character of Western music to know what the dissimilarity of Asiatic music signifies. Infinitely less than Beethoven and Mozart, we were yet more than they were, because of the passage of time, the century and a half during which their music had spread through the world and entered into the very constitution of human beings.

That musical happiness would have been ours in any case, for our mother had given it to us; but we enjoyed it more because we knew these people at the Dog and Duck so well that in talking to them we fell into an analogue of the bland and trance-like condition which we found favourable to our playing. When we talked to them we always expressed the love we felt for them and never made the chilling remarks which the part of us undesirous of friendship sometimes tricked us into making to those who might possibly have become our friends. But we were also much better with strangers because of our beloved familiars. Our mother's light had made us understand that our father's darkness was not mere absence of light; even so the certainties of the Dog and Duck enabled us to be unperturbed by a world that was at that time always announcing its uncertainty. We never feared that our kind was dying, we did not doubt that the sacred patterned snake was still turning and twisting in the heat of the unexhausted sun.

But we might have lost the Dog and Duck had not Rosamund come to us that night to explain Oswald. Without knowledge of what his mother had done to him we would not have been prepared for his tiresomeness, and we might have shown our impatience and so lost Nancy wholly, and the others in part. For Oswald was very tiresome. It was not an exceptional event when, one November afternoon, Nancy having gone up to town to shop with Aunt Clara, I came into the parlour and found Uncle Len and Aunt Lily sitting by the fire, their eyes fixed, and their feet circling on their ankles, while Oswald, with uplifted forefinger, told a cosmic story.

I thought it as well to continue with the task which had been laid on me by Aunt Milly and search the garden for flowers. After I had cut some laurestinus I went to take some of the winter jasmine that was showing yellow round the bar windows, and as I put my scissors on the black and substance-less stalks I heard someone come into the bar, though it was still afternoon. One window was open, and I put my head in; and I saw Uncle Len, his red dewlaps heavy about him, take down a bottle of port from the shelf and select an appropriate glass from the tray below it, look at it, shake his head, and replace it with one of the few larger glasses kept in reserve in case someone wanted to drink wine. He filled it full, nodding in approval at his image in the mirror facing the bar, and raised it to his lips, but paused to say, with the solemnity of a man keeping a lonely tryst with truth, 'B stands for Bates and for balls.'

It was not a moment on which I could intrude, and I meant to go away, but just then the door opened on Aunt Lily. She did not speak, but slowly shook her head from side to side, and clicked her tongue.

'Here,' said Uncle Len, and gave her too a draught of port in a wine-glass.

She raised her eyebrows and beamed at the special generosity but could not speak until she had refreshed herself. 'All that,' she said, 'just for asking how the world began.'

'For mercy's sake, Lil,' exclaimed Uncle Len. 'Is that what started him off? You ought to have a better headpiece on you. That's not a question that would bring a short answer out of Os.'

'Oh, blame me, of course,' said Aunt Lily, 'but it's a short question, and so it ought to get a short answer. That's only logical.'

'Logical?' exclaimed Uncle Len. 'Oh, Lil, that it's not.'

'What, a short question shouldn't get a short answer? What's not logical about that?'

'Never mind,' groaned Uncle Len. 'If you can't see it, you can't.' But they felt better as they drank their port, and presently he asked, 'Has he finished?'

'No. Milly took over listening when I left.'

'We'll get back,' he said. 'And it's a little thing really, when you think how fond he is of Nancy.'

'Yes,' said Aunt Lily, 'now we know she'll be all right when we've gone.'

They emptied their glasses and dutifully left the bar, and when I got back to the parlour they had taken up their burden and were on opposite sides of the hearth, with Aunt Milly in the basket-chair in between, all wagging their heads reverently as Oswald, one elbow on the chimneypiece, brought his story to a confident close.

The perorative cadence of his voice inspired Uncle Len to say, 'Hear, hear,' and Aunt Lily to say, 'Well, it's a comfort to really know,' and Aunt Milly to say, 'Tea, you must need your tea after all that, Oswald,' and they rose to their feet and went about their business. But they had spoken so graciously that he was undisturbed by their speed, and told me happily how sorry he was that I hadn't heard the little thing he had been trying to explain. He said that it was funny to think that when he had started teaching he had found it difficult, now he reckoned that he could make anyone understand anything. He surveyed himself complacently at the chimneypiece and straightened his tie, but instantly lost interest in himself and asked wistfully if I thought there was any chance that Nancy would catch an earlier train. Mary had spoken the truth when she said that no man had ever shown any signs of being as nice as Oswald was about Nancy.

We would not really have liked to be Nancy, because she could not play the piano and she had not been the daughter of Papa and Mamma, nor Richard Quin's sister. But we would have been quite pleased to be Nancy on her wedding-day. It was one of those weddings at which more than two persons are married, which are as general as springtime, which revive the affections of all present. We went to bed the night before with a comfortable feeling that everything was ready for the first step towards a huge advancement in our happiness. Rosamund could not leave London till the morning, so even though Kate had a bedroom to herself there was a room left over, where Nancy's white dress and veil lay on the bed like an unfearsome ghost. We would have liked to leave them overnight on a hanger, but that would have meant pinning the shoulders of the dress close to the wood, lest it slip down to the floor, and we could not bear to spoil the gleaming satin even with pin-pricks. The bouquet, which had been sent from Mr Morpurgo's garden that afternoon, had been left on a table in a disused saddle-room so that the cold air should keep it fresh; and we had surrounded the vase with heavy boxes so that it should not be blown over, though it was most unlikely that a tornado should spring up in a closed room with one high window. We were apprehensive too lest the river should rise and flood the church, in spite of our knowledge that that had happened only once in the last twenty years, and this had been a dry autumn. But all this was a game we were playing. We could mimic insecurity because of the security that let us fall asleep as soon as we got into bed.

But in the early morning I woke suddenly because there was someone moving about in the house. For a moment I thought Papa might have come back. He had gone like a thief in the night, he might come back like a thief in the night. I cried out against the new robbery, the new cruelty he might commit, I asked nothing better than that he should commit it. Then I was fully awake, learned again of my father's death from that strange sense which had told me of it when it had happened, and remembered Uncle Len had said he would get up in the middle of the night to stoke the church boiler; and I rose and kilted up my nightdress and put over it a sweater and a skirt, and tugged on my stockings and my shoes. Mary did not move. She had had a big concert in Edinburgh two nights before, and now lay limp and recipient, drop by drop the night was pouring its fullness into her. Downstairs Uncle Len was on his knees by the door into the garden, wheezing with bulkiness and trying to compel his thick arthritic fingers to free the bolts without noise. As I knelt and slid them back, he whispered, 'You've a quick hand, Rose,' gripped my shoulders, and heaved himself to his feet, the breath whistling up his chest. Featureless in the dark, he was age and weight and infirmity and nothing else. By day he was Uncle Len, and did not seem old or ill, and I felt a sudden fear at this news about him that had come in the dark.

We stepped out into the fierce, silent, still riot of a winter night. The stars appeared not at all remote. It was as if, not far above us, the bare black branches of the tree-tops were locked in combat with the white and sparkling tree-tops of woods growing downwards through the frosty skies with their roots in outer space. But the moon was calm and private in a coign between these two contending forests, and was itself again in a broken road of light across the river. The grass was furred with moonlight and on it each object drew a picture of itself in soft and sooty shadow, but the ground was hard as steel under our feet, and the air was minerally hard with intense cold. We went into the churchyard through the wicket-gate, treading on its shadows as on a grid, and found the graves rehearsing a resurrection, the stones shining as risen bodies might some day. We halted among them and listened to the falling waters of a weir so far distant that we never heard it by day; and I found myself waiting for the cry that should have come from the open mouth of a cherub carved above an epitaph, now forced into high relief by the moonbeams. But if the stone had spoken it would not have been that which made the hour remarkable. The strong light and the December silence were like the sound of a trumpet blown with a single breath in the past, the present, and the future.

Suddenly the church windows were bright. I stared, expecting again that a miracle had happened. It seemed possible that my father and my mother might be standing on the steps of the altar, come to give their blessing to take back to Nancy, who also was to be married. But of course Uncle Len had gone ahead of me and switched on the electric light. He was standing in the aisle, his eyes on the new white sanctuary that Mr Morpurgo's gardeners had made with lilies and chrysanthemums. White flowers were wound round the pillars too, and Uncle Len's hands went up in timid wonder to trace the wires that held them. It would have looked more beautiful had there not been so many memorials in the church. The north and south transepts and the little lady chapel were cluttered with them. A Tudor marchioness and her duchess daughter in their ermined crimson robes and their coronets knelt face to face on a high tomb, their heads bowed over their wide ruffs in recognition of God, their tie of blood, their rank; a Victorian statesman reclined under a coarse imitation of a Gothic canopy; two bearded and armoured brothers of the Renaissance age, who had alike been the King's envoys and were alike killed in his wars, lay side by side; an Edwardian boy in knickerbockers prayed between his two labradors; a heraldic swan spread its wings on an obelisk enamelled with coats of arms. It did not matter that some of these memorials were beautiful, they were still an obstacle to the eye and prevented it laying on the shape of the buildings which signified the meaning of the church. They did wrong in their incongruity, for they were a reminder that life is committed to disorder because all men are not dead and do not die at the same moment. There might have been perfect order round me, had my father and my mother and Richard Quin and Mary and I been contemporaneous, none of us having to wait until the rest were born, none of us having to lose the others. Time, I saw, was the fault of the universe, and because of it grief and expectation, equally mischievous, would prevent us having peace to watch the present. Yet the altar could be seen as never before, because it was decked with white flowers for Nancy's wedding, and the value of the wedding, which gave the flowers their power, lay in time. All the years that Nancy had lived till now she had not been Oswald's wife; and the years that were to come she was to be his wife. That was the marvel of her wedding-day.

Uncle Len had left me. Through the open door of the boiler-room I heard the sober and dutiful sounds of stoking; the deliberate, stubborn push of the shovel under the coal, the prudent, measured tipping-out of the load. I hurried to him. He had propped back the boiler door with an iron bar but it always gave. I held the iron bar in place. He wheezed softly,

'Good girl.' We went out into the churchyard and found ourselves in another night. The river had been unseen when we came in, a mere trough of darkness between the furthest graves and the nearest woods. Now a mist had risen from it, and suffused with moonlight flowed above it like another less substantial river. The tombstones did not shine like resurrected bodies, but glowed softly, like some bright thing that was sleeping. The wind had changed, and the sound of the falling weir-water was even louder than before. The past was irrecoverable. Nancy and Mary and Richard Quin and I would never be children again, eating mealy chestnuts round the fire after we had washed our hair, with our towels on our knees, in our little warm house; Nancy would go to meet her happiness and be borne away from it, and then would only for a short while persist in the memory of a few, and then the rumour of her would become as remote as the sound of waters falling over a distant weir, and then she would be wholly forgotten, there would be nothing left of her in any place. I wept. It was very cold, beneath my sweater my flesh was frozen for an inch below the skin, it was as if I were wearing icy armour. Uncle Len put his arm in mine and, whispering out of respect for the graves, said, 'A cup of tea for us and back to our beds,' and we went back to the wicket-gate. Above us the night sky, hard with vague light, faceted with stars, fitted over the horizon of the sensitive earth like an inflexible helmet. Beyond the gate Uncle Len paused and looked on the inn, frail as cardboard under the strong moon. Stroking my arm, he murmured the names of all that were sleeping under its roof, and said, 'Funny to think of them, all lying there, funny.' I looked up and my sight travelled between the stars to outer space, where there is no more universe. Nothing divided me from it. I was here, I was there, my father and mother and Richard Quin were there and were here, and Nancy would not be destroyed. The light and the silence blew their blast on the trumpet.

We enjoyed the marriage better than anything that had happened to us since we were alone. The only sadness about it was that Mr Morpurgo's youngest daughter asked if she might come, and of course Nancy and Oswald said that they would be very pleased, and she came and watched everything with a certain desperate attention. Also she wore her beautiful clothes carelessly, she slumped down inside them, as if she were not young. We realised that she was in trouble, that she would have liked to tell her father all about it, but she felt that she did not really know him. She was aware that he liked coming to the Dog and Duck, and she had thought that if she found out why, she would understand him better, and could break down the barrier between them. But it was no use. He kept on going where she was not, coming back to see how she was getting on out of kindness; and she was too miserable to make friends with us at once. This was one of the times we missed our mother, who would have flashed her eyes across the dull girl's face and imparted some of her brilliance to it, and fused her with her father by the power of that electric force. But that was the one flaw in the day.

A year later, on Christmas Eve, I met Mary walking along La Salle Street in Chicago, smiling at a memory, almost laughing. I said, 'You are thinking of Nancy's wedding,' and I was right. That was a wonderful meeting. We had both been on tour longer than we liked. Mary had been playing in a Bach festival week that a millionaire was giving to six universities in turn, and I had been going the rounds of the symphony concerts with the French concerto I had played for the first time just before we heard of Nancy's engagement. It had grown dear to me, I thought of it always as the Chestnut Leaves Concerto, for they had fallen bronze about me every morning when I went out for a walk before the rehearsals in Paris, and it built up a stoically pleasant place in my mind, a place such as the Champs Elysées might be; there were no houses there but only the arch at its crown and beyond the arch a wide-open eye, and the first splendid cold of the year. But it was exhausting to play, as all new music is, the audience's incomprehension presses in as a resistant ambient, which has to be beaten back and dissolved by an act of will, a conscious care to explain as well as interpret. So I was tired, as Mary was for another reason, because she had to play only the greatest music for a long period, which meant participating in occasions when people who did not take music as musicians do were excited in a way the nerves could not ignore. Many nice people asked us to spend Christmas with them, for Americans are very kind, but we made a plot with our secretaries and agents and arranged to lose ourselves for three days, to say to the hosts we left before Christmas that we were going straight to the hosts who were taking us in after Christmas, and during the stolen three days to hide together and sleep and eat as we chose in a hotel by the lake in Chicago which we had both liked when we had stayed there on other tours.

Mary got there first. When I arrived in the afternoon the bathroom was already hung with stockings. That is how one recognises the female interpretative artist: on their travels they cannot find themselves near a supply of hot water without immediately washing their clothes. She had left a note saying she had gone out shopping to replace some things she had lost. I found that I had left my manicure set in San Francisco, so I went out to get another, and so it was that I met Mary outside Marshall Fields, smiling to herself over Nancy's wedding, in spite of the high wind that was like invisible ice splinters about us.

We put our arms round each other and kissed, and I said, 'Just look, we're both of us too thin,' and Mary said, 'Yes, it's wonderful, we shall be able to eat what we like during these three days, we will have waffles and maple syrup whenever we think of it.'

'And no squab,' I said.

'Why do Americans like squab?' asked Mary. 'And those horrid clams, embittered spinster oysters. And toast all leathery in a napkin instead of in a toast-rack, as God decreed. But everything else is nice. This is a lovely continent to be given the run of. Shall we go and look at the Christmas trees in the big stores?'

'No, we are too tired,' I said.

'Of course we are,' said Mary. 'Kate would not let us go if she could see us now. But it will be nice just to be alone together in that big room. Can you ever get used to the big hotel rooms we can afford now?'

We stocked up for our days of rest by buying an armful of magazines and a big box of coffee walnuts and several sorts of bath salts, and then took a Yellow Cab back to the hotel, and went into the coffee-shop on the ground floor and had a table by the window, and had our first indulgence in waffles and maple syrup. 'We will have no flowers in our room,' said Mary. 'We cannot buy flowers for ourselves, it is against nature. But it will be good not to have the room crammed with flowers which are given in such a way that one has no occasion to look up the Language of Flowers. They are beautiful, but there's no time to look at them, and the hotels never have the right vases, and one isn't clear who they come from, and so often they come just from people who like our playing.' Dusk fell, and through the window we watched a procession of bright automobiles, cells of privacy in the cold public night, sweeping on their way to homes that would be more warm and private still. 'How good it is to be tired,' said Mary. 'If we were not tired we might feel lonely here.'

'Would you rather have been with people?' I asked. 'Let us go on to the Wallensteins by the night train, they probably would not mind if we telephone and ask if they could have us early, you know how nice everyone is here.' But she shook her head. With her elbows on the table, her smooth face cupped in her fine fingers and nursed by her fur collar and her fur cuffs, she continued to watch the stream of shining cars pass by, or halt at the florist's shop next door. It was amusing to see people hurrying in and out with last-minute presents. One man had trouble in packing a flowering apple tree growing out of a pot into his car, though that was nearly as big as a tram. We drank more coffee, but presently the coffee-shop closed early, because it was Christmas Eve, and we went into the hotel. A clerk at the desk tried to give us our letters but we asked him to send them in the morning. The management had sent us up some roses, so our room was not bare after all. We had long baths, with lots of bath salts, and put on our dressing-gowns and lay down on our beds, meaning to read a little before we ordered dinner, but we fell asleep. When we woke it was nearly nine o'clock and we were not very hungry, so we ordered just oyster stew. There was a lot of it, and we pulled our chairs to the window and drew back the curtains and ate the lovely milky mess, looking down on the long line of steady lights that ran along the black lake's edge, the two lines of moving lights that ran beside them, one line moving north and the other south.

I said, 'When it's this time over there they'll be closing the bar at the Dog and Duck and starting to put up the holly.'

'And Kate and her brothers will be putting it up at her mother's cottage.'

'And poor Mr Morpurgo will have gone home and be sitting in a big chair with his family, after spending all day driving round and leaving presents on people he really likes.'

'And Miss Beevor will be with Constance at Baker Street if her bronchitis is too bad, at the Dog and Duck if she is better.'

'And Cordelia and Alan will be decorating the house. She will do it so prettily, it is a shame they will have to go out to the in-laws for all Christmas Day. What a pity they have no children.'

'No, it is not,' said Mary. 'She wants children more than anything else in the world, but she would not have been kind to them.'

'She might, you know,' I said. 'After all, they would have been hers.'

'But they would not have been her,' said Mary, 'and that is what she cannot forgive.'

'You think she would have fought them as she used to fight us? But she has changed so much for the better. She is always nice to us now.'

'Yes, the battle was drawn. We have our work, she has her marriage. But if she had had children she would have been faced again with the problem of other people existing. Things are better for her as they are.'

We were not being cruel. We did not hate Cordelia any more. But we knew that as she stood at the bottom of the stepladder and told Alan to put the longer spray of silver laurel further to the left of the Wilson Steer watercolour, she would be bound to remember how it had been at Lovegrove on Christmas Eve, how we had heard through our bedroom floor the voices of our father and mother as they put up the holly and the mistletoe and laid out our wonderful presents; and she would, with that white look, push away the thought of Papa, because he was wicked and deserted us, and Mamma, because she was so ugly and queer, and also Richard Quin, because she had always felt doubtful about him, and so she would cut herself off from the glory by which we lived, without which we would hardly exist. She also knew that she let herself think of us out of dutifulness and also out of respect for our success, and we were not exalted enough to forget this.

Mary broke our silence by saying, 'How strange it is that we know exactly what all of our people will be doing tonight except one. I have no idea what Rosamund is doing, have you?'

'No, none at all. But it will be something wonderful.'

But it was strange. She might have a patient, she might not. If she were free then she would drive her mother and Miss Beevor down to the Dog and Duck, unless Miss Beevor was too ill, and then they would all stay at Baker Street. Wherever she was, she would transform the place by her presence. But though we knew her so well, though she was so much more truly our sister than Cordelia, though we had benefited so often from her power to work miracles, we could not conjure up any vision of the nature of that inevitable transformation.

'We cannot imagine what she will do because it is outside our range,' said Mary.

We sat and thought of her until a storm blurred the lake and the lights and blew snow against the window. We were too tired to bother with a storm, so we pushed the room-service trolley out into the corridor and went to bed. After we had turned out the lights we heard people come out of the next room, laughing. One of them wheeled our trolley away, running quite fast, rattling the china and glass, and the rest ran after him, and one of them tooted on a tin trumpet.

When it was quiet again Mary said through the darkness, 'I do wish something.'

'What?'

'I wish that when we get our letters tomorrow there will be one from Nancy saying that she is going to have a baby.'

'There's plenty of time. I don't think Oswald would let Nancy have a baby the first year. He would feel obliged not to, out of respect for birth control, because it is modern, however much they wanted to have one. But they are sure to have several in the end.'

'I hope so. Otherwise, as Cordelia isn't having any, we shall run so short of people when we are old.'

'So we shall.'

The storm beat on our windows. 'No, no,' I said, turning in my bed, 'look at Uncle Len and Aunt Milly. They must have feared that, but they came on Aunt Lily again, and now they have Nancy and us. That's evidently how things work.'

'Something like that might happen to us,' said Mary. 'But one would like to be sure.'

'It will be all right, my darling,' I said, 'it will be all right.'

She did not answer for some time. Then she said, 'I am not really worrying. But when one is tired one is not sure. And how lovely Nancy's wedding was, it was one of the loveliest things that ever happened to us.'

'Nancy looked so beautiful,' I said. 'It was so strange, someone we had known all our lives surprising us like that. She has always looked nice, but not like that.'

'And everybody was so. . . How would we have put it when we were little? I know. Nobody was cross.'

'And Oswald was so good. One saw why Nancy wanted to marry him.'

'I was so glad that he proposed Queenie's health. And he did it so well. He did not make capital out of it by saying anything about her. He just asked us to drink to her, and said how much they wished she was there.'

'I am sure Nancy did not know he was going to do it.'

'No. She was amazed. It made a change in her. Suddenly she looked free. Till then she had a little left of her frightened look.'

'Yes. She held her head up then. And how that wreath Rosamund made for her suited her.'

'It was exquisite. And she and Kate and Constance made it in only a few minutes.'

The people who made the veil had forgotten to send the pearl circlet which had been ordered, and at the last minute had sent the wrong one; it was so big that it fell over poor Nancy's ears. She sat before her mirror and said very quietly, 'Of course I wasn't meant to be married like this, I shouldn't have tried,' and Aunt Lily wailed, 'Poor lamb, poor innocent lamb,' betraying too candidly that she too believed her stock pursued by a blasting fate deserved by only one of its branches. Their sense of insecurity was suddenly revealed, and I cried out, 'Rosamund, Rosamund,' for I knew that she and Constance and Kate were helping prepare the tables underneath. There was at once the sound of the three coming upstairs, and the low room was full of tall women, bending in concern. 'My circlet,' said Nancy, her lips quivering, and Aunt Lily said, 'It's a shame.' Rosamund sat down by the mirror, a smile on her lips, and turned the circlet in her hands, grimaced and threw the useless thing down on the dressing-table. When my call had reached them they had been filling vases with some white flowers, and Rosamund had some on her lap now. 'There is plenty of time,' she stammered, and slowly stripped the wire from the discarded circlet, and remade it in a narrower and more fragile form. Making a teasing mouth at Nancy's anxious reflection in the mirror, she leaned back and handed the circlet over her shoulder to Constance, who turned it about in her hands and pressed it more firmly into shape, and gave it to Kate, who pressed it too and gave it back to Rosamund. 'Give me some thread,' she stammered again, and bound the flowers to the stiff shape. They rested on the wire as the dogwood blossom rests on the bare branch, as the clematis floats on the vine. Constance bent down and freed some buds that lay too close to the wire, Kate made secure a flower that had been grown too gorgeously by Mr Morpurgo's gardeners and stood out stiffly, and the three women raised the crown to Nancy's head, laughing at her in the mirror, laughing at her fear, as a splendid gust of winter wind leaped in riot among the elms that stood beside the inn. That wind joined with the wind that was blowing snow across Lake Michigan a year later, and I slept. Later there were more people running about in the corridor, and this time several of them had tin trumpets, and I woke just long enough to hear Mary turn in her sleep and say, 'Let something happen so that Rosamund can live with us all the time, please, please, Mamma, arrange it,' and I slept again.

In the morning I waited till I heard Mary stirring, and then I felt for my present to her, which I had ready on my table, and I got into her bed.

'Merry Christmas, Sister,' we said, and kissed each other. Then we said, 'Merry Christmas, Papa, Merry Christmas, Mamma. Merry Christmas, Richard Quin,' and I gave her my present.

'It isn't a bit what I wanted, it's much nicer,' said Mary. I had given her an emerald clip, not the most expensive kind of emerald, but the better, lighter kind which looks like sea water over a sandy bottom when the sun strikes through it. 'I say, can you really afford this?'

'Yes, I think so,' I said. 'Gramophone records, you know. And you could always sell it.'

'My present's on the settee,' said Mary. 'I got up when you were asleep and put it out. I saw it in Bonwit Teller's in October, and I said, "I have a sister who would look good in that."' It was an evening coat made of gold damask brocade with a rose mauve bloom on it. I would be able to wear it every time I was asked out to supper at a restaurant after a concert, and that happened a great deal on an American tour. In the looking-glass I looked a stranger, now I had this cloak things might happen to me that had never happened before.

'I will lend you this if ever you want it,' I said.

'I won't ever lend this clip to you or anybody else,' said Mary, lying on her back and holding the clip over her and kicking the bedclothes off and waving her legs in the air.

We rushed at each other and kissed and pulled each other's

hair, and put on our dressing-gowns and ordered a big breakfast with shirred eggs and bacon, and telephoned the desk to send up our letters. We gave the waiter and the bell-hop their Christmas tips and good-luck charms that Mary had found in the Greek quarter in Buffalo, and had the trolley pushed up to the window, for though the weather was still stormy and rough, weather on an inland sea has always an air of futile ill-temper, there was a pure light roving the great grey Middle Western sky. There were a great many letters for us, and we took them as they came; and read them at a comfortable pace; we had plenty of time before we went out to find a church. Though the manufacturers of the water-softener we had just installed in the St John's Wood house sent us greetings which we suspected of lacking personal warmth, the people we really loved had all caught the right post. I got Uncle Len and Aunt Lily, Mary got Aunt Milly. The cards they enclosed each showed a robin; they always did, every Christmas. Kate had been fortunate and found Lord Nelson's *Victory*; and in her big sloping handwriting she told us she would go to Lovegrove on Christmas Eve and stand outside our house, as she did every year, and she was pleased that she had nothing but good news of us to take, though she would have to own that she thought we worked too hard. I could see her while I read, as she had kept that promise a few hours before, four thousand miles away, in the warm sun of the sacred night, threading her solemn path among the people with their armfuls of parcels and holly, and the children leaping at their sides, looking so tall and black and decent and prosaic as she carried out her errand to the other world. But Mary called me away from her.

'Rose, Rose.'

She was on her feet, there was such happiness on her face that it seemed as if there must have been a letter from one of our dead in our Christmas post.

'Rose, Rosamund is going to be married.'

I cried out in selfish joy. I saw Rosamund as ceasing to be a nurse and enjoying the same leisured life as Cordelia, and though I realised that we would have to share that leisure with an unknown man, I was still sure that we would have much more of her than before. I saw her in a little Kensington house, like Cordelia's first one, which we could run into at any time, taking her flowers and marrons glacés and books we thought she would like, while she repaid us by giving life the quality that but for her was only to be found in music and therefore might not in all senses be real. Then I was struck by an impersonal awe. Rosamund, who was above us, had found a companion. It was as if the light that was patrolling the lake, now as a shining ball among the storm clouds, now as a shaft striking down to the pewter waters, had twinned.

'Who is he?' I said.

'The patient she has been nursing at the Savoy since the end of November. But I cannot read his name.'

'Can't read his name? But her writing is so clear.'

'Well, look. It can't be that.'

III

JUST AFTER the New Year we each had another letter from Rosamund, telling us her plans. I was in Hollywood and Mary was at Mount Holyoke; and we were so disturbed that, though we hated talking on the telephone, it is hardly better than spiritualism, we spoke several times on long distance. We were not worried about her; the letters were completely inexpressive, but then her letters always were. She had, however, made a most unfortunate mistake. It appeared that Rosamund's fiancé, whose name really was Nestor Ganymedios, as we had thought it could not be, had for some years made his home in Berlin, and he was therefore anxious to be married there, among his friends. She would have proposed that the marriage should take place as soon after our return from the States as would give us time to travel comfortably to Germany, but as it happened Nestor had urgent reasons for leaving on a tour of South America at the very time of our arrival. So the wedding was to take place a week before our return, and they would return to England three days before we got back and would catch a boat twenty-four hours after our arrival. She was sorry, but there was something important about signing a contract in Buenos Aires, and she asked us to dinner at the Savoy. The trouble was that she had made a mistake about the date of our return. She thought we were travelling three days earlier than we were, by the *Berengaria* instead of the *Ile de France*. This puzzled us, until we remembered that before we started there had been some idea that we might get off by the earlier boat, and we supposed we must have mentioned it to her. But it was not like her to have failed to check her belief by asking our secretary or Kate. Still, she was going to be married, she was

58

going to make a home in a new country, she was going on a long voyage, and to prepare for any one of these things would have been enough to overwhelm her and her mother with business. Of course we could not expect her to alter her plans, so we caught the *Berengaria*. This was not easy for us. We were very tired, as one always is at the end of a tour, and for each of us it meant cutting out the few days of rest we would have given ourselves in New York, and going straight from the hall where we gave our last concert to a train which would get us to the dock in time; and we had to practise exhausting concentration to prevent our last performances being spoiled by our desire to get back to England.

It is always lovely to wake on the first morning of an Atlantic voyage. One is freed from what one did in the continent behind one, as if one had died; one feels certain that one will make no such mistakes in the continent that awaits one. When I opened my eyes there was in the upper air of the cabin the string of wrong notes with which I had defaced Chopin's Sixteenth Prelude at Cleveland. But my bunk was rolling, the great seas were slapping the porthole, the ship was above and below and beside me, I was passing through an area where the clean ocean and the cleansing winds were at work on me. There would be no wrong notes when I played that prelude at the Queen's Hall in a fortnight's time. I felt no further remorse about them, my mother's face ceased to blaze contempt at me as she heard them. I would play well at the Queen's Hall and differently, for I would be a different person. By then I would have met Rosamund married, I would have met Rosamund's husband. I wished Mary would wake up so that I could ask her if Rosamund had told her anything about Nestor in the letter she had got, for in my letter Rosamund had said almost nothing about him. But Mary was sunk in sleep. Fatigue had set such shadows on her eyelids and under her cheekbones that I remembered how ill she had been during the first years of the war, and I resolved I would try to make her drink more milk. Anyway it was not likely that there was anything more in her letter than in mine, for Rosamund could not put down on paper anything but the most immediate facts. It was hard not to be impatient, but I closed my eyes and let the waters rock me, and as a squall came up I remembered, as I had remembered in Chicago, how the elms by the Dog and Duck had groaned under the winter wind, while we dressed the bride for that minor wedding.

In the afternoon Mary shook me awake, to show me a radiogram from Berlin. 'We are married. I love you. Rosamund.' We slept all that day, though the stewardess made us eat some dinner, and we stayed in bed for the next two days, because we were passing through a full gale, and we were still too tired. It was always a pleasure for us to be on a boat. It was like retreating into childhood, not such a childhood as ours had been, hag-ridden by poverty and miracles and music, but the kind of childhood that is described in children's books. We were in a warm and comfortable nursery, and we had a kind nanny who said we need not get up, as we had been doing too much lately, and brought us nice things on trays, and let us play with our toys. We lay and looked at the flowers people had sent us, which were lovely except for the microcephalous roses that American florists grow, with long stems and tiny flowers that make one worry about their intelligence quotients, and we read our letters, which were all friendly, and turned over the pages of the books other people had sent, and talked about Rosamund's husband.

'I wonder if he will be like the doctor,' said Mary.

I too had been thinking of that summer afternoon long ago when Rosamund had stretched her tall fairness on the lawn at Lovegrove and lain with a long blade of grass between her teeth and, it might have been thought, the hesitance of awakening love muting her voice, her smile, her movements.

'Robert Woodburn,' I said. 'But how do you know what he was like? She never brought him to see us, did she?'

'No, but I always felt I knew all about him,' said Mary. 'Taller than Rosamund, fair like her, and quite perfect. Never cruel.'

'But if he was like that, why did she not marry him?'

'She never told me. I thought she might have told you.'

'Rosamund would never tell me anything she did not tell you,' I said. 'Never once in all our lives have I felt, "Rosamund likes Mary more than she likes me," and I would be apt to think that, because I know you are better than me. Rosamund would take precautions against either of us being afraid like that, not that you would have to be afraid about me.'

'Why on earth should you think that I am better than you?' asked Mary.

'You should listen to our gramophone records some time,' I said, 'and look in the glass when we are both standing in front of it. You are just a little better than I am in everything. I do not mind, but I might have minded it if Rosamund had cared more for you than for me.'

'All this is nonsense. I always feel you have something I have not got,' said Mary. 'But to get back to Robert Woodburn, he cannot have been perfect, for Rosamund did not want to refuse him. I came on her once being sad on her own account. It was so odd to find her caring about herself for once.'

I looked back on that afternoon in the garden at Lovegrove, and though I had had no lover, I felt sure that Rosamund had been in love. 'Yes. Yet she was quite determined not to marry him.'

'I wonder why. I feel he had not that queer thing about him that all men have who want to marry us.'

'What is that?' I asked.

'Why, enmity, of course,' said Mary.

We were silent for a minute, and let the kind sea rock us. Mary took up a comb from her bed-table and brought her dark hair back to sleekness. I said, 'And Nestor must be without that too.'

'Yes. He will be quite perfect, as we thought the doctor was.'

'How things turned out right! Do you remember how in Chicago on Christmas Eve we were frightened that we would run short of people? You see, here is someone wonderful.'

'But in what way is he wonderful? It is maddening of Rosamund not to tell us more, but she cannot help writing bad letters, it is like her stammer.'

'What can he be?' I speculated. 'Ganymedios, Ganymedios, have we not met people in Sweden and Finland with odd names like that?'

'Yes, he might be a Scandinavian. Then he would be tall and fair like her.'

'Mamma would be pleased. She liked men to be tall. She thought Alan tame, but she was proud of his height.'

'This is all she hoped for,' said Mary. 'She did not expect us to marry. With us at our music, and Rosamund with the right husband, she has all she wanted.'

'But do you think they will live where we can see a lot of them?'

'Probably his family has moved to England, lots of Scandinavians do, and if they haven't we could spend our holidays where they are. It will be all right, she will be much freer than when she was a nurse.'

On the last three days we got up and walked about the ship,

though the weather was still very rough and many people stayed in their cabins throughout the voyage. We were so happy that we could not feel sea-sick. We had played really well in America, we were sure that we were going to play better in Europe, we had made a lot of money, the people we met had been nice to us and warm as they are not in England, and there was this immense pleasure at the centre of our lives. We were again to have a man in the family, as we had not had since Papa and Richard Quin left us; and that was in itself a precious recovery. Kate kept a man's hat and overcoat hanging in our hall, and pretended it was to intimidate burglars, but it was really a complaint to the gods that we had had to eat our meat without salt for many years. We had not thought that we would ever see good salt on our table again. But this man who was now coming to us must be male indeed. We saw few proofs that there was any truth in the traditional view of the relationship between the sexes. Only at the Dog and Duck did we see a man who took it for granted that it was his duty to protect his women. Papa had done all sorts of things for Mamma but he had not protected her, and most of the men we met in our profession and at parties seemed not to have been fitted at birth with any apparatus for cherishing. We could believe that those who were homosexual had become so simply in order to evade any such obligation. But this man must indeed be ready to accept it, for when he took Rosamund away from her nursing and gave her a home where she could have children, he was protecting someone who was not helpless but was herself a protectress. The work was grander than was ordinary, and our imagination saw it carried out now in a long white farm on one of those rocky islands between Finland and Sweden, where the autumn maples burn red among the dark firs, now deep in the Swedish forest, in a baroque castle beside a lake on which they and their children would skate by torch-light, now in a tall and narrow eighteenth-century house in the ship-invaded elegance of Copenhagen. We obstinately set the scene of Rosamund's happiness always in the North, perhaps because of the crystalline chill of Nancy's wedding, perhaps because we were so greatly enjoying this winter voyage.

Every day it continued its peculiar pleasure. The Atlantic seas were so tremendous that often our prow hung on the crest of a huge wave while the stern hung in mid-air until another wave rolled on to take its weight, and during these seconds the substance of the liner quivered like frightened flesh. It was as if we were travelling on the backbone of some marine animal, which was about to break. We were not afraid then, nor when we found a glass door that enabled us to look obliquely across the deck at the approaching waves, which came on like black marble mountain-faces, veined with foam, so high that they cut off the sky. Then we could see, as well as feel, the successive moments of our danger and our salvation. For we would have been engulfed, had it not been that at the last moment the human intelligence which the shipbuilders had incorporated in the hull took notice and assumed control and made it ride the waves. But every day we were losing hours in fighting the gale, and we soon realised that we were going to get into London just in time for Rosamund's party. There was always the hope that we would come into good weather in the Channel, and indeed for an hour or two the West Country smiled at us with the lying innocence of landfall, showing us cliffs and fields sweet as a nursery frieze, and the sea was gently green like spring pasture. Then another storm struck us, we lurched and hesitated into Southampton, it was evening, a hurricane howled round the Customs-sheds, everything took much longer than usual. Before we got off the boat, we knew that we would not be able to change for the party, before we got on the train we knew that we should not be able to get to the Savoy till half past nine or ten. We were not depressed or exasperated, we saw that the forces of evil were trying to prevent us from meeting Rosamund and her husband, and thought that natural enough, and we had beaten them, we were nearly there. We dined in the Pull-man and gave ourselves sherry and a half-bottle of champagne, though usually we did not drink unless we were with quite a lot of people. When we got to Victoria our secretary, Miss Lupton, was there, and we left her to deal with the luggage and took a taxi to the Savoy. The lights were shining back from the streets, London had the snug look it wears when one comes home to it. We drove along the Embankment; the palely illuminated lion by the pub at Hungerford Bridge seemed childlike and modest beside the huge clamant electric fantasies of Broadway. About us we could divine miles and miles of little streets where people enjoyed moderate happiness in front of glowing open grates, and were unlikely to be guilty of cruelty or violence. When we reached the Savoy vestibule we passed through crowds which looked worn and innocent; American hotels at that time were

63

frequented by people formidable not only because they were so gorgeously dressed, but because they were unacquainted with grief. When we waited with the page-boy outside Rosamund's suite we were breathless; and it was a second or two before we realised that the buzz of a large party sounded behind the door.

'What, will there be other people?' asked Mary.

'His family, his friends, I suppose,' I said.

There was a burst of laughter within. We had to ring again, and then it was a waiter who opened the door. We saw a very large sitting-room; Mary and I had been staying at hotels for years now but we had never had a sitting-room as large as this. At one end, where there was a fireplace stacked with flowers, about twenty men and women were standing about. We knew none of them except Cordelia and Alan, who stared at us angrily, as if something unpleasant were happening which was our fault. All these strangers were looking at a small fat man who stood in the middle of the room, exactly in the centre of a Persian rug, with his back to a table at which two men sat and ate among the coffee-cups and wine-glasses left by a large dinner-party. This little man was so small that the sleeves and tails of his evening coat were like fins and he was, indeed, fantastically marine in appearance. He had dark red hair that grew away from his forehead and low down on the nape of his neck, if a fish tried to wear a toupee it would slip back into this position. His face was flat but mobile, one could imagine it applied to the sea-bottom, the nose and mouth attracting by suction small organisms from the crannies of the rocks. We supposed him to be some sort of entertainer, and we supposed too that he had said something improper, as Cordelia and Alan looked so cross. There was at that time an odd fashion for entertainers who sang songs and told stories that treated with coy facetiousness habits that were in fact taken for granted by everybody present. But because we could not see Rosamund anywhere we listened to what he was saying.

'In those days,' he was telling his audience, in a rich foreign voice, 'I was a poor young boy, and I did not know what to do, so I joined the Istanbul Fire Brigade.' He turned for confirmation to the two men who were eating at the table. 'Was it not so, Mr Ramponetti?' Mr Ramponetti, who had the long, prudent, and obstructive face of a mule, paused reluctantly as he lifted a laden fork to his lips and impatiently nodded. The fat little man swivelled back to his audience, rays of light emanating from his

collar-studs and cuff-links and a ring on his finger. 'Mr Ramponetti was a poor young boy, too, and so he too joined the
Istanbul Fire Brigade, and together we did many deeds. Ah,
the poor little Moslem girls, how they used to run from the
flames, blind in their veils. Come in, come in,' he said to us.
'Waiters, give these two young ladies champagne, give them
all they want, and then listen, young ladies, I am telling the
story of my life. Already I have told of my father and my
mother, and how each for long believed the other dead, and we
were all little children. My God, my God, you are Mary, and
you are Rose.' He came towards us and stretched wide his
arms. 'So I must kiss you, for I am Rosamund's husband.'

We looked past him at Cordelia and Alan, and we saw that it
was true. They looked at once angry and exultant.

'You are one of my family now,' said the little man. 'My God,
my God, I marry a beautiful woman, and my life becomes a
rose-garden, with her she brings so many beautiful women.
Already there is Cordelia, who is beautiful like a rose, and so is
Mary and so is Rose, and they are as beautiful though they are
not married, why is that, and I will kiss you as I kissed her.' He
gave us a smack that made the strangers about us laugh, and
turned about and ran from us towards a door. He beat on it
with both hands, crying, 'Rosamund, Rosamund,' before he
remembered that he could open it by turning the handle.

On his departure the laughter and chatter of his guests fused
into a fountain of something just decently short of derision.
Like many of the most disagreeable occasions of adult life, this
party made us feel we were back at school. These people were
like the girls at Lovegrove High School when they gathered
round us and asked about our music examinations and said
how glad they were we had first-class honours, but said something else after we had left the room so that we always heard a
burst of laughter through the closed door. Alan and Cordelia
crossed the room towards us, and Cordelia said to us, with her
white look, 'Was it really quite impossible for you to change?'
We looked round and saw that all the women had very good
dresses and jewels, and the men had the slow and bulky look
that is given by certain sorts of riches. There was nobody there
we recognised, though by now we knew many people in
London. We recognised in Cordelia's panic the respect she
paid to people who were not of our sort. She would instantly
think that, because we did not know these people, they must

be our superiors; that they might be our inferiors would never strike her. From an armchair in the corner there rose Mr Morpurgo who came to us and without offering any greeting said, 'He is not a Jew.'

We said to the three of them, 'Where is Rosamund?'

Alan said, 'She tore her dress, Constance is mending it.'

'How is she?'

'Very happy, I am sure,' answered Cordelia, restored for a moment by malice.

It was a curious thing that even now when Mary and I were angry with Cordelia we wanted to hit her and pull her hair as if we were still little.

I lowered my voice and said, 'Who are all these people?'

Alan shrugged his shoulders, Cordelia pursed her lips. Mr Morpurgo said, 'They are all coming up. Some are City people, there are two Members of Parliament, and a lawyer or two, and some newspaper people. I have never met any of them before.' He looked at them coldly out of this pouched eyes. 'Some of them will get through. Some will not.'

Mary whispered in my ear, 'But why did she ask anybody but us?'

'She could not help it,' I said. 'You know she could not help it.'

The fat little man was back with us. He returned to his stance on the rug in the middle of the room, although he addressed Mary and me in an extremely personal manner. It evidently appeared to him as an advantage that the party was too small for any person present to remain unaware of what he was doing and saying. 'My wife Rosamund is so happy that her cousins have come. "Oh, it is Mary. Oh, it is Rose," she cries.' He spoke the words in a falsetto voice and clasped his hands in a cloying attempt to imitate an ecstatic feminine gesture. 'And how wonderful it is for me too to see these young ladies. Look, I have married the most beautiful woman in the world, and I say to her, and you know how you say anything when you love a beautiful woman and you are first married, "Your family shall be mine," and I mean it, for which of us English is not good with our families? But it might be a hard vow to keep, for not all families are easy to be good with. But all my wife's family are as my heart desires, they are nice, they are beautiful, look at these two young ladies, you can see how they are, and they are that and more. Do you know who they are? Look hard. For they are famous. They are the greatest pianists in the world.'

He said our names, and the guests murmured politely. They had of course never heard of us, they were the kind of people who never go to concerts; and that was perhaps as well, considering the idiotic description. But even so, a voice said, 'Give the little girls a hand,' and some people clapped, while others knew one another well enough to know it was all absurd, and tittered.

'They play,' said Nestor Ganymedios, voluptuously closing his eyes, 'more beautifully than anybody has ever played since anybody invented the piano, not counting the harpsichord. Do I know, since grandfather's cousin was Anton Rubinstein?' He suddenly grew sad and his chin dropped on his chest. 'Alas, that great man is dead. We must all die.' Cheerfulness, however, immediately brought his head up again. 'But many people are dead. Good God, when one thinks of it, all people are dead except those who are actually alive. It is an immense number, we cannot worry about them, let us think of Mary and of Rose, they are alive and they play everything. Continually they play in Berlin, no artists are better known in Germany, and from now when they come to Berlin they will stay with my dear wife and me at my house at Dahlem that was built for me by the great Schaffhausen. I tell you, it is a thing only I can say, my house which was built by the great Schaffhausen. For he builds town halls, and art galleries, he builds, and universities, and huge concert-halls, and a cathedral, yes, in Thuringia he has built a cathedral, but dwelling-houses he does not build. For why? They are too small, and he is a great man. So he will build none, until he meets me, and then he says, "For you, Nestor Ganymedios, for you I will break my rule and I will build a house." And now there it stands in Dahlem, it is the wonder of all, there is a huge window of glass, people do not know what it is, they guess, a factory, a hospital, and these young ladies they will stay with me there, and so will all of you.' Somebody said, 'Right, Nestor, we'll take you up on that, old man,' and the little man flung out his arms, 'You shall all come. Waiters, waiters, let there be caviare. But, my friends, it cannot be now. Not till I have returned from South America where I go to buy twenty-eight hotels.'

'Twenty,' said Mr Ramponetti, suddenly, from his seat at the dinner-table.

'Why do you say only twenty?' asked Nestor Ganymedios irritably. 'That old man is eighty-seven, he will die soon.

Maybe,' he said, growing chubby with optimism, 'he is dying now, we will buy those eight hotels from his heirs.'

'If you are eighty-seven you may be eighty-eight, you may be eighty-nine, you may be ninety,' said Mr Ramponetti. 'Otherwise how are there all those old men?'

'But I am very lucky,' said Nestor.

'So too is Arturo Arahona,' said Mr Ramponetti, 'or he would not be eighty-seven.'

Everybody laughed. 'Mr Ramponetti is very witty,' said Nestor, beaming round the room. 'He has what foreigners so much admire, the English phlegm. For like me he is English in spite of his name. But who shall say how a man gets his name? But we are quite English, Mr Ramponetti is very English. Though he came late he could have had what I gave you for dinner, the oysters, the mushroom soup, the sole, the duck, but he is so English, he would have only eggs and bacon.' He looked affectionately at Mr Ramponetti, and bade a waiter, 'Give my friends much coffee, and take round again the champagne and the brandy.' Suddenly his eyes fell on us, he gaped, he struck his forehead, and wailed, 'My God, my God, I have forgotten. Rosamund wants you to go into the bedroom to see her, she is with her dear mother, who is to live with us in Berlin, all my wife's family shall be as mine. Her dear mother is mending her dress, so tall is my wife that she trod on the hem of her long skirt, and she bade me send you in to her. Go, go at once, she will not forgive me, for she loves you as if you should be her own sisters.'

There was but one Constance in the bedroom. She was sitting stiff-backed in a chair by the window. Her body had always been an effigy representing the kind of woman that she was, but it had never revealed what she was thinking or feeling at any particular moment. So she looked us full in the face and we looked back at her, and we learned nothing except that whatever course of action had brought her to this room, she would persist in it until it was achieved, for such was her habit, not to begin what she did not finish. But because there were many panels of looking-glass in the room, we saw six Rosamunds. Each was sitting with back a little bowed on one of the twin beds, and wore a dress of pale sea-green satin with huge, shining, spreading skirts. Its body was closely and deeply cut, and the shoulder-straps were narrow for her splendid breadth. But she did not look naked for she was wearing a diamond necklace so massive and so remarkable that it clad her as decently as if it were a scarf. She was breathing slowly, and with each breath the diamonds rose and fell, and in the mirrors a dazzling multicoloured brightness flickered over her breast and shoulders. Some hairdresser had seen that her beauty was outside the sphere of fashion and had piled up her hair into a helmet of curls, and one golden ringlet fell past her ear and rested on the diamond necklace. She hardly moved as we entered, and it was not possible for her to speak. She threw her head back to look at us better under her heavy lids, and we saw her stammer beating like a huge pulse against her mouth. But we knew why she had left the party. The curtains were pulled back, and against the glass, only faintly patterned with the reflections of the room, was the darkly shining Thames with its barges, and the innocent and trivial electric signs, and the south-side factories with their smoke-stacks wearing the red oval blotch of their reflected fires above them, and the Houses of Parliament, with Big Ben as a second moon; and these things made the London which she and we had known all through our childhood and our youth. That window made the room a refuge to her disgraced flesh.

I became aware that she had lied to us about our Atlantic crossing. She had known that we were planning to sail on the *Ile de France*; she had pretended that she thought we were travelling on the *Berengaria* simply in order that she might spend her one night in London too early for us to meet her husband. It did not matter. We sank on our knees beside her and put our arms round her and kissed her, and looked up into her face, and waited for her to explain.

But she said nothing, only smiled faintly and stroked our faces with her beautiful hands, which, now that she had stopped nursing, were as white as ours. She was wearing a huge diamond engagement ring.

Mary said, 'I am sure he is very nice,' but still she did not speak.

I asked, 'Where are you going to live?'

She could just force out the words. 'Germany. Always Germany.'

'Oh, Rosamund. You are forsaking us. But we shall see you often?'

Surely the meaning of her expression was pure pain. We turned to Constance but her face was blank. It occurred to me that perhaps Nestor Ganymedios was a lunatic whose misfortunes

69

Rosamund had resolved to share; that this suite and the diamonds were extravagances he could not afford, and that Mr Ramponetti was a rogue who was using his employer's lunacy as a decoy. Then there would be poverty and humiliation, perhaps involvement with the law, to take her back to her accustomed destiny.

'Tell us,' begged Mary. But at that moment Nestor Ganymedios burst into the room, crying, 'Come back, come back, my darling, the Lord is coming.' He embraced her so roughly that his lesser weight rocked her backwards, and gave her such a smacking kiss as he had given us. 'See, Mary, see, Rose, does she not look beautiful? You are now of my family, some day I will tell you what her necklace has cost, but I grudge nothing to my beautiful wife, though I know she has always been poor, and would have been content with cheaper presents.' She rose slowly to her feet and gave him her hands, smiling. She could not have made it more plain that she wanted to be with him, that she intended to stay with him, that this was a marriage which would never be broken.

I was enraged. It was against nature that she should be happy with this man, who was a head shorter than she was, who was ridiculous in form, whose head ran down with almost no neck into his body, which dwindled from plumpness to his tiny feet so gradually that he was like a fish standing on its tail. And indeed she was not happy with him. She was ashamed and repelled, so deeply that she felt almost nothing else. The one emotion that had not been driven out of her by this distress was, against all reason, this resolute loyalty towards the cause of her distress. This man could have no such rights over her unless he were going to go mad or starve; and indeed there was already the froth of madness on his phrases.

'There will be coming in at the door, he has telephoned from his house, one of the richest men in the world, let me not lie, let me tell the strict truth, one of the richest men in the universe, and he is coming to drink my wine and eat my caviare and see my wife, and he is bringing with him the little one, but he is the big one, that I have dropped in the Bosporus this afternoon, that my janizaries tied up in the sack. How I wish,' he suddenly howled, 'that you could wear more of your jewels, that you could wear all of your jewels, but here people do not know how to live. Come now, my rose of the world; but come first, Mary and Rose, my family, my own family, which shall be round me like the vine, come first. For my wife she must make the big entrance when the rich man is here.'

We did not really think that any new and important guests would come. The party was from one point of view just like school, and from another it was like certain musical parties. While we waited on our return to the room we got the feeling of the people, and they were certainly rich and might be powerful, but they were not supremely so. They were as Mr Morpurgo had seen them; and they had accepted Nestor's invitations because it seemed to them possible that his strange strategic assault on them might have had some chance of success, and they would not yet disdain any connection which might be useful. But they felt no certainty, and they were careful to mock him a little in the sight of their own kind, so that, if he failed, they would be able to claim that they had never believed in him. They were taking out this insurance every moment of the party. As each lifted his glass of champagne from the waiter's tray he smiled slyly over the brim at his neighbour, however slight their acquaintance; each listened to Nestor's stories with the laughter that he asked for, but changed it to a grin when he looked away. Had these people been satisfied with their position they would have stayed at home. So I was sure that no prodigious millionaire was about to appear; and I was wrong.

After about a quarter of an hour two men came into the room who were certainly very rich. One was Lord Branchester, a tall lean man with silver hair, rather like Lady Tredinnick's husband, but not leathery, for he had not been in the tropics, he was a private banker. We knew him because his wife liked music, and though they did not really understand it they tried very hard, and they were generous and were on the list of guarantors of all sorts of concerts and operas. The other was Lord Catterock, whom we did not know so well, but had often met, for he was always at parties. He was a little man who hunched his shoulders to look as if they were broad and had a huge mouth, and spoke with a strong American accent, because he had been brought up in Texas. He had made a fortune in oil and was supposed to be one of the richest men in Europe. He was disappointing. You could see him saying to himself, 'I am so rich that I can behave as I like, nobody dares punish me,' and he was perpetually advertising, by a whimsical expression, that he meant to use this immunity in some impish and entertaining way. But it never came to anything except some violation of good manners, a too abrupt departure, a noisy demand for some food or drink or companion not available, or a sudden boorish quarrel.

Mary and I had dined with the Branchesters just before we had sailed for America, but he looked into our faces blankly. A muscle was twitching in his lean cheek. Lord Catterock was grinning widely and saying to him, 'Come on, man, come on,' though in fact he was not hanging back, he was simply behaving as one does when one comes to a party late, and is not sure where one's host may be. But Lord Catterock was organising this arrival with cruel intention. He met Nestor on the Persian rug in the middle of the room, and the two small men, by their terrible need for attention, made it a stage which everybody watched. Rosamund came out of the bedroom and stood unnoticed behind them. She had disguised her misery and was blank. It might have been supposed that she was a stupid and beautiful woman who thought and felt little more than that she was wearing a beautiful sea-green dress and a beautiful diamond necklace.

Lord Catterock belled in his deep Texan voice: 'All my friends will tell you that I never leave my own home in the evening. But I broke my rule to come and see you, Mr Ganymedios.'

'You are like me, Lord Catterock,' said Nestor, forcing his voice down to Lord Catterock's level. 'Never do I leave my own home except to see a dear friend. It is a great thing to have friends.'

'Friends,' echoed Lord Catterock richly. 'Only thing worth having in the world.' The corners of his huge mouth began to twitch, the room was intended to notice this. 'I've brought you a new one tonight. Come on, Branchester, where have you got to?' Lord Branchester was still behaving like any other guest and was waiting quietly to shake hands with his host. But Lord Catterock gave a guffaw which was meant to be a giveaway, which suggested that the other man was hiding like a sulky child, and pulled him forward by the arm. He watched the handshake with self-conscious puckishness, and said in a roaring chuckle, 'You'll be the best of friends. It's only that you gave him a bit of a surprise this afternoon. By God, you were surprised, weren't you, Branchester?'

'Yes, I was surprised,' said the other.

'By God,' said Lord Catterock, 'I don't think I've ever seen a man so surprised. And the whole shareholders' meeting was surprised. You fairly stole a march on them there, didn't you, Mr Ganymedios?'

'I had my men dig by night and change the course of the stream,' said Nestor modestly. Then his eyes and Lord Catterock's met, and for a minute they were two small fat men mocking a tall thin one.

'And mind you, it's not easy to surprise Branchester,' the huge mouth continued. 'Though I once surprised him myself. Didn't I, Branchester? Do you remember how I surprised you?'

'I have not forgotten it,' said Lord Branchester.

In my ear Mr Morpurgo murmured, 'Excuse me, Rose, I must leave you, you will find me in the corridor, I need fresh air.'

'I surprised him so much that he's been on his guard ever since,' Lord Catterock persisted. 'Haven't you, Branchester?'

'I thought so,' said Lord Branchester.

'And, mind you, he took it in good part, and we're the best of friends now, aren't we, Branchester?' There was no answer, and the huge mouth was irritably licked by a huge tongue; but after a second the Texan accent went on. 'I've brought him here tonight to make friends with you. Nothing like a surprise to make a foundation for friendship. But it has to be trodden down before it makes a foundation.' He repeated this, as if he were reading Today's Great Thought off a calendar. 'And by God that was a surprise and a half you sprung on him this afternoon. It should be a great friendship between you and him that starts today. A great friendship. Yes, yes. And you know,' – he chuckled suddenly – 'it surprised me too. I don't think I've ever been more astonished in my life.'

Again the two short men giggled together.

'But there'll be no bad blood,' continued Lord Catterock. 'I can say that,' he added with a judicial air, 'for of course it cost me something to be astonished. I would have chosen that that meeting took a very different course. I would, indeed,' he pronounced, shaking his head. But he sighed and threw off his momentary sadness, though he remained solemn. 'But it's no use resenting what you did, and I know it. We'll all forgive you. It'll pay us to forgive you. You're a grand man, and this age belongs to you. You have special qualities, Mr Ganymedios, special qualities that our age respects. You've got the world at your feet, and I would give a lot to be you. I am an old man now, and my sun is setting. But yours is rising. A splendid dawn, Mr Ganymedios. Everything is coming your way. In a few years everything you want will be yours.'

'In a few years?' asked Nestor. 'But I may have it already, everything I want. In a few years I may have more than everything I want, and that it will be good, it will be very good, it is perhaps that also that I want. But as for everything I want, I got the last piece of it four days ago, when I married the most beautiful woman in the world. Where are you, my dear, where are you, my Rosamund?'

Rosamund moved slowly forward, her blindish look on her. For just an instant the two men were amazed by her beauty, and by its kind. Then Lord Catterock assumed an expression that again he was hoping would be recognised by everybody in the room as puckish, which he retained while he paid her a string of compliments. He was savouring the joke which comes into being when any tall woman marries a little man. But Lord Branchester's amazement passed coldly into nothing so kindly as obscene laughter. Yet he must have admired her very much, for he liked women to be good-looking, he had a special fondness for Mary, and Rosamund was the type he liked, for his wife, to whom he was devoted, resembled her. But wherever Rosamund went with Nestor, the more people admired her, the more they would despise her.

'Forgive me if I cannot take my eyes off you,' Lord Catterock was saying to her, stretching his mouth as if he meant to eat her, 'but I adore beautiful women and I adore beautiful jewels, and that diamond necklace might even be said to be worthy of its wearer.'

Poor Rosamund bowed slightly, and Nestor, low at her side, cried out: 'I was dying, here in this hotel I was dying, I had worse than double pneumonia, I had triple pneumonia, and when the doctor came in every morning he did not say, "You are going to die this evening," I was so bad that he always said, "Surely you died last night?" and my Rosamund came to me as my nurse, and when she came into the room in her white cap and apron I said to myself, "Pray God she is a good nurse, for if she is a bad nurse I will die, and I want to live, to give her the diamonds, for on her the diamonds would look better than on the velvet case in a jeweller's window," and she was a good nurse, and I have given her the diamonds she deserved.' Lord Branchester's glance grew harder still. He was not the stuff of which martyrs are made. Being treated with contempt, he

74

found some relief in thinking contemptuously of the good-looking nurse who, when her rich patient grew amorous, could turn the situation to her advantage.

Of course Rosamund was aware that he was despising her. I saw her grasp his error to its last false implications; and I knew she would grasp all the cruelties and treacheries of this horrible party. She could not be called observant. That would be too sharp a word. Simply she became conscious of everything which happened where she was, as a looking-glass reflects the objects within the angle of reflection. She would know that the people in the room regarded her as having sold herself to a freak of dubious origin and morals, and she would only have to look from face to face to realise what base variations of conduct each, according to his or her baseness, would ascribe to her. She would understand, as even we, with our ignorance of business, had understood, that her husband had committed a fraud, not less repulsively fraudulent because it was within the law, and that there was a depth of fraudulence below that. We did not know what Nestor Ganymedios had done at the shareholders' meeting, but we were sure that it had not surprised Lord Catterock. He had not even troubled to sound sincere when he talked of his astonishment. He had been conveying to Lord Branchester: 'The first time I cheated you I got you so thoroughly in my power that now I am cheating you a second time you dare not say a word in protest, and I can make you shake the hand of the little rascal from nowhere that I made my instrument.' To every fine shade in the judas-colour with which the moment was suffused Rosamund would be as sensitive as Mary and I were sensitive to tones and half-tones and quarter-tones.

Our eyes met. I knew she knew that I was thinking: 'No wonder we were not touched by this man when he said he would consider us as his family, for he is a cold-hearted little thief and liar.' Her eyes left mine. They travelled slowly round the room. She can have seen nothing that she would like. Since the arrival of Lord Catterock and Lord Branchester the atmosphere of the party had been emptied of irony. The guests were now no longer taking out insurance in sly smiles. Their insincerity was not in a pure state. They looked at Nestor Ganymedios with an affected admiration, but felt under no necessity to reveal that it was affected. Now the time would begin when they would press on her without reserve friendship that she knew was worthless.

It was not fair that Nancy should have had so beautiful a wedding and that Rosamund should know such want as a bride. That night before Nancy's marriage-day Uncle Len and I had stood in the wealth of light that fell from the winter moon and stars, giving even the graves their share of living glory, and had listened to the waters, pouring over a far-off weir, abundant as the moments of time; in the boiler-room his shovel had searched piously for its due burden among the loose coal, and would have counted no labour too great to serve his dear Nancy; and the inn where all our people slept had lain under the clear night as the centre of a great estate, stretching to the walls of the universe. But this room was hot and full of smoke; and the people who sat in it, half-seen, were a part not of life, but of its scum. I got up and went out into the corridor, and Mary followed me.

We found Mr Morpurgo walking up and down. He said, 'I am so glad that your Mamma and Richard Quin are not here to see this.'

Mary said fiercely, 'I wish they were, for they could tell us the explanation.'

We walked the length of the corridor and back, and Mr Morpurgo timidly asked pardon. 'It is quite some time since your Mamma died. Sometimes I forget what her world is. But, of course, there must be an explanation.'

Presently Lord Catterock and Lord Branchester came out of the party, and walked past us. 'There, that wasn't so bad, was it?' asked Lord Catterock. He got no reply and he asked again, 'It wasn't so hard, was it?'

'No,' said Lord Branchester.

Some people barred our way, and we had to stand beside the pair as they were waiting for the lift. 'He's an able fellow,' Lord Catterock was saying, 'and nothing will get him off the horse now he's in the saddle. No use crying over spilt milk, you know. We all have to take a knock sometimes, particularly as we get older. Ah, we all lose our grip in time, Branchester. I've lost mine. Well do I know it, for I never should have let this little fellow spring this surprise on us.'

The party was breaking up, other guests came out. We went back, and Nestor took us by both hands, and waved us to a sofa in a corner where Alan and Cordelia and Constance were sitting. We stayed in silence while Nestor said goodbye to his guests. The last to go was Mr Ramponetti. 'He is my London representative,' Nestor explained, 'and if ever any of you should want money suddenly, he will give it to you.'

'And if ever he wants money suddenly,' said Mr Ramponetti, grinning, 'he will ask you for it.'

'He is always a very witty man,' explained Nestor, when he had shut the door on him. 'A very strange character. His mother was an Albanian. But where is my wife? Where is my Rosamund? Rosamund, Rosamund!' He ran into the bedroom and led her out by the wrist. 'Strange girl,' he said as she sat down in front of a little table covered with used glasses and coffee-cups and ash-trays, on which she bent her eyes with a curious intentness. She was perhaps telling herself that these were emblems of her new kingdom. 'She was standing by the window, looking out over the river, with not a light in the room. She is poetical, she will like it when I take her to Istanbul and to Syria. The Syrian Riviera is superior to the French. But we have many other things to talk of than tourism.'

This should have been true. Yet there was a silence before Mary said, 'Rose and I have been wondering what to give you for a wedding-present.'

'How difficult a question,' said Nestor, 'since she will have all. I am giving her everything. What indeed can you give her?'

'Give me your Mamma's work-box,' said Rosamund.

'But Mamma never sewed. She could not, any more than we can. It is so bad for the hands.'

'Yet she had a work-box,' said Rosamund. 'Her grandmother had given it to her. None of you thought much of it. It was not very pretty. It was mahogany and it had a band around it of inlay, and it stood on brass claws.'

'I remember the thing,' I said, 'but it isn't pretty at all. It's a clumsy brute, we never had it anywhere where it could be seen. If you want anything that was at Lovegrove you can have anything you choose.'

'I want that work-box,' said Rosamund. 'You kept it in the dining-room cupboard, under the shelf where you kept the table linen, and one day when I was helping your Mamma to put away a heavy cloth she took out the box and showed me what was inside. There are little ivory spindles and tiny scissors and a mother-of-pearl needle-case and a tatting-shuttle, and they had not been used for a long time, if ever. And your Mamma said, "When I was a real pianist I could not sew because of my hands, not that I am too busy, but I would like to

77

have not just another life but so many lives that I could spend one being lazy, and could do embroidery and fancy needle-work, and could sit for hours using these little things."' Rosa-mund laughed. 'I like to think of that, of having so many lives that it would be safe to idle one away.'

'I will fill your life so full that you will not want more than one,' said Nestor, 'and work, never think of it again. Poor child, I think she does not realise that someone has come to take her away from her nursing, as Alan has taken Cordelia away from whatever it was that she was doing, as someone will come to take Mary and Rose away from their piano-playing.'

'I remember elderly ladies tatting when I was young,' Constance told the silence in her flat, informative voice. 'The movement was supposed to show off a pretty hand.'

'All women look beautiful when they are sewing,' said Nestor. 'I have six sisters younger than I am, and they are all beautiful, and when my father and my mother had found each other again they had a house in Salonica, and on the flat roof my six sisters would be sitting, and they would all be sewing, and my heart would turn to water, they were so beautiful. Alas, that all this turned out not so good.'

'Why, what happened to them?' asked Alan, with a laugh that was supposed to show that he was not finding the situation brought on him by his wife's relatives too much but was actually enjoying it.

'Well, I am rich now, and I think I will always be rich, for I have seen to it that if I fall others will fall with me, and they will rather save me and save themselves. That Lord Catterock has got me, but he will see soon that I too have got him. But in the past I have sometimes been rich and sometimes I have been poor, and the condition of my sisters would not keep pace with my condition. They became marriageable without regard to my purse, and you cannot say to a woman's figure, "Go back, it is not time to show yourself, lie flat till the rate of exchange is different." So some of them are married to rich men, which should be so, and some are married to poor men, which should not be so. For poverty is a kind of sickness, one would not choose to be with the sick, and there is also a fitness of things, a beautiful woman should have a rich husband, if she is not a fool, a rich man should have a beautiful wife, if he is not a fool. Such harmony is in immortal souls, as our great Shakespeare says. But this marriage thing with my sisters goes better. The poorest of their husbands is sick, and I think he will die.' He rose and went and stood in front of a mirror and took a comb from his pocket and combed his hair. 'If he should die I will arrange it well and will marry her to a rich husband. That will be better, for this poor one is a most miserable man. Thinking of him I had the need to get up and arrange myself to see that I was not as he is. But enough, let us have more champagne and let us finish those caviare tartlets. You eat nothing, Rosamund. Eat something, my beloved, it would not suit you to be thin. You must not lose those fine shoulders.'

'For our present,' said Alan, 'we have sent down to the boat a picnic-basket.'

'A beautiful present,' said Nestor, 'just the present people should make to other English people. We shall use our picnic-basket much, when we go to our cottage on the Wannsee, for you do not know how fortunate Rosamund is, she will have two homes. I have told you how the great Schaffhausen would build only cathedrals and town halls but not dwelling-houses, they were too small, till he met me, and then he became humble, and built me a house at Dahlem. Well, coming to know me during the building of the house, he became more humble still and built me a cottage by the Wannsee. There I have a boat, a beautiful boat, and I am very skilful in navigation, I could also have been a sea-captain, and I will take Rosamund all the way to the Baltic by the waterways.' Rosamund's eyes were perhaps set on the end of that voyage; but indeed whenever he spoke for any length of time she stared into the distance. 'It will be like Wagner, it will be like *Tristan and Isolde*,' Nestor went on, lowering his eyelids and dilating his nostrils, 'only nobody will die, we will live and we will love, and we will take your picnic-basket, because you gave it to us. It will be dear to us for that reason, so we will never leave it behind, though of course the boat is fitted up to give all food and drink. Have more champagne, my new family, let us finish up the caviare.'

'And what shall I give you, Rosamund?' said Mr Morpurgo.
She said, 'Give me a drawing of yourself.'

'But I am dreadful to look at,' said poor Mr Morpurgo, humbly.

'No, you are not!' cried Rosamund and Mary and I; and Rosamund added, 'You see, it seems that I am to spend my life abroad, in Germany or else in South America. I must have a picture of you to take with me. Not a photograph. Think how Mary and Rose never look quite themselves in a photograph.'

Mr Morpurgo was about to answer when Nestor exclaimed, 'How is it possible that I should have forgotten anything so important! No, not a drawing of him. But a portrait of my wife. Is it possible that not till this minute did I think that I must have, it is absolutely necessary, a portrait of my wife, life-size, and that diamond necklace, also life-size. Tell me, Mr Morpurgo, your pictures are worth millions, who can paint this beautiful woman and this beautiful diamond necklace.'

'Rosamund should have been painted by Paulo Veronese,' said Mr Morpurgo.

'But naturally it must not be someone dead,' said Nestor. 'Above all it must be someone alive.' But he struck himself on the forehead. 'Yet, dead or alive, who can paint a diamond necklace? I have been many places, and museums I have not spared, and there are many pictures which show beautiful women as they are, but there are no pictures of diamonds which are truly like diamonds – never do you see a picture of a diamond which is so that you would buy a diamond of which it was the picture. How can that be? But why do I ask? It is plain. Artists do not think of diamonds. They are poor, particularly when they are young. When one is poor one does not think of diamonds. I know. I have been very poor, if I had had a coin to bite between my teeth would I have joined the Istanbul Fire Brigade? So I know that when one is poor one does not think of diamonds. There are days and weeks, and in bad times even months, when the thought of diamonds does not cross the mind, though not years, for the heart of man is full of hope. Only if one is rich can one think of diamonds all the time? Which of you in this room thinks often of diamonds except me and Mr Morpurgo? It would be waste of time. So it is with artists, they do not think of diamonds, they paint what they think of, they think much of women, for the poorest man must think of women all the time, so artists paint women and again women and again women, and they get much practice, and they learn to paint them very well. But they do not think of diamonds, and never they learn how to put them on the canvas as you see them on my wife's shoulders, not shining blue and green and red but white all the time. To people like me and Mr Morpurgo it is hardly fair.'

Mary and I laughed, and stopped because our laughter made him look cross. Cordelia's short upper lip became very short. Because of her training as an art dealer she took art very seriously.

'There is another reason,' said Mr Morpurgo.

'No, believe me there is not,' said Nestor. 'I know. I know. It is only by accident that I am a businessman. All I could have been, musician or poet or sculptor or painter. Oh, how I wept the first time I saw Venice, and it is not unnatural, for among my mother's brothers were all gifts. So I am very artistic and I understand what is in all artists' minds.'

'No, there is another reason,' insisted Mr Morpurgo. He spoke in a bored but firm tone, as an Englishman might if, captured by Moslem enemies, he found himself under some necessity to assert his Christian faith. His ultimate loyalties went to Mamma and his pictures. 'Painting sets out to do certain things and it leaves everything alone which interferes with its task. It does not represent various sorts of matter which are so arresting in their difference from all other sorts that it would be difficult to harmonise an exact representation of them with other objects in a picture.'

'You do not believe me,' said Nestor, 'because always you have had money, you have had diamonds as you have had a wife. But this does not matter, if we cannot get the diamonds painted well but we have them. Take off the necklace, my dear, and let your beautiful cousins look at them.'

Obediently Rosamund raised her hands to undo the clasp. 'Look,' said Nestor, 'the most beautiful arms in the world.' Her downcast face told us that she did not think the clasp would ever open. 'I must help, little intricate things she does not understand as well as I do,' he said. As he worked at the clasp he rolled his eyes at us over her head. 'The nape of her neck is like a child's.' But he grew grave with respect as he felt the weight of the necklace in his hand. He put it down on the table in front of Rosamund, drew up a chair beside her, and cried out to us, 'Come nearer. You shall not often see such a wonderful thing, even now, and you certainly never dreamed of anything like it in that little house at Lovegrove where all you four beautiful women were children. No, very surely there can have been nothing like this here,' he chuckled, but broke off to look over at Mr Morpurgo and wink, as one shrewd man at another, 'and yet what a success-box was that little house! Remarkable, was it not, *hein*? Not one but has done well for herself one way or another. And now this little piece of good fortune, come close and see it. Do you understand such things, what is your name, Alan? I will explain it to you, for I could also have been a

81

great jeweller. See,' he said, rising to his feet, for he was too short to speak to us all unless he stood up.

His zest had filled his mouth with saliva, so he had to stop and wipe it away; and as he stood with his handkerchief at his lips he looked down on his wife. She was to us misery made visible. Her eyes had gone into the feared distance, and her defeated body slumped within her clothes. 'But I am a fool,' he cried, 'to buy this woman a diamond necklace! How beautiful she is without it! How specially beautiful are her shoulders.' An impulse quivered through him, he resisted it for a moment, then it forced him down to her, his mouth munching. It seemed certain that he was going to bury his face in her shoulders and rub his babyish cheeks against the bare flesh. For only a second was she less aware of this than we were. Then disgust pulled down the corners of her mouth so that we saw the gums under her lower teeth, and pushed up her cheeks so that her eyes became slits. A twitch of her head showed that, like us, she knew exactly where his face was going to touch her, at a point below her ear, at the base of her neck, and we could feel abhorrence travelling over the skin of her body. Helpless, we watched her increasing nervousness and fear, and did not at first remark that he had drawn away from her.

He was standing quite upright, holding out the necklace and laughing, 'My God, my God, I love my wife so much that I nearly dropped it.' She raised her head and smiled at him as tenderly as she had ever smiled at any of us.

We got up and said that we must go, and asked when the boat train was leaving, so that we could see them off. But Nestor said, busy clasping the necklace on his wife's neck, 'It goes in the afternoon, but we will not be there. All I do is so important that I cannot make anything in the ordinary way. My secretaries yes, the boat train is for them, but Rosamund and I go with Mr Ramponetti in his fine car to lunch with the great Lord Catterock. But so it is, you cannot see Rosamund off, and you must kiss her and make your lamentations with her tonight.'

The three of us went into the bedroom with Rosamund to get our coats, as Nestor was saying to Mr Morpurgo, 'Will you not have a last glass of champagne while the women say goodbye, for we know they will be long, hahaha, the little ones. I would like to ask you many things, including whether you know of my grandfather, who was of Baghdad.'

In the bedroom we took Rosamund in our arms and kissed her, although Cordelia was there, and we told her how much we loved her, and hoped she would be happy, and wanted to be with her when she came back. But her face under my lips, her body in my arms, was preoccupied to that total degree impossible in the mind. I could have drawn a sentence or two from her that would have shown regard for our plight, if I had forgotten the decencies and spoken of it. But her body had no pity, it said, 'I have gone from you.'

Cordelia, very pretty and neat in her squirrel coat, her red-gold curls combed so that she could go out through the foyer looking as she should, said, 'Well, it has all been very nice.'

I looked back into our childhood and cried out, 'Rosamund, that time you pretended that you had told fortunes as well as me, and you were whipped too!' And Mary said something I did not understand about a parcel. But, of course, she too must have had her temptations to traffic with evil, though she would have yielded less than I did, for I was the darkest member of the family. I cannot give certain passages of music their true grace. But dark as she was, and darker as I was, Rosamund had lent us her light.

Cordelia said, 'Come, we ought to go. Remember they are leaving tomorrow.'

In our arms Rosamund was alive again, she kissed us with a real mouth, her eyes shone, and she tried to speak, though her stammer would not let her. 'Lovegrove!' was all she could say. Her firm flesh trembled with recollected joy, it was as if marble should feel happiness.

Constance, coming into the room at that moment, repeated, 'Lovegrove.'

We asked ourselves again how she was taking this marriage; and again her smooth and colourless exterior remained simply an exterior. She slowly crossed the room, saying again, 'Lovegrove,' and sat down by the window. 'It was a great privilege to be there, and many marvels happened to us. But do not forget that it all rested on a firm foundation.' She had often reminded us of the sort of statuary that is found on Victorian town halls, and now she seemed as if she might be reading from such an inscription as is sometimes carved on these buildings. 'Your Mamma took in Rosamund and me when we had nothing and she had little more. But neither she nor any of you children grudged sharing with us, though there was no margin. None at all. It meant less for all of you. More wonderful things happened in your house, but that was wonderful also.'

Rosamund, choked with her stammer, nodded, and wound her fingers in ours.

'When things are complicated,' Constance went on, 'it is often a help to think of something quite simple. I shall often think of the generosity of you and your Mamma, for it is the simplest side of what you did for us.'

She was paying us and our mother a moral compliment without the smallest doubt of her right to do so; and she would have been aware if she had lost that right. She was right. She had had nothing when she came to us. But I remembered how, more than once, she made some slight, hardly visible error in her needlework that had threatened to make the finished garment just less than perfect, and she had gone out and bought new material at her own expense and started the work afresh. And this was how soldiers going back to the front used to talk. 'I shall often think. . .' There must indeed be some sanctification of this marriage. But at that moment there was a knock on the door, and Mr Morpurgo stood on the threshold. 'Rosamund, I am sorry, but I think we should be going home. Mary and Rose have had a long journey, and it is late.' Something that Nestor had said had made him very angry. He had been polite, of course, and Nestor did not know it, but stood behind him, as pleased as he could be. But we knew it, and so did Rosamund.

Her eyes went to our faces, and we must have gone back to doubt. She grew grey, and said, 'You are quite right, it is late, dear, dear Mr Morpurgo,' and held out her arms to him. 'Now it is goodbye,' she said, and bent down and waited for his kiss.

He gave it very coolly.

She straightened herself, and looked round at all of us. For the first time in my life I saw her visibly wish to make a claim for herself, to take her own part, like the rest of us. She sighed and tried to renounce, but could not quite. She put her hand under the diamonds at her neck, so that they blazed, and her eyes went from face to face. It could not be that she was saying what she must be saying: 'Whatever you may think of him he gave me these.' And indeed she stammered words none of us could have predicted. 'I should so like Richard Quin to have seen this necklace.'

Mr Morpurgo stepped back. 'Would you?' he asked incredulously.

She nodded, smiling at us all.

Slowly he gave her another kiss, and Nestor asked, 'Who is this Richard Quin?'

'Our brother, who was killed,' said Mary.

'Ah, yes, she has told me of him, she tells me all, even the little sentimental things. But he was a young boy. Did he know about the precious stones? Had he taste?'

'Marvellous taste,' said Mr Morpurgo, and slowly we moved towards the door, and out into the corridor, and stood by the lift, and faced the knowledge that we were to have no knowledge.

'But your address in Berlin. Quick, has anybody got pencil and paper?'

'You do not need them. I left the address with Kate this morning.'

'And Mr Ramponetti will tell you any day where we are. In each of my offices there is a huge map with many flags on it, and one red flag bigger than the rest. That is me.'

'I am so glad you managed to see Kate.'

'Of course I did, and we went down to the Dog and Duck yesterday.'

'Was Nancy there?'

'No. We missed her. We missed Miss Beevor too. You must give them all sorts of messages.'

'I will send you a drawing, Rosamund. I think I know a man who could do it.'

'I have many pictures and drawings, but we will take down one to give your portrait a place.'

'Oh, goodbye, dear, dear Rosamund.'

'Do not worry about her, I will be the best husband, and you will stay with us often in Berlin, and I will make you more famous than you ever hoped to be in Germany.'

The lift dropped, and we were carried down in silence. While Alan and Mr Morpurgo looked for their cars we three stood in the foyer. 'Now,' said Cordelia, and stopped, because she was choking with tears. 'Now. I hope you see that I was right all the time.'

'Right? About what?'

'Why, about Rosamund.' We said nothing and her voice rose to a high whisper. 'I always knew.'

'Knew what?'

'Why, this,' she said. We looked coltish, and her foot drummed on the floor. 'Why will you never admit that I was the only

85

one at home who ever showed any common sense about anything? I was always right about everything. I was right about Rosamund. I would have expected her to do just this.'

For a while she was silent, and we stared at the swing doors, waiting for the men. Then she broke out again, 'Are you not ashamed? Are you not ashamed of always having put her before me?'

We could not be angry with her. She was frightened, as we were, because Rosamund was acting out of character, and Rosamund's character was the ground we lived on. Cordelia's honesty made her recognise this, and she said, swallowing, 'Not that she was not very kind to me when that horrible man pretended I could not play the violin and you all believed him. But this is dreadful. It is so hard on Alan. I felt so ashamed at having brought him here tonight to see one of our family and finding that Rosamund had done this awful thing. Oh, there you are, Mr Morpurgo. I saw you were as upset as I was, as we were. Now Mary and Rose are pretending that there is nothing wrong, but I feel so humiliated because of Alan. It is all right for Alan to have to treat Aunt Lily and Nancy as if they were members of our family, they are so unfortunate. But this man is so dreadfully the opposite, there is no question of feeling sorry for him.'

'Wouldn't you want to know Aunt Lily and Nancy if they were fortunate?' asked Mary, smiling.

'You and Rose are hopeless,' said Cordelia. 'You see what I mean, don't you, Mr Morpurgo?'

'I should,' he said, 'I have known so many Jews who preferred to have no relations with their own people except as members of the Jewish Board of Guardians.'

'You are teasing,' said Cordelia. 'I have nobody but Alan, really,' she exclaimed, with a flash of anger, and walked away from us, but turned back after a step or two to say, 'Come to dinner tomorrow night, if you can.' Mr Morpurgo said he could not, though he always liked to dine with her, and we said we would try, so she told us, 'Eight o'clock, and do try not to be late.' It was a belief of hers, from which she derived much pleasure, that we were very unpunctual, though as public performers we had to cultivate a fussy sense of time. As Alan came through the swing doors she hurried to him for comfort; we saw him bend down to give it.

We expected Mr Morpurgo to take us to his car. But he stood

still. 'Was it not rather neat, what I said then about the Jewish Board of Guardians?' he asked us, dimpling, and did not move until we told him that it was not rather neat, but very neat. We knew why he was lingering. Like us, he wanted to get into the lift and go up to the suite we had just left and say to Rosamund, 'Why have you married this man?' But it was not a question that could be asked of any bride, no matter how good an answer she might be able to give; and Rosamund could have no answer at all within the limits of probability. To explain Nestor, she would have to say: 'Do you not understand? We are two Signs of that different Zodiac, which follows the path of the sun not seen here but by other stars. We are now in conjunction, that is all our marriage means.' Or again: 'Be easy in your mind. It is only that we are two cards in a tarot pack, drawn by an invisible giant who is holding them close in his hand while he ponders some divination, naturally not to be read at a first glance, in view of the peculiar circumstances.' When I thought that, I was thinking of magic as if I knew nothing of it, but when I remembered what I knew of it, I could believe that the explanation was indeed rooted in magical practice. Again it seemed possible that Rosamund was marrying this man because she had looked into the future and had seen him beggared or insane. But again I saw the altar decked with white flowers as I had seen it on the eve of Nancy's marriage, as I stood alone in the church, which smelt as stone does at night, and in the boiler-room Uncle Len's shovel lurched through the coal till it got its due burden and tipped it prudently on the furnace; and as I had seen it during the marriage, when the day, that commonly makes things obscure which are clear in the darkness, could not destroy the mystery of the cross and the table. I was aware that there is no wall between magic and the common law of operations of cause and effect; for if Rosamund had looked into the future and seen Nestor beggared or insane and had married him, against that day, she was performing the same sort of act as Nancy and Oswald, when they had taken each other for better or worse. The essence of the situation between Rosamund and Nestor was that they were husband and wife; and that situation would have been, whatever their circumstances, incredibly strange.

We were foolish to stand there, asking questions that could not be answered in terms within our comprehension. We went out with Mr Morpurgo to the huge nest of his car, and settled down on each side of him, deep in rugs. It was so late that when we left the West End and approached our home there were no people in the streets, we might have been entering a zone deserted because of disaster. Outside the classical church opposite Lord's the girl on the monument was praying obstinately under slanting shafts of rain. She reminded us of the existence of a technique that might have helped us if we had ever had time to master it. When we reached home Mary got out of the car first, and I found her standing quite still on the pavement looking up at the house, though she had the key in her hand; and I too stood still.

'What are you looking at?' asked Mr Morpurgo.

'The house is dark except for the drawing-room and the hall,' I said. 'Kate is not in her little sitting-room in the basement. Usually she sits up for us when we come back from a tour.'

'But it is very late,' said Mr Morpurgo, 'and like all of us, she is older than she was.'

'However late it has been,' Mary said, 'she has always stayed up for us before.'

'You are tired,' said Mr Morpurgo, 'it has all been too much for you.' He took the key from Mary's hand and went up the stairs to our front door, and led us in. 'Look, your lovely room is waiting for you. They have put flowers in all the vases. Some I sent, but other people sent more, though you know what I am, I tried to send most. But too many people love you, I could not succeed. And there is the biscuit-box, and there is the milk in your electric saucepan. Everything you want. I will sit with you till you eat your biscuit and drink your milk.'

'And for you,' said Mary, 'there will be a bottle of Perrier in the refrigerator.'

'How well you know me,' he said. 'Yes, I feel myself a hot and greasy little man, when I am faced with the prospect of going to bed and seeing myself through the small hours I like to cool myself down with very cold water.' He sat down heavily on the sofa and Mary went down to the kitchen. I stood by the hearth and took off my hat and looked through the door she had left open at the table in the hall, stacked with letters I would not want to read, because they were not from Rosamund. 'She will write,' I told him, speaking as if there at least we had gained a victory over fate.

'She writes bad letters,' he said. We let the clock make all the noise in the room for some moments. Then he sighed, 'She will write no more than your mother does.'

'What, is she going to die?' I asked in consternation.

'I did not mean that, it is not me who knows such things,' he said. 'But, like your mother, she has gone.'

'Yes, like Mamma. And it was right that Mamma should go, and it is...'

'Yes,' he said mildly, 'but she has gone.'

Mary brought in the Perrier water and poured it out for him, and repeated, 'She has gone.'

'Well, it is glorious,' I said.

'It may be, but all the same, we are alone,' she said.

'We have each other,' I protested, weakly.

'But we are by nature children. We do not know how to live alone. Mamma and Rosamund and Richard Quin are by nature parents. They have gone away. However many there might be of us left behind, we are still deserted children.'

'Yes, I am by nature a child,' said Mr Morpurgo.

'We may be children but we are not deserted,' I objected. 'They would have stayed with us if they could.'

'It has been agony for them to leave us, but what difference does that make? We are none the less deserted children. The power that uses them has pushed us off alone on a raft.'

'It will be hard to be without her help when Queenie comes out of prison,' said Mr Morpurgo.

'Yes, down at the Dog and Duck they are by nature children too,' I said. 'But we will just have to imagine what Mamma and Rosamund and Richard Quin would have done and act it out. And this may all be over by then. Something may have happened, she may be back with us.' I repeated it confidently, 'She may be back with us.'

Neither of them answered until Mr Morpurgo said, 'That milk is boiling over.'

It was too hot to drink at once. We each took a biscuit. Mary wiped the crumbs from her mouth to ask violently, 'Where does this man come from? What is he?'

'His grandfather was of Baghdad, he tells me,' said Mr Morpurgo, his mouth pulled down at the corners, 'but more recently there seems to have been a Levantine connection. And he said something about Polish relatives. But one could not tell. He is not a Jew.' Coldly he added, 'I think he is what the Jews, who come from the same quarter of the globe, feared to become, and that is why they all took the tiresome precautions that add up to Judaism.'

We drank our milk, and the clock ticked. He burst out, 'The creature is too ugly. He is ugly in such an ugly way. I always thought there was pitifulness in ugliness, like the pitifulness of death, but in him there is none.' He ran his hand over his face and shuddered. Suddenly it appeared what divided him from his family. He loathed his wife because, being beautiful, she had found it possible to marry a man who looked as he did, and he felt his children to be strangers, because they were not ugly like himself.

'But she has married him for a reason,' said Mary.

He answered, 'Oh, I know that. I have not forgotten your Mamma, and how it went with the people about her. And she would not have spoken of Richard Quin if this marriage was what it looked like.' He thought for a long time; and he was surely thinking of his own marriage. He said, 'I wonder,' and stopped. Then continued, 'Oh, we know that Rosamund is immortal among the mortals, and that incorruptibility has raised her above corruption. But we are not sure of it, we wish to know it as we wish to know that Big Ben will strike the hour. And anyway she is gone from us. My dear children, I must go home. I have a great trouble of my own. Shall I tell you what it is? It is not my own dear old chauffeur who is driving me tonight, it is the young one. I will not feel it possible to ask him if I may sit beside him as we drive home. I might feel it more possible if he were a Jew, but he is not. Why do I always have goys around me? But anyway I shall sit in the back of the car all by myself, and I shall feel, oh, you know how I will feel, for it is how you are feeling. Good night, my dears.'

We kissed him and helped him on with his coat, and opened the front door. 'You must have noticed,' he said, 'how much I have been talking of Jewish things tonight. I am driven back on my last defences.' We watched him go down the steps, looking up at the red moon that was appearing through two storm clouds, shake his head, and get into the car, the back of the car.

In the drawing-room Mary went and stood beside the sofa, and said, 'She lay there that night she came to tell us of Nancy's engagement. Oh, in this world of miracles, do one that is an act of grace, set her down there again, let us have her here. Let us keep her here. Let us see her hair first, then her face, then her

90

hands, then her body, all of her, and let us keep her here for ever. But look, there is nothing. There is never anything but these demands, this harshness, this avarice for pain, never generosity.' She went back to the fire, tried to pick up her cup of milk, but her hands were trembling, she had to set it down. 'When we first went in and saw her sitting on the bed it was terrible. I understood why Lucretia had to kill herself.'

'Yes, but she was glorious too,' I said.

'I wish such glory had passed her by.'

'But she thinks nothing better than such glory. So did Mamma.'

She said softly, 'Oh, poor Mamma! Oh, poor Rosamund!' and wept. But she broke off and pointed to the open door, and said, 'Hush!'

'What is it?'

'Kate has come out of her room. Do not let her find us crying.'

I could hear nothing. But Mary's senses were almost more acute than mine.

'Now she is coming downstairs.'

'Yes, I hear that. But how slowly she is coming. Oh, but we're wrong. I don't think we really heard anything. Surely there's not a sound now.'

'She has stopped. She is standing quite still on the landing.'

'Well, let us go and meet her.'

'No, wait. Wait. Listen, she is going upstairs again.'

'Yes, I can hear that. Now she is closing her door. Mary, what does it mean? Can anything be wrong with the old dear? Hadn't we better go and speak to her?'

'No. No. Oh, Rose, I am frightened. When I went down to the kitchen to get the bottle of Perrier, there was a wet circle on the scullery floor.'

'You think she has been looking in a bucket of water as her mother used to do?'

'Of course. Nestor and Rosamund came to see her this morning. She thought of him as we did, and she could not bear it, and looked in the water and saw the future.'

'And because of what she saw she dare not face us. I understand.'

Mary took up her cup of milk with a steady hand and said, 'There is everything in this universe except mercy,' and began to sip it, but set it down again. 'Surely this is nonsense. Are you

91

sure you heard Kate on the stairs? Are you certain you did not merely think you heard her because I suggested it to you? After all, we are dead tired because of that tour, that voyage, that abominable party. It may simply have been that someone had put some floor-cloths to soak in a bucket that was over-full. All that we know is that Rosamund is what Mamma and Richard Quin are, she is eternal, she is part of what keeps the stars from rushing away from each other, and now she is doing something we cannot understand. Let us go to bed, we must get some practice in tomorrow.'

IV

THE NEXT MORNING Kate herself brought up my breakfast tray, as she always did the day after we had come home, and at first I judged that there had been nothing in our suspicions. For she at once owned, with her stiff, ship's-figurehead forthrightness, that she had not felt able to wait up for us the night before because she had been so upset by meeting Miss Rosamund's husband. She had known we would be distressed when we found our cousin married to a heathen who was not a gentleman like our Papa, even though there must be a good reason for the marriage; and she had not wished to add to our distress by her own tears. But I had a later intimation that our doubts had been well founded. I told her of our stormy voyage, and she said she had guessed how it must be with us, for she had never seen so many seagulls about. Everybody knew, of course, that year by year more of them were settling down as river-gulls, but even so there had been such a flock of the creatures about, all acting like strangers, that she had been sure they were true seagoers, taking refuge from bad weather. There had been some on the garden-wall of the house opposite nearly all week, she said; and she went to the window to see if they were still there. So they were; and she sighed deeply, and said, 'Ah, well. It is promised in the Bible, "And there shall be no more sea."' Nothing was more certain than that Kate would have been a sailor if she had been a man, and she would not have repeated that cruel text unless she had been brought up to tolerate it by foreknowledge of a storm which would not be weathered by one she loved.

Down at the Dog and Duck, I found a few days later, they had much to think of besides Rosamund's marriage, for it was a year of floods. The Thames had not been so high for thirty years. I went in, waiting till men said 'To you, from me,' at angles of the passage, effectively enough for the piano to get by, and stepped over rolls of carpet to get into the denuded tearoom, where Aunt Milly and Aunt Lily were standing at the open french window, looking down at the river that was lapping the grass not three yards away. They were excited both by the peril to their goods and by the demented beauty of the inundated landscape. 'Look at the ferry-bell hanging there!' they said; the post was standing in the midst of the glassy rushing current, with no sign that it was supposed to be on the other side of the Thames and on dry land. The fields beyond were now a lake, steel-grey under violet storm clouds, and across it a line of willows, their budding branches a rich crimson, marked a submerged dike. In its lee thirty snow-white swans and their smoky cygnets rode at anchor, and were so still that they must have apprehended danger. But the sunlight was caught in the bronze woodlands on the banks that ran along the downward flow of the river, and I said, 'Surely it's going to be good weather now?'

'Not blooming likely,' they both wailed, and went on at once to talk of Rosamund's marriage.

'Mark you,' said Aunt Lily. 'That girl's the victim of a plot. She couldn't have married him, not him, if there hadn't been foul play somewhere.'

'What plot could there be?' asked Aunt Milly, reasonably enough. 'You've got it wrong. It's that nursing that's done it. I never thought it right for a pretty girl like Rosamund, and she taking everything so seriously, to go in for doing good that way. She's just thought herself into such a state, always living in hospitals, and treating accidents, people who've been run over and lost a leg and got their faces smashed up, that she's forgotten what ordinary people look like. She probably doesn't even see this little chap the way we do.'

Inside the bar Uncle Len was wondering whether to move the grandfather's clock. 'I'm going to leave it till the last moment. It's as heavy as the Nelson column and both times we've moved it before somebody's set it down too hasty and there's been a bill as long as your arm. Funny little fellow, that Ganywhatsisname. Now, am I a fool to leave that clock where it is, or am I not? But Ros knows what she's doing, of course. No need to worry about her. I'll leave that clock.'

'Len,' cried Aunt Lily, rushing into the room, 'you said the river's falling, well, it isn't. It's coming up while you look at it.' She rushed out again, pausing to tell me, with a censorious air, 'It's so dreadful to stand and watch it turning against one like this.'

'Bless her heart, she's always wrong,' said Uncle Len. 'I'll leave that clock where it is. No, hang it all, that's the awkward thing about Lil. You can't even rely on her always to be wrong. Once in a while she's right, which throws one out. I'd better go look for myself.'

This happened to be one of the times when she was right. We spent the next few hours helping to move the remaining furniture and some stores and the lines, and making up beds in the stable lofts. As the January daylight failed Uncle Len came in and said, 'Girls, we're all going off to Nancy's for a good high tea. I've telephoned, and it's all right, she'll be glad to have us.'

'Oh, but there's lots to do,' whimpered Aunt Lily. 'And there's turning things off. You ought always to turn everything off, when things like this happen.' She yawned and moaned through her yawn, 'Always merry and bright.'

'My feet are awful,' said Aunt Lily, 'but we ought to go on.'

'No, we're going to fold our arms and let the insurance take over,' said Uncle Len.

'But what they pay won't make it any easier to clear all that mud off everything,' said Aunt Milly. 'Like brown toothpaste, it is.'

'Pity you didn't take that little place at Uxbridge,' fretted Aunt Lily. 'Anywhere inland. It's so awful, watching the river turn against us like this, after everything.'

'You can't talk about the river like that, it isn't logical,' said Uncle Len. 'It isn't a person, it means no harm.'

'Yes, but we've trusted it,' said Aunt Lily. 'We trusted it, that's what makes the difference.' She was nearly crying. I had forgotten that, really, they were all getting old.

'Have a minute's sit-down before you put your hats on,' said Uncle Len, 'and don't miscall the river either. There's a lot goes on Saturday nights in a town pub that never happens on the Thames. You should count your blessings.'

'Blessings or not,' said Aunt Milly, 'my feet are like raw steak.'

'I don't feel like going out to tea,' said Aunt Lily, defiantly.

'Well, I do,' said Uncle Len. 'There isn't anything I hate on earth like evenings when there are floods. When the sky goes black and comes down as low as these ceilings, and it's doing that very thing now, and the water goes grey and shines and covers everything as far as you can see, and seems to raise up towards that damned sky, and you can feel the damp coming off the water and passing into your own breath, but you can't breathe it out, it goes back into your chest, I could cut my throat. I'm getting out of the place till it's all dark.'

'But we're too tired,' said Aunt Lily. 'Let's stop off at the Red Lion at Haxton. It's half the distance to Nancy's and they do a fish tea. We can put Nancy off.'

'No,' said Uncle Len. 'We're not going to the Red Lion at Haxton, we're going to Nancy's. You two have got the willies too, and I know it, and I don't blame you, for you haven't got the strength I have and if I got them you got a right to them too. But I'd rather you had the willies at Nancy's than at the Red Lion.'

'If you're thinking. . .' Aunt Milly began vaguely.

'Get on your bloody hats,' shouted Uncle Len in sudden rage.

I had never seen him lose his temper before. He had lost it too easily, with these two tired and ageing women.

They went silently up the stairs. Uncle Len called after them, very softly. 'Milly. Lily.' They turned and looked down at him, tears on their cheeks. 'All the same you're a couple of good old gazooks,' he said, and blew a kiss at them. Without speaking, they blew kisses down to him, and turned about and went on upwards.

We got into the car and sped off through the dusk, past the fields where floodwaters lay like sheets of white metal on the darkening earth, towards Haxton, a village so swollen by the building of two factories that it had spread out and acquired the polluted quality of a suburb.

'Young Os will be giving us all that science he knows about the causes of floods,' said Uncle Len, grimly.

'Well, that should be very interesting,' said Aunt Milly, with an air of reproof.

'Unfortunately science doesn't know more about the causes of floods than a man living on the banks of a river, and therefore interested in floods, can read in his spare time,' said Uncle Len.

'You been reading books about that too? You sly thing,' said Aunt Lily.

'The books he gets from the library, Rose, you wouldn't believe,' said Aunt Milly.

'You ought to have had an education, you ought,' said Aunt Lily.

'So's I could be more like young Os?' chuckled Uncle Len.

We had reached a crossroads, and had to halt, where a light switched off and on a crimson cast-iron lion standing on the porch of an inn larger and more urban than the Dog and Duck. A sudden hush fell on the three in the back of the car.

'They do do a fish tea,' said Aunt Lily suddenly. 'Quite a good one. That's really why I mentioned it.'

'I know, I know, Lil,' said Uncle Len, gently.

There was evidently a long-standing family dispute about the Red Lion at Haxton. I looked at the narrow oblongs of its windows, gold on the ground floor, where the bars were, and on the floors above black and printed with the flickering reflections of the light behind the lion. Those upper windows had the secretive and sinister look of dark spectacles, but I felt not much curiosity about the secret that they hid, for since it concerned these people it was bound to be simple and creditable, and indeed to lack all the ambiguous character that would seem inherent in a secret. I smiled to myself in the dusk at the unearthly innocence of these most earthly people.

As we drew nearer Uncle Len said, 'I always like going to our Nancy's home. You couldn't have anything more decent. In its own half-acre.'

'The Laurels was bigger,' said Aunt Lily. 'Poor Harry wanted Queenie to have the best. But this will last. There'll never be any trouble in this house.'

When we got there they stopped and looked at the house before they opened the garden gate. 'What I like,' said Aunt Milly, 'is that the house and the garden aren't exactly like the house and the gardens on either side, but they aren't really different. The people in those houses wouldn't have the slightest excuse for looking down on this house.'

'I wonder if they do all they might with that greenhouse,' said Uncle Len, his steps lagging as we went up the crazy-pavement path between the standard roses. 'But there, nobody likes getting advice.'

The door was opened by Nancy's servant, Bronwyn, in black dress and cap and apron. She was a child of seventeen from South Wales, and she looked up into our faces and told us, her eyes growing rounder and, it seemed, her little nose growing snubber with every word she spoke, as she told us that the master and mistress would be happy we had come, for they were all terribly afraid we should all be drowned. Uncle Len said that he personally had been drowned, round about two o'clock, and it was his own ghost, come along to have a last look at a pretty girl, and Bronwyn giggled, and Milly and Lily told her she was a clever mite to have got up her cap and her apron so beautifully, and Bronwyn was explaining that she had understood nothing of the laundry work, but the mistress was teaching her, when Oswald and Nancy called to us from the dining-room.

They looked very young, far younger than they were, and they were laughing, and could not quite sober themselves even when they greeted us and told us how they had grieved over the inundation of the Dog and Duck. The dining-room looked Victorian, for it was dominated by two enlarged photographs, one of Oswald's father, his handsome features blazing with impatient yet contented evangelism, and the other of Oswald's mother, she who had been a drunkard and was dead, a pretty woman with smooth hair and an oval face, and troubled, staring eyes, and a tiny mouth, so tiny that it seemed hardly broader than her nostrils. There was an early-Victorian clock, an early-Victorian wall-bracket bookcase, a mid-Victorian mirror over the chimneypiece, none of them very good, but all showing signs of a restrained taste, a provincial nonconformist purity. The rest of the room had been decided by Oswald's taste, and was garden-suburb. The tables and chairs and sideboard were rough-hewn of unpolished wood, the curtains were hand-blocked linen, the ingenuously designed pottery and glass and the table silver made reference to some sort of peasant in another country. The room exhibited a clash between the generations. There was a brooch at the breast of the woman in the photograph which showed that she would not have understood why her son should have chosen to own any object in this room. It even exhibited a clash within Oswald's generation, or rather an unresolved harmony. The early-Victorian bracket bookcase was filled with the works of Shaw and Wells, and it was certain any house where the dining-room was furnished in the peasant tradition would contain their works. Yet there was really nothing in the writings of either which would have led anybody to agree with them to think it logical that oak should not be polished or that pottery and textiles should ignore the achievements of the last four centuries. But there was another disharmony. Nancy and Oswald seemed to have at this moment nothing to do with their own room. Surprised in their enjoyment of their secret joke, they were not as I had ever seen them. They were classical, they were idyllic, they might have been outside time, actors inside art, who had no private lives but perpetually performed. They even recalled what was not human, the winter sunlight on the bronze branches of the woodland, the crimson buds of the willows rising from the waters.

'We've had to alter the table, Oswald's father is coming too,' explained Nancy, smoothing the laughter from her face. 'We see a lot of him, now that Brother Clerkenwell has come to live at Haxton. He rang up just after you did, it's funny, it really is –' She and Oswald took the flimsy excuse and surrendered to laughter again. 'Oswald, you look after Uncle Len, and I'll take the others to get their things off.'

She ran up the stairs lightly before us, giving Oswald a last smile over her shoulder. As we went into the bedroom Aunt Lily pointed a reproving finger and said, 'Who's been a careless girl? Tchk, tchk. You should take care of your good things.' There was a wide Heal bed, with a headboard of unpolished oak running out at each side into bookcases; and on the floor at its foot Nancy's fur coat lay in a semicircle. 'I threw it down anyhow when I came in,' said Nancy, and again broke into laughter. The rest of us gathered round the triple mirror on the dressing-table, and patted our tired faces with our powder puffs.

Nancy's smiling face floated in the darkness behind our reflections. 'I threw it down anywhere,' she said, 'because I heard Oswald come in, and I had to run down at once to tell him my news. And now I'll tell you. I've been to the doctor and he says I'm all right.'

I slipped my arms round her and we kissed.

'But here, what's this?' breathed Aunt Lily.

'We thought you wanted one!' exclaimed Aunt Milly.

'Well, I've got one,' said Nancy. 'I'm telling you, that's what the doctor said. It's coming in July. Something went wrong at the beginning, so we weren't sure till now.'

They squealed for joy and hugged her. 'Forgive us for being stupid,' said Aunt Milly, 'but when we were young and a girl

99

went to the doctor and came back saying she was all right it usually meant she hadn't got a baby. But, oh dear, oh dear, isn't this lovely?'

'Won't Queenie love this?' cried Aunt Lily.

'I know, I know,' said Nancy, 'she'll come back to a proper, ordinary family in working order.'

'Do you want a boy or a girl?' asked Aunt Milly, while Aunt Lily said, 'Coo, I'm a grand-aunt. Are you going to have it here or in a nursing home?' and then both began to sob.

'You old sillies,' said Nancy, 'none of that. I want to cry too, and it's ridiculous, as there's nothing to cry about. I am nothing remarkable, but millions and millions and millions of women have had babies since the world began, so presumably I can.'

'My God, and you so slim,' marvelled Aunt Lily and broke into sudden panic. 'And we let you pick up that fur coat yourself.' She threw it on the floor and picked it up again, and we all laughed at her. But Nancy hushed us with an uplifted finger.

'Listen, that's the doorbell. It'll be Oswald's father.' She began to giggle. 'We'll be able to tell exactly when he's heard. Ordinarily you can't hear in this room what's said in the room underneath – unless it's Oswald's father speaking. It comes up like what you sometimes hear on a cliff by the seaside, when the waves rush into a crack. You know, a sort of booming. Just you wait a minute. It'll come. Boom, boom-boom, boom-boom-boom boom-boom-boom. That'll be "Well, I just thought I'd look in and see how the Lord is dealing with this little household", and then we won't hear anything, and that'll be Oswald saying we're all quite well, but deliberately not bringing the Lord into it, and then there'll be little booms which will be Mr Bates saying that yes, he will take a glass of tomato-juice, and a bit about may he have his favourite chair that's big enough for his long legs.' She paused. 'That,' she said coolly, 'is to make Oswald realise that he's not as tall as he is, and that is the real reason why Oswald won't say anything about the Lord.' Then she went on, 'After that there'll be a silence, and that'll be Oswald telling him about the baby, and then, you listen, there'll be such a boom.'

She pointed to the floor and we all bent down towards it. Aunt Milly was a little deaf and she cupped her ear with her hand, but said, 'Well, I don't need any help to hear this,' as the rich belling came up through the boards. The little booms went on in the order predicted, and she said, 'Funny how you can nearly always tell what they're going to do.'

'Isn't it?' said Nancy, and they exchanged a cynical nod.

'Funny, I always think they're so deep,' said Aunt Lily.

'Yes, they're *deep*,' said Aunt Milly, 'but at the same time. . .' But the great boom rolled and echoed under our feet, and we clung together in silent laughter as it went on and on, rose and fell, fell and rose.

'Any idea what he's saying?' asked Aunt Milly, drying her eyes. 'Len will be as pleased over the little fellow as if it was his own grandson but he won't go on about it like that, thank God.'

'Oh, it'll be a great thing for Father Bates,' said Nancy. 'It's a great thing, you know, when a child is born to one of the Heavenly Hostages.' I listened to her with irritation, for she spoke these words in an affected tone, quite uncharacteristic of her, which I had heard her assume once or twice before. It was borrowed, I think, from her Uncle Mat and Aunt Clara and their friends, for it carried a trace of the Midland accent. But it was nothing so innocent as regionalism. It was a lethargic defence of mediocrity, it indolently ridiculed all acknowledgment of the prodigious, and all attempt at interpretation of the ordinary. She told us that the sect held that membership conferred access to special means of grace. Each Heavenly Hostage could be perfect if he could but keep his mind on it; but nobody ever did. If anyone could he would die; but even in imperfection their members were better than other people and were recognised by God as His best beloved children. 'So each member is a hostage held by sinful humanity, and it's a good thing for the world, since God will be more reluctant to destroy the world for its wickedness if he knows that some of those he specially loves are captive on it.' She seemed to be speaking with the cheapest irony, and I was about to protest that at least the sect saw that the world was a battlefield of forces not confined to this world, when she smiled timidly and gloriously, and I remembered that she borrowed this horrid way of speaking only when she was very shy. 'Surely it can't be like that,' she said, in her own voice, 'it seems too far-fetched. But there's something. There must be something,' she told us, her eyes wide. 'It's all so strange. You can't think how strange it is having a baby.'

'I've always thought it must be a funny feeling,' said Aunt Milly.

'You see, the thing isn't a bit reasonable,' Nancy went on. 'Oswald keeps on telling me how it happens, ovulation and all that, but it doesn't explain anything. It's not logical that two little things without any sense can get together and make a third thing, that suddenly gets sense and thinks and feels for itself and gets born and has a will of its own, and is a person. How can there be a person, suddenly, when there wasn't one before?'

'It's a mystery,' agreed Aunt Milly.

'Yes, put it like that, it's against nature,' said Aunt Lily.

'And think of it happening all the time,' Nancy went on. 'And all these people that come into the world in this extraordinary way clinging on to the earth, which is just a star like any other, and nobody knows how the stars come to exist. It's all so odd that anything should be here.'

'I never thought of it before, but it would be more natural if there wasn't anything at all,' said Aunt Milly.

'Yes, it's all so unnatural that there must be a meaning to it,' said Nancy, glowing. 'They always say so in church but you only half-believe it, but having a baby, it's more extraordinary than anything they tell you in church. I don't know what it all means,' she proclaimed, 'but I feel that I might know any minute now.'

Through the floor came a supreme BOOM boom boom boomboom boom-boom BOOM BOOM BOOM. We laughed so loudly that we had to gag ourselves with handkerchieves. '*He* knows, he ain't half telling Oswald,' gasped Aunt Milly, and Nancy begged us, 'Oh, please hush, there's someone coming upstairs now, if it's Oswald he'll want to know why we're laughing.' But Aunt Milly and Aunt Lily said together, 'No, that's Len's tread,' and presently there was a knock at the door, and a hoarse voice, repelled by the apocalyptic, whispered, 'For pity's sake, girls, come down.'

But as soon as we opened the door Uncle Len forgot the distaste that had made his wattles blood-red, and he was with us in our contemplation of Nancy and her exultation, that was faintly bright, like moth-wings. He put his arms round her, but not close, and said, 'Why, Nancy, what we've been hearing downstairs is what we've all been hoping and expecting, yet now it's happened it seems so strange I can't believe it.'

'Yes,' she said looking up at him, 'that's what I was telling them. It's strange.'

It appeared possible that Uncle Len might weep, so I went to the dressing-table and took my comb out of my bag and ran it through my hair. I looked towards the triple mirror, and saw that it was reflecting this room in which there were five persons, and indeed six, if one counted Nancy's child, as though it were empty. I was kneeling to the right of the mirror, and Aunt Lily and Aunt Milly were far to the left of it, and Nancy and Uncle Len were in the doorway, so the central panel of the mirror saw nothing of them, and the others, loosely screwed, had swung towards it and reflected only its reflections: the images of the broad bed, which was covered with that furrowed material known as candlewick, and a wardrobe of unpolished oak beyond it, and the edge of a green rug and a foot or two of parquet floor. The mirrors reflected my private truth. To me the room was empty. Nobody was real to me, as people had been real to me till then. I saw before me a man and three women whom I had known since my childhood, and I had no direct apprehension of them. I had to tell myself, 'That is Nancy, she says she is going to have a baby, and from what I remember of her she should be very happy about that,' but I had to work it out in my head, and when I had deduced her happiness I did not share it. I was in the same wretched state that I had fallen into once or twice before when I had had to play at concerts too soon after I had had influenza, and I found I had to get through the programme entirely on my technique and my recollection of the meaning that the music had had for me when I was well. Though it had been my opinion that music was as important as any other part of my life, I now knew it was better to feel like that when I was playing Beethoven's Piano Concerto in C minor in the Usher Hall in Edinburgh than when Nancy was announcing that she was going to have a baby; and my present sickness was graver than influenza. This room was empty for me because Rosamund was not here. For me all rooms where Rosamund were not were empty. I could not be sure whether this did not mean that henceforward I was to find all rooms empty. For there could be no room where Rosamund was if there were no Rosamund, and I had reason to doubt whether the Rosamund I had thought I knew had ever existed.

But of course she existed. When I left the house Nancy murmured to me, while the others were busy with their good-byes, 'Poor Rose, you have kept up so well. But I know you are hardly able to see or hear, you are so miserable about

Rosamund marrying that little man they say is so awful. I was often like that when I lived in Nottingham.' She was my friend, and it was Rosamund who had given me continued friendship with her, by making my impatience halt and understand how she had feared to expose her fragile happiness to my sweeping judgments; it must have been Rosamund who had told Nancy, herself too timid and too respectful towards my career to make the discovery, that I was impatient because I always feared to be overtaken by the darkness, and was not arrogant but pitiable. Rosamund had existed, and since she had not died must still exist. Nancy came closer to me and whispered, 'The Heavenly Hostages like all children to have one Old Testament name and one modern one. If we have a girl, it will have to be Janet Ruth, Janet after Oswald's mother, Ruth because I like that bit about "Intreat me not to leave thee", though it has nothing to do with the rest of the story which is a dull thing about barley and landed property. But I will have another girl, I will call her Rose Mary. And, Rose, if we have a boy it is to be Richard Adam, Richard after Richard Quin. I think of him so often.' Her face was glorious because she spoke of him. In my obsession I passed from delight in her love for him to recollection that Rosamund had said that she would have liked Richard Quin to see her necklace. She had sworn by his name. I was nearly happy as I drove my party back to the Dog and Duck, I could laugh with Uncle Len when Aunt Lily, who had been dozing on his shoulder, woke up and said, 'Salads. She ought to eat plenty of salads now. Perhaps that's the reason I've never been able to abide lettuce, me never being meant to have a family.' All the rest of the journey he kept on chuckling and saying, 'Straighten that one out if you can.' That night I did not go back to London, but slept in one of the stable lofts, for Milly and Lily were fearful of the morning and I felt so well that I was sure I would be able to help them if, as they feared, the river was into the house by morning.

But I woke in wretchedness, and the view from my window was terrible to me. The effacement of the land by the steel-grey waters seemed the confirmation of some bad news I had heard in my sleep. Fortunately I did not need to stay, the Thames had fallen in the night, and Aunt Milly and Aunt Lily had nothing to distract them from the cheerful business of telling the staff and the neighbours the news about Nancy. So I went back to my music-room in London and practising was an effective anaesthetic. But when I was too tired to work any more I again had the illusion that the room was empty; the house was empty; the city was empty; the world was empty. I had thought that I could go on living without my father and my mother and my brother, but now I was not sure that I was right. My power to do so was perhaps conditional. It had perhaps been given me by Rosamund, and might be taken back by Rosamund. For the first time I understood how people could kill themselves. When Mary came in that night, back from an afternoon concert at Bournemouth, I saw that she too was suffering from the hallucination of solitude. I had left the door of the sitting-room open as lonely people do; so I saw her from my seat by the fire as she came in, put down her attaché case, and laid on the hall table the flowers she had been given. Then she looked up the staircase as one does when one lets oneself into an unoccupied house and thinks, 'How am I to make a home here? There are only the bare walls.'

When she saw me, she said, 'Oh, Rose, you love white lilac, a nice woman has given me an armful of it,' and came over to lay it on my knee. It gave me no special pleasure, though she was right, I liked it best of all the flowers we were given in the winter.

I thanked her and thought to myself, 'Flowers are no great matter, I may do better for her than she has been able to do for me, by telling her about Nancy's baby.' But she could not make herself feel any great interest, though it delighted her to hear that if it were a boy Nancy was going to call it after Richard Quin. We sat for a minute in silence after we had spoken his name. I thought of the stars blazing in the black winter sky above the house. But when I went on to say that if the baby was a girl it was to be called Janet Ruth, she cried out, 'Not Ruth. I wish she would not call it Ruth.'

'She likes it,' I said. 'It is because of that passage about "Intreat me not to leave thee".'

'I hate that passage,' said Mary. She pulled off her gloves and fell on her knees by the bookcase and pulled out our big Scottish Family Bible, that had Mamma's people in it up to her great-grandfather, who was born when his parents were on the run after the rebellion of 1745.

'Between Judges and Samuel,' I said. But she had found it. There was nothing I knew that she did not know. We had a common stock of information.

105

'Listen,' she said. '"Intreat me not to leave thee, or to return from following after thee: for whither thou goest, I will go; and where thou lodgest, I will lodge: thy people shall be my people, and thy God my God: Where thou diest, will I die, and there will I be buried: the Lord do so to me, and more also, if ought but death part thee and me."' She closed the book. 'Oh, it is terrible,' she said, and went out into the hall and fetched the rest of the flowers, and came back and sat with them on her lap, sorting out the narcissus and daffodils and tulips from several mixed bunches.

'Why do you think it so terrible?' I asked. 'People say that it is strange because it is said by a woman to another woman, instead of to a man, but if one thinks of the men one meets at parties one can't imagine saying it to any one of them.'

'It is what every human being ought to be able to say to some other human being,' Mary answered, 'if life is to be worth living. But there is nobody to whom it can be said safely. One cannot trust anybody. Not anybody at all.'

'Why are you dividing those flowers?' I asked.

'Because the narcissus have so strong a scent I do not want them in the same room as the lilac, and these big daffodils are wrong in this room. But you are right. It does not matter.'

At least we could work. There lay our great good fortune. Our love for music might have weakened now, but we were still under the compulsive power of our mother's voice, angrily bidding us to the piano, angrily exposing our incompetence, angrily exhorting us to play better than she did, proudly supposing that we could. Mary continued to develop her special understanding of Beethoven and worked hard on Skriabin, I went on with Mozart and waited for every new piano composition of Stravinsky. It might seem strange that Mary, who was so coolly classical, should choose to interpret Beethoven and the ecstatic Skriabin, and that I, so much rougher and less controlled, should prefer the crystalline concertos of Mozart and the legalistic compositions of Stravinsky. But any serious interpretative artist seeks out the composer who lacks the faults he has learned to deplore in himself: the composer is to him a symbol of creation itself, and by lacking these faults he suggests a universe in which they do not exist, and in which there are therefore no moral or aesthetic problems at all, and indeed no problem except the technical difficulty of making the body execute the conceptions of the mind. We both

106

eagerly attended the disclosure of Bartók's genius which was going on at that time, though only a very few people wanted us to play his music. I also worked on some sonatas by Oliver, and joined with friends to play two quartets and a sonata for piano and violin of his.

Oliver was the grey-eyed man whose songs were played at that concert in a house on the Regent's Park canal where Mary and I heard that we had got our scholarships; he had stayed with us that first summer of the war, in Norfolk, and we had seen him from time to time ever since, though he had suffered that separation from his friends which is the result of domestic tragedy. He had married a singer, quite a good contralto, and they had never been quite happy; and their unhappiness had not taken an easy course. She had left him for another man, and had not been happy with him either, and had got ill, and had come back to Oliver to die. He was now so taciturn that very often he did not follow a conversation to its end, but just got up and went away; and his music too never seemed finally written. But perhaps I felt this because it nearly coincided with my way of thinking. Had I been a composer, I would have written just this kind of music, and it was possible that my dissatisfaction with certain passages simply meant that, though our musical minds were alike, they were not identical, and in case he, being a composer, had to recognise limitations of which, as an interpreter, I was nearly unconscious.

But once our work was over we were faced again with the fact of Rosamund's desertion, and nothing came to explain it or mitigate it. Mr Morpurgo had been right: she wrote to us hardly at all. We got some picture postcards from South America, but they were addressed in Constance's large handwriting and inscribed with messages hardly more informative than R.I.P. They left our wonder where it was. They did not, it is true, confirm our doubts. To look on that handwriting, though it was steady, the a's and o's moonfaced as they always were, was to see Constance, old now and in a foreign country, unable to speak the language and galled at the failure, for she liked to be the mistress of every situation, and lodged in a hotel suite which she would not like as much as she had liked her flat in Baker Street. These were such postcards as one would sit down and write for the sake of company. When she had achieved one she would fumble among the tiresome foreign stamps to find the needed one, and go into the bathroom and hold it under a trickle from the tap. None of our family ever licked a stamp; it was to us an action of debauched unfastidiousness. Then she would go along the corridor to the mail-chute beside the elevators and watch the white card fall down behind the glass at the speed of suicide. Then she would slowly find her way back to the room where Rosamund sat at the window, her hands idle on her lap, because neither sewing nor knitting could make the moment better, her eyes fixed on the lizard-coloured mountains beyond the skyscrapers, because it was pleasant to contemplate any place other than that where she was. Mary and I saw such a vision of stagnancy whenever we took these postcards in our hands. But it might have been a peevish fancy, born of resentment. We were sure of nothing, not even of ourselves. But we were not without resources, we could take shelter under that nativity which grew like a flowering tree all that summer, shading us from all heat and distress.

Aunt Lily, seeing us as we came into the garden one late-spring day, turned towards the house and cried, 'Milly, they're here,' and then turned to us and said, 'She's well,' and Aunt Milly came out of the house, nodding and confirming the good news. 'She couldn't be better. Well, you dear girls, twenty minutes before lunch, duck and green peas, have a sherry?' We four sat and preened ourselves and watched the river running by and felt friendly with time, as if we as well as Nancy were engaged in the creative process even when we were idle. Though, indeed, there was a good deal of activity going on in the Dog and Duck these days. 'She says she's going to have quite a family,' said Aunt Lily, 'so I'm making everything in pink as well as blue. First a girl then a boy.' A pink pram-coat was lying on her lap, a horrible pink that made more horrible her horrible dress, which was the colour of pickled cabbage. Aunt Lily's clothes were as regrettable as they had always been, in defiance of the vast commercial development that made it possible to buy cheap and inoffensive dresses in almost any part of England. Nothing like Aunt Lily's raiment was exposed in any shop-window I ever passed, and it seemed possible that in hidden places, say among the peep-show machines at the back of the fun-fairs round Leicester Square, there were clothes-dens that catered for sartorial perverts.

'She says she doesn't care which it is,' said Aunt Milly. 'That's what's so nice to see, she's taking it all so easy.'

'They came over on Sunday night,' said Aunt Lily, 'and she

was as cool as a cucumber. Told us to get poor Mr Morpurgo to lay off with his specialists, she'd have one if the local man thought anything was wrong, and wouldn't if he didn't.'

'And young Os is very good to her, and that's a help,' said Aunt Milly. 'Very helpful. He was as excited as a kid when he came over, he had a great idea about a new type of Moses basket he wanted to ask Len's advice about.'

'It wouldn't work,' said Uncle Len, coming out of the bar with Mr Morpurgo, bringing a tray of sherries.

'Len, you are mean about young Os,' said Aunt Milly. 'It might have worked.'

'Not unless the force of gravity acted quite different,' said Uncle Len.

'But he was trying to be a good husband,' said Aunt Milly.

'Oh, he tries hard over that,' said Uncle Len, chuckling. 'He keeps on telling me that he's doing all he can to make Nancy feel it's a natural event.'

'Well, why shouldn't he?' asked the two aunts, indignantly.

'No reason at all, no reason at all,' said Uncle Len. 'Only it strikes me as a damn funny thing for a man to say when his wife's having a baby. Well, I must be getting back to my customers, and I wish they'd move out.'

'I wish I could understand why Len always picks on Os,' said Aunt Milly.

'It's not like him, either,' said Aunt Lily. 'Len's a fair-minded man. But over Os he just gives way.'

'I know why it is,' said Mr Morpurgo. 'And it isn't what you think it is. You think it's because Len is getting on and Oswald is young. You know you do. And of course we grow bitter. But there's something deeper than that, and quite creditable to Len, though what he finds intolerable in Oswald is not Oswald's fault. I suppose nothing is anybody's fault. It is how we are made. But the trouble between Len and Oswald is that Len has a scientific mind, and Oswald has not, though he has a scientific degree.'

'What do you mean, Len has a scientific mind?' asked Aunt Milly. 'He left Church School at ten, you know.'

'That doesn't matter at all,' said Mr Morpurgo. 'He has the scientific approach by nature. I know it, I have watched him with his puzzles for years now.'

'But go on, that's just his fun,' objected Aunt Milly.

'I think his fun might have been mathematics, if he'd had the chance. Remember he was a bookmaker, and a successful one, particularly considering he started from scratch. All bookmakers have to be mathematicians to some extent, you know. But I think Len might have been outstanding if he had had the advantages my own children have had. He has a real feeling for the theory of numbers, and he can manage most of all the books on the subject I've been able to find for him. He enjoys algebra, too, in a way that means a special talent. He has an instinctive realisation of these things, but Oswald only knows what he reads about them in books.' He spoke with a grumbling connoisseurship, and would have gone on to further grumbling, had his eye not suddenly caught the pickled-cabbage dress. He was silent for a moment, then asked, 'Lily, do you find it difficult to distinguish between blues and greens?'

We had often thought of that too.

'Course I can,' said Aunt Lily. 'Why do you ask?'

Mr Morpurgo swallowed. 'I only wondered. I sometimes find it not too easy myself.'

'Coo, I always can,' said Aunt Lily. 'But funny thing, someone else asked me the very same thing the other day.'

'Write me down a dumb bunny,' said Aunt Milly, 'but how can you know about such things except by reading about them in books? You said yourself, you bring Len books.'

There was a rabbinical streak in Mr Morpurgo which made him feel that he must teach. The books should come second. 'If you are a scientist you think about the structure of the universe in a certain way which is not like the way of thinking we use in ordinary life. And if you can think in this extraordinary way then you can learn a great deal by reading books written by people who also have that same trick of thought. But the important thing is that you should start off with that unusual approach. Which you have, Milly. I have seen you cut out loose covers for the sitting-room armchairs without a pattern. That means that you know a great deal about the shape of things. You have, in fact, an inborn capacity for understanding plane geometry. You are a scientist too.'

'What, me? Girls, is he teasing me? Look at the swans. Those are the ones that nest up by the bridge. Those last year's cygnets of theirs are almost white. Well, Len and me scientists, I never did.'

'Only me that isn't anything,' said Aunt Lily.

'That is untrue,' said Mr Morpurgo. 'You belong to the company of Mary and Rose. You, like they, are excluded from the world of science, and you, like they, are an artist.'

'Well, I do think I could have been a dress-designer,' said Aunt Lily.

Mr Morpurgo's eyes bulged. He could not help but enjoy the remark, just a little, but he loved Aunt Lily so much that he wished she had not made it. But again he was so perfectly honest that he could not bear to give it the faintest shadow of assent. After a second's thought he said, 'Women think too much about dress. I meant something else. I meant that you were an artist in your relations with your family and your friends.'

'I'd like to think it, but I'm sure I'm gauche, if that's how you pronounce it,' said Aunt Lily.

'That duck will be charred if you don't start the lunch,' said Uncle Len, at the bar window.

'Here's Mr Morpurgo saying you and me are scientists and Lily's an artist,' said Aunt Milly comfortably, taking her time to finish her sherry.

'No doubt he has his reasons,' said Uncle Len, 'but if he's a man and a brother he'll get your situpon out of that chair, and see to it that we get that duck before it's a black bone. Milly, I mean it, shift.' He leaned on his crossed arms and beamed over us, over his garden, over the river. 'Not a thing wrong with today.' But soon he began to chuckle. 'Trying to make her feel it's a natural event. I mean to say.'

For hours we did not think of Rosamund when we were with them, any more than when we were playing. She was not in our minds that afternoon, a week or two later, when we drove down to Nancy's, without notice, for we suddenly found we had the rest of the day to ourselves. But we had forgotten that when we got there she would be having her afternoon rest. The little Welsh girl told us that we must sit in the drawing-room till four o'clock, or the master would be angry. But Nancy heard us, and rang, and called down to us in her endearing, light voice, which was just not thin, and told us to come up.

'I must stay in bed till tea-time because of the fuss,' she said, when we went into her bedroom. She was lying with her hands clasped behind her head and her lovely hair spread loose on the pillow. Now her face was as interesting as her hair. 'But I have already slept. And I had such a funny dream about this

111

fuss. It is the only part of this I hate. I dreamed the monthly nurse had moved in, and the baby was just going to be born, and Oswald was in a terrible flap, and Aunt Milly and Aunt Lily and Uncle Len were all in the way being frightened. So I decided that I couldn't stand it any longer, and that I would take some sandwiches and run away and hide and not come back until the evening. It seemed to me quite natural that the baby would have been born while I was out, and sensible of me to keep away till the hubbub was over. I went into the larder and found some very nice ham and cut some sandwiches, very carefully, spreading the butter very thick. I am always hungry just now, you know. And then I went to your house at Lovegrove and told you all about it, and you were very sympathetic, and we cut more sandwiches, you found some turkey in your larder, and we went and played on Lovegrove Common, and it was nice. It is funny, I have no idea how long I stayed with you after Papa died. It was just a patch of – of what? For I was very unhappy, yet you made me happy. And that reminds me. I have heard from my brother in Hong Kong.' She found an envelope on her bed-table, took out a letter and spread it flat, and then put her hand over it. 'Tell me what you have been doing,' she bade us. We saw that there was something painful in the letter, and that she was moderating the pace of her approach to it, as a rider gentles his horse to a difficult gate.

Before we could answer she had grown bolder. She lifted her hand from the letter and said, 'I wrote to Cecil reminding him that Mamma would be released in August, and asking him to write to her a welcoming letter, and make plans to come home on leave to see her soon. This is his answer.'

Cecil wrote that he did not think she had ever understood how awful the scandal had been for him. For one thing, he had been older and had realised more, and it had been worse for him, because he was a boy, and had had to go out into the world, while she could stay at home. He said he had had to remind himself as he wrote of her more sheltered position, which had saved her from the full impact of their mother's crime. It was in any case hard for him to forgive an attitude which could mean that she had forgotten what a dear old sport Daddy had been. And anyway he hoped she was not losing her sense of proportion. There must be some places where people in the situation of their mother were taken care of, and it would probably be better for her and for the world at large if she were left in skilled hands. It could not be helped, he supposed, that Nancy had no real feeling for him or for his father.

'It is so silly,' said Nancy, 'because it has been one of my great difficulties that I loved my father much better than my mother. But what am I to say to Mamma when she realises he has sent her no message?'

We did not answer because we did not know. After a minute Nancy folded up the letter and put it back in the envelope. She had fully realised we did not know the answer. Rosamund would have stammered some words that would have told Nancy what to write to Cecil which would soften his heart; but Rosamund was not here, she would never come back to us.

'I do not think he is unhappy,' pondered Nancy. 'Ordinarily, of course, that is what one would think about a letter like this, that it was written out of misery, which always makes one silly. But this is a very collected piece of writing. It is just the kind of letter Uncle Mat would write, poor man.' Gently she tore it up. 'Not that I am angry,' she explained, with her faint smile, 'but I might come on it when I was feeling ill or tired, and then I might be angry.' She felt for her hand mirror and restored her pale mouth with lipstick. 'That is one of the difficulties of the job I am doing now. One does not have one's own children. Cecil is Uncle Mat's child, he has nothing to do with our papa and mamma, I am nearer them. But I feel that Aunt Lily had a hand in me somehow. And where did Cordelia come from in your family? And whose baby am I going to have? Perhaps I will have Cecil's. But it does not matter, I will have several, amongst the lot of them one will surely belong to Oswald and me. And I understand I shall have an unreasonable liking even for the others.'

She was far stronger than any of us had ever thought, and her strength derived from a cynicism that made no exceptions. Like everything about her, it was delicate. When she doubted whether her brother was as unhappy as he said, or whether her child would be the kind of being she desired to bear, it was as if her long fingers were unscrewing the stopper of a fragile scent-bottle, and raising it to her nostrils, while she raised her faint, arched eyebrows and said, without complaint, simply remarking a fact, 'There is not a drop left.' She was nearly immune to the dangers of childbirth. Even if the child died she would smile and make her plans for another day. But it might not be so well with her when Queenie was released. Nancy had visited her often enough at Aylesbury and at Reading, where she was now, and she agreed with Aunt Lily that she had grown away from her crime. But Queenie's crime was not all that was terrifying in Queenie. That was only an explosion which had occurred when Queenie's force had escaped from the small space in which it had been confined and had come in contact with what was, for it, a flame. That force had again been confined in a small space under pressure, and it was going to be allowed to escape again, and even if she had become holy, as my mother hoped, it might still find objects to ignite it, of one sort or another. I could see Nancy's slight body crumpled in a heap, such a burden as firemen carry, because of the incendiary effect of her mother's penitence or drunkenness or featureless despair; and, as she turned in the bed and, always with that little smile, laid the fragments of the torn letter neatly on her bed-table, I thought, 'But surely Rosamund must come back.'

She was indeed to return soon afterwards, but not for Nancy's benefit. One morning I was interrupted in my practising because Mr Ramponetti had called with a message from Mr and Mrs Ganymedios. He exercised a curious magic on the drawing-room. We were secure enough financially, his large, seal-shaped body was handsomely clad, and his car waited at our gate like a cream-coloured tram, yet it was as if a broker's man had been put in. I asked him eagerly if Rosamund and Nestor were coming to London, and he said amiably that things were never as simple as that in the Ganymedios family. 'Come to London, that would be too easy. But we give four big parties slap in the middle of the season. One in London, one in Paris, one in Brussels, one in Rome. You may come to one, you may come to all. Your tickets will be booked, your hotels. You may have all. Now the dates.'

He read them from a crimson leather notebook, and I could tell him at once that we would be able to go to the London party and no other. At that he took out from a foolscap envelope four quarto envelopes, bound together by a rubber band and with the air of doing a card-trick gave me the one on the top. It contained a very thick card printed in silver with an invitation to go at ten o'clock one night in June to a house near the Albert Hall. Mr Ramponetti watched me while I read it, as if there

114

were some interesting feature about the card which would presently astonish me, as if the lettering would change from silver to gold and from gold to bronze. But it was the address on which he wished to comment. 'A marquis lived there who won the Derby, but it is nothing to what we have in Paris, we have a palace in the Avenue Foch, and in Rome we have a palace by the Pincio, and in Brussels we have a palace built by a millionaire, very mad. Pity you cannot come to Paris and to Rome and to Brussels.' He indicated by a smiling nod that it would always be so for Mary and me, the second-rate would be our portion.

I asked him if the London house were lent them by a friend, or if they were leasing it and staying in it for some time. 'Na, na,' he said, 'we take it for three days only. We get in, we get out.' His hands performed a meaningless but proud pantomime, showing such delight in mobility for its own sake as an ape might feel. 'I make all the arrangements. Nestor is too far away. They went from South America to Australia, they go now to China. You should see the fares they pay. It hurts. And Nestor has told you, like me he was once a very poor boy.' To my alarm he transferred his curious delight in instability and loss to the room in which he found himself. 'Nice place you got here,' he said, looking round the room, as old-fashioned actors do on the stage when they are supposed to be visiting a house they have never seen before, running his eyes round a line very high up on the walls. 'Have you been here long?' he asked, meaning, 'I suppose you think you can stay here for ever, my poor girl, but it doesn't last, it never lasts.'

When he rose to go he said, 'Now I go to engage the wild animals for the party. Nestor will have wild animals, to be different.'

'What wild animals?'

'All that are tame enough for a party. Elephants, camels, dromedaries, for certain. Giraffes and zebras, lions and tigers, if they will come. A whole zoological garden they tell me to get. I tell them that some day they may be pleased if they have a canary in a cage.' His smile disclosed large yellow teeth that seemed to confirm his pessimism. 'Look', he might have been intimating, 'I am a man now, but my teeth tell you I was once a horse, and I shall be a horse again.'

We hoped at first that Rosamund would stay in London for some days before and after the party, but she was to fly over from Berlin that day and to leave the next morning for Paris, as the parties were to be given on four successive nights. This she told us on a picture postcard from Ceylon, and did not write again. But we were to read in the newspapers much more about the peripatetic court which was going to be constructed for these unknown royalties without title, in paragraphs written in envenomed doubt. There had emerged since the war a new kind of journalist who wrote on social events, in the most restricted sense of that term, and were employed because they had been born into families of social importance. They were the children of people who had been hosts and could be so no longer, and they themselves were exclusively guests, and were not gracious in their new role. Uncle Len had told us compassionately of fly-by-nights, as he called them, who had sunk so low that they could only hope to sell to those who had sunk too low to buy, and therefore always asked to be paid in advance and bit the coin to see that it was not counterfeit. The gossip-writers too suspected the credit of those who promised to entertain their kind. They wanted another house to be open where they could drink champagne, they were inflamed by rumours that the English guests who found the date of the London party impossible were to be given their plane tickets and hotel reservations to Paris or Rome or Brussels. But since they saw the world growing mean about them, they feared that this might not be true, and for all their greed would not have been disappointed if it had been false. As Mr Ramponetti half hoped that the Ganymedios fortune would not last, the gossip-writers half hoped that it did not exist, and probably for the same reason. Mr Ramponetti had almost no ideas, and not enough to help him to perceive a pattern in life; so it gave him a certain degree of philosophical satisfaction to recognise instability; and there was something in many people now that liked the thought of loss. Indeed they liked the thought of every kind of ugliness. At a luncheon-party Mary heard a man say, 'They have asked Lady Bentham to bring thirty people, they know nobody.' Lady Bentham was a friend of ours, we had often played for her, we rang her up and asked her if it were true, and it was not. We had wondered many times why certain women who liked to entertain were hated almost as much as if they had brought people together for the purpose of hurting and insulting them rather than to give them good food and wine and hear their talk. We were to see Rosamund and

Nestor, the targets of hatred more vicious still because absolutely nothing was known about them except their intention to ask people to a party; and those who aimed the arrows would not have found Nestor questionable as we did.

We were invited to dine with them before the party, but both of us had to play earlier in the evening. When Rosamund heard she wired to us that it did not matter, there were forty other people coming, we would not have been able to talk. But she did not say anything about seeing us privately at any other time; and of course she could not, if she was to fly in the morning of the party and fly out the next morning. We were not to see her except at the party, and we went there knowing that. We found ourselves approaching the hired house in a queue of cars so slow that we got out and walked; and from the porch of another house a woman whom we knew, though we could not remember her name, called out to us. She was saying goodbye to a man, and as soon as he had gone she explained that the hired house was blocked with guests, and that as the party was being held in the communal garden behind the houses we could go to it through her back door. We followed her through her hall, which was hung with watercolours of the kind that ambassadors' wives used to paint in the nineteenth century, studies of the Parthenon and the temple at Luxor, and the Kremlin, all looking as if they were in Surrey, while she lamented the excessiveness of the party and blamed the committee in charge of the communal garden for having given their consent to it, even though the sum would, she said, pay the bulb and plant bill for years. Crying, 'It's like a fair,' she led us into her garden, which someone had remade in the Italian fashion, leaving it all stone. It was a terrace, decorated with amphorae, from which some flowers of creeping habit, pale in the night, fell to the flags.

'If you do not want to go into the party at once, you can watch it from here,' said our unknown friend. 'Look, I have laid a rug over the balustrade here, you can lean on it without spoiling your gloves and your lovely dresses. Ah, I remember you both when you were so young you did not wear proper evening dresses, you wore little muslin frocks. You were so charming, so simple, you must have been brought up in a very sheltered home, you would have been overcome had you known you were going to grow up into such a world as this.' Wondering where adults situate the alternate universe,

117

virgin and secure, where they imagine children live, I thanked her.

We looked from the darkness into a bright theatre. On the ground underneath the terrace were great squat lamps, part of a pioneer effort at floodlighting. Their harsh brilliance turned the many trees in the communal garden the prodigious green of vegetables I had sometimes eaten in my childhood, which had been boiled with pennies by cooks who knew nothing of metallic poisoning; and it made the solid Victorian houses insubstantial and colourless, like stage sets awaiting their last coat of paint. Many houses seemed to have pale thick window-boxes, with blurred edges, in their upper storeys; these were the heads of the curious who had thrown up the sashes and leaned out to see better. All over the lawn there had been erected tall gold and silver masts, to which were attached metal streamers painted with heraldic devices and curling horizontally, so that they looked like pennants blown by the wind. It was as if there had been a battle or a tournament here, and the tents had been dismantled, leaving only the tent-poles. These tents might have been set up within a greater tent, for the intemperate lights annulled the sky above, though it was a clear night, and substituted a discoloured haze, which might have been the ceiling of a vast marquee. This glare made monochrome of the crowd of human beings walking about among the masts, to the sound of music played by an unseen band, and the animals which here and there towered above them. If Mr Ramponetti had not found the variety of wild animals he had hoped, he had at least found quite a number of elephants and camels and dromedaries, all of excellent behaviour, who were moving with the cautious, humanitarian gait of the circus-trained beast, to the peril of no one.

The tangle of cable which ran from the lamps just below us kept a segment of the ground quite clear, so that we looked straight across at a spotlit group of these animals. There were three camels and an elephant, who was shifting from foot to foot, perhaps because he was accustomed to perform his act to music and heard the band as a call to duty. White-clad attendants were standing by but the men in charge of the lamps were alarmed, and shifted cables further from the animals, leaving a fairway along which there then streamed innumerable people, some of whom we knew or at least recognised, so strongly illuminated that the expressions on their faces and the essential

118

character of their bodies and movements were emphasised to the point of caricature. Lady Tredinnick strode between us and the light, her arms swinging and her head bowed; she had brought her melancholy solitude with her, she might have been a castaway walking on a lonely beach. Then came Lord Catterock, the little millionaire with the Texan accent, strutting along with his hands in his pockets and his habitual look of devil-may-care roguishness, which as always promised that he was about to blow up the whole of the elaborate occasion by some gay and imprudent act, although the woodenness of his face and body betrayed that he had no fancy, it was beyond his power to think in the mode of gaiety and impudence. Behind him spread out in a fan the young people he always took with him wherever he went, beautiful young women of good family and their husbands, who were suspected of mercenary participation in orgies of vice. In this cruel light it could be seen that this was not true, and that what they were paid for was to endure boredom.

Two men came along with a girl whose dress was almost fancy dress, whose movements spoke of a desire to attract attention. She came to a halt at the sight of the elephant, as a housewife might pause in her cleaning of the larder shelves because she had seen some left-over that could be used for soup. She had bethought herself that the contrast between her fragility and the elephant's huge mass might be amusing and exciting, if it were dramatised. She coquetted in front of the great beast, and when it bent its knee she made a court curtsy, and when it raised its trunk she raised her lovely arm in salute. She was exquisitely made, an almond of a girl. Lord Catterock came back and watched her. His flock stood behind him and watched her with some concern, wondering whether their number was to be increased by one, and wondering too what was considered to be their full strength, whether this meant that one of them would be dropped. But the elephant could only lift its trunk and bend its knee, and other young women tried to prove the same point as the initial exhibitionist, which was however not susceptible to proof by larger numbers. They proved the more general and not interesting point that women are smaller than elephants. Lord Catterock moved away. There was a blare of trumpets somewhere among the gold and silver masts. Everybody moved away. There were left only the camels, the dromedaries, the elephant, the white-clad attendants. A soprano rose in the distant night, hideous in the deformity imposed on the voice of any singer fool enough to sing in the open air. An old man and a young woman came slowly along the fairway and came to a halt in front of the animals. The woman wore a sari, the old man's skin was nearly black against his white suit, they and the animals had travelled a long way to this place. The attendants stepped forward and bowed deeply.

There was an outburst of woe close to us, about the level of our waists. An ape was standing on the flagstone just behind us, rocking itself from side to side, and holding its head between its hands and moaning. It had broken free from leading-strings, a crimson tinsel ribbon was looped round its neck. It was very tame. It came for comfort to us and gripped our skirts round the knee, exuding that strong smell which is not altogether physical, which makes a wail through the pores, a complaint. We sang softly to it, an air by Ladmirault. It liked that and stayed quietly by us, and we were able to turn our eyes back to the party. The old man in the white suit and the woman in the sari were still standing beside the animals. They had impressed one of the attendants to act as a messenger and sent him in search of the host and hostess. He had now returned, followed by Nestor, who stepped into this spot of special brightness as if the lit ground were an elastic substance on which he could bounce, but turned back to give an encouraging arm to Rosamund, who was walking slowly and heavily. Now it could be seen that the old man was a great king among his own people, for his greatness was reflected in Nestor's excessive obeisance as in a distorting mirror. His little body stretched voluptuously while he chattered greetings; he was thinking, 'We both have money, you have more money, but I have much. We both have power, you have more, but I have much. We have houses and gardens, automobiles and yachts and planes, you have more, but I have much.' But a delicious tremor ran through him. He had, of course, a unique treasure this man could not possess. His short strong arm drew Rosamund forward with a competitive pride. She wore the diamond necklace and a dress, white or nearly so, of chiffon draped in the Greek fashion; there was at that time a dressmaker in Paris called Alix who made clothes of this sculptural kind. Rosamund's hesitation, her anxiety, her distress, were like a mist about her under the strong light.

We looked at her, wishing it were not so, making sure that it was so. The disregarded ape between us cried and clutched, but we hushed it till we were quite sure. We saw four people very clearly in the circle made by the elephant, cloud-coloured under the strong lights and standing very high against the stained and hazy sky, the flimsier, lower, sandy camels, the frail and erect white figures of their attendants. The old man and the woman in the sari watched Nestor and Rosamund with the close and impersonal attention they might have given to a complicated gymnastic feat. Nestor was springing from foot to foot, and caressing the air, he was enacting the praise of all women and of this supreme woman. He folded his hands and held them horizontally and laid his face against them, and groaned and pouted. He was plainly depicting himself as a sick man on his pillow, and must be describing his first meeting with Rosamund, who was all this time standing quite still, as still as the circle of animals. He reached the climax of his story, stepped nearer Rosamund and put his arm round her. We lived through a moment we had lived through once before. Standing on tiptoe, because he was so much shorter than she was, he strained up his round flat face, which resembled the sun in a medieval carving, and it seemed certain that he was going to press his mouth against her shoulders and rub his plump white cheeks on her flesh. Of course he did not. But before it was sure that he would not the old man and the woman in the sari moved sharply, as if about to flee from these curious hosts. At once Nestor changed himself into a clownish *tourbillon*, he spun about and spread out his arms as if to turn a cartwheel, and he said something which made his guests laugh. He thought this would make them forgive him. He was mistaken. It would only make them remember it longer. Before they had stopped laughing they turned an inquisitive and censorious glance on Rosamund, who made no attempt at an ingratiating defence. She remained quite still. Her body was an ideograph which signified: 'I want to die. This is a wretched moment, and not less wretched than the one which came before it, not less wretched than the one which will come after it, not less wretched than all the moments which will come after that.'

There were some steps leading down from the terrace and an iron gate into the garden. The ape ran after us, squalling, but was comforted when Mary led it by the crimson tinsel ribbon. We walked over the white grass in front of the arc-lamps, our

121

shadows long and black before us, touching the feet of the people we sought as soon as we started. I hoped we could take Rosamund home with us that very night. Somewhere in the crowd that sauntered between the gold and silver masts there would be Cordelia, her prettiness pursed in contempt, her white gloves clenching and unclenching and twitching the pearls about her neck, as she raged to Alan that all the things she had said about Rosamund were true. She would be on the point of weeping for fear, lest they were indeed not the lies she had always known them to be. But there would be an end to her fear, and to all our fears, if Rosamund came back with us. But as we drew nearer the group it was not the same group that we had seen from the terrace, and did not permit the same conclusions.

The elephant and the camels ceased to be familiar and credible. We no longer saw them from the distance, as painters and photographers see such great beasts, in order to fit them into their canvases or lenses. The creatures lacked the unity the further vision gave them. Surely each camel's front legs belonged to a tall and supple Negro runner, the hind legs to another; and the two had joined together in fame under some shabby hides, older than themselves, and were carrying before them in play a great swag of a neck and a mask made with great clacking teeth taken from other beasts, which they had stolen from a medicine man's hut. It had long fair eyelashes, which surely it had failed to darken not because animals do not make up but because it was unworldly; and behind these lashes were distressed myopic eyes, which showed these odds and ends to be inhabited by one spirit, at a loss. The elephant had seemed smooth and cast in a mould of flowing lines, we now saw the deep corrugations of its trunk, the rough linen-like surface of its tusks, the wet pink formless gash of its mouth, the shapelessness of its ear, clapped on the sides of its head like bits of sacking; and from the stuffed tent of the vast bulk protruded a small mean tail, belonging to a smaller beast. But again there was the eye, little and genial and self-possessed, to show that all these things were one.

We had forgotten the inherent strangeness of the world. Though human beings are less strangely shaped than the great beasts, what is within keeps the balance even. The strangeness of these people, to our distress, was not where we would have preferred it, among the strangers. The old man and the woman in the sari were a king and queen from the East as they are pictured in a thousand children's books. Nestor had been seen almost as often, as the rogue who went out of the gabled city riding backwards on an ass. But Rosamund was not to be recognised, not to be understood. She was staring towards us but did not see us, for she was blinded by the lamps. She was therefore not veiled by any pretence. It was her true face that we saw; and its meaning was not the meaning of her body. That still told its story of complete disgust. But the straight bar of her eyebrows and the curved bars of her lips showed her as much at peace as if she were sleeping. The dejection of her spine, the weary clumsiness of her arms and hands, which worsened the moment by making her seem unworthy of Nestor's ecstasy, spoke of an accumulation of sick perceptions. The old man and the woman in the sari could keep their opinion of her secret no better than Lord Branchester and Lord Catterock; indeed she had an even sharper knowledge of their misjudgment, for the last few months had given her practice in measuring contempt. But as we drew nearer, it became more certain that her peace was untroubled by the least bad dream. In her eye there was no explanation that disunity was unity. Her pure blank gaze simply stated that disgust and serenity could lie down in her together.

When she saw us she cried out, 'Mary! Rose!' and Nestor said, 'Ah, it is the great pianists come to see how the poor boy who married their cousin can give a party.' He drew us both to him and we shut our eyes, since he intended to kiss us. But he suddenly stepped back and pointed his finger at something behind us. Mary had let fall the crimson tinsel ribbon, and the ape was now lamenting its abandonment, holding its head in its hands and rocking itself and groaning. 'What, it is a monkey!' exclaimed Nestor, in loathing. He watched it for a moment, then put his hands up to his head and rocked himself and groaned. 'This is the most horrible thing I ever saw, it looks like a little man, it looks so like a little man.' He covered his eyes, 'Rosamund, Rosamund, get them to take it away. It should be killed, it looks like a man being sad.'

The woman in the sari looked at the old man and raised her eyebrows, as if to say their host was even stranger than had at first appeared. But he ignored her and said, 'Yes. It looks just like a man when he is sad.'

Rosamund put her arm round Nestor's shoulder and

soothed him. But she did not have to do anything about the monkey, for the attendant standing beside the elephant silently came forward and held out his arms to the little creature, who jumped up into the embrace. The attendant wheeled about and held it up to the elephant, who threw out his trunk to grip it and lifted it on to his back. There the monkey bowed to the four quarters and began to somersault, over and over and over, and Rosamund said, 'Nestor, look. You can look now. Up there.'

He was instantly enchanted. 'Ah, the little one! Up there on the big one! He is not afraid!' The attendant said, in a shallow, sweet, quick, oriental voice, 'No, they are great friends, they spend nearly all day together.' Nestor, his eyes on the somersaulting, took a note from his pocket and held it out to the attendant, mistaking the direction by a wide angle. When he realised this he made no motion to move it nearer the attendant, who had to walk to him to get it. His generosity became a proclamation of indifference to its object. 'Ah, nothing so comical as a monkey,' he said.

'Yes,' said the old man, 'there is no animal more comical than a monkey.'

Later we sat with Nestor and Rosamund beside a stage in the centre of the lawn and watched two great dancers without seeing them. She sometimes stroked our hands and once asked with terrible candour and humility, 'Can you enjoy anything of all this?' We stayed till nearly the end, and would have stayed longer had it not been that Mr Ramponetti had sat down beside us and wearied us.

'Tomorrow morning, when the sun comes up,' he said, smiling at the glittering scene, 'how bad all this will look. All the lawn trodden, bits of broken champagne-glasses, and where the animals have been. Shocking it will be.' He glowed with a sense of co-operation with ruin. 'We will pay, of course, but it will be a long time before the poor people in all these houses have a nice garden again, a long time indeed.'

124

V

ROSAMUND did not speak of staying in England, or of visiting it again, and in the next day's evening papers there were photographs of them leaving Croydon Airport for the second party in Paris. We were tormented and we were alone. Our only consolation was the perfect efficiency with which the business of most importance in our world was transacted, without the aid of Rosamund. Nancy gave birth to her son, Richard Adam Bates, without trouble to herself or anybody else. She even contrived that he should be born not at night but a most convenient period of the day, at an hour which allowed Oswald to go off to the school in the morning without suspecting that there was anything unusual afoot and to return home in the evening and find everything in order. It was represented that she had sent for Aunt Lily as soon as she felt the first pains, but there had been some finesse there, for it was all over when Aunt Lily arrived.

A month later, Nancy said, 'There was almost no fuss. It was important.' She was pouring out tea for Aunt Lily and me in the dining-room. 'I wanted to keep Oswald calm. He worried himself ill thinking I was going to die. It's all his father's fault, those everlasting sermons about the Last Day. The old man didn't mean any harm, of course, but it is a pity to bring up a sensitive child not to realise that there are a lot of days as well as the Last Day.' Aunt Lily wistfully objected that it was nice to have a husband who made a fuss of his wife, but Nancy shook her head. 'No, it is tiring too. If I am to have four we cannot have all this fuss.' Her upper lip rose from her teeth, she was gay but she was weak, she warned us that she could not work beyond her strength.

'Why must you have four?' I asked.

'Oswald will feel so grand with four, and we can afford to keep them.' She meant, 'I will take this bullied child that has been terrorised by eternity and make him at ease in time.' She did in fact love him. He was not simply the sole companion her circumstances allowed her, not the one instrument by which she could make herself new company. Yet she was honest and was obliged to add, 'And I have always thought it would be nice to have four.'

The baby had been stirring and squeaking in its Moses basket. She rose and picked it up without passion, with a movement that was neat and debonair. 'Nothing the matter with you, my lambkin,' she said. 'Only a minute's cuddle and down you go again. But how beautiful you are, oh, how beautiful.'

'Maybe you won't have as many as four,' said Aunt Lily, 'but I'll be glad when you have another. For the mite's sake. It would be awful to be an only child. I couldn't have borne it myself. I should have been so lonely without Queenie, it would have been past bearing.'

'Yes, you have a sister, I have a brother, Baby must have a sister and brother,' said Nancy. Her cynicism was really enormous.

'Bless him, he's the image of Mr Bates,' said Aunt Lily.

'Yes, he'll be a handsome man,' said Nancy, 'but he mustn't preach silly-willy sermy-wermons. Mummy won't let him. Look at his little puds, aren't they sweet.'

It was remarkable how she practised the ritual in spite of her cynicism.

'Nothing to worry about, his being like Father Bates,' said Nancy. 'And nothing to worry about if the next one is Janet Ruth, and looks like Mrs Bates.' Our eyes went up to the enlarged photographs: to the preacher, not defying the lightning but taking it into his bosom, to the preacher's wife with her oval face, her troubled brows, her tiny mouth. 'I wonder why she drank.'

Aunt Lily winced. 'Oh, hush. Don't say it out like that.'

'Yes, I will,' said Nancy. 'Skeletons must feel hurt at being kept in cupboards all the time. If we're not to forget Oswald's mother, as I shouldn't like to be forgotten, we have to own she drank.'

'The poor thing, it's a madness,' said Aunt Lily. 'Your

tongue goes up to the roof of your mouth, and then you're
gone. So they say. But you're right. I wonder why she should
have had that weakness, though. She had her own home and a
husband. You might say she had everything.'

'Nobody has everything,' said Nancy. 'But my Richard, my
Dick, my precious, I have you.' She and the baby were fused in
an embrace which had no tension in it, not even warmth; it was
as if a spring wind had blown a flowering branch back against
the tree that bore it, and rocked them together.

'Queenie isn't coming home to something lovely, not half
she isn't,' said Aunt Lily, and then sighed. Hesitantly she
began, 'Talking of your brother,' but Nancy said, 'We all want
another cup. Run and get some more hot water, Aunt Lil,
there's a dear.' As the door closed she put the baby back in the
Moses basket and looked at me through tears. 'I am stupid
since Baby came,' she said, 'I can't do anything more. I can't
rise to it. Please tell Aunt Lily what Cecil wrote to me.'

In the kitchen a kettle had been put on to boil, and Aunt Lily
was passing the time by comparing methods of tea-leaf-
reading with Bronwyn. 'Well,' she was saying, turning a cup
round and round between her hands, 'my mother would have
said that meant a commercial traveller. I'm sure she would. But
your mother may be right. And in a way it's the same thing.' I
took her out into the hall, and we sat down side by side on the
stairs, and I wished very much that Rosamund could have been
there.

I began, 'Nancy wants me to tell you that she has heard from
Cecil. She wanted me to tell you because she still feels weak
after the baby.' My arm was round Aunt Lily's waist. I felt her
meagre skeleton adjust itself to withstand a blow, and her teeth
chattered. I could not imagine how Rosamund would have told
this story. I followed what I supposed would have been her line
by saying that Cecil was very unhappy and had suffered much
from the family tragedy; but what I said had no power. I did not
myself grasp the precise mode of his unhappiness. I thought it
probable that Nancy was right and he was not really unhappy
but moved by an ungracious temperament to take advantage of
what was clearly an exceptional opportunity for ungracious-
ness. My words were therefore only words and worked no
transformation of the news I gave; and when I finished Aunt
Lily groaned and struggled to her feet and clasped the newel-
post.

127

'The little bastard,' she said. 'Not that he was, mind you.'

I implored her not to upset Nancy, and she sobbed that she would not, she always remembered that Nancy was feeding the kid. She put her head against the wooden ball she hugged, and swallowed her sobs. I said, still without force, still knowing what I said to be so inexact that it could have no value, that Cecil had to be excused for not forgiving his mother because, after all, it was his father who had died. She burst into a torrent of whispered words, pointing a gnarled and useful finger, incongruously frivolous with scarlet nail polish, at the dining-room door, to remind us both that Nancy must not hear. What Queenie had done, she told me, was not just hard to forgive; it was impossible to forgive it. Her own blood often ran cold at nights thinking of Harry, who had never harmed a mouse, and how his insides had been wrung out of him by what she gave him, and he had grudged her nothing. She had been in the house, she had seen it. But we had all done the impossible thing and pushed on with the job. How could we leave Queenie alone with what she had done? It would be like leaving someone to freeze to death outside the door on a winter's night, only she wouldn't die. And my Mamma had made it quite plain to her that it had been a special sin to make away with Harry for the very reason that he wouldn't lie quiet in his grave if anybody was persecuted just for doing him an injury. Why couldn't the silly little shit Cecil come in with the rest of us on this? She clapped her hand over her mouth and asked me not to tell Len she had used that word, but muttered, 'Oh, hush,' as the dining-room door slowly opened.

Nancy looked out, immense shadows under her eyes. She swayed as she saw us and hung on to the door-handle.

'Why, Nancy,' said Aunt Lily, her voice cracking, 'you look such a kiddy, and you've got a kiddy yourself now! Listen, Rose and me have had a bit of a pow-pow over young Cecil. Don't you worry. Men grow up late. He'll come round in a couple of years, and Queenie won't be put out. She'll wait. Now let's see about the kettle, I'm dying for my other cup.'

I was still young, so I thought that after a certain period of time events, however violent, retired and lived on a diminishing emotional pension accorded by those they had affected. I knew this was not so in my own life. I was aware that my father's desertion of me had never ceased to happen; when I went to Cordelia I knew that there was a Wilson Steer over the chimneypiece and a certain timid exquisiteness about her dress and the food, because there still rang in her ears the brutal comminations of a long-dead German violin-teacher, pronouncing her a barbarian. But I believed that other people were able to travel out of the orbit of experience, as easily as they could leave a town so far behind them that they could not hear its church-bells. I was surprised that the murder of Harry Phillips was still so appalling to his family that the return of his murderess was to them a domestication of horror, a confusion of this world with hell. The language of my friends was banal with a banality which was perfect, with a perfection which admitted no exceptions, which often wearied me, although I loved them as much as if I were forced to listen to a mindless tune in C major in two-four time strummed hour after hour on a poor piano. They cultivated also a banality of mood, a cheerfulness which might have proceeded from stupidity and which often was stupid, because it was automatic, which often prevented them saying what their courage and serenity and shrewdness had to communicate. Nevertheless I knew they were standing in a desert place, like people in the Bible who are being tried by the Lord.

It was about this time that Kate came into the drawing-room when I was eating sandwiches after a concert, and stood with a distant air, her hands folded in front of her spread skirts, as she always did when she was asking a favour. The proud intention of this stance was to present herself simply as a servant, and renounce all advantage to be drawn from our affection for her. Yet it was so she melted our hearts, for she was then most Kate, most a sailor dressed in skirts. The years were working on her, as they had long worked on Lady Tredinnick, to harden her out of unfemininity. But there was a difference, for Lady Tredinnick was becoming male in aspect, while Kate was changing into some sexless natural substance, say wood of a ship long at sea. She made her voice impersonal as if she were answering roll-call on deck; and she told me that because she had heard Mary and me say that we had not heard from old Miss Beevor for some time, she had been down to Lovegrove to visit the old lady, and had found her sad and ill. She wanted us to ask the old lady to stay with us.

'What has tipped the balance is that the old half-Persian cat has died,' said Kate, 'and that now she cannot play the piano at all. Her fingers are too rheumatic. She has nothing to do but sit and think of your Mamma and all your family. It is such a life as not a dog should have. But you must understand that if we have her she will never leave. She will not come, of course, unless you pretend she is only to come for a short time till her bronchitis mends, and she will mean to leave. But she will never be well enough in her body or her mind to go back and live by herself. And she will be curst when she is old, she is fretty now. But I hope you will ask her to come.'

'We would like it well enough,' I said. 'But you, Kate, would it not be too much for you? Can you arrange it with the help you have?'

'It would be a kindness to me,' she said. 'It would take my mind off things.'

'What things?' I asked.

She sighed. 'The world is not going very well.'

There was a hangdog look about her. Surely she had done what my mother had forbidden and opened a door that ought to be kept shut. Surely she had been looking into a bucket full of water, whether after Rosamund's visit, whether to assure herself about one of her sailor kin. I was afraid, I would like to have asked her, 'Kate, Kate, is something terrible going to happen?' But it was my mother's voice that drove me to the piano every day, and my mother's voice now spoke with abhorrence of magic. I remembered too a beating that had struck me now as curiously cruel. My sudden shocked realisation of its cruelty made me resentfully suppose that it must have been unnecessary. It seemed to me that many of the things I thought I remembered happening in my childhood could not have happened, and that we must simply have been imaginative children who made up fairy tales and painted the visible world with them so that we could not see things as they were. Surely I could not have raised a paper eighteen inches off the ground and kept it steady in mid-air by willpower alone? Surely dogs that had been long dead could not have played about our feet, surely the hooves of ponies ridden by my father and his brother in their distant boyhood could not have sounded on the stable cobbles? Surely I could not really have gone to a children's party and put my hands on each side of a little girl's face and did something that felt like casting my mind to the front of my head and tell her the number that she was saying to herself? Mary and I never spoke of these things now, and the life that went on around us was plainly lived on the assumption that they did not happen. But after all it was not only we four children at Lovegrove who had seen and enacted these marvels. There had been the evil things that had invaded Rosamund's home, there had been the spill of salt from the chimneypiece in the kitchen when they were routed, there had been the hare that talked with us in the garden. But I remembered, with deep misery, that I had often read of poltergeists since, and it was always said that none ever troubled a house unless there was in the family a plausible and unscrupulous little girl or boy.

But really it did not matter if as a child I had practised magic, or not. I might be deluded into thinking that I had raised a paper from the ground and held it in mid-air by supernatural means. But I was not wrong when I remembered that Richard Quin had turned from me and wept when I made him watch me at this trick, whatever it was, and had grown sick and nearly died. For he had been a saint. For he had been a saint whose repulsion from evil had been absolute; and at that time I had been evil. I had used that other trick, thought-reading, to confuse poor Queenie. I had shown her that for me life was not so rigid as was supposed; and she, crazed by her hunger, had drawn the conclusion that it was in all ways more flexible. She had seen me knock down the wall between one child's brain and another's, she had believed that I could knock down the wall between the present and the future, and she had rightly divined that all walls would tumble down at a touch. She had not perceived that unless that touch is withheld, unless the walls are left standing, the universe collapses, we are back in chaos again. So she knocked down the huge wall running across eternity and infinity which is the existence of a human being. She killed Harry Phillips, and would not have killed him had I not imparted to her my false belief that if one can break down walls one should break them down, that if one can alter the universe one should use that power of alteration to its uttermost. I had not then learned that one must move delicately, since creation is plainly a last and desperate resort, a danger improvised to avert another of a more final kind.

Kate said, 'You are so often out in the evenings. The evening is a sad time. The girls are good, we get on well together, but I have known them only a short time. If I had someone in the house I had known a long time and had to wait on them, it would be a great comfort.'

She was a hieratic being, intensely conscious of degree. As children we had always known when she was baking a birthday cake, though that rite was supposed to be performed in secret, for her demeanour was solemn as it would never have been had there been only scones or pastry for the oven. If I were right and she had peered sideways into the future, she had seen more than a personal tragedy; she had stood on the steps of a temple and looked down on a centrifugal flight of fire, that left the gutted palaces behind and leaped through the blackened city walls and spread over the scorched countryside to the horizons, which would also be ashes.

I said, 'Of course she must come. Mary will think so too. Sit down and we will talk about how she is to come over and what room she is to have.' A look of happy cunning came into her eyes. She believed herself to be in a beleaguered city, and she was smuggling in a sick old woman to whom she could be kind, as others would store up food and wine.

The catastrophe she had seen was too large to be poor Queenie's destiny; yet that seemed catastrophic enough when I met her. I recognised her as soon as I went into the garden of the Dog and Duck, although her deck-chair had been put far across the lawn, right over by the gate into the churchyard, to be out of the way of the people who had come in for lunch. Her lank body was stretched out under a coverlet, her head was thrown back on a cushion, and one hand hung down and plucked at the parched summer grass; and the long lines of her body, her bared throat, and her dangling hand made the same diagram of avidity that I remembered from my childhood. She was motionless, but for the twitching fingers; and when I stood beside her chair I saw that her face too was still, though not tranquil. She was staring at the sky, and one hand held a crushed sprig of southernwood under her nostrils. It astonished me that she was so young. I should have known better, I was aware that Aunt Lily was her elder by several years and was even now not an old woman, and that she had been young when Nancy was born, and that her prison term would not have carried her past the early fifties. But I had only seen her in the bulky clothes which women wore in my childhood, and these made youth as lumbering as middle age; and I could not have allowed for the curious false youth bestowed on her by her imprisonment. Her strong hair was still black, the yellowish skin was still unlined. It was as if she had been laid by in a box.

'You're Rose, aren't you?' she said, in the slightly mocking tone, the careful but not quite accurate imitation of an educated accent, that she had used to Mamma and Constance so many years ago. 'I've been reading about you and Mary.' Aunt Lily's album of press cuttings about us was open on the grass beside her deck-chair. 'I'm sure I'm not surprised, you were always clever little kiddies.'

Her eyes went back to the sky. It was not I for whom she had been waiting. I had expected to find myself able to talk to her, because we were linked in guilt. But in that instant I knew that we had nothing to say to each other.

I was to learn that of all those who had waited for Queenie only Aunt Lily was to escape this paralysing conviction that it was impossible to communicate with her; and Aunt Lily owed that immunity to a terrier strain in her which enjoyed laying at her sister's feet everything that had come into common use since she had gone to prison. The *Sunday Express*; shaped brassières; a crystal wireless set; flesh-coloured stockings instead of black; she did not wait to see what her sister made of them, she was off on a chase for the next marvel. That the others were daunted I saw that very afternoon. Aunt Milly brought out her mending and sat beside us, but soon went back to the house. Uncle Len came out with the wireless set to tell us that there would be the racing results, and meant to wait for them, but went back to the bar, though it was between hours. The trouble was that Aunt Queenie imposed her own pattern on the conversation, and it was a forbidding one. It was not easy for us to raise a subject; if it failed to interest her she looked about her with opaque eyes that made the world a desert, and oneself lost in it. She asked us questions, and when we answered them she made some comment that deprived of life everyone we mentioned and put every fact outside the context of reality, while at the same time we were confounded by our excessive sense of her own life and reality. She spoke to me of the people who had been kind to her and Nancy and Lily, with curiosity, wondering why they had done it; and all of them, even my father and mother, became waxworks arranged in some tableau illustrating charity. She said how glad she was that in spite of what she had done her daughter had a good husband and a nice home; and Nancy and Oswald became wax models in a shop-window displaying a suite of furniture. This transformation was the worse because there was a furnace breath about her, that would have melted any waxwork.

Mr Morpurgo came and sat down beside us, the pouches under his eyes enormous, as they were in times of adversity. He had brought a parcel with him, and he set about undoing it.

'Cut the string,' said Queenie, without ill temper. Simply she told him to cut the string. 'Don't go fiddling with it like that. It makes me nervous.'

Meekly he brought out a knife, though unravelling knots was one of his chief pleasures. She was touched and surprised by his compliance. She had perhaps been speaking to herself, as if she were still in a cell, and without expectation of having her own way. She explained that she was very nervous, as she could not sleep as well as she had done in there, and the food out here still worried her, she hadn't got used to it. Mr Morpurgo said that he understood, and went on unpacking his parcel.

'I shall be disappointed,' he said, when he had finished, 'if you do not find something here you like. One of my daughters chose them for me.' It was just about that time that the French dressmakers who had come up since the First World War were bringing out their own scents. They sat on the brown paper on his lap, Chanel's *Numéro Cinq*, Lanvin's *Pétales Froissées*, Patou's *Golliwog*, and two or three of the old Floris flower scents. 'Which will you try first?'

She looked on them like a quiet wolf. 'That was a kind thought. I have been longing for some nice perfumes. I haven't dared ask, for everything seems too dear. But there were no smells in there except kitchen smells and disinfectants. How did you know that? It's a funny thing for a gentleman to guess.'

'I have noticed that you always have a sprig of southern-wood or lavender or a walnut leaf in your hand,' said Mr Morpurgo.

'You are the noticing kind,' said Queenie. 'You ought to have been a detective. Some people might think that that's no com-pliment. But if people do things that are wrong there have to be detectives to see they're punished.' She had pointed her finger at the Lanvin scent, and Mr Morpurgo had unpacked it. 'I like that black glass,' she said, and when he had freed the stopper she raised the bottle to her widely dilated nostrils. 'There ought to be more detectives,' she mused, her eyes going back to the sky, and she passed into a state of harsh meditation, which we did not interrupt until Mr Morpurgo said, 'Nancy and Oswald have just come, I see them talking to Milly at the window.'

'Since you're both so kind,' said Queenie, 'there's something you might do. I've noticed that Cecil's never written and there wasn't a message, and Nancy and Lily seem upset if anything we say seems likely to come near him. I would be obliged if you would take some opportunity to tell them that I don't hold it against him. It's right and proper that Cecil shouldn't want to have anything to do with me.'

'We will tell them,' said Mr Morpurgo. 'But, Mrs Phillips, it may not last.'

'I should think less of him if it didn't,' said Queenie.

Nancy came down the lawn to her mother and laid her lips on a cheek that remained mere flesh under her lips, and Mr Morpurgo and I saluted her and went into the house to seek Uncle Len and Aunt Milly. On the kitchen table there lay a gingerbread, full of crystallised cherries and mixed peel and walnuts, baked that morning, and the four of us ate thick slices of it, going back to the comfort of sugar, as if we were children in a house chilled by grave adult events which we could not hope to have explained to us. As we ate our eyes were drawn to the window. Queenie was still stone, though there was much that might have softened her in this moment. The Thames landscape was as gentle as anything in nature. The river was breathed on by a summer wind, and the flattened and wavering reflections showed what the world would be like if it were slightly diluted, if edges were not so sharp. On a deck-chair in front of her, leaning far forward, sat Oswald, pouting like a baby, surrendering himself absolutely to her mercy as a baby to the breast, while he gave her the gentle domestic news which would have come pleasantly to the ears of the troubled girl in the enlarged photograph over his dining-room chimneypiece. Nancy was crosslegged on a cushion at their feet, faintly smiling. Her enormous cynicism was amused by the inappropriateness of her husband's tendering offerings, the inappropriateness of her mother's mineral reception of them. But her gentleness refused to feel despair. She looked about her at the shaven lawn, the moderate river, the tamed woodland, as if there were no desert anywhere. Yet Queenie remained stone, with all this gentleness about her.

It was to be supposed that it was prison which had turned

her to stone. We watched therefore with hope and admiration her attempts to annul her imprisonment. During the first week or two she rested for most of the day; her body was shocked into excitability by the cessation of routine, and she was sleeping badly. She forced herself to eat good meals; she found a choice of long-forbidden foods not a gratification of appetite but a wearisome demand on her will and her digestion. Then she asked for some fashion magazines and those weekly papers which publish photographs of actresses and society women, and she huddled over them, lifting her wolfish eyes from time to time to compare what she saw with the women and girls who were eating at the tables on the lawn. Her gaze would stay with some of them only a contemptuous second, and on others would linger with a diagnostic fixity, and her judgment was never wrong. She had grasped what the contemporary woman looked like, as her sister Lily had never done. In a few more days she transformed herself into that image. She made up her mind easily enough to have her hair bobbed, but her face twitched when she learned what the new miracle of the permanent wave involved. But she steeled herself to sit in a little room, bound by antennae to the chandelier-like machine for three hours, as was then necessary. Then she went to London for the day with Milly and Lily, and in the evening they showed her off proudly, standing between their artlessness, wearing a straight and short dress and a cloche hat, and stamped with the hallmark of the fashion of the age. She was of course not really elegant. She was not the polished Malacca cane that Chanel made of a rich woman in those days. But she was a straight staff of dark wood.

Nancy, seeing her for the first time in her contemporary uniform, exclaimed, 'Your name suits you, Mamma! There is something very regal about you.'

Queenie murmured, 'Am I all right? I feel all wrong. I could look a sight more regal if I could wear a big hat. These little things squashed down on your head couldn't help anyone. And there are no violets. No violets anywhere. We had such lots of them. The Parma violets were the best. They're the paler sorts. We used to put violet essence on them and wear them on our furs in winter and put them where we pinned our feather boas to our blouses in summer. They gave a lovely finish to a turn-out.' Her eyes were caverns of nostalgia. They roved and fell on her image in the mirror over the chimneypiece, and

136

blazed with delight in the present. 'But there,' she said. She was not stone. She was full of gusto at ranging herself with the living.

She often rose and sombrely left us to go to church; and then she too was not stone. Once we went together to early communion. She walked through the wicket-gate with a certain disdain; the repentance which was harsh about her might have preferred our path not to follow easy contours among the tombs and the long summer grasses under the morning sky, but to run under vaults along distempered and scentless corridors, with a file of the punished shuffling before and after us. We were much too early. Fidgeting, she frowned about her at the grey church and its gilt and enamelled monuments, its richly coloured heraldic glass, blaming them for not being as haggard as herself to suit the gravity of what was to happen at the altar. When the vicar and his server came her hungry expectation brought her sharply down on her knees, and I could feel her faith as if she were playing very loud on some spiritual instrument like a cornet. At the altar rails her expectation was fed, and she walked victoriously when we left the church. The inn was now awake. Uncle Len was singing 'He went on swinging her higher' in the bathroom, and Aunt Milly and Aunt Lily and the potboy were carrying on a dispersed trio from the bar, the coffee-room, and the staircase, concerning the best way to remove nicotine stains from table linen, the women's voices old but fresh with undefeated hope, the boy's voice fresh with youth. Queenie and I had the kitchen to ourselves and the secret we had brought back from the church.

I made the tea strong as she liked it. 'One lump,' she said, 'I haven't got my sweet tooth back yet. Well, that was nice. A lot of rot there being no God.' She gave me a twisted smile before she drank. 'Many's the time I've wished there wasn't.' She drank deeply, wiped her mouth, pushed back her cup and saucer, put her elbows on the table and rested her brow on her hands. 'How early it is,' she said. 'A day's a long time.'

She was stone again. She knew we were not going to fill her day with what she wanted.

Later that morning Mary and I found her in her deck-chair on the lawn, tears on her cheek, ambushing with her hard gaze two boatloads of young people who were letting their craft swing round in midstream while they shouted and laughed

137

and splashed water at each other. The sun turned the spray to silver, one of the girls had red hair that flamed.

'This isn't a very nice part of the river,' said Queenie.

Mary was naïvely angry. 'We think it very beautiful.'

'I don't mean that. It's a lovely spot. I mean only the riff-raff come here. Look at them rowing in their braces. I never could bear to see a man rowing in his braces. I don't think they would do that in other parts of the river.'

Mr Morpurgo spoke from behind us. He was often at the Dog and Duck these days, and never far from Queenie, though he was no more successful than the rest of us in keeping conversation with her alive. He said gently, 'I believe there's a hotel near Maidenhead where. . .' He did not know what word to use. Just as the pause grew too long he found it. 'Where the toffs go.'

'Well, Maidenhead, I mean to say,' said Queenie. Her swarthiness glistened.

Why should anyone think of Maidenhead with that degree of appetite? It was not a suburb taken over by the river and transformed into scenery for a masque, like Richmond, nor river-country, where the woodlands and the meadows are so green that they give the eye the same pleasure that the throat derives from a draught of cold water. Yet Queenie was so eager for the expedition that she dared not tell us so, but lay languidly in her chair, plucking at the parched grass, but looking at us with the gaze of a dog that wonders if its master is truly thinking of a walk. Mr Morpurgo said that we had better all drive to Cookham and take a launch to the hotel, which was, he remembered, past Maidenhead, at Bray. Hoarsely she objected that she had not the right clothes, and did not answer when I told her that we would go as we were. Her gaze ran down us not disrespectfully, conceding that our dresses and our shoes and stockings were good, but making no pretence that we looked as she would wish to look. She sighed, 'Well, of course, it doesn't matter,' yet took a long time to get ready and came out in a state of considerable elegance, in a dress of a sort we all wore then, beige and cut straight as a chemise, and a little hat pressed down over the eyes. There were only occasional traces of her long enclosure. When the car started she took a pair of gloves out of her bag and drew them on and buttoned them. It would not have occurred to any woman of my generation to wear gloves when she was going on the river, unless she found herself playing a ceremonial part at Henley Regatta. I remembered how Papa had refused to take me out with him one day, when I could not have been more than nine, because I had lost my gloves, although the day was warm and nothing could have been involved except an obscure principle of propriety.

Queenie gave us a flashing smile as she went aboard. Yet it was not for the trip on the water that she had hungered. We passed into the long marvel of Cliveden Reach, the curled trench of woodland volute round its image in the river, all contained within the miracle that is a day on the river, the light above us pure because it reflected only water, the water shining purer because it reflected this pure light. Surely this was the opposite of prison, yet she gave it the briefest inventory-taking stare and lowered her eyes again to her left-hand glove, which she had buttoned wrongly and was rebuttoning.

Her glove arranged, she looked at the stream before us. 'Isn't it Saturday? I lose count now. There's nothing to help one keep the date right in one's head. Not the same meals coming up. But if it's Saturday, why are there so few people about?'

Two eights were practising. In! Out! barked the coxes censoriously; the oarsmen, their flesh bronze against their white singlets, pretended that human beings are nothing but lever and fulcrum, pure as diagrams; the clean-cut boats cut clean lines through the water that gave back the pure light of the sky. A rowing-boat nosed into a backwater, another hugged the bank; the girl in one wore scarlet, the other a dark and penetrating blue. In a punt a girl wore another blue, the blue of anchusa. Each of these idle boats kept its own pace, none moving much faster than the current; the variations in their leisure were the more perceptible, the more delicious because of the metronomic bark of the coxes, the backward slide and dip of the oars, the forward and backward slide of the white singlets. The rowing-boat that was entering the backwater passed into shadow; the girl's scarlet dress became crimson.

'So few people? It is not yet lunch-time. We would not expect more.'

Queenie's brows knitted. She sat straight-backed, her gloved hands stiff on her lap, curiously unrefreshed. On Cliveden Heights the woodland lay unexhausted under the noon, and on the water's edge the willows were as green as if there were no smoke anywhere, and nothing on earth had yet been defiled. 'Slower, slower,' said Mr Morpurgo to the steersman in his glass box, taking the bright river under his pouched eyes, as deliberately he would take his Watteau drawing in his hands. Queenie liked it better when we came to the big houses. 'There's nothing nicer than red geraniums,' she said, and exclaimed at the garden furniture. 'In my days we only had hammocks, they were horrid things,' she said. She liked the shining launches that were moored at landing-stages or gleamed in the shadow of boat-houses. This too was better than what she had known. But when the river narrowed and Mr Morpurgo said that we must line up for Boulter's Lock, she cried out in hot and thirsty irritability.

'This can't be Boulter's Lock! Where's everybody?'

We had for company half a dozen rowing-boats and punts, full of boys in grey flannel trousers and girls in cotton frocks, and fathers and mothers and their children, sitting with their picnic-baskets and their Thermos flasks at their feet, and a couple of launches. The smaller of the two was steered by an old man with a long white beard and an orange homespun shirt, whose wife in a window-curtain dress with a long necklace of amber beads was setting out a meal of fruit and nuts and salads. The other belonged to plain parents and their six children, all in khaki shorts. Queenie said again, 'Where's everybody? Where's everybody got to?' It was as if she had gone to a theatre and found half the places empty, and demanded why this should be so, for fear she had made a mistake and booked seats for a failure instead of the popular play she had designed to see. It was odd to feel this about the river, or indeed anywhere in the open air.

'Perhaps there will be more people in the afternoon,' said Mr Morpurgo. 'I hope there will be. It's nice to see a lot of people.' He was not lying in expressing an opinion which he did not hold. He was looking earnestly into her face, and seeking to enter into her nature.

'It isn't only that,' said Queenie.

He tried to understand what she meant and could not succeed. 'I rather think,' he said, at a venture, 'that you're disappointed because you remember things not quite as they were.' His hand turned over on his lap. If it had been Mary or I who was troubled he would have slipped his fingers into ours.

140

But none of us dared to caress Queenie. She would have wondered why we were touching her.

'I wouldn't forget anything about Boulter's Lock,' said Queenie savagely. 'Some things I remembered all the time. The Derby. The City and Suburban. We always went to that. And a ball at Covent Garden. And Boulter's Lock. I used to go over them again and again.'

The lock gates closed behind us. One of the schoolboys on the domestic launch began to play a toy xylophone, pouting very earnestly as he struck each note, trying for the Londonderry Air. 'That sounds very nice,' Mary called to him, leaning over our rails, 'but your G is flat.'

He sounded it and listened, and looked unconvinced.

'No, play the scale, and you'll hear it,' said Mary.

This time he heard the falsity. 'Oh, what shall I do?' he said sadly.

'Take it to a musical instrument shop and they'll tune it for you,' she answered.

His smallest brother, a red-haired little boy, thrust forward his contentious little face and asked, 'But what does it matter, the G being flat?'

Mary and I laughed. This was a frontal attack on the foundation of our lives. The bigger boy exclaimed in disgust, 'Oh, you are silly!' We really could have made no better answer. We smiled across at Mr Morpurgo to see if he had heard the joke and found that he was watching Queenie. She had turned greenish, and her clothes looked too young for her, and yet there might have been nothing of her except her clothes. She could have been an Aunt Sally propped up in her basket chair.

She said faintly, 'It's the water sinking, and these walls going up higher and higher round us. I don't like it.'

Mary and I put our arms round her, but it was like trying to comfort stone.

Mr Morpurgo said, 'Put your head back and look at the sky.'

She murmured, 'Yes, that makes all the difference. This is silly of me. I made up my mind to the permanent wave, but the lock, I hadn't thought of that. Naturally, when I was here before,' she said, smiling grimly, 'it didn't strike me quite the same way.' She breathed deeply till the lock gates slowly opened and we chugged out under the stucco bridge into the bright stream. 'That was silly of me,' she breathed happily, 'and now we'll be seeing Skindles in a moment.'

As we drew nearer Maidenhead Bridge she looked down at her gloves to see if they were rightly buttoned. Her feet had turned inward as she sat, as the feet of the middle-aged are apt to do; she straightened her ankles and pointed her toes. An alert and modish look came on her as if she were an actress, experienced in her art but inexperienced in life, about to give a performance as a duchess. Also beauty reappeared in her, sallow and helleboric, but real. It was not possible to know what bugle was sounding the reveille in her ears. She looked to the left at Skindles, where there were some people lunching at tables outside the hotel, and others sitting nearer the water's edge with glasses in their hands, and she gave them one of her hard stares and turned away. She had in her time been judged, and she judged. Then she looked to the right, at Murray's Club, where there was a greater affluence of couples, most of them lunching, some dancing on a floor built round a tree. The crowds had the granular look of human beings casually assembled under strong light and not under the governance of any overwhelming emotion: a light sprinkling on the lawns of a wayward sort of sand. Perhaps Queenie, so inconveniently important and unique, had wanted to see trivial and undifferentiated specimens of her kind.

But she found no contentment here; and this was not the place which she had desired to see. Without disappointment she said to Mr Morpurgo, 'This bit of river isn't what it used to be. But I don't think anywhere can be like what it was now that there's so much people don't care about any more. I don't like it,' she pronounced in her judicial tone, 'the way it doesn't matter now what women look like, provided they're skinny and have their hair cut right. It's a pity, you know, that Lil couldn't have been young today. When we were girls you had to have looks, and she was out. But if she had her time over again now, she could get away with it, particularly if someone else dressed her.' We slid under the bridge and her voice spoke under the arches with ghostly inhumanity. 'It wouldn't matter, that horse-look she has.'

Beyond, alders and willows on an island, and the circle of images round it, were a confusion of gentle greens, and the water that was their looking-glass was a kindly grey. It was good that there was tenderness in the world if only in colours. After that there was the curious railway bridge, grim and grudging in line, and painted a deep, absorbent crimson.

142

Queenie said, 'This bit we are coming to is what I wanted to see, really.' She spoke in her habitual, quietly hammered measure, but her beauty became extraordinary. She was more vulgar than before, she might have been posing to some mediocre artist who wanted to paint a gipsy, but her face was a light-house, like the faces of the young. Her eyes were brilliant darkness, astonishingly pure in their setting of lined flesh; her lips and teeth shone; she was not yellow any more, she glowed. It was strange that she should have cast off years and be flushed as if she might run further back towards her youth, simply because we were coming into the water that lies between the railway bridge and Bray Lock. For if the Thames can be dull, this is dull. On the right bank is a line of vapid villas in gardens spitted with notices that say 'Private' yet look like public recreation grounds. On the left bank there is only a towpath and the plains beyond. 'Her memory has mixed it up with somewhere else,' I thought. 'The Temple at Henley, or Hambleden Mill and its cedar, or both, she has transplanted them and put them down here. Never mind, we can take her to see them where they really are some other day.'

But as we came out of the arch we forgot her. That is a strange saying, 'Unstable as water, thou shalt not excel,' for water, by its variability, perpetually excels itself. There had been an infinity of green images, printed on a grey mirror. Now there were no images, and nothing was grey. The midday sun rode in a high sky empty of cloud, and it poured down light on water shuddering under little winds. The river was milk-white and scaly like a fish, with a fleck of deep blue in every scale. We exclaimed in joy, and Mr Morpurgo said, 'My Sisley.' But Queenie wailed, 'Where are they? Where are they all?'

Mr Morpurgo slipped from his seat and knelt beside her. 'Oh, hush. Hush, my dear. Where are what?'

'The houseboats. What's happened to them? There were hundreds of them. All along the towing-path.'

We looked down the reach. There were some rowing-boats and punts and canoes and launches moored by the villas, and some craft on the stream. But there were no houseboats anywhere.

'We passed some, by the islands,' said Mary.

'Yes, and nasty scrubby things they were,' said Queenie. 'But the ones I remember were lovely, and they went all the way along from Maidenhead Bridge to the Lock. Oh, don't tell me I've forgotten. If there's anything I got right, it's this. I've seen them so often in my head. Some of them had funny names, like *Dewdrop Inn*.'

Mr Morpurgo called to the steersman. 'Can you tell us, please, were there ever a lot of houseboats moored along this bank?'

The man turned round and faced us. He was as old as Queenie. His face was deeply engraved with discontent. 'Yes, they used to go the whole way along to the lock. When I was a young man.'

'Well, where are they now?' asked Queenie, angrily. 'Why did they move them?'

Mary took the wheel from him so that he could give his whole attention to this lament, this invocation. 'They didn't move them,' he said. 'They went out of fashion. They weren't worth anything any more. Most of them's broke up long ago. There's a few left, for the sort that want them for cheapness. There's some live on them to dodge taxes, and there's queer people, riff-raff, you know. And there's schoolboys and that. It's a cheap way of having holidays. But people with money won't look at them now.'

'What?' Queenie begged him. 'Not Gaiety girls? Not stockbrokers?'

'Oh, it's a long, long time since we had any of them about.'

'Do you mean that nobody has houseboats all painted white, with wire baskets full of red geraniums hanging along the front, and a deck where you sat and played the banjo in the evening?'

He shook his head. 'I haven't heard anybody play the banjo for years. They've got this new thing called the ukulele but it doesn't sound so good over the water as the old banjos used to.' He faced her anguish with a stolid discontent that confirmed it. 'The river's gone down,' he stated in so flat a tone that it seemed as if he must be speaking of a material fact, and we all glanced away at the water to see whether it had suddenly fallen by some inches, and we had been wrong in supposing the Thames not to be tidal at this point.

Mr Morpurgo said to him, 'Now we will go on to the hotel as quickly as possible, please.' Then he knelt at Queenie's feet. 'Here is a clean handkerchief. Is there nothing else than houseboats that you specially wanted to see?'

'Oh God!' she said, throwing off her little hat and holding

144

her head between her hands. 'I knew I'd never go to one again, but I did like to think of them still being there.'

I stroked her hair, which was curiously strong and coarse, but I did not know what to say. 'We will have a good lunch at this hotel,' said Mr Morpurgo. 'I haven't found out yet what you really like to eat or drink. And then we have the whole afternoon before us. Is there nothing else you want to see, Queenie? Where you would like to go, we can take you, Queenie.'

VI

IT WAS A DAY OR TWO afterwards that Oliver and I had to go
down to the West Country for a charity concert, to be given at a
house that was supposed to be very beautiful, Barbados Hall,
just after Goodwood. There was so much reason why we
should attend this concert, and there is so much of the accident
in all events, that I did not think we would ever go. Oliver's
interest in the occasion was his passionate desire that I and a
violinist named Martin Allen, who had been a fellow-student
of mine at the Athenaeum, should play a sonata for piano and
violin written by Kurt Jasperl, a Swiss composer in his early
thirties. Why it was imperative that this should happen Oliver
explained to Miss Beevor and Mary and myself one afternoon
when he came in for tea. It was no trouble having Miss Beevor.
She had to stay in bed perhaps one day in ten, which gave Kate
something to distract her from growing melancholy. For the
rest Miss Beevor was cheerful, and men liked talking to her.

'Jasperl,' Oliver said, to her rather than to Mary and me, 'is
consumptive, and he is just about to come out of a sanatorium
after two years of treatment.'

'Oh, poor young man,' said Miss Beevor.

'It would be appalling if he were to come out and throw away
the strength he has got back by going out and taking some
wretched teaching job,' said Oliver.

'Of course, of course,' said Miss Beevor, 'the poor young
man.'

'If he could get one,' added Oliver, 'which is doubtful. You
see, he has much against him. It is impossible to collect money
for him in Switzerland or Germany or France, because his
earlier compositions aroused keen controversy and were

146

widely discussed, and were in fact quite worthless. They were cheap and nasty experiments in atonality.'

'Tchk, tchk,' said Miss Beevor, looking across at Mary and me, over her tea-cup. She had made the journey all the way from Mendelssohn and Massenet to Debussy and Ravel and Fauré, and even to Poulenc, under pressure from our family, but she liked sometimes to make the point that travel can take one too far, that it may land one among the head-hunters.

'The performance of these horrors had given him the reputation of a charlatan, whom nobody was going to be anxious to maintain. Moreover,' said Oliver, a knot of trouble appearing on his forehead, 'he is a violent and irrational man.'

'Oh, tchk, tchk,' said Miss Beevor. She would have made a superb accompanist. 'But perhaps it is part of his illness.'

'No,' said Oliver sadly. 'He is just one of those people born with a taste for hurting other people. He enjoys contriving monstrous situations without issue. The last thing he did, which makes it impossible to collect money for him in Switzerland now and will make it impossible at any future time, I think, was quite bad. The wife of a rich industrialist, a Madame Kehl, who was herself quite a good musician, persuaded her husband, though he detested music, to subsidise Jasperl. But after a couple of years of this, it seemed to Jasperl that in giving him this money Kehl was showing signs of bourgeois complacency not to be borne. He also began to feel deep pity for Madame Kehl, whom he saw as tied to this bourgeois brute so insensible as to have kept him for two years, and he ended by imagining that he was in love with her. This was a pity from every point of view. He had a wife himself, and a mistress, and he had taken the mistress – and this is what makes collecting money for him anywhere in central Europe quite difficult – from a man called Pfleister who is one of the best known and best liked and most influential of German conductors.'

'Oh, tchk, tchk, tchk,' said Miss Beevor.

'His next step,' said Oliver, with increasing gloom, 'was to write a letter to Kehl refusing to accept any further benefits from a source so degraded, and expressing in inflamed terms his passion for Madame Kehl. And the trouble is that his genius got into this letter. He is a genius, you know. That is why I want Rose to play this sonata at Barbados Hall. He is a great genius. And, as I say, some of his genius got into this letter. Kehl was not only infuriated by it, he could not help believing what was said in it. Naturally this made him anxious to believe the worst of Jasperl, and he ran round Switzerland asking various critics and musicians what this chap was really like, and they all said that he had not a scrap of talent. They were quite right in saying so, on the basis of all they'd heard of his work. For those earlier compositions, they really were jackassery.'

'Mmm,' purred Miss Beevor.

'The trouble was that Kehl drew from these quite honest and reasonable opinions a totally false conclusion. He knew his wife was really musical, and he thought the only reason she could have had for getting him to support Jasperl was because she was in love with him, since every musician he asked told him that the man was a charlatan. As she had never had any personal liking for Jasperl, and had indeed come to detest him during the period when she had to hand over her husband's cheques to him, I imagine she could not have denied the charge more strongly. But there was that letter of genius between them. Ultimately they separated.'

'Why do you take any trouble about this horrid man?' asked Miss Beevor.

'Because just about this time he began to write good music. He threw overboard his nationality.'

'Ah, he found his keys,' exclaimed Miss Beevor in rapture; and though this is an accurate enough rendering of a return to normality it made us all laugh.

Oliver went on, 'He wrote a symphony, a violin concerto, and an opera which proved that he was a genius beyond all doubt. I think he may be better than Bartók.'

'Well, isn't he all right now?' asked Mary.

'No,' sighed Oliver. 'He specialises in never being all right. His symphony is so long that it is almost impossible to play it. A watch-manufacturer finally put up the money to get it performed in Geneva, and they started it much earlier than most concerts, but all except a handful of the audience had to go home long before it was finished, I think it went on till well after midnight. But that handful went mad about it, they were so excited about it they walked about the town singing and cheering until the police ran them in.'

'I should have enjoyed doing that,' said Miss Beevor, her glasses shining. 'Think of hearing a piece of music that seemed like a revelation, and being so excited that you had to walk about making a noise in the streets. I dare say some of them

148

didn't even go to bed. Dear me, girls, it all makes me think of your dear Mamma.'

'I wasn't able to go to bed for hours after I had read the score,' said Oliver. 'But all the same the length writes the symphony off as a way of spreading Jasperl's name and fame. The violin concerto is also too long, that matters a lot, for it is horribly difficult. So difficult that I think few soloists would risk it even if it were normal length.'

'And the opera?' I asked.

'Oh, it is too short. It also has an extremely disagreeable libretto by a German poet. The very heavy principal part is written for a little girl of ten, which in itself raises a serious musical problem. But apart from that what happens to her is enough to keep the opera out of any opera-house. She is adopted by the childless wife of a farmer in Silesia, and the farmer rapes her in a hay-loft. An idiot farm-labourer informs the wife of what is going on, and she climbs the ladder and sets fire to the hay. She and her husband and her child are burned to death, and the curtain falls on a crowd of villagers rushing in and falsely concluding that the idiot farm-labourer is guilty of the crime and lynching him.'

'But how unnecessary!' breathed Miss Beevor.

'Indeed, indeed, how unnecessary,' agreed Oliver. 'But the orchestration of the lynching is sublime. All this, however, gets Jasperl no further. These compositions cannot be performed, as you see, and it is difficult to read the scores. They have not been printed. It will be difficult to get them published, since Jasperl has this reputation of an excessively backward member of the avant-garde. It is hard even to read them in manuscript, for he copies his work himself, very inaccurately, and often refuses to lend them to those few who are interested, on the ground that they are unworthy. So there is nothing to do but collect some money for him, some of which he can spend on publishing these works, and maintaining him in the hope that he writes some more which will be easier to perform. And that is why I am taking Rose down to Barbados Hall.'

'Why?' I asked. 'Does it belong to somebody very rich?'

'No, no. The Mortlakes have all they can do to keep the pediment and cupola over their heads, the wolf from the colonnade. But somebody rich will be there. The Mortlakes have to give this concert for some charity that is dear to royalty, I forget why. All sorts of people who have been at Goodwood are going to it. And one of them is Lady Southways. She is an example of the connection between love and music of which we have often talked before.'

At that time a curious pattern of musical susceptibility was appearing among the women of the upper classes. In an earlier generation the most respectable peeresses and bankers' wives played a tutelary part towards music; they were ranged in the boxes round Covent Garden opera-house as if virtue had an acoustic value. Now such a part was played by wealthy women with many lovers, who turned to music as soon as age began to take their lovers from them. It did no harm, though it was odd, after a concert to find that Beethoven and oneself had been for some members of the audience acting as surrogate for the duke who was the great lover of our day.

But it made Miss Beevor angry. 'I call it disgusting. I read in the newspapers of Lady This and Lady That getting divorced again and again, and after a year or two there they are, popping up to tell Mary how wonderful her Skriabin is and telling how Stravinsky is, and what impudence and hypocrisy that is, pretending to understand always the most difficult music, when they have spent so much of their time in ways that cannot have helped on their musical education. And anyway it is all wrong. Music should be so elevating.'

'But so is love-making,' laughed Oliver.

It was strange to think that of the four people in the room only Oliver knew what it was like to make love.

He went on, 'You are too hard on them, Miss Beevor. They are good old girls, only not at all vegetarian. And there is a similarity between love and music that makes them very generous in a certain direction. You must have noticed that there are really very few famous composers, compared with the number of famous authors and painters. The composers that are known to the mutt in the street are a very few – Bach, Beethoven, Mozart, Handel, Haydn, Chopin, Mendelssohn, Schubert, Schumann, Wagner, Bizet, Puccini, Elgar, you have the lot. It is a short list. We know more but they don't. And there are apparently only a few great lovers, for when I ask about the pasts of my particular old girls, I am always told the same names.' He mentioned the active duke, and gave other men. 'It is a short list too, and I suppose it was a great credit to add a name to it. That Armenian painter who is going round London with every edible peeress, if you know what I mean, I suppose the first woman to discover his charm feels a certain pride. I always find these women take a great pleasure in putting up money for unknown composers, and I am sure they must be fascinated by the idea of adding a new name to a short list, associated with excitement and prestige. And that is how I have got hold of Lady Southways, who has promised to give me quite a reasonable amount of money for Jasperl, if she likes his music.'

'But does she know one note from another?' I asked.

'Oh, yes,' he said, 'I stayed with her in Scotland, when they performed my opera, *The Useless Sacrifice*, at Glasgow. She has a beautiful music-room, looking out on a firth, and she plays a great deal. One might say that her hands are always wandering over the keys; and really often they wander in directions which indicate some musical feeling. For example, when I was there she was constantly playing the piano score of *Turandot*, and all the wrong notes had the effect of making it sound more like *Madam Butterfly* than it actually is. Surely there is a certain sort of musical feeling there? It was, to be truthful, just that feat of transposition that gave me the idea that Rose and Martin Allen should play this sonata of Jasperl's at Barbados Hall.'

Mary interrupted. 'You are taking another slice of cherry cake, Oliver?'

'Well, yes, I was,' said Oliver.

'But you crumble all the cake and pick out the cherries,' said Mary. 'That is absurd. The cake is quite good, I will go down and get Cook to give me some crystallised cherries, and you can eat as many of them as you like, without wasting the cake.'

When she had left the room, Oliver said, 'How can it be that a sensitive woman like Mary does not see that eating crystallised cherries by themselves would not be at all the same thing as picking them out of a cake? But that is really the reason why I asked you and not Mary to play this sonata with Martin. I had better explain first why I asked Martin. This is one of the easiest of Jasperl's compositions to understand, and dear Martin plays everything so that it sounds as if it were Brahms. The result should be something that will enchant the ears of Lady Southways. But I couldn't trust Mary to be my accomplice in such a – well, one might call it such a light-fingered business. But you, Rose, you are a realist. You won't object to taking part in what is really a parlour game, "In the manner of", I think it's called, when there's such a good object in view. You won't mind just for once playing the piano in the manner of Martin Allen, in order to keep Jasperl going.'

Just then Mary brought in the cherries, and he ate some out of politeness, but of course I quite saw it was not the same thing. And Kate followed Mary in to tell her so. She was quite cross. 'I made the cake,' she said, 'and if anybody should mind your picking out the cherries I should, and I do not mind at all. They are quite different after they have been cooked with all the good butter and eggs and sugar. Anyway people sometimes like to push something away and say, "No, I will not have that." When I take Miss Beevor her cup of milk when she is in her bed she always takes the skin off and says, "Ugh" and rattles her spoon on the saucer to get rid of it. But she wouldn't like it if I took the skin off the milk before I brought it to her, she would not know where she was.'

'Oh, I'm sure I wouldn't mind,' said Miss Beevor, and Kate said firmly, 'Yes, you would, Madam.' But Mary's eyes widened and she laughed and exclaimed, 'How stupid I am!' It struck coldly through me that she was taking too much pleasure in this gloss on the process of rejection. It was as if I had suddenly seen the first signs that she was growing deaf and blind. We were not a big enough household to keep ourselves in perfect health. Kate and Miss Beevor were better than just Kate and me; but Mamma and Richard Quin should not have died, Rosamund should not have gone away.

'How kind you always are to me, Kate!' said Oliver. 'You know I see through you, you are only teaching the children that they must let the little boy that has come to tea do anything he likes. I am really at fault, Mary was right, it was intolerable to crumble such a lovely cake. But forgive me, and help me. I want you and Miss Beevor to tell me what you think of this photograph of Jasperl. I took it on the sanatorium veranda. I wondered if I should send it to Lady Southways.'

Kate went behind Miss Beevor's chair and they both peered at it.

'Oh, not a nice face,' said Miss Beevor. 'Not a nice face at all.'

'He is as cold and sharp as those snow peaks in the background,' said Kate.

'I do not think I would send this to Lady Southways,' said Miss Beevor. 'From what you say, she should be experienced in reading men's faces, if anyone is.' She handed the photograph back to Oliver and sat back, rubbing her glasses clean of the image they had just magnified. 'But, you know,' she broke out, 'surely some of this modern music is really degrading and horrible.'

'You forget,' said Oliver with a smile, putting the photograph back in his wallet, 'he has found his keys.'

'And the man who fetches the laundry looks much the same,' said Kate. 'No modern music for him but he is a nasty beast.'

'Let me see what he is like,' I demanded. But Oliver did not seem to hear me, and said, 'You see, Rose, to impress Lady Southways I have to rely solely on you and Martin doing your best at Barbados Hall.' From his expression I knew what was now going to happen. Abruptly he stood up and said goodbye and left us. That was what always spoiled his visits, he suddenly got tired of us and went away.

I found our rehearsals amusing, though I felt ashamed, when I looked at Martin Allen's good, kind, trusting face, which always, when he was playing, although he was entirely masculine, bore the expression of a woman tending domestic apparatus such as a sewing machine or a mangle. He got the sonata back into the nineteenth century all right, as he would have got the selvage seamed, the pillowcases fit for drying. But he did not approve of the enterprise, though he did not understand his own dubious aesthetic part in it.

'What is the good of this?' he asked Oliver, cutting in on his praise for our first finished account of the sonata. 'You know that Jasperl will bitch everything up the first time he meets Lady Southways.'

'Perhaps he never will see Lady Southways,' said Oliver. 'I doubt if she will go to Switzerland much now. She is too old for winter sports. I have thought of everything. And if she invites Jasperl to England, he will probably get into some altercation with the immigration officers and not be allowed to land. Oh, it should be possible to spin the thing along for a year, or even two years. And that will be perfect for Jasperl.'

Martin asked abruptly, 'Where is Madame Kehl?'

'Living alone in a large villa in one of those little towns between Geneva and Lausanne, charming country but baked without salt.'

'Should we not,' said Martin, 'be thinking out something that would be perfect for Madame Kehl?'

'Nothing can be perfect for her now,' said Oliver. 'All one can do is to get some more music out of Jasperl.'

I said, 'But how old is Madame Kehl? She does not sound as if she had come to the end of her life. She was young enough for her husband to be jealous of her, to think it possible that she might have had a love affair with Jasperl. Probably she will fall in love again, and forget both of them.'

The two men did not like me saying this. They did not take it as a simple statement of fact, and after a second laughed, as if I had made a pleasing show of spirit, a gallant feminist protest against unalterable conditions favouring the male. I thought how little I liked men, and said, not too agreeably, 'Shall we try the sonata again? The second movement is still quite rough.'

The rehearsal had to stop a week before the charity concert, for Martin had to go off to run a music summer school. But this was in the West Country too, so we arranged that Oliver and I should go down to Barbados Hall the night before the concert, and meet Martin there, and spend the evening in a rehearsal of the Jasperl sonata. Lady Mortlake wrote all three of us letters saying she would be so glad to have us, she had admired us all for years, and although we knew she had probably not done so, she obviously had had the intention of being nice, all over four pages.

Oliver and I met on the platform at Waterloo, just about two o'clock. We had to take a very slow train, for the faster ones did not stop at the junction where we had to change to get to Barbados Hall. We arranged not to eat before we started, and I brought a luncheon-basket, with some of Kate's special sandwiches, the ones with chopped chicken mixed with mild curry sauce, and smoked cod's roe beaten up with lemon and a very little whipped cream, and some cherry cake, so that Oliver could eat it the way he liked. At first we talked about some records that a young American composer had sent us both, tone poems about the Great Lakes, very nice orchestration that showed he had studied in Paris, but nothing much to say, though that might come. Then we passed a wonderful nursery garden, and the train ran across Maidenhead Bridge, and we looked down on the reach where Queenie had found no houseboats, and I was too miserable to speak.

Oliver said, 'Why have you suddenly stopped talking?' and I was irritated, it had happened so often when he came to see us that he himself suddenly stopped talking, and got up and went away, too. Then came that stretch of railway where there are more nursery gardens. We began to eat, and looked out on fields of roses, the cross-looking little plants set far apart on the rich earth, in the midst of their crossness the small flowers so bright that it could be seen even at that distance whether they were red or yellow or white. It was the time when the herbaceous plants were in their prime, and a full brush had painted broad blue bands of delphiniums and purple bands of Michaelmas daisies. Blue and purple comes out of the earth everywhere as July goes towards August, and in the hedgerows there were chicory and mallow and thistles and vetch. They reminded Oliver of the fields round the house in Norfolk where we had spent the first summer of the war, we always thought of it now as the last summer.

'That is one of the things I always remember about that visit,' said Oliver. 'Either there were an extraordinary lot of flowers there, or I had never noticed them before. And there were wonderful ones down on the sea-shore too. Your brother once took me to a part of the dunes where there were miles of yellow sea-poppies. You cannot think how beautiful it was, with such a restrained beauty. Not many flowers on each spiky plant, and the leaves a wonderful blue-grey, that sometimes melted into the tongues of water that lay among the dunes.' He spoke as if he were sure that Richard Quin had taken nobody to this stretch of sand except himself. But of course he had taken Mary and me there as soon as he found it. I found myself saying to my dear brother, 'Really, you should not have been so ready to please, you came near to pretending.' But of course this was nonsense, he had no faults.

After that the railway runs for a long time beside a trout-stream and a canal, set in a pale green landscape like the background of a Rowlandson drawing; and Oliver and I found that both of us had again and again looked out at them, and resolved to take a train to the district the first free day we had, and walk along the clean buff towpath and over the clean grey bridges. Of course we had never had time. Our own country was covered for us with a nexus of work; to get a holiday we had to take refuge in another country, it was impossible for us to travel in England. But this present journey, though there was to be a concert at the end of it, was half-way to a holiday. As we munched, the great downs, stretched out like sleeping dogs, came up between us and the South. In a field an elm lay

155

prostrate, that had been felled by a winter storm but had brought its root with it, sticking up like its feet, so that it still lived and had brought forth its summer foliage. Among its leafy branches children played and waved to the passing train. They looked like the children in children's books, genuinely different from adults, and preoccupied with other interests, as our family had never been. I waved back to them, though the sort of child I had been, not yet dead in me, despised them. Yet I wondered if such children grew into adults happier than Mary and myself; and instantly noted that this afternoon I was almost happy.

So was Oliver. 'It should all go well,' he said. 'I have had several letters from Lady Southways, and really they sound very good.' He took them out of his pocket and read me passages. 'It is funny how all rich women write letters in scherzo form, and funny too that they evidently want to give the effect of a scherzo played by a pianist of imperfect technique, for they always end out of breath. But you see what hope uplifts her, she sees herself as godmother to a prodigy, as Diaghilev to Nijinsky. And that is really what she will be, if we can get her to keep him for a couple of years, if we can get him to be kept for a couple of years without biting the hand that feeds him and infecting it with a specially deadly microbe, which he has obtained by seducing the wife of a pathologist who once had done him a good turn.' He laughed and, folding up the letter, said, 'But I do not really think this funny at all. Why, why, I ask myself, why,' and he sang the theme out of the second movement of the sonata.

We had left behind the neat little river that kept company with the canal, now there ran beside us a broader and wilder stream. Our train halted where it widened beside the ruins of a mill. We looked out of the windows on the other side and found this was our junction. We had to hurry to get out our suitcases and the lunch-basket, and reach the little train that took us, through wet fields veined where they were wettest with drifts of late meadowsweet to foothills that were golden with the afternoon sun. This was the West, almost as foreign as France. 'It might be true,' said Oliver, looking out at the cottages that sat with clumps of hydrangeas like footstools at their feet, and wore late clematis and roses and fuchsias like excessive jewellery, 'that here they knew of no other ways of killing cats but by choking them with cream.'

But there was no car waiting for us at the station. We both took out our letters to see if we had made a mistake, but no, we had been told to be at this station, at this hour. There was no taxi in the village, so we left our luggage with the porter and crossed the road to an inn, the Huntsman's Horn. The innkeeper's wife said that we could have tea in the garden, and we warned her that a chauffeur from Barbados Hall would be coming to find us. She smiled at us as if we held a secret in common, and offered to make us scones if we would wait, but we reminded her that we might be fetched at any moment. We found a rustic table facing a bed of dahlias that were now transfixed by the horizontal shafts of the late sun. Crimson and scarlet, orange and yellow, purple and lavender, white and grey, burned the great lamps of incandescent velvet; and while we sat staring the innkeeper's wife came along the paved path, tenderly bearing something white in her arms, smiling down on it. She spread it before us with a transparent affection of the casual, and we looked down on the phantom of a tablecloth, covered from hem to hem with darns. It was a disconcerting exhibition of toil and thrift in the midst of this profligate floral splendour, this velvet that had not been woven, these lamps that burned no oil. But it was her treasure. She smiled so proudly that I said, 'What a wonderful cloth,' and she said, 'Why, yes, it is. It comes from Barbados Hall.' She had been a kitchenmaid there in the time of Lord Mortlake's father and mother, and when she had left to be married Lady Mortlake had told the housekeeper to give her any linen that there was to spare, and she had found a wonderful damask tablecloth that had been used for big dinner-parties but had had some hot candlegrease dropped on it. The hole had been right in the middle, so she had cut it into four, and she was still using them, though that was forty years ago. She could well believe, she told us, that we had never seen lovelier linen.

We sat among the fiery flowers, and drank strong tea and ate bread thick with strawberry jam and Devonshire cream, and followed with our fingernails the pious intricacies of the network of darning cotton, and talked of music and that summer in Norfolk and what Richard Quin might have done if he had not been killed. A bumble-bee came about us, making the very sound time would make if it did not pass silently. Almost an hour had gone, and the chauffeur had not come for us. 'Martin will be going mad,' said Oliver, 'we should have gone through the sonata at least once before dinner. I will go and find a telephone.' But he called from the house that there was none, he would have to go to the rectory up the road. I waited happily, for I was engaged in an adventure, I was doing something quite unlike anything I usually did. I was not in our home at St John's Wood, I was not going to a real concert, I was not at the Dog and Duck, which was now more troubled than my too empty home or any concert-hall, because of the unresolved misery of Queenie. I was moving in a free place where my movement would have no consequences, for in three days Mary and I would go on our holiday, and there would be no more reason for me to see Oliver until he wrote a new composition which I could play. And that might be a long time, for he had spoken of beginning another opera, though for some reason I felt that that might be a mistake.

Oliver came back a little disconcerted. He always had his pride that with him everything went smoothly. 'It seems the car they sent for us broke down. We cannot be fetched until another car comes back and is sent out again. It will perhaps be another three-quarters of an hour before it comes. That is all right, though it seems a little strange, but what worries me is that I could not speak to Martin. Evidently the butler could not find Lady Mortlake, it was a pansy who spoke to me, I think it was Lionel de Raisse. He was very much concerned at the thought of you being left high and dry like this, but he really did not seem to grasp what I meant when I asked for Martin. But we will be all right, there is no reason to worry.'

The old inn-keeper came out and took us behind the dahlia-bed to show us his rabbits; blue Angoras, making a great show of sensibility. Just at the right time, when the light had left the garden, his wife hurried up the path, explaining that the Admiral who was the second husband of Lady Mortlake's mother, and lived at the Dower House, had called in for some soda-water, and would be pleased to take us up to Barbados Hall, just as soon as he had fetched some medicine for his invalid wife at the surgery. 'It will be nice for you,' she breathed, 'to be driven by one of the family.' She made us feel like the donors of an altarpiece, elevated above their station by being represented in proximity to sacred personages, and, smiling, we waited for the instrument of our elevation on a bench outside the inn, our luggage at our feet, resting on a strip of cobbles, set shining grey in a network of blue shadow that edged the rose-red road.

'That is a superb suitcase of yours,' said Oliver. 'An oddly superb suitcase, if I may say so. It is more what I would have expected of Lady Mortlake or Lady Southways.'

'I bought it in Paris,' I said. 'It is the product of terror. When we were little our family luggage was awful, Japanese baskets that had broken at the sides, and pockmarked tin trunks. People used to laugh at us at railway stations, and the land-ladies at seaside lodgings used to sneer like Dickens characters when our things came off the cab.'

'What, were you poor?' exclaimed Oliver. 'I never knew that.'

I stared at him. I felt as if he had lain indifferent on a beach while I drowned in the surf. 'Of course we were poor. How could you know us and not know that we had been poor?'

'I knew only that your mother was a widow, and that you had had an isolated childhood, and that you and Mary seemed unlike other people,' said Oliver. 'But you had that nice house in Norfolk, I supposed you were all right and always had been so. Weren't you? You always seemed to have so much of everything. I told you, there were more flowers in the fields round that house than I had ever seen anywhere else.'

'We had nothing,' I told him angrily. 'Oh, it was so dreadful for Mamma. We had less than nothing. There were always debts, duns came to the door, we had the most horrible clothes, and shoes were the worst thing of all, they were so dear that we always went on with the old ones long after they had begun to hurt. Ask Mary, she will tell you.' I was enraged, but what I said was wide of the mark. I was angered not so much by his ignorance of our poverty as by his remark that Mary and I seemed unlike other people. I hated that he should share the obstinate persuasion of the world that there was something strange about us. But as I saw the pity on his face anxiety struck through me, I asked, 'And you? What sort of childhood did you have? Were you poor?'

'No, no,' he said impatiently, 'we were not rich, but we were not poor. But why were you so poor? How did it happen?' He shook my arm to make me tell, but it was then that the Admiral came up in an old Daimler, driven by an old chauffeur, it might have been a chariot in a masque representing honourable old age. He hobbled out and introduced himself, and we were at

159

once torn by that conflict which, for us, usually raged in the shadow of a great house such as Barbados Hall. The Admiral's blue eyes were hard in the wrinkled waste of his old eyelids, he was hard and stupid and obsolete. There was impertinence in the candour with which he conveyed to us that, though it was not surprising that I was reasonably elegant and a pianist, since women were condemned to be entertainers of all sorts, it was surprising that anybody as masculine as Oliver should be a musician. But Oliver explained with perfect civility that from his earliest childhood he had never cared for anything but music, as he might have confessed to congenital asthma. The Admiral was so much nearer death than we were that it was not becoming for us to correct him; and indeed it is necessary that some people should be insensitive to music. All musicians know that a community in which everyone was susceptible to musical excitement would run mad. The old man's deafness let sound speak its meaning in safety. Also he and the chauffeur, and all the crowd of servants one could divine behind him, had their own mystery. We drove into a park flooded by the setting sun, and on a knoll of golden turf, before a golden hanger, a herd of deer, bright brown, amber-bright, stood fixed in fineness, a line of attention running taut from each raised muzzle to the same point of the compass. 'It's easy to know what's coming to them down the wind,' called the chauffeur, and the Admiral gave a connoisseur's chuckle and grunt. We had no idea what they meant. For these men the earth was covered with forms and embodied motives of which we were ignorant, as for us the air was a complex of sounds and articulated motives which they could not hear. They were also our associates in art, practitioners of a craft we could not undertake. Their kind had not built the house that lay in a sudden garden amid the deep folds of this part; but their kind had caused it to be built and had preserved it, as our careless kind could not. We reached it as the sunset blazed. The central wing had two storeys of deep red brick divided by stone pilasters; the brick was glowing, the stone was stained the colour of ripe peach flesh. In the windows flamed small reflected sunsets, their wildness bridled by good taste, for each window was so right a shape. Pilaster, strip of brick, pilaster, strip of brick, might have made too simple a pattern had not the pilasters burst into capitals under the eaves, capitals ornate as the heads of the heavier flowers, the stronger lilies or the Datura. On each side there was a wing in a later, classical mode, faced by a colonnade; the one not flushed by the sunset was lilac-blue. Time had not been allowed to spoil one square inch of this.

We could not drive up to the door, for there was a car in front of it. On the broad steps three menservants were coloured by the sunset like the stone, and might have been architectural details of the huge and highly decorated doorway. They looked at the Admiral's car with a certain distaste, and the Admiral cut through our goodbyes with an enquiry as to whether we were quite sure that Lady Mortlake expected us to arrive tonight, and telling us that he had only wondered, and that he must be getting on, his wife had had a special salmon sent from Ireland, and some friends were coming in to share it at an early dinner. It might have been that there was the fog of a family quarrel in the air.

As we mounted the steps the butler remained standing against the carved framework of the door, his face and hands and shirt-front glowing in this remarkable identity of colour; he might have been a *trompe l'œil* butler painted on the stone. We found it odd that his silvered handsomeness should be discomposed, that he should regard us with what seemed like open reproach, and should abruptly exclaim, 'We would have fetched you!' and should make no motion to usher us into the house. But just then there came through the door a woman whom I could not doubt to be Lady Mortlake, and not for a moment could we believe that she was there with the intention of welcoming us. She was dressed for departure, and she burst out of the house as if it were a constraining bodice and now her bosom could be bare and free. She looked at us with frank impatience because we were in her way, then recognised us, and after a hostile pause repeated our names loudly and with ecstasy. Some faces had shown behind her in the darkness of the doorway, and with a freshet of laughter these disappeared. It had been obvious that she had raised her voice for other ears than ours, that she had been giving what she knew would be a cue for that laughter, which was not good-natured, which she had known would not be good-natured. On us she turned the full brilliance of her appearance in a greeting far too cordial, to listen to it was like looking at a pattern material from too short a distance. Like many women of that time, she spoke with a cat's voice, and overstressed certain words, introducing into each sentence an affectation of unbounded enthusiasm and a satire

161

on all spontaneity. She explained to us that she had to rush to the bedside of a sick relative. To convince us of her regret she leaned towards us and we were lapped by waves of an intoxicating scent, surely more useful at the bedside of the well than that of the sick. She had not seen the Admiral's car, so she identified the invalid as his wife, her mother-in-law. The doctors could not tell, it seemed, what was the matter with her.

'Well, she has a special salmon tonight,' said Oliver, but Lady Mortlake was not attending. She ran on into the orange light as if it were the sea on which she was embarking for Cythera.

We went through a circular hall, where gods and goddesses stood on pedestals round the curved wall. Some people had a second before been looking down from the gallery above, but they had stepped back. We went to our bedrooms, which were the usual thing one finds in old houses, big square boxes with Queen Anne furniture and needlework pictures and 1860 watercolours, and I gave the housemaid my keys and washed and made up, and was ready when Oliver knocked on my door. His room was just round the corner of the corridor, I had heard him singing the theme of the first movement of the sonata as I washed. We went downstairs and found the butler, and before we could ask him where Martin Allen was, he told us with a bizarre hauteur, as if he were acting a butler in a film, that if we followed the footman to the small music-room we would find the violinist. As we went along the corridor Oliver hung back and muttered, 'I wonder what this means. She was going to a lover, of course.' It angered me that he spoke as if I would not know that. 'But to the girdle do the gods inherit. But there is something else wrong: I cannot understand why she should think we cared whether she was here or not tonight, our time will be taken up with the rehearsal. Still, Martin will be able to tell us.'

But when the footman opened the door Martin was not there. It was a shabby little room with an upright piano in a corner, and in front of the fireplace stood a stout and sallow girl of seventeen or so, dressed in crumpled bluish-pink linen, and holding a violin and a bow.

'Oh, it's you!' she said, scowling. 'I thought you would never come. Why have you been so long? I am Avis Jenkinson. What, do you not know who I am? Didn't that horrible woman tell you? Oh, I know I should not call her a horrible woman, for we are in her house. But I told her I would not come unless she telephoned you both and heard it was all right. You see, Martin Allen cannot come. He has had an attack of appendicitis and is having an operation tomorrow morning. I am supposed to play instead of him. Oh, do not trouble to stop looking like that, I know how awful it is. I should not ever have consented to it for a moment, but I wanted so much to meet you both, and I did make it clear that I would not think of it unless she telephoned to both of you and told you who my teacher was and you could telephone him and he would tell you how good I am. But of course she did not do it. Everybody here is a beast, and she is the worst beast of all. They have been such beasts I did not dare to go in to tea. But I suppose,' she said bitterly, 'by this time you think I am a maniac.'

Oliver stood silent. He raised his right hand to his lips and bit the knuckles, then whispered to himself, 'Jasperl.' Then he shook himself, as if he were a dog coming out of the water, smiled at the girl, and said, 'Let us sit down and then you can tell us all about it.' She looked so awkward and bedraggled as she dropped into an armchair, one foot beneath her, that I had to ask, 'How long have you been here?'

'Since yesterday afternoon.'

'Alone?'

'Of course. How would I know people like this? There are some professional musicians here, but they are as horrid as the rest. Of course I do not mind what they do to me, but I want to kill them.'

'But there are three of us now,' I said.

'Yes, yes, and we are the real people, and they aren't,' said Avis. 'I have been telling myself that, ever since I got here, I have been reminding myself that in a hundred years' time I shall be remembered, and they will be forgotten as if they had been sheep or horses. Spavined horses, they say in books, though I do not know what it means.'

'But how did it all happen?' asked Oliver.

'I live near here,' said Avis. 'My father is clerk of the gas-works at Aysthorp and I went to the music summer school were Mr Allen has been. When Mr Allen had to go into hospital, because he had appendicitis, the people at the music summer school telephoned to Lady Mortlake, and she was in a panic, she wanted you to come to the concert whatever happened. It is something to do with someone called Lady

Southways. Oh, it has nothing to do with music, Lady Southways likes you,' she said, pointing her bow at Oliver in a censorious manner. 'And Lord Southways has a lot of money and breeds wonderful racehorses, and Lord Mortlake is poor, or what these people call poor, and anyway I wish the Mortlakes were so poor that they would starve, and Lord Mortlake is trying to breed horses, and he has a mare that is very good, and he wants it to have a foal by a horse that belongs to Lord Southways, so Lady Mortlake wants to please Lady Southways by getting you here. She knows nothing about music, though she talks about it all the time. She went on and on about a concert of Beethoven's later quartets, and I think Beethoven's later quartets are jolly difficult to understand, don't you? Don't you? But she came to me just because they told her at the music summer school that Mr Allen had been practising Jasperl's violin and piano sonata with me, she did not see how impossible it is that I should play it with you; I should not have said I would, of course, but she was so nice to me when she came and asked me to do it, and I did so want to be with you. So I came here, and I have been practising it, and I see how impossibly difficult it is, I cannot get the hang of it at all, everybody here has been foul, when I come into the room they stare at me and stop talking. I must have been mad when I said I would come, though really I am quite good, I am exceptional, my teacher would have told you so.'

'Who is your teacher?' asked Oliver.

I shut my eyes. It seemed to me inevitable that she would answer 'Silvio Sala'. For many years I had not thought of the poor old humbug who had sat in a gilt armchair, once part of a touring company's *Rigoletto* set, between two panels of machine-made tapestry, representing Mascagni and Verdi, in a house on the Brixton Road, pretending to have been a professor at Milan Conservatory and charging Miss Beevor huge fees for lessons to Cordelia. Inevitably he must by now be in his grave. But this girl's air of foredoomed failure was so great that I could not doubt a parallel between her fate and Cordelia's; and it would not be a true parallel, for this girl had no last resource of loveliness, no alternative career. Her defeat would be absolute.

But she answered, 'I have two really. Kingsley Torbay and Pietro Pedrucci. But I like Kingsley Torbay better. There is

164

almost nothing more that Pedrucci can teach me, and so he does not like me.'

'What, you are at the Athenaeum?'

'Yes, yes, I have a scholarship there. You haven't been to a single students' concert since I've been there,' she accused me. 'But if you had you would see that I am pretty much what you were when you were there, allowing for the difference between a violin and a piano. Why did you choose the piano? Surely the violin is a better instrument. I would be happy at the Athenaeum if it were not that nobody likes me much except Mr Torbay. But I expect they liked you.'

'No, they did not like me much.'

'Did you ever find out why?'

'No, never.'

'I wish, I wish people were not such beasts,' the girl raged. 'But how extraordinary they dared to be beasts to you. You must always have been good-looking. How horrible that I am going to fail you, for of course I cannot play this sonata.'

'Play us something, anything,' said Oliver, 'then we will know where we are. Though I think I know where we are.'

She sighed. Instead of a plain and harsh adolescent, she looked a pretty and timid child. She put her pad under her chin and picked up her violin and bow, muttered through her teeth, 'I am no good, really,' and began to play. I was right that she was foredoomed to failure. She would perpetually suffer the same defeat which was the lot of Mamma and Mary and myself and all our company of interpretative musicians. Her body could not produce the sounds which would make others hear the music which her mind knew the great composers had intended to convey; nor did her mind fully grasp what their intention was. But her body was so nearly obedient to her mind that it was aware of the extent of its disobedience and was ashamed; and she understood so much great music that she could see where she had a blank space on her map. She would possibly be a better player than I was. I could hear signs that she would ultimately possess that sublime lucidity which made Mary my superior.

She lowered her bow and grumbled, 'I played that like a carthorse.'

I said, 'Let us get one thing out of the way at once. You are our equal except in experience. You have not learned quite a number of things that you need to learn, but that is only because you have not had the time. Oliver here will agree, we are all three on the same level.'

'That is quite evident,' said Oliver in the casual tone that was needed, for the tears stood in the girl's eyes. She had used mascara on them, with a marked lack of skill, and they were smudged already. 'If anybody of your age could play the Jasperl sonata with insufficient rehearsal, it would be you. But you must not be disappointed if it turns out that the feat is impossible, and we call the thing off. It does seem like trying to go down Niagara in a barrel, the chances of being smashed and submerged are terrific. But let us get down to it.'

'But that's another thing,' sulked Avis, 'you cannot get down to it here. This piano is out of tune. They only call this the second music-room for an excuse to put me here. It is the schoolroom really, the footman calls it that. Apparently Lady Mortlake has children, nobody remembered in time to say, "Hear, nature, hear; dear goddess, hear! Suspend thy purpose, if thou didst intend to make this creature fruitful!" There is a lovely music-room with a good Steinway, but they did not want me in there, there is a horrid little peer who plays the piano like a musical box and he is always in there.'

'Show us where it is,' said Oliver.

'No, no,' she begged. 'They are too horrible. Yes, of course, I see that we must.'

It was in one of the two classical wings: a large room with a tremendous chimneypiece, where Apollo was playing his lyre before an audience of gods and goddesses enthroned on mounting marble clouds, and grey and white walls embossed with flutes and trumpets and viols and harps in plasterwork, and high windows looking out between bluish silvery curtains to a lawn and a distant prospect of the park. One of these windows was open and swinging on its hinges, and the wind had sent some sheet music drifting across the carpet, which was also patterned with musical instruments. 'Have you tried this Steinway yourself, Avis?' said Oliver, going towards the piano. But he came to a halt. A slim man was sitting on the stool, his face pressed down on the keyboard, his arms clinging to the music-rest, his shoulders shaking. Oliver went back to the door and shut it noisily. But the man continued to sob, more noisily than before, and did not lift his head. Oliver crossed the room to the piano, Avis and I behind him. We were all insensible to the little man's sufferings, partly because there was an indefinable air of habit about his paroxysm, but chiefly because we were no longer three human beings, we had become a rehearsal of Jasperl's sonata, and we saw him simply as an impediment to our full being.

We came to a halt beside him. Oliver was about to speak but paused in embarrassment. There was a circle of baldness on the little man's head, and the long wisps of mouse-coloured hair that he had combed across it bore traces of golden dye. Oliver sighed and put a hand on his shoulder, and the little man sat up with a jerk, but did not look round. Staring in front of him he cried: 'Of course you've come back. I knew you would. But it's no use. I've finished with you. I couldn't start again even if I wanted to. You're hopeless. You're so base. So utterly and so vulgarly base. If you hadn't said you never wanted to ski with anybody but me, I wouldn't have minded what you said to Lawrence at luncheon. But you did say it. And I never asked you to say it. You insisted on saying it. I remember putting my hand over your lips when you said it because I didn't want you to commit yourself. It's never been me who asked for assurances. It's always you who gave them. Who thrust them on me. And I couldn't help believing them, though everyone warned me against you, because I'm that sort of person. You should know that by now. And you should know what skiing means to me. And Kitzbühel. Our place.'

Oliver said through his teeth, 'Oh, God. Please, please, Lord Sarasen, get off that piano.'

The little man swivelled round and gaped at us. 'Please go away,' he said fretfully. 'How dare you interrupt us?'

'But there is no one else here,' said Oliver.

The little man looked round the room and buried his face in his hands.

'Please, Lord Sarasen,' said Oliver, 'we want this piano.'

'And if it is Mr de Raisse you want,' said Avis, 'I think that's him out in the garden, lying face down on a lilo by the herbaceous border.'

The little man bridled, and rearranged his collar and tie, and swallowed, and suddenly sprang to his feet and ran through the open window.

'God forgive us all,' said Oliver. 'The poor little beast. Now let's get down to it.' While I altered the stool he pushed forward a music-stand for Avis, who said, 'I don't understand about homosexual men. I know they're supposed to be like women

167

but they aren't, really, are they? Their voices are higher than ours, and quite differently produced, and there's the funny tone no woman ever gets, as if they had plush tongues. And women don't move like that, look at him now, it's like a loose-limbed corkscrew, not like a woman. And all that he was saying, no woman would talk like that, about giving assurances and believing them, and no woman would have got so excited just because that awful man de Raisse said to the flautist that he ought to go to Kitzbühel for winter sports. You wouldn't, would you?' she asked me, and turned to Oliver, 'Do you understand about homosexual men?'

'Afterwards, afterwards,' said Oliver. 'Rose, are you ready? But, Avis, aren't you at all sorry for that pathetic little brute?'

'No,' said Avis. 'Why should I be?'

'You are a horrible brat,' said Oliver. 'But we will go into that later. Now for our dear Jasperl.'

She had known that Martin Allen's interpretation of the sonata was wrong, and had disregarded it, but she had not understood it any better herself. But her error partook of her magnificence. I had only known musical misapprehension rise to the empyrean on such strong wings once before, when I heard 'Jardins sur la pluie' and 'Les Danseuses de Delphe' and 'La Fille aux cheveux de lin' played by a schoolgirl who had never heard any Debussy, and played them as if they had been written by Beethoven during an attack of cerebral anaemia. Although only thirty-five years had passed between the death of Beethoven and the birth of Debussy this confusion of the two composers played such havoc with their essential qualities as a historian might equal if he ascribed to Napoleon the same motives for conquest as inspired Julius Caesar. Avis's error about Jasperl was also temporal. She had not heard this kind of contemporary music, and though she had wit enough to see that Jasperl did not belong to the past she played the sonata as if it were jazz, as if it were an improvisation, whereas its character was, if anything, over-deliberate.

She was furious with herself for her mistake, which she immediately perceived from my performance. 'But wait,' said Oliver, 'you are simply leaving something out of your concep-tion of the work. Once you get it in, the whole thing will become easy to you. You are used to music that has melody and an accompaniment to that melody. Here the melody has its own rhythm, and the whole work has its own very strong rhythm, which encloses the other as in a casket. We want the wild, adventurous thematic material, which is always lunging off into dissonance, to be kept in order by this overreaching rhythm. Listen. This is part of something which was written this year by Bartók.' He played it to her twice. 'Now this is something I wrote.'

'Play it again,' said Avis, and when he had played it twice she said, 'But are you sure you have really anything to say there?'

'Whether I have or not, you can't give me a chance to say it at all, unless you give the overall rhythm its chance. And I may have nothing to say. I mean I may have nothing more to say. I know I once had something to say, but perhaps I have gone bad lately. But quite certainly Jasperl has a lot to say. Now try over that second movement, you will get the trick of it better there than in the first.'

She began to understand, and we took her through the whole sonata.

Then the door softly opened, and someone looked in, and softly closed it. Then it was opened again, quite noisily, and a voice called my name and Oliver's. We pretended we did not hear, but in a minute they were standing in a crescent round the piano, a dozen or so of them, including three girls. We knew most of them. They belonged to a circle very prominent at that time, which was paradoxically at once rubbish, and as certainly not without value. Half of them belonged to families that were rich or aristocratic, and sometimes both, and the rest were the friends they drew from every class, either because they loved them or found them gifted in the arts. They were in all things paradoxical. Nearly all, except some of the younger homosexuals, had plain faces, with protruding eyes and receding chins and colourless skins, but their bodies were graceful, and they had slender wrists and ankles and a dancing walk. Individually each had an air of distinction. Yet, seen together, they recalled the poorest sort of touring theatrical company which one saw sometimes waiting at railway junctions if one travelled to a concert on a Sunday, tawdry and insecure. They spoke always in captious voices, as if their pride lay in their capacity for constant rejection; yet they enjoyed life, and they had to be admired for the strength of their enjoyment, which sent them all over Europe to see a beautiful church, a beautiful harbour, a beautiful people, or an innovator in the arts. They had a moral code so confused that the nature of the confusion could not be guessed. Their fastidiousness plainly did not exclude conduct from its range. They bore themselves with the confidence of those sure that they had guarded their honour, who value their honour.

There were a number of things they would not do; but it was impossible to guess what these might be. I was often perplexed by these people and I was perplexed by them now. Amongst them, much loved, standing at this moment with his arms cast about the unreluctant shoulders of the most aristocratic of them, was a young man who had tried to sell me a Matisse which had turned out to belong not to him but to the elderly peer who had lent him his house while he himself was away on a world tour, and who would not have dared to prosecute him for theft. It was not that his friends did not know that he was a criminal in both the narrower and the broader sense, a thief and a betrayer of a vulnerable lover's trust, for they often joked about his enormities. But there they were, enlaced with him, and it might be that tomorrow I should hear of them crossing the world, not necessarily in comfort, to admire a work of art which in technique and argument depended on honesty.

I always found them mysterious, and now they were presenting us with a mystery particular to this hour. They greeted Oliver and me with cries that were in part their own tribal version of the convention followed by Lady Mortlake, which at once pushed effusiveness to its extreme and mocked it, and were in part intelligent enough references to our recent work. But soon their conversation was muted, and they became, for them, curiously immobile. They were like the bright herd we had seen on the knoll, all looking one way, all braced by a common perception. But we understood them hardly better than deer and could not guess what was coming down the wind to them. Presently they left us, saying, with gaiety that rang as queerly as the laughter one hears as one goes along corridors to a swimming-bath, that they would see us later.

Avis said, 'They wanted to say something to you that they did not want me to hear.'

They had indeed averted their eyes from her and had said none of the pleasant things that would have been natural in such circumstances, they had not asked us how we found our new colleague and given us a chance to compliment her.

'Come on, you silly little girl,' said Oliver. 'They do not like you, and why you should mind that I cannot see. Rose does not waste her time regretting that she has never been elected Beauty Queen of Clacton-on-Sea.'

'As a matter of fact I do,' I said. 'Passionately. But let us get on.'

The sonata went much better this time. At the end we sat back and Oliver smoked a cigarette, and nodded his head at us as if he were a pasha, and said: 'But it must be late. Yes, it is late. I wonder when they have dinner.'

'Not so late as this,' said Avis.

We had to ring several times before anybody came, and then it was the handsome silver-haired butler, who was still flushed, not now by the sunset, but by the glow of slight intoxication. He was surprised to see us. 'Oh dear, oh dear,' he said. 'You were not expected to dine. I'm afraid there is nothing ready for you, and the rest of the staff has gone to the Fire Brigade Ball at Aysthorp. There is nobody here but young Alice the kitchenmaid. This ball is our great social occasion, Lord Clancardine himself, the Lord Lieutenant of the county, attends it. My own wife would never miss it, she has gone every year since she was a kitchenmaid herself, bless her, poor soul. It is a pity,' he said censoriously, ducking his head to see himself in a mirror and sleeking his hair, 'that her ladyship never now honours us with her presence. The dowager Lady Mortlake always made it her duty, so long as she could get about. But who am I,' he said, with an effect of impersonation, 'who am I to cast the first stone?' He was perhaps admiring some debonair guest he had admired while waiting at table.

'What were we intended to do about dinner?'

'Why, her ladyship thought you would be going with the other guests to the party Mr Oswald Sinclair is giving over at Great Barn,' said the butler. 'You were all invited, to be sure, and I thought you had gone and we had the house to ourselves, for I believed I saw Lord Rothery and his friends come in here to tell you it was time to be leaving.'

'There has been a mistake,' said Oliver.

'You have not missed much,' said the butler dreamily. 'Mr Sinclair has not an inherited cellar. But it takes all sorts to make a world.' He returned to the study of his image in the looking-glass, bowing as if in gallantry.

'Can you get us something to eat?' asked Oliver.

'Nothing hot, I fear,' said the butler. 'None of the staff will be back till midnight, and please God they are later. The time will pass like a flash, I fancy.' He remained for a minute suspended in a smiling reverie. 'But you must have a bite. What a pity I did not know before! For young Alice the kitchenmaid and I cooked something for Mr de Raisse and Lord Sarasen. They have had a falling-out and have made it up again, so they had a fancy not to go to Mr Sinclair's party, but asked if they could have a meal private like, in the pavilion beside the lake. So young Alice and I cut them some cold chicken and gave them some white burgundy, just the same as I had got up for Alice and me, and a bit of the raspberry cream we had for lunch, and a nice piece out of the Stilton just the same as I'd got ready for Alice and me, and we carried it over. Very agreeable it was, going down to the lake. I would have done that for you and the two ladies with pleasure, with greater pleasure, for after all it is the way we were all brought up. I would like to do everything I can to make people happy tonight. Who is the better for it if things go wrong? So I will put out some cold meat and salad for you, and what is left of the raspberry cream and Stilton, and some of the peaches, and this white burgundy, this Montrachet, all in the Parrot Room, for that is where we have our little late suppers. It is opposite the foot of the staircase that takes you to your bedroom, and you cannot miss it, but I will leave the lights on and the door open, so that there can be no mistake. This is a confusing night.'

The door closed behind him, and Avis cried, 'I told you they had something to tell you that they did not want me to hear. They did not want to take me with them, they hated me so much that they even ditched you so long as they could leave me out. It is partly this awful dress, it is the wrong colour, and it is no use ironing it, it gets crumpled at once, the housemaid did it for me this morning, she is nice. It was a bad buy, but I have no time. I have to rush through my work, and there is nobody to look after me, I have to be squalid. And I have almost no money, of course my clothes are awful. But I do not think that is the only reason why people hate me. There is something else. What does it matter what it is, it means that I have brought something horrid on you. You will not want to have anything to do with me.'

But the butler was back with us.

'If there is anything you want, say it now,' he bade us, 'for now I will lock the door to the kitchen quarters. I will lay you out the supper, but then I will turn the key.'

He looked hard at us and assumed a look of grave responsibility. 'It is to protect the silver,' he said. He scrutinised our faces and told us, 'The Mortlake silver is famous.' Then bowed and walked backwards, as if we had been royalty, then turned about, and made an eager scuffle to the door, rising on his toes, as if he were a king bee about to take off in a nuptial flight. Some consideration struck him, and he called across the room, 'Is there anything more? I am muddled tonight, it is all the vexations. Her ladyship is terrible,' he said to himself. 'When she has a new one, such a pack. And I have only one thing on my mind.'

The door closed on him.

'See, Avis,' said Oliver, 'see what a kind of universe we live in! Not the grim cage of hate which you imagine, but a lovely warm swimmy place, with stuffy little rooms in the kitchen quarters where young Alice the kitchenmaid can be fed on chicken and white burgundy and learn what is good for her. Now, what shall we do until our supper is ready?'

'Go through the sonata once again,' said Avis. 'I am not hungry any more, now I know that supper will be there. Let us get it as right as I can do it, so that I can sleep. Last night I cried for hours and was all swollen. I do not look so awful as this usually.'

'Rose, could you do it?' asked Oliver. 'Right. Then let us start, and, Avis, never let your sense of the importance of the rhythm leave you.'

We started off again, and knew the combination of tense effort and serene relaxation that is a good rehearsal. I thought as we came to an end, 'What is the good of a performance? Why do we not retire at the first possible moment and simply play good music with our own kind?' When it was over I was in that state of exaltation when the intelligence that lives in one's hands and in the depths of one's mind suddenly visits one's lips, and I was able to speak to Avis of technical tricks that I had long practised without ever realising it. This ugly child; who thought only of herself, was so wholly committed to beauty, so selfless, that she made immense additions to the treasure I had been seeking to lay up for myself for twice her lifetime.

But soon there was a distant sound of banging on wood, and the clanging of a bell, and I went out to see if someone was trying to get into the house. I thought it might be that our fellow-guests had returned from their party and that the butler, in his desire for privacy and his slight confusion, had locked more than the door into the kitchen.

I went along the corridor past the circular hall by which we had entered the house. All the lights were extinguished but two torches held by bronze boys at the foot of the staircase, and the gods and goddesses cast on the curved walls huge shadows which the curve made comical, leviathan. At the door, on which some people were still beating, were the man whom we had found crying over the piano and another, in very beautiful dressing-gowns, one mulberry, one rich blue, who were pulling at the heavy bolts of the front door, and crying, 'Darlings, we are doing all we can. But they're frightful, too frightful!' The bolts gave way so suddenly that the three people who had been beating on the door were precipitated into the hall. I stood behind the pedestal of Artemis and her hounds and watched with fascination because these people were not only performing certain movements and speaking certain words and creating an incident in the ordinary course of living, they were also acting the incident in the convention, or what we suppose to be the convention, of eighteenth-century Neapolitan opera.

The bolts were heavy, but the two men pulled them as if they were still heavier, as if they were of a weight such as would not have been put on the door of any house built later than the Middle Ages. The three people who fell into the hall affected to have lost their balance as would have been impossible unless each had been leaning all his weight against the door and had had only one toe on the ground. Recovering themselves, they rushed together and, engaging themselves in stylised embraces, made of their coloratura greetings a quintet. Their meeting, which could not have been less planned, was the more like a scene on the stage because the last person to fall into the hall was a famous beauty, Lady Phyllida Dane, whose natural fairness emitted as much light as any actress gone forth in make-up under the limes, and whose dress was of the particular greenish rose that any theatrical designer might have chosen to set off the mulberry and the blue of the two men's dressing-gowns. The friends who accompanied her were both stock characters from early opera. One was a tiny and emaciated elderly woman with black ringlets, named Sukey Herzegovina, a pet of Lady Phyllida and her set, for

174

whom she acted as interior decorator and fortune-teller and go-between. The other was pantaloon, an old retired diplomat called Sir Geraint Something-or-other. Without doubt he would be forced to marry Sukey in the second act, but it would turn out in the third act that it was all right because the priest who had performed the ceremony was really somebody's serving-maid in disguise.

The quintet then developed into something so formal and so rich in invention that it actually recalled certain scenes in *Così fan tutte*. Standing to the left of the semicircle and crying out a sort of melody, Lionel de Raisse pinned Phyllida's elbows to her side and cried, 'Oh, darling, but you must stay the night, you must indeed,' and she replied, 'Oh, darling, we simply can't, we are on our way to Carl,' and Lord Sarasen and Sukey Herzegovina and Sir Geraint, standing at about the same position in the right semicircle, repeated this theme, with adaptations of the thematic material appropriate to their characters, for about the same number of bars. There was one delightfully anachronistic feature in the ensemble; I had been teased because Lord Sarasen's manner of speech as he wept over the keyboard had aroused in me a musical memory which I could not quite identify, but I now realised that the plangent sweetness in his voice had the exact quality of the boy soprano's rendering of 'Oh, for the wings of a dove', which was the favourite record of Aunt Lily and Aunt Milly and Uncle Len, and, I believe, about a million other people at that time. But his barley-sugar smooth tenor twists and turns made delicious dramatic contrasts with Sukey's refusals which were uttered in rapid triplets, denying extravagantly but keeping strict yet conciliatory time, and Sir Geraint's falsetto runs, which were almost in the nature of an accompaniment. I felt some of the fascination they exercised on themselves and their friends, and did not, as I had intended, slip out of the shadow of Artemis and her hounds into the deeper shadows of the corridors and go back to my friends, but came out and smiled at the newcomers and greeted them before I went away. Lord Sarasen asked me if I had any idea how to get some food for these poor people who must be starving; he and Lionel had rung the bell and nobody had come. I explained that the staff were away at their revels but would be back at twelve, which could not be far off. I remembered how long Avis had worked, and how she had said that she had had no tea, and I turned back to them, and said, laughing, 'If you find our supper in the Parrot Room do not eat it. Oliver and Avis and I have been rehearsing all evening. That Jenkinson child is a genius.' 'What, that dingy child?' said Lionel de Raisse, and Lord Sarasen, the wings of the dove suddenly renounced, asked sadly, 'Oh, do you *think* so?' The newcomers caught an intimation that there was an issue between their friends and me, and for a second they stared at me like ill-natured children. But de Raisse and Lord Sarasen went on to talk about the possibility of getting food for his friends. In a trio Lady Phyllida and Sukey Herzegovina and Sir Geraint said that they had had an early dinner at Bracegirdle and that anyhow Carl would have champagne and oysters lying about the house. I left them laughing happily at Carl's extravagance.

I went back to the music-room and found Oliver and Avis still busy with a problem that might be solved by an alteration of fingering. 'What was all that, Rose?' said Oliver, looking up. 'Only Lady Phyllida Dane and Sukey Herzegovina and Sir Geraint,' I said, 'paying a call.'

'Not staying here?' asked Avis. 'No? Oh, I wish I could have seen her. Is she really beautiful? I thought so. But if she comes here she is sure to be a beast.'

'No, she is not a beast,' said Oliver. 'You really are a little ass, Avis. Phyllida Dane is a good girl, devoted to her plump little tea-cosy of a husband, and a great help to good causes. She takes a lot of dumb oxen to the ballet and to the right concerts that would just otherwise stand in the fields and low. Put your mind on your work and stop wasting your energy on your harmless inferiors.'

They did not need me. I went to a sofa at the end of the room and lay and watched them, and thought how well they were getting on together. I closed my eyes and set out on a backward journey through dreams to Papa and Mamma and Richard Quin. My heart ached as I found myself going through the dark corridor of that direction and I knew that when I turned this corner I would come on these three, but not on Rosamund, for though she was no longer in my life she was not dead. But I hurried on knowing that those who were safe in death would explain to me what had happened to her, and I was folded in one of those dreams so happy that they are not remembered on waking, for where they are experienced never sleeps, never wakes. I woke once to hear several cars drive out, and then the chatter and laughter of people passing the door. Our fellow-guests had come back from Mr Sinclair's party. Sometimes the music Oliver and Avis were playing forced itself on me, as music does on sleep, not as sounds, but as ragged multicoloured streamers of light across the dark backcloth of the eyelid. I was at rest, I was not at rest, I was happy, I was distressed, that is to say I was alive. I shared in the peace of the dead, I was exiled from death in this state where I swayed on the balance, and then I was aware that two people were confronting me who were not dead, for they laughed, and laughter is the sign of our astonishment at this perpetual state of insecurity. I did not want to come back, but I was delighted at the faces of Oliver and Avis, they were so deeply familiar to me. I did not have to wonder for a minute who Avis was, though I had met her only that evening.

Oliver said, 'I am pointing out to Avis that though you have been asleep and we have had our backs turned to you this last hour or more, nobody had crept in on all fours to steal your rings, so she need not think this such a house of evil. Now come on, we must find the Parrot Room and eat.'

We went through the corridors with our arms enlaced, as if we were all students, and Avis said, 'This is a great adventure. Nobody at the Athenaeum will believe it when I tell them except Mr Torbay.'

'It has been a great adventure for us,' said Oliver. 'Nobody will believe us when we tell them how well you play.'

'My sister Mary will,' I said. 'She sits waiting for news of people like you. She reminds me of the religious people who long for more and more children to be born so that they may serve God. She wants more and more musicians to play the works of the great composers.'

'Will I be able to meet her too?' asked Avis, but took it for granted she could, and burst out, 'Oh, it is all right now! I will always remember how horrible it was and that you came and it was all right.'

'But I see no door open on a room with all the lights on,' said Oliver. 'Can that old villain have forgotten us?'

'This should be the room,' I said. 'He told us it was exactly opposite the foot of the staircase. But the door is closed.'

Oliver opened it gently and felt for the light. 'This is it,' he said, and we followed him in, Avis exclaiming, 'Every room in this house is better than the last! They do not deserve it.'

There could be no doubt that this was the Parrot Room. It was a vague and languishing little library, the sort of place where a charming but ineffective man might write a sensitive diary of his empty days, or two egotists meet for courtship that would lead to nothing, however far it went. The curtains were sea-green and shining, and the walls were covered with the kind of old paper which has a pile like plush, and were the colour of green distance, of grassy hills seen afar in summer twilight. Against three of the walls were low bookcases, painted greenish white and cut very delicately, so that the many-coloured inlay of books seemed to float in lines rather than be packed on shelves; and on the fourth wall was a mantelpiece of sea-green marble, patterned with a pale orange stone in starry shapes that made it seem insubstantial. The centre of the mantelpiece and each bookcase had its *blanc de chine* parrot, each caught in a different moment of raucous and ruffling comment. They were the only objects in the room that gave back highlights, that were positive and recalled the action of the will, the reaction of criticism. This was the Parrot Room to which we had been directed; and under the chandelier was a table with a white cloth and set with silver and glass and china.

Avis said, 'Will it always have been like this? Or has she done it, though she is so horrid?'

But Oliver and I were looking at the table. Round it five chairs were set askew. The glasses held wine at different levels; on the plates were peach-skin, peach-stones, the buttery mess where somebody had scraped off the rind of a cheese like Camembert and Brie; there were emptied coffee-cups standing on saucers full of wet cigarette-ash. On a butler's tray set up against a bookcase there were more dirty plates, a dish with a chicken's carcass on it, another with some aspic to show there had been cold meat there, an empty salad-bowl, a glass dish with some ooze of whipped cream in it.

'We are like the three bears,' I said. 'Who's been eating my porridge?'

'They have left us some bread,' said Oliver. And he fingered some bottles at the back of the tray, 'But nothing to drink.'

Anger blinded me and choked me. 'They have taken your supper. How dare they!'

'What!' said Avis, who had been touching the parrot on the mantelpiece with her fingertips and now turned round. 'But they all went out. Why did they want our supper?'

'I told them it was our supper,' I raged.

'But who were they?' asked Oliver.

'When Phyllida Dane and Sukey Herzegovina and Sir Geraint came Lionel de Raisse and Lord Sarasen let them in, and they wanted to give them something to eat,' I explained, 'and I said, "There is some supper for us in the Parrot Room, please do not eat that, we have had no dinner." They knew!'

'What a prep-school trick,' said Oliver. 'Oh dear, Rose, how can I get you something to eat?'

'It is not me,' I said, 'but it is you, men always ought to have lots of food to eat, and Avis, she is young, at her age she should have lots to eat.'

'I could not eat now,' said Avis. 'I want to kill them, I wanted to kill them before you came, now I want to kill them and torture them as if I were a Red Indian. How dare they eat your supper and make a fool of you, when you told them where the supper was? They did not like you, of course. They kept saying you were a virgin.'

'Oh, Avis, and you did not protect Rose's good name by saying that you had heard different?' said Oliver.

She gaped and asked, 'Oh, should I have?' and I said, 'It is all right, he is laughing at you. Oh, Oliver, do not laugh at us. This is really horrid.'

'Yes, it is horrid,' said Oliver, 'because one does not know what to do. I feel it is absurd to be angry because three pederasts and a blonde and a procuress have eaten our supper. But I feel that if I am not angry I really am a little too docile for something that walks on two legs. I feel I shouldn't have let this happen to you and Avis. But it is all so silly. Must we be angry?'

'Must we be hungry is what we had better ask,' I said. 'Do you think that when that butler's wife came home he forgot his care for the cellar and unlocked the door between the house and the kitchen?'

But the padded leather door down the passage was firmly closed. Avis said, 'I told you they were beasts, why did you tell me I was wrong?'

'We did not quite tell you that they were not beasts,' said Oliver. 'We suggested to you that they were not beasts to such an extent that you had to worry about them. But just at this moment they have been beasts enough to get us into a situation where we are thoroughly hungry.'

We walked back towards the Parrot Room, and hesitated at

the door while Oliver asked us if we would care to eat the bread, and I exclaimed, 'Oh, I remember now! There are some sandwiches we did not eat in my picnic-basket, and some coffee. Let us go up to my room, and we will eat them before we go to bed.'

'That will make up for everything,' said Avis.

'It will make up for everything, and we will play our sonata tomorrow afternoon and go away.'

'But I shall never see you again,' said Avis.

'Nonsense, we are saddled with you, and you are saddled with us, for the rest of our lives,' said Oliver. 'We know how good you are, because we are so good ourselves, and you know how good we are, because you are so good yourself, and we cannot get rid of each other. Now, up these stairs, for Rose's sandwiches and bed.'

But when we came to the landing we stopped. Mine was the first room: and outside it were my suitcase and my picnic-basket, draped with my nightdress and my dressing-gown, and my sponge-bag and my beauty-box and my bedroom slippers on the floor beside them.

'By God, it cannot be,' said Oliver. He turned the door-handle, but the door was locked. 'But by God it is.'

'Phyllida and Sukey and Sir Geraint meant to go on to Carl's, wherever that is,' I explained, 'but Lionel de Raisse and Lord Sarasen wanted them to stay. Well, they have stayed.'

'But are they all in one room?' said Oliver. A suspicion crossed our minds. 'My room is just round the corner.'

But as we went to see if what we thought had happened Avis caught us back. 'If they wanted three rooms, they would take mine too,' she said. 'Mine is beside yours, oh, I cannot bear it if they have put my things outside my room. They are so disgusting. It is a hateful thing they have done to you, because you are a goddess, but your nightdress is lovely, your dressing-gown and everything is lovely, my suitcase is brown-paper, but my nightdress is cotton and my dressing-gown is flannel and it isn't even clean. Oh, why did I ever come to be tortured like this?'

'Oh, this is hell,' said Oliver.

'You are a silly little fool,' I said. 'How should you have decent clothes before you have earned any money? And even now when I go on tour I get my things in an awful mess. Come along and we will see.'

We went to the corner of the passage; and there was Oliver's suitcase with thick silk pyjamas of a curious violet-blue and wine-coloured dressing-gown on it. It was odd to think of him doing his shopping. And in front of the next bedroom was Avis' brown-paper suitcase and her poor things, thrown out with special contempt. She could not help crying, and I too found tears of rage on my cheeks.

'I do not know what to do,' said Oliver. 'I should kick in the doors, beginning with yours, Rose. But when I had done that I would have to roll out whoever was in your bed, and I don't think you would care to sleep in sheets warmed by Phyllida or Sukey.'

'But how could they do this?' I wondered.

'Because they are all drunk,' he said.

'Yes, de Raisse and Sarasen were a little drunk when they let the others in,' I said.

'And there were three bottles of burgundy there, and a brandy-bottle,' said Oliver, 'all empty. Yet I would have thought this hardly old Geraint's mark, even drunk. But let that be. We will find bathrooms to wash in, and I will carry down your cases and we will pick ourselves the most comfortable sofas downstairs.'

'No, no,' said Avis. 'Let me carry my own things down.'

'Let that be,' said Oliver. 'That is not what really troubles you. What do you want to do?'

'Why, run at the doors, and kick the panels in, and then run at whoever I find inside and scratch their faces and pull their hair out by the roots and hit them till they fell on the ground and then jump on them,' said Avis, 'and there is something out of the Bible about bowels gushing out that I would like to happen to them.'

'I am so angry that I would like to do that too,' said Oliver, 'and yet I do not want to do it at all. And neither do you. You simply want to go away and get on with your work. And that is all Rose wants too. But that makes us more Quakerish animals than we like to be.'

'There is something,' said Avis, and choked.

'What is it, my dear?' I said.

'I do not want to play to these beasts tomorrow afternoon,' she sobbed.

'There is no question of that,' said Oliver. 'Neither Rose nor you can play here.'

'We will go home and play together later,' I said.

We made her sleep on a very fat sofa in a little library, and when she was settled under a rug we had found in the hall, we gave her the sandwiches that were left in the picnic-basket. We had to say we had had some while she was washing. She tried to prevent us seeing her flannel dressing-gown, which was indeed quite dirty. I could not wait till I got her home to Mary, who would see her through all this. Then Oliver found me a sofa in a long drawing-room and a tablecloth for a blanket, and we said goodnight. Since leaving Avis he had grown silent and looked unhappy; and beyond telling me how sorry he was he had let me in for this insult he made his goodnight brief enough.

After he had gone I shuddered with fury at the humiliation we had suffered, and was exasperated at the beauty of the room. There were vague pictures of mountains sloping to plains and fused by them in golden sunshine, temples on seas themselves swimming underneath seas of light, a heroic vision of earth, floating on walls made vaporous by raised plaster-work, which suggested a ghostly growth of flowers up an invisible trellis, and on the faint golden ceiling above me showed plasterwork and Venus and Adonis. I lay on golden brocade and there were deep falls of golden brocade at all the tall windows. There was something very displeasing in suffering such an extreme humiliation in these gorgeous surroundings. The fundamental flaw in the world was that there was no drama worthy of the setting at the Dog and Duck. Green trees, each shapely as if turned by some craftsman neat as a potter but in love with wilder shapes, leaned over the mirror of the Thames, and should have witnessed some serene consummation of the lives of Uncle Len and Aunt Milly and Aunt Lily, but they had to stand still and be scorched by the fire of Queenie's unassuageable and even unidentifiable longing. The house where Mary and I had our home should have seen some event that had never happened within its walls, that should have happened if we were to be quite sure that music was real, that it was an honest interpretation of life and not a legend to be told to distract our attention from intolerable features of existence. It was not right that these worthless dilettantes in this house, who were taking refuge from life in perversity, who were going further than perversity into the pure mischief of monkeys, should have the power to make me doubt the value of the world, the value of art. And there was not Rosamund to reassure me. I tossed and turned and put out the light.

Perhaps I slept a little. In any case I was awake when the door opened and the light was turned on. Golden light flooded down on the golden room from great chandeliers, faintly tinted. I sat up and saw Oliver standing at the end of the room in his dressing-gown. I noted the jut of his shoulders, which was strange, for they were not broad, yet he held them as men with broad shoulders do. I put on the reading-lamp on the table by my sofa and he switched off the chandeliers. I was a little cave of light in a hall of shadows, and he came to me out of the shadows. He looked wretched.

'Were you asleep?' he asked.

'No, I don't think so. What is the matter? Have they done anything else?'

'No, no. All quiet on the barbaric front.'

'But there is something worrying you.'

He stood by the sofa, and sighed deeply. 'Rose, Jasperl means something more to me than I have told you.'

The lamp shone strongly on his anguished face. I looked up into the darkness that hung about the upper walls, past the landscapes of sunny plains and mountains, of seas incarnadined by sunset, faintly glossed, to the ceiling, at the huge black shadow his standing figure cast across the golden brocade curtains. I had not thought Oliver was homosexual. He had spoken of men that were with mockery. But then homosexuals often mocked their own sort. I drew the table-cloth that was my coverlet more neatly round me, and straightened myself. I felt too tired to talk about this, and thought how peaceful it must be to lie quietly in a coffin.

'You knew my wife? You knew Celia?'

I nodded.

'She was very beautiful and she was a good musician and I loved her very much. And it was all right for a time. We could not have been happier.' He sat down and turned the lamp away so that it shone on neither of us, only on a little marble sphinx that lay on the table. 'Could we have been happier? That is one of the things I do not know. I am not sure whether she was ever happy. One is an idiot,' Oliver said, 'however little one is an idiot about other things, one is an idiot about love. I used to come into our house at Hammersmith and pass through the

183

square hall we had, and in the middle of the hall there was a highly polished table and Celia used to put flowers on it, in a round dish, a little raised, so that it cast a big reflection on the shining wood. I remember specially that every spring she used to fill it with those very brown wallflowers and forget-me-nots, and when I came in I used to see the blue forget-me-nots reflected on the wood. When I wonder whether Celia was ever really content with me, I think, "Of course she was, just think how wonderful it was when I used to shut the door behind me and see the curved garland of reflection of those forget-me-nots blue among the highlights and the brown depths of the wood, and I felt I was home, that everything in the house was going to be like that. Of course we were happy!" But that is stupid. All that that meant was that Celia liked putting forget-me-nots in that particular dish, on that particular table, and that I liked the look of them when I came in.'

Rosamund had come back into my mind. It was no argument that she loved us, that she had liked to eat cream and honeycomb with Richard Quin, all people not dyspeptics like to eat cream and honeycomb, nobody had suffered from spiritual dyspepsia badly enough not to like being with Richard Quin.

'But of course I have more reason than that to think that we were happy,' said Oliver.

'Yes, that I understand,' I said.

'But if you love anybody does it not last for ever?' asked Oliver.

'It does with me,' I said.

'It does with me,' said Oliver. 'You and I are the same sort of people. Celia is dead but I still love her. I cannot love anybody else.'

'The person I love is not dead,' I said, 'but it would be easier if death was what divided us. But I could not love anybody new.'

'When they take charge of you like that, they should not go away,' said Oliver.

'What do you mean? Was it not you who went away?' I asked.

'I?' said Oliver. 'I could not have left her any more than I could have cut off one of my hands or feet. What is it?'

'Ah. I made a mistake,' I said. 'But it does not matter. Go on. Go on.'

'I have to tell you all this because it is all so strange, and nobody else that I can think of would understand. I cannot think of anything you would not understand. I must have bored you a lot lately because I come and see you and derive a stupid satisfaction from the thought that if I told you what was troubling me you would not think me a fool.'

'Oh, Oliver, my dear, I wish you had told me long ago. I would never think you a fool.'

'Most people would. You see it was Jasperl who took Celia away from me.'

'Jasperl!' I looked about me, at the glowing suggestions of the sunlit plains and mountains, the flushed temples, on the darkness of the walls, the faint moulding on the darkness above that suggested the beauty of Venus and Adonis. 'But he is so horrible.'

'Yes. He is horrible.'

I wanted to cry out that Celia must have been horrible too. I had to bite my knuckles.

'He is horrible as musicians are not. He is horrible as few really good artists of any kind are. He is horrible like a bad French painter living at St Tropez might be, with a wife and a mistress quarrelling in a small kitchen and their children, mixed with the children of a seduced servant, playing in a yard with ironmongery, dragging an old tin bath about. He has thick black hair with a wave like a woman's and a jaw like a boat, and a huge Adam's apple, and he mocks and leers.'

'How could she?' I breathed.

'Am I so bad, Rose? Tell me frankly,' Oliver asked.

'You are quite good-looking and you are nice, you behave properly,' I said.

'I thought I made her happy,' said Oliver. He stopped and pondered. 'Looking back, I cannot believe it. Also we had enough money. I've always had this house, which I thought quite lovely. We could go away when we wanted. We had pleasant friends. What was it that I did not give her? But I could not give her what Jasperl gave her, for it was vile.'

'Did she run away from you with him?' I asked incredulously.

'She went to Switzerland to give three Fauré and Duparc concerts,' said Oliver, 'and when she came back she was quite different. She made some excuse to go back to Switzerland quite soon, and this kept on happening, she was supposed to be giving lessons. She was unhappy. Anyone could have seen that. She enjoyed nothing. Yet she seemed well, even more vigorous than I had ever known her. But her work went off. I thought that was what was worrying her. She did not care about it any more. She sang quite without genius for the last four years of her life.' He passed his hand over his forehead. 'I would not have thought she could have existed without her genius. But there was a lot more than that. She suddenly stopped being well. She went to Switzerland and was away far longer than usual. Then she came back, utterly miserable. And I got an anonymous letter telling me that she had been the mistress of Jasperl. What made is specially disagreeable was that the letter came from Jasperl.'

'How did you find that out?' I asked.

'I gave it to Celia at once,' said Oliver, 'and she recognised the writing. I realised that moment what was to be our tragedy. You never were at the Hammersmith house. There was a room at the back that was almost all window. I have a feeling that a grey river flowed through my head at that moment, carrying barges with it. I thought it unlikely that Celia had spoken of me in any way that would lead Jasperl to suppose I was not likely to give her an anonymous letter about herself. If he had not disguised his writing it could only be that he wished her to know that he had written it. He was, we both thought, trying to get rid of her finally. It appeared from what she told me that he had told her he was tired of her some time before. She had made not only her last visit to Switzerland, but the one before, in order to persuade him to take her back.'

He fingered the marble sphinx and fell silent.

'Oh, Oliver! Oh, Oliver!' I breathed.

'I was at first terribly angry. I could not bear it that she had not told me. It seemed to me vile that I should have shared her with him. Not because I minded that, though of course I do, but because she minded it, I knew she had, looking back on it.'

I wished furiously he would not talk of such things. But his voice cracked with misery as he said, 'I asked her why she had done this, and she said that Jasperl had asked her not to tell me. I said she need not have told me who her lover was, she could just have said she had a lover. Then she told me that she had put that to Jasperl, and he had forbidden her to tell me that she had a lover, even when she offered to give me lying details, so that I would think that it was someone quite unlike Jasperl. When I asked her what reason he had given for this monstrous prohibition, she said he had given none. It had seemed to her that if he told her to do something it was right for her to obey;

and as we sat there in this window by the river, with this letter he had written to torture me and dismiss her, lying on a table between us, I saw that it still seemed to her a law of nature that she should do anything that he told her to do. I was in the presence of what I then called madness. I would not call it that now. But anyway the agony was something I could not understand.'

'I know, I know,' I said. 'That is it, not being able to understand.' This was far worse than Rosamund.

Oliver suddenly laughed. 'How I should hate to tell this story to our forthright little Avis,' he said. 'By God, she's good, isn't she? But to get on, I stopped being angry with Celia, and I must have been fairly irritating to her, because I was patient with her as one is with people who are mad. We separated for a time. She cancelled her engagements and went to stay with some people in Italy, and I went over to America and stayed with old Lowenthal in New England. I was full of confidence, for a damn silly reason. I had got all his early compositions and I had quite rightly thought them worthless. This gave me a feeling of superiority. Then we started all over again in the Hammersmith house. And in six months Jasperl got her back again.'

I cried out.

'Well, he would want to,' Oliver said. 'It is his aim, his constant aim, to hurt people. By getting Celia back he hurt me, and he had by now a considerable interest in me; and he humiliated her, and humiliated the German conductor's wife with whom he had eloped in the interval, and then had all the fun of humiliating Celia again when he left her. As he did a few months later. That was a peculiarly horrible business. He had fallen ill with phthisis, and Celia had felt that she was of use to him, looking after him during his haemorrhages. She was very kind to people when they were ill. It also made some sense of their relationship. She was not just there to be the object of his sadistic passion, the subject of her own masochistic passion. She was his wife, his mother. At this point, and of course it was inevitable, he threw her out. He professed a sudden loathing for her which, he said, made him feel excited and ill, so that his doctors ordered that she must go away. This was at Lausanne. She did not leave the town at once, for there was no longer anybody to look after him. By this time all that horrible business of Kehl I told you about was over. But Jasperl did not send for her, and she decided to kill herself. It was unfortunate that she was one of those people who are compelled to read everything in print that comes their way, if a parcel came to us wrapped up in sheets of newspaper or pages of a book she would flatten them out and see what they were about. Somewhere she had read that some quite common medicine which is quite easy to get a doctor to prescribe is fatal, if one takes it over a period of a week or so and stops oneself from drinking anything. She got a prescription of the stuff and sat in a grim little hotel taking the dose and drinking almost nothing. If it had not been that her eye had caught this wretched piece of information I think she would still be alive, for she was so kind, she would not have hurt her family and me by causing the scandal of a suicide. Her family do not yet know either that she ever left me or that she killed herself.'

'Oh, my dear,' I said. 'Did she kill herself? I heard only that she came back to you and got ill and died.'

'She killed herself,' said Oliver. 'But it took a very long time. She got so ill that she fell into a coma and they took her to a hospital, and I was sent for. I was there for weeks, and then I took her home. But she had done the job, her kidneys were destroyed. She died dreadfully.' He slipped forward from his chair and buried his face on the cushions of the sofa where I lay, just below my feet. I sat up and leaned forward and stroked his hair, and presently he raised his face and said, 'During the time when she was dying she often spoke of Jasperl, but she never told me anything good or pleasant about him. When she was delirious and cried out for him it was not as if she longed for him, it was more as if he was a torment against which she was protesting. It was simply as if he were the disease from which she was suffering.'

'This was madness,' I said.

'No,' he said obstinately, 'it was not. She had been horribly disfigured by her illness, but after she was dead her beauty returned to her. I stood by her body and I was intensely conscious that she looked as she had done until she went to Jasperl, but that she was gone from me; while she had been with me, unchanged, my wife, till the last moment of her life, though she had been puffed and swollen and slow. All these strange dealings with Jasperl had been carried on by the Celia that I had loved.'

I thought to myself, 'Yes, what Rosamund has done she herself has done, she is not changed.'

'Then, when I had buried her, I heard that Jasperl had written these new works, this symphony, this violin concerto, this opera, and I went to great trouble to get the scores. My motive was part curiosity. I had a feeling that perhaps I might find what she had seen in him. But I also was being base. I had derived great satisfaction when I first knew she had been Jasperl's mistress in reading his early compositions and finding they were worthless. I am sure I hoped that those later compositions would be worthless too.'

'I wish they had been,' I said.

'No, that would have done no good. It would have left the mystery of Celia's love for him unsolved. And you know, Rose, that no good can be done by there being more bad music in the world. Even when I read the stuff and hammered out the important passages on the piano and realised that Jasperl had genius I was glad that it was so. But it added to my perplexity. I had loved Celia, Celia had seemed to love me, we had led a happy life together, she had lied to me and degraded herself and walked into a bog of cruelty for the sake of a man who had nothing good or even agreeable about him, who was a fiend out of hell. That was one mystery. Now there was another. To me music is contrary to hell, the annulment of evil, but this fiend out of hell was a better composer than I am.'

'No, no,' I cried.

'As we stand now, he is the better of the two,' said Oliver obstinately. 'Rose, what does that mean? You see what the problem is. I don't mean that I think music ought to help people to be kind to their mothers or pay the rent regularly, and I am sure that at the very moments when mutts are most sure that Bach was ecstasising over the Christian mysteries he was thinking of sound and nothing else. But music is what Celia and I were, and not what Celia and Jasperl were. And it is strange, it makes nonsense of it all if Jasperl is a great composer. Doesn't it?'

'Yes,' I said. 'I thought of the person I loved as being the same as music, too. And all my doubts seem doubts of music, too.'

'You know, I always knew you understood,' said Oliver. 'How strange we should have the same experiences. But I must tell you what I want to ask you. After Celia died I fixed about

189

selling the house at Hammersmith and I went to Switzerland, and I sought out Jasperl. I did it to show that I did not believe Celia's love of him was simply madness; and I did it to show I still believed in music. He was not sure when I found him that I had not come to kill him, so you can guess what he did. He stammered out that Celia had from the first pursued him and that his motive in sending her away, the first and the second time, was to send her back to her lawful husband, partly out of respect for holy matrimony, partly out of respect for my compositions, which he professed to admire. I think it may have been true that Celia pursued him. He was her destiny, the martyrdom to which her cruel God called her, it is possible that when she came face to face with him she followed him as an early Christian saint might follow a bishop whom she knew was to lead her to the stake, the grid, the lions of the arena. That is not, however, how Jasperl put it, but there were the three damned scores, unperformable, perverse, magnificent. I explained that I had not come to talk about Celia but to see how I could keep him alive and get him on to writing more music. He was miserably unhappy in a state sanatorium which was good enough for the ordinary patient, but no good for him. He could do no work. I got him out of that to a more comfortable private place, where he could have his own chalet and a piano and strum away as he pleased. I have been keeping him going ever since, and, Rose, I cannot do it any more. Not a day more.'

'Of course you cannot,' I said. 'We must think of something.'

'Oh, Rose, he is so vile!' sighed Oliver. 'He cuckolded me, and I, the funny English cuckold, come over and save his life. Of course it is funny if such things are funny; and to Jasperl they are enormously funny. Or rather he pretends that he finds them so. He knows everything. He has chosen to be evil with his eyes open. He knows that in a marriage such as Celia's and mine the husband is not a cuckold. That is the main difficulty. There are others. Twice I have had to go out to Switzerland, just to find him another sanatorium, because he has made himself intolerable to the quite decent and kindly people who were looking after him. But this is the chief source of trouble: that the man whom he cuckolded is now helping him. The jest chokes him every time I go to see him. I know he has roared over it with the nurse or the poor little patient who is the last seducee on the strength. His silly little wife has always shown that she is sorry for me. But once he is out of the sanatorium the temptation to carry the joke a little further will be irresistible. It will be fun for him to run up enormous bills, at hotels, with tradesmen, with wretched copyists, that will be paid by me, the funny English cuckold who grudges his dead wife's lover nothing. Rose, Rose, I cannot bear it. For one thing, it gives Celia such a dreadful immortality. I should remember her for what she was at Venice on our honeymoon, what she was like in our house at Hammersmith, other people should remember her for her singing. She will be remembered in Switzerland, in Switzerland of all places, where they make milk chocolates and watches, where they ski and yodel, as the discarded mistress of a vulgar freak, as a suicide. I cannot bear it.'

Again he buried his face in the cushion by my feet, and this time he sobbed. 'Come nearer to me,' I said, and he moved along till I could let him rest his head on my arms, and presently wipe his eyes with my handkerchief. I said in my heart to the shadows in the angles of the walls and the ceiling, 'Celia, if you are there, come back and tell him it is all right.' It seemed to me she must be all right, for it was surely impossible that anyone would go such a strange journey, the measure of its strangeness being that it took her by her own free will away from Oliver, except to find some extraordinary prize. But it is forbidden, they do not return. At least he raised his head and said, 'I wanted to stop giving him money and get Lady Southways to give it him instead. But we cannot play at that concert, we must go in the morning.'

'I suppose we could stay,' I said. 'Avis would do it if we asked her. After all, it was not Lady Mortlake's fault that this happened.'

'No,' said Oliver. 'You know you are only offering to do this to help me. And it would be wrong. That Mortlake bitch should have stayed to see we were properly treated, she is no fool, she is quite well aware that she has her house full of rubbish that might misbehave. If we do not pack up and leave, we are going over to the side of Jasperl. I know what I have to do. I have to go on keeping Jasperl, but I want to do it without him knowing that I have anything to do with the money. He is so clever, he will guess if I send it through any of my friends. But you, you have played so much in America, do you know anybody who could impersonate an anonymous admirer and send him the money in dollars?'

I knew that Mr Morpurgo would arrange it through his American lawyer. I said, 'Very easily. Tell me your bank and I will get somebody to do it in two days' time. But do not give him too much. You are too good.'

'No,' said Oliver. 'You do see this is something I must do?'

'Yes, yes,' I said. I wondered how I could show I still believed in Rosamund. 'I see it might be the most important thing in your life.'

'I have let it run on too long,' he said, 'it should be settled soon. He will be out of the sanatorium in a fortnight's time. I have such hateful, civil, mischievous letters from him. I have one in the pocket of this dressing-gown now.'

'Burn it,' I said. 'Take it out and burn it. Oh, please, Oliver. Celia would not like it to be there now.'

'Celia is dead,' said Oliver.

'She cannot be so dead that she would want you to have that letter in your pocket,' I said. 'Nobody is as dead as that.'

'I wonder what you mean,' he said, but took out the paper and put it on an ashtray and burned it with his lighter. The flame went higher than one would think. It was a long letter. Our shadows wavered madly on the wall.

He continued to watch the ashes until they were quite grey. Then he raised his eyes and looked at me steadily and said, 'You will see to the money, and I will write to Jasperl and tell him I will have nothing more to do with him. And I will never write to him or see him again. But that is the least thing you have done for me. Sitting with you in this room where we have never been before, where we will never be again, is like being out of life a night and knowing everything. I know why Celia had to go to Jasperl. She had a genius for love. I was all right. I could love. But Jasperl cannot love, he is the negation of love, he is hatred, he is nonsense, given time he would uncreate the world. His state was a challenge to her. She had to win his soul from Satan. She went to him as to a battlefield.'

After a silence he said, 'I have kept you up for hours when you should be asleep, worrying you over a perplexity I never need have felt. If it comes to that I have been howling like a dog and not getting on with my work for years, because I have had no sense. I should have seen why she had gone to him if on that first day when I read the anonymous letter in that room with the window on the Thames I had not forgotten that she was love itself. She could do nothing vital except for the sake of love. I have remembered it only sitting in this room with you.'

'No, you knew it all the time,' I said. 'You said to me something about it being possible that your wife had pursued Jasperl, because he was her destiny, the martyrdom to which her cruel God had called her.'

'So I did,' he said, and thought for a while. 'Yes, I knew it with my mind, as I might a fact about a stranger that I had read in a book. But now, sitting here, I knew it with my whole being, as I know that we were once happy. I never should have forgotten.'

I never should have forgotten how Rosamund had been the peer and companion of Richard Quin, how they had laughed together in an innocence that nothing could destroy. I never should have forgotten how, immune from perturbation by any external event, she held up my mother's body as it ejected her soul. We smiled at each other.

'Oh, dear Rose, I have been terrible to you,' he said. 'Bringing you down to this hell-hole. Telling you this beastly story of Jasperl, which I might well have kept to myself; and keeping you awake. But I was selfish. I wanted my soul saved. Well, you have done it. Now, will you be able to sleep?'

'Indeed I will,' I said. 'Will you?'

'I think so,' he said. 'Though, curiously enough, I should like to go out for a walk.'

'So should I,' I said, 'but we dare not. I have a feeling that there is just one thing this household has still got up its sleeve, and that is to let loose big dogs on us. But I should go to the window and look out at the night.'

He found my slippers for me under the sofa and slipped them on to my feet. It seemed strange to have a man do that, but he seemed to find it quite natural and even to take some pleasure in doing it. We shook back a great fall of golden brocade and looked out at a smooth lawn deep in the bluish frost of moonlight, where one tall tree stood incandescent.

'It seems to be in blossom,' said Oliver, 'but are there trees that blossom now?' We stood for some moments side by side, and then he said, 'And you, Rose?'

'And I?'

'You said there was someone you loved with whom you were not happy any more.' He looked at me. 'I would have thought that a man whom you loved would never leave you.'

'Oh, it was not a man, it was not that sort of love!' I told him impatiently. 'It is my cousin Rosamund. But you have made me happy about her.'

'Your cousin Rosamund? I remember her. Beautiful, golden-haired, stammered, so never spoke.'

'Mary and I loved her more than anyone in the world. She was the nearest of all of us to Richard Quin, she looked after Mamma when she died. At any time she was utterly lovable. We thought her perfectly good, but she has married someone repulsive. Not like Jasperl. But dwarfish, and, we think, dishonest and queer. And very rich. But when you said what you had forgotten about Celia, I knew we had forgotten the essential thing about Rosamund too. She was good. When she married this man she must have done it for the sake of goodness.'

'You are sure to be right. You would not have loved her so long without knowing her. And forgive me with saddling you with a faithless lover.'

'I could never have a lover, faithful or faithless. I cannot love anyone except the people I have loved since I was a child. My father. My mother. Richard Quin. Who are dead. And Mary. And Rosamund. There are others I love, Kate, whom you know, and old Miss Beevor, and three people who keep a pub on the Thames called the Dog and Duck, and a girl called Nancy, and even they were all given me by my family. But for deep love, the sort you felt for Celia, I cannot get past those five people. I shall not ever love anybody else as I love them.'

'I have only three. My father and mother, and Celia. Who are all dead. And I too know that there is the end of the list. I have lost my power to love.'

We looked out for some moments on the tree that blazed white on the white lawn under the liquid starry sky. I said, 'I would not be any different. Would you?'

'Not for the world. Yet it is a very curious fate, to have the book closed so early when other people read in it so much longer. But now go back to your sofa and sleep. I will call you early, I will telephone for a taxi and we will all get out of this bawdyhouse at the first possible moment and get breakfast at the inn.'

VII

WHEN I WOKE I could not think where I could be. I was so delighted to be there. Even after I had remembered I was still ecstatic. My arms folded behind my head, I lay and watched the framework of light round the dark and stolid window-curtains, and thought of the morning outside which I conceived to be hazed with heat under a pale dome, the trees and hills standing half-created, mere outlines. There came back to me knowledge of the human hideousness that had come my way before I went to sleep; the insults to which we had been subjected in this house hardly affected me, for Oliver's story was so much more strong. Celia's singing was loud in my ears; it was almost all I remembered about her. She had an extremely pleasing legato which she took with her into quite difficult music, and much more besides. Indeed her voice was of the sort that suggests immortality, that promises to sound some-where after a singer and audience are dead. Yet she had lost her voice before she died. I was grieved by that and by my failure to divine Oliver's unhappiness, and I looked forward to telling Mary his story and getting her to help me with plans for his distraction. But at the same time I was thinking of none of these things. I was absorbed in my sense of the morning that would receive me and bathe me when I should leave this house. I got up and stretched and laughed at nothing to the four corners of the shadowed room, and went through the corridors, which were still dark, for the curtains had not yet been drawn, to the cloakroom where we had washed the night before. I did not mind that the water was cold, although I always made a great fuss if that happened at home.

When I came out into the corridor Oliver and Avis were

195

coming towards me. She was carrying her violin-case with just such a mother-and-child concern as Cordelia used to show; it is not fair how one should be taken and the other should be left. Oliver was kind, it showed in the way he walked beside this girl, his arm was curved, he knew well she was clumsy and would knock into something, and he did not count it against her, he only tried to save her the humiliation. They were both as happy as I was. It seemed they had learned from an early-rising footman that a lorry was taking milk-churns to the station, and the driver was waiting for us now. But first Oliver and I went into the little library, which had not yet been set to rights, and was still a sea-green tent of brocade curtains, enclosing the smell of tobacco and the exhalations from the half-inches of wine in the glasses on the disordered table. I wished we could have gone straight out into the morning. But the delay was necessary, we pushed away the chairs the diners had left askew and spread our cheque-books among the dirty coffee-cups and glasses and plates, of which those that were smeared with peach-skins were peculiarly sordid, and we wrote out cheques for the benefit of the charity we were now not going to serve by playing at the concert. The four *blanc de chine* parrots looked down on us from the heights of the greenish bookcase with an irony that was too apposite, for it was hard to write these cheques without feeling a vulgar satisfaction at being able to buy one's way out of this barbaric household in currency they recognised.

We left the envelope on a table in the round hall. Then Oliver and Avis took me through a passage with a vaulted roof, which had an amusing echo, and we came out into a courtyard built of the same blonde stone as the pilasters on the house, with that air of the classical drama, of Coriolanus and Troilus and Cressida and Sejanus, which people of the past often thought appropriate to stables. As Avis climbed up on to the high lorry, cradling her violin, I said to Oliver, 'You should write an opera about some lovely stables.'

'Yes,' he answered, 'about an elopement frustrated by some respectable horses who would not draw the coach in which the guilty pair were fleeing.' I could have got on the lorry by myself, but he lifted me, gently but so strongly that I shot up from his arms and was suddenly beside the churns. He looked after women so well that he might have been an American. I was foolish ever to have suspected that he was homosexual.

'An opera with instrumental choruses of neighing horses,' he said, jumping up beside Avis and me. 'What instrument do you suppose?' We thought the cor anglais, though perhaps one would have to put something inside it, to get the right equine tone, as one puts tissue paper across a comb to get a harmonica effect.

We lumbered through an archway carved with trophies, into the full morning which was not as I had expected, but was also glorious. The world was rough and golden, like Rosamund's hair when she first awoke. The turf in the park, bleached and glazed by the dry summer, gave back the yellow sun, but every low tuft had its shadow because the sun was still not high, and when we went out into the open country the standing crops were more yellow than green, and chalk-laden red fallow lands were luminous; but nothing was smooth, each of these fields was broken by the short shadows of what grew close to the ground, or the long shadows of the trees, or the hedges distorted images of themselves which they dropped on their westward side. This was not the strong light I had imagined, pouring down from a zenith blanched with its strength, blinding the eye to all but essential forms. Yet I felt myself bathed in such a light. I was in a trance, sealed from the world, yet I followed Oliver's pointing finger and saw the rabbits loping far out in the open fields. Even more definitely than when I first awoke, I was living a twofold life.

We found that there was no sense in taking the same train as the churns, it only went to the junction to meet a train that was going west, and we wanted to go east. We could just as well wait till the next train, which left in two hours and a half's time. There was a curious pleasure in watching Oliver settle all these details. As we came out of the station we saw the innkeeper's wife standing at her front door, shaking a mat, and we hurried across to her.

'What, back so soon?' she asked, kindly. She was afraid for us. Perhaps we had not been good enough for Barbados Hall, perhaps we had been sent away.

'These ladies were sent for,' said Oliver. 'They were called away to play at other concerts.'

The innkeeper's wife nodded. She was glad there had been no awkwardness. 'You can't have liked that,' she murmured, 'having to leave the lovely place so soon.' She told us, as if to comfort us, that she would give us breakfast, though it was so early, and we took Avis into the garden to sit at the table under the apple trees where we had had tea. Oliver said, with a wonder which would have seemed excessive had I not felt it too, 'Rose, it is not twenty-four hours since we were here.' We sat down and rested our elbows on the table and drowsed in the sunlight, until Avis said suddenly, 'Damn!'

We looked at her, and she swallowed. 'Yesterday, at that horrible place, I knocked over a beastly table and broke something. I could not help it, they were all staring at me. Should I send a note saying I will pay for it?'

'No,' said Oliver, shutting his eyes again.

'But they will say I am dishonest as well as clumsy.'

'The thing will have been insured. Probably with two companies. Never think of it again.'

'How can I help thinking of it? It was so awful.'

'Think of those bloody people, remember how bloody they were, call them what Othello did. "Goats and monkeys! Goats and monkeys!"'

'Goats and monkeys,' I echoed sleepily, my face in my hands.

The peace of the garden was sweet about us. 'There is honeysuckle somewhere,' said Oliver. 'Sniff it, Avis, and say, "Goats and Monkeys". And the dahlias; surely they are more beautiful than they were yesterday?'

I said, 'It is because we are here so early. Mr Morpurgo says that two hours of sunshine take away the genius of the colour in every flower but the rose. The night remakes it; but the genius is gone till the next day. That is why when his favourite flowers come to blossom he has himself wakened at dawn.'

'Who is Mr Morpurgo?' asked Avis.

For a minute I could not answer. Then the innkeeper's wife came back and spread on the table a darned cloth from Barbados Hall, smiling slyly, knowing that this time we would understand, having seen Aladdin's cave for ourselves; and Oliver was returning her smile with a deceitfulness I did not like. Then his hand went out to the sugar-bowl she had set down before him, and took out a lump: and I was revolted by the hair that grew from the third joint of his fingers, just above the knuckles. He had of course far less hair than many musicians had on their hands, but it would have been better if he had none. I could not help remembering that it was he who had taken me to Barbados Hall, and for an end which, now I

198

thought of it in the morning light, revolted me. He should not have brought me into contact of any sort with that vile man, Jasperl. I fell back into the world of frightening fairy tales. It appeared to me that to play music written by such a man might spoil my hands, in which my sole value lay.

Oliver's eyes, still smiling, held mine. 'Tell Avis about Mr Morpurgo,' he said, speaking with masculine impertinence, as if he had a right to give me orders. I told them how he had called at our house in Lovegrove long ago, to help us when we had lost our father, and how Mamma had come into the room, carrying a box of keys and had practically ignored him, because of her astonishment that she had in her house so many more keys than things that locked, and how she had not recognised him, and he had been hurt, and she had somehow put it right, by saying with what singers call attack, 'Well, I knew there was no great difference,' and he was entirely satisfied. But when I went on to tell how he had helped us with our careers, Avis cried out, 'What, you had someone to help you?'

'Yes,' I said, 'he was always there to help us.'

'You and your sister did not get on just because you were geniuses? Then how will I ever be able to get on?'

Her anxiety was terrible. I had to give thanks for the idiot confidence that had inspired my youth. I could not think how to comfort her, but Oliver's hand closed over hers, and he said, 'Here comes a symbolic answer. Look at the trays they are bringing us. Bacon and eggs. Tea. Toast. Butter. Marmalade. We ordered all that and had a right to expect it. But there's a glass bowl full of raspberries, and we said not a word about them.'

'Oh, and cream!' breathed Avis. Her house must be as poor as ours had been, we had talked of cream like that.

'Let this be a lesson to you,' said Oliver. 'Remember that the Lord will provide. Good God, you are a tiresome noisy little thing. You start squealing long before you are hurt. Actually, Rose and Mary started their careers by getting scholarships like the one you are holding, and though Mr Morpurgo helped them by giving them such trifles as an odd music-room when they needed it, the trick was already done by the time he got there. Nothing could have stopped them. Nothing will stop you, unless it is your tendency to rampage and riot instead of getting on quietly with the business in hand.'

He was very kind, I should not have disliked him. But I was sick with loathing of him, even though he was in a trusting

199

state of happiness that would ordinarily have disarmed me. When we had finished breakfast he asked me to pour him another cup of tea, though he did not drink it, just so that he could go on sitting at the table, pretending that breakfast was not finished, that our adventure was not nearly over. He scattered some crumbs on the grass a little way off and we kept quiet so that the birds would come; and as we sat we could hear in the next field the clatter of a reaping machine, the gentle tempered calls of its driver, the whinnying of the horses and the slow soft blows of their hooves as they turned just beyond the hedge, the diminuendo as the machine went off round the curve of an unseen hill, the crescendo as it came back again, the rhythm repeating itself over and over again, each time with a slight difference in pitch, as the swathe went further down the hill. Oliver listened to this reaping machine and watched it as if it were a special part of creation he had known for a long time and always liked; and when two wagtails strutted across the grass and see-sawed the black and white slivers of their bodies over the crumbs they might have been pets he had lured to him throughout a summer.

I wished I was back at the Dog and Duck. I wanted to see the familiar discord of Aunt Lily's dress as she gave the bar its morning dues – the girl can sweep, it takes one of the family to dust – and watch her as, frowning with earnestness, she laid down her check duster that was good enough for the tables and the counters and piously applied a chamois leather to the glass on the prints of dead racehorses and jockeys because they were dear to Len. I wanted to see Aunt Milly, as she stood at the larder door and looked at yesterday's joints and tapped her upper lip with her forefinger, and calculated what could be got off them for today, and sighed that Len had made a proper mess of that leg of lamb, but what could you do, there wasn't a man alive who didn't think he could carve. I wanted to see Queenie who as she came downstairs and sat down in front of her cup of strong tea, with four lumps of sugar in it, jutting her brows at it, knew nothing could let her taste sweetness in her mouth. She would have resembled a great figure from Racine, had it not been for some fact, which was perhaps simply the fact that she really existed. I wanted to see Uncle Len, padding through the garden to see how his roses were growing and if anybody had left any bottles and glasses outside, his red jowls dripping the irascible peace known to old bulls. I wanted to see

Nancy and Oswald, holy in their mediocrity. I wanted to see Mr Morpurgo, who would certainly come in towards evening, for he rarely let a day pass without visiting Queenie. Before he went we would stand side by side on the riverbank in the next field, while he dropped his line to the dark waters, which mirrored our images and flowed on and on, out of sight. Everybody in the Dog and Duck had either never been able to live, or had done with life, or lived well within their means and was calm and kind. I wanted to be there, not here.

The innkeeper's wife had brought the bill and Oliver had put his hand into his pocket, and was taking out silver, and I was embarrassed at the thought that he was paying for me and Avis, I could not offer to pay.

'Now we must go,' sighed Oliver with a regret which I felt to be idiotically presumptuous. 'We must not lose that train.'

'We will only be together till the junction,' said Avis with angry grief. 'There we will have to say goodbye, I take a bus. I suppose I shall never see you again.'

'Nonsense,' said Oliver. 'Rose and I will take you home, and we will explain to your family how right you were in leaving Barbados Hall and refusing to play at that concert.'

'No,' I said. 'I cannot come.'

'Oh, Rose!' said Oliver. 'Oh, Rose!'

Avis cried, 'But it's you they'd be impressed by.'

Oliver and I had to exchange an amused glance at that. But I loathed him. I was hardly able to speak, to force out the words, 'I cannot possibly come with you.'

'But why, Rose! Why?'

'I must go back to that inn by the Thames we have often told you about.' My words struck me as so final, so forbidding, that I relented them. I supposed that was because they must give offence. I did not want that. To make the moment seem more casual I took my powder-puff out of my bag and passed it over my face. My hand was shaking. I said weakly, 'They will be expecting me.'

'They cannot be expecting you this afternoon,' he objected. 'You had arranged to play at that vile concert.'

'Yes,' I said. 'But it was always inconvenient for me to leave them.'

He was sulky for a moment, but it was not his way. He said quickly, 'Rose, I have been stupid. You have put yourself out to help me with this Jasperl thing! Avis, you squalling little

201

egotist, take note of this. Rose has been doing a job for me for weeks, and looking every day as if she liked it, and suddenly I see that it has been a burden to her, and she has done it all just because she is nice. Oh, Rose, forgive me!'

'No, it is not that,' I stammered. 'Ask me to do something really difficult, I would do it, that was not difficult at all. I would do anything for you, any time. So would Mary.' It embarrassed me to hear these too friendly words. But they poured out of my mouth. I was so anxious to dissimulate this nauseated loathing of him.

It made it worse that he believed me. 'Look, Avis,' he said. 'As you go through the world of music you will meet goats and monkeys, they are not all kept at Barbados Hall. But you will meet friends. Here I have plagued Rose with a dreary job for weeks, for my own purposes, and kept her up late last night, long after you were asleep, listening to a story which I wanted her to hear, but which she had no reason to want to hear. And all this time I have disregarded the obvious fact she must have obligations and troubles of her own. In fact, I am an egotist like you, Avis, and have behaved in the beastly fashion of our kind, and here she says that she will do anything for me any time I ask. Come, we must go.'

Outside the inn, while Avis was fetching her violin-case, he said to me, 'How Celia would have liked you, if she had known you better,' and walked away, his eyes on the ground. I stood trembling with fury, and he turned back to say, 'Not that she did not like what she saw of you, and of course she admired your playing, but you met her so seldom.'

I was still tingling all our journey to the junction. I would not have wanted Celia to like me, she was so polluted by this world of masculinity. It now seemed not so absurd to me that the Victorians had taken women who had slept with men to whom they were not married and shut them up in rescue homes. Marriage, inviolate marriage was the only way by which the traffic between men and women could be rendered tolerable. If two people went to a church in festive dress and took part in a pretty rite in the presence of their friends, and then shared the same house and always went about together, then one could think of these public things as all that was happening. But women like Celia forced the most reluctant mind to follow them to the private horror of their pollution. Why did she leave Oliver? To go into a room with Jasperl. Why? You know, you cannot help but know. It is the ugliest thing for a woman to know, for such pollution spoils women to the destruction of their essence, they become rubbish. Celia must have become rubbish when she had confused her life with Oliver and Jasperl, and though I would have thought it could do nobody much harm to be with Oliver, the germ of Jasperl was in Oliver, for Jasperl's offence was to have carried masculinity to its logical conclusion. All this rank stuff, that made one remember stenches, must end in wickedness. Not only had Oliver brought Celia into the orbit of masculinity and thus been responsible for all she had done there, he had chosen to wrestle with Jasperl, to be smeared with the shine of what was worst in himself carried to a worse stage by a man with a worse self than him. He was not internally vile like Jasperl but he was now externally defiled.

I sat back in my corner-seat and shut my eyes and pretended I had gone to sleep. It was all right, for Oliver was quite happy talking to Avis. It would be a good thing if he married her. His kindness would help her solve the difficulties of her genius, and he would have something else to think about than Celia and Jasperl. The coarseness in Avis, her greasy skin and her greedy over-anxiety about her career, made me not regret it if she married, as I would (I now realised for the first time) have regretted it if Mary had got married.

Oliver said, 'Rose, we are running into the junction.' I did not open my eyes. I feared he might touch me, and my body stiffened in an agony that was not allayed when he did nothing of the sort. Simply he said, 'Rose, poor Rose, you are so tired, but you must wake up.' In spite of my violent disgust I was delighted with the words as if they had a specially intricate rhythm; yet of course they had none.

The Reading train was in the station, but it did not start at once. I had to spend some time standing at the window and looking down at Avis and Oliver, in a state of embarrassment because they were plainly so disappointed at my departure. This was new for me. I always wanted people more than they wanted me. It was my great sorrow that so few of all the men and women I met sought to be close to me. Evidently, this was something that happened as one got older. Of course I did not enjoy the act of rejection, but I knew it was inevitable, I was glad I had the strength to perform it. I belonged to others, to a

203

small group that was forever complete and closed. These two people could mean nothing to me.

Oliver broke off something he was saying about Avis's fingering and stared at me, and asked sharply: 'What tree can that have been?'

'What tree?'

'The tree we looked at through the window in the moonlight. It seemed to be in blossom. What can it have been? Surely no trees are in blossom at this time of year.'

'Oh, that tree!' I said. 'How strange I have not thought of it before! How could I have forgotten that tree?'

'It was the most beautiful thing I ever saw in my life,' he said. 'Did you not think so?'

'Yes, yes, it was the most beautiful thing I ever saw,' I said. 'But it went out of my mind. How could that be?' The memory was a ringing in my ears, I felt the same prickling of the skin that comes in listening to certain high notes played on the trumpet.

'I meant to look at it this morning, but I felt such a need to get out of that house that I forgot,' said Oliver. 'Shall I go back and ask the gardener?'

'No, no,' cried Avis and I. 'Please do not do that,' I said, 'Barbados Hall is bad magic. The tree would be gone and they would say it had never been there,' and Avis said, 'There is a market gardener near us at home, who is famous for his trees and shrubs. I will go and ask him what it could be, it will be an excuse for writing to you.'

'Curse it, the train is going to start,' said Oliver, speaking with an absurd impatience, as if it might be supposed never to do so. 'Rose, what are we doing about meeting again? You are going to the Dog and Duck now, but you said that you were going on a holiday with Mary almost at once – does that mean that you will be at home any time tomorrow?'

'Yes, yes,' I said, leaning far out, 'I will be there in the afternoon.'

'Damn it, there the green flag goes. Quite early in the afternoon?'

'Yes, yes,' I said.

'Do not forget,' said Oliver, running beside the train.

'Oh, he is lucky,' panted Avis, bobbing just behind him. 'He will see you so soon again.'

They ran right to the end of the platform and stood there

204

waving, and so long as they could be seen at all, they kept their character, which was unique, and uniquely pleasant. They belonged to the same order of existence as everything I liked, and I realised this with an exquisite acuteness for I was again in that exalted and divided state that I had experienced earlier in the morning. I found myself able to remember several pieces of music at once, and they all seemed changed and new, so new that as one theme travelled through my mind's ear, I said to myself, 'What, have I suddenly become a composer?' My state of excitement might be adequately explained if I had undergone the huge fundamental alteration that is necessary if an interpretative artist is to become a creator.

Oliver's face appeared before me, and I saw no other sight. He was, I reflected, exceptional in his appearance. It was not simply that he was fairly good-looking, there was something better than nature about the carving of his face. The brooding lines across his brow, the slant of his cheekbones, which made him look Russian, the fineness of his nostrils, and the fairness of his lips, which were, however, not thin; all these were exactly as one would have chosen them to be, and it seemed impossible that a face could simply happen to be as right as that, it seemed that a master craftsman must have worked upon it.

I was still thinking of Oliver's face when I found that we had come to Reading station. Though I knew very well that I had to hurry to the bay where the local train was just about to start, I made my way instead to the open space outside the station. I was seized with laughter.

It was an area given over to chaos, neither a square nor a triangle nor a circle; and as I stood on an island in the middle of its sprawl I raised my eyes and saw that Reading station, above the postered walls on ground level, offered an amusing incongruity. Its upper elevation was of prison-coloured brick, pierced with mean windows overhung by heavy mouldings of sooty stone, pointless dream of one of the millions of stupid men who have sat in England and thought about Rome, for no particular reason; and this was surmounted by a trim little clocktower, of unmistakably marine character, the sort of thing that ought to decorate the Customs-house in a small port such as Ramsgate, and house an eccentric Dickens character in a yachting cap with a telescope to his eye. I hoped I might show it to Oliver, I knew he would be delighted.

I went further and found, at one of the outlets from this formless open space, a statue of Edward VII which represented him as a slim man with projecting teeth holding his body under a regal robe in the attitude by which wax models in cheap tailors' show that the trousers they wear are of an easy fit. Laughter seized me again; this too I wished to show Oliver.

I made my way back to the station and asked a porter where I could get a taxi to take me to the Dog and Duck. He was a wrinkled man with a preacherish air, and he told me shrewishly that I should hurry to the bay, for the train was only just due to start. I would not do it, and he grumbled sourly that it was a waste of money to take a taxi for so long a journey, and that there was another train in two hours, and if I could not wait all that time I could go by bus with only two changes. I could not help hurting this man, for when I obeyed my natural impulse and told him that I had ten pounds in my bag and knew that the fare would be less than that, and anyway I could afford it, he was enraged that anybody should have ten pounds in their bag, that anybody should have enough money to hire a car. He was glad when we had to send to a garage in the town for a taxi that would go so far, and it did not come for nearly an hour; and when I overtipped him he hated me for my power to do so, he did not even give me credit for doing my best. I could not even feel sorry for him because he showed an innate peevishness that, glutted with good fortune, would simply have made him another Lord Sarasen. Yet still I was happy. I felt that such people would not always be and that there was an answer. I sang bits from the *Messiah* and the *Creation* all the way as we drove through the winding lanes, their margins starred and delicate with the huge white heads of cow-parsley, past crops that were greener than the crops in the West Country and only half-possessed their ripeness as a faint gold immanence, through woods where the heaviness of midsummer foliage cast a shade as dark as storm. But indeed as we drew nearer the Dog and Duck the skies grew duller. I liked it, the colours of the landscape were the richer for it.

The Dog and Duck was very busy. There were some motor-launches moored alongside, the school holidays had begun, there were many people having tea in the garden round the house, and through the coffee-room window my eye was caught by Aunt Lily's new frock, a flower print in magenta and viridian green, and I watched her tenderly as she crossed the room holding high a loaded tray. She and Uncle Len and Aunt Milly would all be too busy for me, and I felt it a pity, since I had this soaring and swelling happiness to share. I looked down the slope and saw Mr Morpurgo sitting out at a solitary table at the water's edge. He looked dejected and in front of him a little box was lying across its wrapping paper. Evidently some present he had brought for Queenie had failed to amuse. I ran across the lawn to share my soaring and swelling happiness with him, and as I sat down at the table a sword went through my heart and I burst into tears. It was extraordinary that I should have only a moment before imagined I was happy. I knew nothing except grief.

'Rose, poor Rose,' said Mr Morpurgo. 'Take this other chair, then nobody will see you. Lean your elbows on the table, and your face on your hands, and it will not look as if you were crying. Don't try to stop.'

It was a long time before I could speak. My weeping was hideous and painful. My face was screwed up and sodden, my nose ran, my sobs hurt me like violent hiccups. At last I whispered, 'Such a horrible thing happened to me at Barbados Hall.'

'Barbados Hall?' said Mr Morpurgo. His eyes rolled against their yellow whites, then fixed on a point in the distance. 'Why did you go to Barbados Hall?'

'To play at a charity concert,' I sobbed.

'There is something to be said for keeping women in purdah,' said Mr Morpurgo. 'Free to come and go, they may be subjected to unpleasant experiences. You should not have gone to that house. Lady Mortlake is a whore. She will sleep with any man who can make her some money. It was even once made plain' – his hand ran over his face in fascinated self-loathing – 'that she might sleep with me. She should be stoned,' he said, with terrible hatred.

'No, no, Morpy,' I said. I put out my hand and caressed his face where his fingers had coldly passed. 'Oh, no, Morpy, anyway I don't care if she is a whore, what happened had nothing to do with that. All she did was to go away.' But I choked and could not go on.

'Shall I go up and get you a cup of tea or some brandy? But of course not. You and I do not respond to irrigation, like the rest of the world. Take your time.'

But he was not indignant when he heard that Lady Mortlake

had insolently picked a substitute for Martin out of the hedges, he was amused.

'You should smile at that,' he said. 'There is a Yiddish word, *schlemiel*, a man who falls over everything, who buys brass for gold. There should be a goy word for the elegant *schlemiel*, who has been born to handle gold but never knows it from brass and calls it gold with the weight of authority, who falls over everything but does it with such assurance that the fall is taken for a curtsy.' He was amused too when he heard that the substitute had turned out to be a genius.

'Life defeats them, brass defeats them, it turns out to be gold, we acquire it,' he chuckled. 'Where is this girl?'

But when I raged on with my story, his amusement went from him. 'They stole your supper and laughed at you,' he said. 'Look at those two swans coming along on the dark water. How white they are, how calm their bodies make them for all the vicious temper that lives inside.' He ran a finger round his collar to loosen it but his cold anger broke out. 'By God, they treated you like Jews without money. If I can make them pay for this I will.'

'No,' I said. 'Nothing could make it better now, it happened, but they did something worse.'

When he heard of our stolen bedrooms he leaned over the table and took my hands in his.

'Dear Rose,' he said, 'this will hurt for a long time. I wake even now and think of some of the things the boys did to me at school. Idiotic of my mind to go back so far. There have been plenty of incidents which have happened to me since.' His teeth bared. 'There is no wound to pride that does not fester. A bite from an ape, I believe, always goes septic. But you must remember that it was an ape that offended, not a force you need respect.'

'"Goats and monkeys," Oliver kept on saying,' I snuffled.

'They were wise words,' said Mr Morpurgo. 'That is why Shakespeare is so restful, he never pretends that human beings are not horrible. All other writers pretend that we are all good fellows if we are looked at from the right angle. We are not.'

I was better now, the sobbing had stopped, but the tears were streaming down my face.

'How this has hurt you, Rose,' said Mr Morpurgo. 'I am so stupid, I keep on thinking can I not give her something that will distract her? But who should know better than I that

208

humiliation is something that will not permit distraction, it makes first claim on the soul. It is like certain kinds of physical pain. The tooth, the throat, the belly, the foot. I know I cannot do anything. But I cannot bear the daughter of your mother to have been insulted. I feel there is some visible inheritance of honour that people should respect. And you are such a good girl, Rose. You do so little to offend, you do so much to please. I wish indeed this had not happened.'

There were tears in his eyes, and I felt, as I had done all through our conversation, very guilty. For I knew I was not weeping about the tricks these inept people had played on me at Barbados Hall. I would not have lifted a finger to save them from a painful death, but I would have thought of my crime as insecticide; I knew that these people were so alien to me that they could not hurt me. But though I was well aware that I was weeping for another and deeper cause, I did not know what it was.

I tried hard to speak the truth. 'But there is more than that, I am so miserable. Not just over this. I am miserable all the time.'

'Dear Rose, dear Rose. Tell me what is wrong. Surely I can do something?'

What could it be? 'I do not like people,' I found myself saying. 'I hate all people except Mary, who is more or less me, and the people here, you, and Aunt Lily and Aunt Milly and Uncle Len and Queenie, and Nancy, and the baby, and of course Kate and Miss Beevor. I am so lonely! I am so lonely! I am only happy here.'

'That I can understand,' he said. 'Your mother has gone, and the world could never be the same after that. It has lost the sources of its wealth. Richard Quin has gone. And so has Rosamund.'

'Yes, she has gone, much more than Mamma,' I cried. 'She has gone to that man.'

'And your sister Cordelia was never really one of the family.'

'Yes, she would have been on the side of the people at Barbados Hall,' I said. 'If I tell her she will ask me what I did to annoy them and will say, "But you must have done something, dear."'

'One has sisters that are not of one's blood, some antipathetic children that are strangers, the facts of biology are not properly understood,' said Mr Morpurgo. 'But perhaps we understand them as well as is necessary. Yes, I can realise that you are very lonely, my poor child. But we are here. We wait for you. We talk of you when you are not with us. You and Mary are very fortunate, my dear. You are greatly loved. These dear people here love you... I cannot tell you how well they love you. It is a treasure they lay up for you. You are rich.'

'Only when I am with them,' I cried. 'Morpy, I hate my work. I want to give it up.' That was what was troubling me. I had found it at last.

'Your playing?' he asked incredulously.

'You are surprised? But what does my work do for me? These horrible people come and listen to me, and they pay me money, and they send me presents, but they give me nothing. I give them everything that I can and they give me nothing in return. It is not fair.'

'They give you money, you have said so, and they send you presents, and they admire you,' he reminded me. 'And you love music.'

'But that is not what I want,' I said. 'I want them to give me something. I feel empty without it. I never get it from anybody but the people here, and Kate, and Miss Beevor.'

'But you have it from them,' said Mr Morpurgo. 'I do not see why you cannot go on with your playing, because you are a musician, and music is a part of you, you are your mother's daughter, and at the same time take what Len and Milly and Lily and the rest of us can give you.' His sharp, connoisseur look lit on me for a second. 'You have not got it clear yet.'

He was right. There was another terror in my mind I had not recognised before. 'It is the people, I tell you. The people I play to, and, oh, yes, the people I have to work with. I am frightened of them. I said they gave me nothing but money, nothing but presents, nothing but admiration, and that what I value is not that, but what I get from the people here, at the Dog and Duck. But what I would hate most of all would be if these people I play to, these people I work with, started to try and give me what I get here. I could not bear it if they stretched out their hands to me, and touched me, and tried to come near me – oh, I should be sick, I could not bear it, if they persisted I should kill myself.'

'I wonder what you really mean,' said Mr Morpurgo, frowning into the distance.

'I mean what I say,' I cried, raising my voice angrily. 'I could not bear the thought of these people laying hold of me, feeling they have rights over me.'

Aunt Lily was standing beside my chair, and she bent down and kissed me. 'I saw my Rose when I came out to pick a sprig of mint for the high tea, and I had to come down to give her a hug. Thought she wasn't coming down till tomorrow.' She smoothed my hair, which was no doubt disordered, and looked about at the calm afternoon, the level river, the reflections of the brightly painted rowing-boats and launches, the August uprush of grasses and flowers and dark enrichment of foliage on every tree. 'Funny that with everything so lovely and abundant people should want to eat rock cakes. Miserable things. But you can't give them enough.'

She was gone. I repeated in a lower voice, 'I tell you I cannot bear the thought of these people coming nearer to me. Mixing me up with their affairs. And such disgusting affairs. Only the people I have always known are clean and innocent.'

'Oh, come, Rose,' he said, gently. 'You will understand how much you may be misjudging the people you do not know if you reflect how hard it might be to convince strangers that the Dog and Duck is the home of purity. If anyone knew only the beginnings of Len and Milly and Lily they might harbour a good many doubts about them. And there is Queenie.'

'But that would be only because they did not know,' I objected. 'Just because some people would make a mistake and think that Len and Milly and Lily and Queenie are bad, it does not follow that no people are bad. "Goats and monkeys," you said that Shakespeare was right when he wrote that. Why do you not believe me when I say that I want to run away from people? I want to give up playing, I want just to live here, never seeing anybody but us.'

'My poor Rose, how long have you felt like this?'

'For a long time,' I said. I was lying but I could not tell the truth, it was clouded in my mind. 'It comes to me when I am playing. I look at the audience, and I think how detestable I am and I am afraid they will rush the platform and take me to themselves, and I go blind with disgust.' It sounded as if I were mad. I wished I had not told this silly lie, because my distress was sane. I was right to fear the unknown thing I feared.

'I would not have thought your professionalism would ever break down to that extent,' said Mr Morpurgo, with a puzzled air.

211

'Well, it is not quite like that,' I owned. 'I invented that. But of course you knew it. But you see,' I said, weeping again, 'I am so terribly miserable, and I do not know why. And what I said is roughly the truth. I want to have nothing to do with anybody except the people here. I should like to give up my playing and never see any strangers. Why will you not believe me? Why do you force me to go on?'

'My little pet runaway steam engine, I have never forced you to do anything in my life,' said Mr Morpurgo. 'I do not think that in all my life I have ever forced anybody to do anything they did not want to, except by the means of money, an instrument which could not be used on you. If you want to give up playing and come and live here, there is nothing to stop you. But you are not talking entire nonsense. It is certainly true that you are very troubled. Let us go for a walk along the river and we can find out what it is all about. There is a thing so pretty there just now that it will help me to understand.'

We went into the adjoining meadow where he always fished, passing first by a tangle of meadowsweet and purple loosestrife, and then to an open path on the river's edge. A steamer full of people went by, with the harpist that all Thames boats used to carry, making the thinnest music possible, that sounded as if the strings had got hoarse in the damp air, that somehow gave the crowded boat an air of ceremony, that made it dignified like the swans. We walked in silence till those waif-notes and the plumper gush of the wake could no longer be heard, and then I burst out, 'I want to stop living, I have had enough of life, I want to shut myself up with what is left of Papa's and Mamma's life, everything else is detestable.'

'You may be right,' he said. 'But I doubt if your mother would have gone to the trouble of having four children if she had wanted life to stop with her.'

'She went to the trouble of having four children,' I said bitterly, 'and one, the best, died before she did, and before he had time to do anything or enjoy anything.'

'Oh, what Richard Quin did was infinite, and what he enjoyed was the absolute of enjoyment, which could not have been increased if he had lived to be a thousand years,' said Mr Morpurgo. 'You are not going to be vulgar and think his life was not accomplished because he left nothing that could go into an inventory for insurance?'

'But he died,' I raged. 'He died, while vicious people, gross people go on living. Let the whole thing stop, let me detach myself from the whole hideous business.'

'As you will,' he said. 'But why are you arguing about it if you are sure that is what you want? I am not stopping you. I do not think that I have ever really succeeded in penetrating life myself, so I am not likely to take great trouble to keep you there, or be very effective if I should do so. But perhaps we had better find out who is the other party to your argument, since it is not I.'

'Yes, Mamma would have wanted me to go on playing. She would not have liked me to settle down and hide myself and be nothing. She believed in life, but I cannot imagine why. Oh, we in our family know much more than other people, we know there is a life after death, and that mind can speak to mind through walls and that there is a war between good and evil, but still we do not know the meaning of it. If we live for ever does that give life a meaning? How can good win the war, what then, when human beings are what the war is fought through, and they are so vile? How cruel Mamma was not to let Papa go on his way to death long before he did! Oh, poor, poor Papa!'

'The thing I want to show you is this,' said Mr Morpurgo. 'Oh, it means nothing, it is not a symbol. It is just so pretty.' At a certain point on the riverbank the purple loosestrife grew in a thick hedge between the water and the bank, level and neat as if the pruner's hook had disciplined it.

'Yes, that is beautiful,' I said. 'I could be content to live down here with Uncle Len and Aunt Milly and Aunt Lily and Queenie, and you as a constant visitor, and see lovely things like this. This is enough, and so it ought to be, for it is so much.'

I looked at the way the sun, now it was sinking, struck on the silver under-edge of the willow leaves, and on the coarse long grasses that stood higher than the rest, so that the trees seemed interpenetrated by light, and the ground too. And the river, how calm it was!

'How I love the river!' I said. 'It is something I have known all my life. It flows back to London where I was a child. I feel as if I could get into a boat and glide down till I came back into my childhood, and Rosamund would be there.'

'But nothing of the sort could possibly happen,' said Mr Morpurgo.

'No, but I could come here again and again and think it

might,' I said. 'You see, you are against me. You do not like me to do what I want to do and come here and see nobody I did not know when I was a child.'

'I am sure it is not what your mother would have liked you to do,' he said with quiet obstinacy.

'Why, because she was cruel to my father, should she be cruel to me too? Why did she marry him? Why did she get mixed up with all this horror?'

'You rave if you question the wisdom of your mother's life,' he said, without anger.

I looked over the river, over the meadow, to the clear yellow western sky. 'So I do,' I said.

'It is a measure of your unhappiness, poor Rose,' he said.

'But why am I so unhappy?' I wept.

'I wish I knew,' he said.

'What do I want?' I asked him.

He shook his head in perplexity.

'It is so dreadful, I cannot go forward or back,' I whispered hoarsely.

'What did all your mother do mean except that there is a God, as they said in the past?'

'How does that help?' I said. 'Of course what she did must mean just that. But she never talked as if that meant that everything went well. It only says in the Bible that are not two sparrows sold for a farthing, and not one shall fall on the ground without your Father. That is all it says. The Father does not save the sparrow. He only knows it has fallen.'

'But He may be calling the sparrow to great things,' he muttered. 'Your mother was not something we were told about, she lived.'

The fish were rising, there were silver circles on the dark waters. 'I love this field, I love walking here, let me live at the Dog and Duck,' I said.

'Look at those trees across the river,' he said absently. 'That line of poplars at the back, then the beeches below, then those weeping willows, with their tumbled branches in front of them, and in the foreground the flat meadow, and the same hedge of loosestrife on the water's edge as we have, and then the water. It is a composition!'

'It is so beautiful,' I said. 'But I am so unhappy.'

'Has your unhappiness anything to do with the beauty?'

'I think it has,' I said uncertainly.

214

'It has often seemed to me when I have been very unhappy and looked at beautiful things that there was a relevance,' he said. 'But I am babbling. Why have I made my collection if I do not know it is an answer to the pit? Why do you play if you do not know music is an answer to the pit?'

'I do not want to make that answer any more,' I said. 'Oh, my dear, I would like it if this dark water was flowing over me, if the meadows on each side were far above where I lay.'

He put his arms round me and his connoisseur look came on him. 'No,' he said, letting me go, 'there is nothing of death about you. But let us go back. It hurts me that I cannot help you.'

I bent down and kissed the curiously loose flesh of his face. 'I would give the last drop from my veins for you, or any of her children,' he whispered. 'I mean it. I longed to die instead of Richard Quin and keep that grief from her. But the idea of sacrifice is a myth, we make it to keep ourselves happy, delightful to imagine a god that can be bought off. Oh, Rose, Rose, what a woman your mother was! If she had been any other woman, it would have been right to say that I was nothing to her. But being what she was, she gave me such kindness, such grace, she spread such light in my darkness. . . .'

My mother was huge across the skies, the peaceful fields, the peaceful waters were her footstool; I wanted always to be here.

'Rose, she would not want me to think of her when you are suffering. But all I find to say is, let us go back. You want to be at the Dog and Duck, then sit there quietly. You want to be near them. You will be near them. It may calm you, and I am doing nothing for you. Oh, Rose, I have never seen anybody crying as you are crying.'

'It must be horrible,' I said.

'No, there is a certain style about it.'

'But that I am crying is so strange at my time of life,' I said.

'You tell them about Barbados Hall, they will find it natural enough that you should have wept with rage.'

On the way home I paused all the time to take handfuls of meadowsweet and sniff them, to bend down and strip the leaves from the peppermint stalks and crush them on my palms. 'Yes, scent is a kind of medicine,' said Mr Morpurgo absently.

'But I am not ill,' I wept, 'I am only unhappy.'

'Even so,' he said, nodding. 'Even so.'

In the garden we sat down at the little table at the water's edge and looked up at the inn, which was now not so busy as it had been. The teas had gone, scampering away in their multi-coloured simplicity. There were now only a few people who were having drinks before an early dinner. Of a more sedate sort, they were mostly couples, and there was one pair, a man and a woman about my own age, and of our kind, the sort of people one sees at concerts, the man with a nice smile, the woman in a rough silk dress of a sympathetic shade of lavender grey, who were evidently not married, for they looked at each other with amused and delighted surprise. Either I had met one or both, or people who resembled them, in unpleasant circumstances, which my distracted state prevented me from recalling, for I felt great distaste at the sight of them, I had to turn away.

The little packet still lay on the table among its wrappings, and Mr Morpurgo sighed when he saw it, and slipped it into his pocket. As he was such a virtuoso in benevolence I did not draw attention to his failure by seeking to know what this object might be, but I asked how Queenie was, and I got a grave headshake. She was helping in the kitchen, it seemed, at the moment. Housework bored and tormented her; her past was too much for her, she could not set about to clean a room without baring her teeth as if at any moment a wardress would come to censure her. But Mr Morpurgo told me what I had not known, that of late she had taken to baking and made excellent though extravagant scones and simple cakes, and quite elaborate breads. 'Bread,' said Mr Morpurgo, in the belief that he was telling me something, 'still made with yeast, one of those things one thinks must nowadays only be metaphors. She greatly enjoys working with it, I have watched her. One has to make the dough with it. It behaves like a living thing, and that has to be beaten, she hits it with her fists quite hard, and then it is put in a warm place and it rises, oh, incredibly. Then it has to be kneaded again and put into tins, and it rises again, and she puts it in the oven, and it is a great victory when it comes out good bread.'

I could understand that, and I was glad as I was whenever I heard of Queenie being happy, for I was still quite well aware that I was responsible for Queenie's crime. I might have been a child when I teased her with my power of fortune-telling and inflamed her with the idea that the universe is not so rigid as

216

she supposed, had inspired her violent and impulsive mind
with the aspiration to change it in such a way as would favour
her desires; but I was a child who had been warned. I knew I
was trafficking in forbidden things, and I knew there was a
justice in the prohibition. I was a murderess by proxy; and I had
condemned the woman who did the murder for me to a life of
torment. Yet it seemed to me at that moment that had I been
able to go back to my childhood I would not have been able to
refrain from committing that crime. For that would have
altered my childhood, which I loved so much that I could not
bear it to be different in the smallest respect. If Queenie had not
killed her husband the light from the gas-jet in our hall at
Lovegrove might not have fallen on my father's high cheekbones as it had when he brought in Aunt Lily after a day in court,
and holding her by the shoulders, disregarded her babbled
absurdities about the unfairness of the judge and told her
softly, almost in a whisper, to go and lie down and not to talk,
Mamma could wait till afterwards to hear about it all. Usually
when I thought of my childhood it was Mamma who appeared
with the solidity of real forms, Papa was only a dark presence,
but now it was he whom I could nearly touch, and for whom I
so longed that not to touch him was a sweet pain.

I had not noticed that Mr Morpurgo had left me, but we were
drinking double sherries. I said, 'But Uncle Len does not like
women to have more than one glass of sherry,' but Mr
Morpurgo said, 'It will be all right tonight. I will explain.'

I had had no lunch, so the world grew liquid as I drank. 'How
wonderful those scarlet snapdragons look in this light,' I said.

'And better still the mixed crimson and scarlet ones Len has
in the beds beyond the bar,' said Mr Morpurgo. 'Look at all that
flaming and smouldering colour, that precise form to every
flower, the splendid bravura lift to the first, inaugurating the
design of later stems and lesser supporting growths, all that to
be stored up in an annual, it is not possible, it is against the
principle of the conservation of matter. Look, dear Rose, you
will like them.'

I turned in my seat and, though I liked the sight, my heart
still was sore; and then the potboy lit the Chinese lanterns that
were hung above the tables and I became subject to the strange
law by which the spectacle of lights burning by daylight, in
agreeable surroundings where people have gathered together
to take their pleasure, causes an aching hunger for the past.

217

I kept my face turned away from Mr Morpurgo so that he would not see that I had begun to weep again. But he knew, his gentle voice advised, 'Look, Rose, at this company of swans, how they seem whiter than ever now the twilight is falling.'

I cleared my throat and said, 'Here is Queenie.' She had come out of the house and was strolling down the lawn, towards the river, not towards us. We were not in her mind, she was absorbed in her own lack of ease. She did not present her usual careful copy of elegance. Her hair (and how astonishing it was that it was still dark) was a little disordered, and as she came nearer we could see a streak of flour across her shirt. She was frowning, and her hands looked discontented. For a little time she had forgotten her misery in the work of baking, and now tea was over and no more scones were needed, and she was back again where she had started. There was no grey in her hair, she was unbowed, she walked loose-limbed like a girl, her face surprised with the virility of its sullenness. It was probable that she would live for many years to come.

As she came near the river her eyes were on the dark flowing waters, but a shadow passed over her face and she looked at the table where we were sitting, at Mr Morpurgo and at the parcel lying among its wrappings, as if she had to take up a burden again. I did not trouble to wipe the tears from my face, she would not notice them, so distracted was she by the tedium of finding a response to another of the futile kindnesses that were being offered to her. She laid a hand on my shoulder and said my name, flatly as if it had no meaning for her, and said to Mr Morpurgo, 'That thing you brought me, I would like to look at it again.' With effort she added, 'It's so tasteful, so –' In her search for another adjective she let her eyes wander into the distance, where they instantly became fixed, while she asked faintly, 'Who's this?'

She was looking at a tall old man with silver hair who had halted as he was about to enter the garden by the wicket-gate on the meadow side. 'What's he staring at like that?' she said, her voice no stronger. 'Why's he coming in by that gate that nobody but the family uses?' The carefully woven tissue of her reticence suddenly ripped. 'What's the old bugger think he's playing at?' she demanded, with fury, though she did not raise her voice.

'Why, Queenie,' said Mr Morpurgo, 'that is Oswald's father. He will have guessed that you are Nancy's mother. He will have recognised you from the photograph she has in her drawing-room. He has always been anxious to meet you.'

She said words we could not hear, her tongue and her lips moving but making no sound, and remained quite still while Mr Bates strode down the lawn towards us. Mr Morpurgo stood up and put out his hand in greeting, but was ignored. As Mr Bates had approached his gaze had been set on Queenie's face. Now he leaned on his staff and looked at her, and then asked, 'Are you the woman who has been a great sinner?'

Queenie was trembling, but she did not lower her eyes or her chin. 'I am the woman who is a great sinner,' she answered.

He leaned on his staff for a long moment while their eyes burned into each other's. Then he came closer to her and said, 'Come with me and I will deliver you bound and gagged to the mercy of the Lord God,' and he laid his arms across her shoulders. Side by side they went up the lawn and passed through the wicket-gate.

When I had gaped after them for some moments I started to my feet. 'Come on, we must follow them!' I cried to Mr Morpurgo.

His face had expressed such astonishment as mine, but he replied, 'Follow them? Oh, no.'

'But he may kill her!' I exclaimed.

'Oh, no,' he said. 'I do not think he will kill her.'

'But the way he was looking at her,' I stuttered, 'the way he spoke to her! Surely he sounded dangerous!'

Mr Morpurgo's black eyes rolled over to the opposite point of the compass from the wicket-gate, and rested on the company of swans that were patrolling the blackening waters before us. 'Oh, no,' he breathed, 'oh, no.' I felt suddenly no disposition to argue with him. It was not that I was careless of what might happen to Queenie, but it appeared possible that Mr Morpurgo was right. I felt in relation to her destiny and my own, that there was some element in the situation which for the moment I could not identify, but which guaranteed the safety of both of us. But perhaps this was merely the effect of the double sherry. I said to Mr Morpurgo, 'What a pity it is we are sitting on this side of the river and not on the other, for over there we would see the reflections of the Chinese lanterns in the water, and it must be lovely,' and felt my irrelevance. But Mr Morpurgo had left me. I did not care. I was alarmed to the extent to which I cared for nothing. I reminded myself of the horrible sanctimonious arrest to which I had seen Queenie subjected, but I felt no emotion. Presently Mr Morpurgo returned with another double sherry, saying, 'Not for you, considering you have had no lunch. But for me.' He drank it slowly, sometimes saying, 'My God, my God,' but with less and less intonation of distress.

'When will they come back, do you think?' I asked.

'That no one could tell,' he answered. Darkness fell round us, the swans grew still more spectral, the laughter and conversation of the diners at their tables under the Chinese lanterns sounded like a bird-song, and I was contented, though very tired. I folded my arms and rested them on the table. Something in the air was very sweet. 'It is that bed of tobacco-plant,' Mr Morpurgo explained, and I dozed, waking for a moment because he was laughing, slowly and softly. 'Why are you laughing?' I asked sleepily. He answered, 'I am not exactly laughing. Well, yes, I suppose I am.' My mind did not want to unravel his subtleties, I felt that all the essentials were so clean. I breathed, 'How glorious those tobacco plants are,' and went to sleep again. Then I felt Uncle Len's hand on my shoulder and heard him happily fulminating over roast lamb and the first of the runner beans.

In the light of the parlour I stood blinking. The electric bulb in the lamp over the table seemed too strong, and the reflections from the polished glass and plate and the white cloth glared. I would have liked to go to bed at once without any dinner. I rubbed my eyes, and Aunt Milly gazed at me critically and nudged Aunt Lily. 'You don't look well, love,' they said in unison.

'She's been crying,' said Mr Morpurgo. He placed himself at the table with an air of appetite.

'That's what we thought,' said Aunt Milly, 'but it's not like you, Mr Morpurgo, to say a thing like that out loud.'

'I don't mind,' I said.

'The tears came of nothing but hurt pride,' said Mr Morpurgo, 'and she's going to tell you a story of gangster life that may entertain you. But let her eat first. She's had no lunch.'

'No lunch? Silly girl,' said Uncle Len. 'That way madness lies.'

As we sat down at the table Aunt Lily asked, 'But where's Queenie?'

Over Mr Morpurgo's face passed the expression he always wore when he enjoyed witnessing a drama that he knew he should not enjoy because it was so serious for its participants. He answered smoothly, 'Gone to Nancy's, with old Mr Bates.'

'Glory, how did that happen?' asked Len, the carving-knife in mid-air.

'He came down to our table when she was with us,' said Mr Morpurgo, sucking his secret knowledge like a jujube.

'Was he civil?' asked Lily nervously.

'He was just right,' said Mr Morpurgo. Obviously this was a monstrous assertion. Yet I found myself unable to quarrel with it.

'Len, go on carving but for Pete's sake turn the joint upside down and begin where you ought,' said Milly.

'Wait a bit, wait a bit,' said Len.

'You go ahead and do as I say,' said Aunt Milly. 'I've a feeling for joints.'

'You make me nervous, looking at me with that thought in your eye,' said Len.

'I'm not looking at you,' said Aunt Milly. 'Looking at you when you are carving makes me think of something I once read about an explorer, his plight was horrible, they wrote, he had lost his compass and had no natural sense of the North.'

'If old Mr Bates hadn't been civil,' began Aunt Lily, in a menacing manner, and stopped.

'If old Mr Bates hadn't been civil and you'd been round he'd have found he had lost his compass and had no natural sense of the North,' said Len.

'Why would Mr Bates have either?' asked Aunt Lily. 'He's not an explorer.' She took it well when everybody jeered at her, saying, 'You know, ever since I've been a little thing people have laughed at me, because I'm so logical. But I can't help it, it's the way I'm made.'

There was then some thoughtful conversation as to whether there was or was not a natural sense of the North, which lasted until Uncle Len said, 'But what about Rose's story?'

I had no desire to tell it, not because it represented me as the victim of humiliation, but because I was no longer a part of it. I had this massive conviction at the back of my mind that some great event had taken place and the course of life was now altered and clear before me, with the result that everything that had yet happened was unimportant. It was as if I were

221

spending the night in a camp stuck by a broad river which was spanned by a huge bridge, built to a great height, span upon span, like the Pont du Gard, which I must cross tomorrow morning very early, to make my way along a road to the mountains where my life was to be, not because I had chosen to live there, but because my life had been transported there, without my consent, without my previous knowledge, by forces not to be resisted, not to be judged.

What did it matter what had happened yesterday in another continent? It was utterly beyond me why I should have this illusion of change that could fill my mind with images of vast architecture, of journeys from which there could be no return. If my double sherry had made me drunk its power must since have worn off. But then I had been a little mad all day. Why had I stood by the Thames and wept and said I wanted to give up playing, a step which now seemed to be hideous? I was conscious too that I had committed some other folly earlier in the day, which I now felt reluctant to remember. There was a singing in my ears and I found thought difficult. Yet I was not simply feverish. This sense of some enormous event, a huge pillar suddenly erected in the middle of my landscape, joining the earth to the clouds, was not a delusion. For as Mr Morpurgo sat eating his roast lamb he was hoarding just such a recognition of the tremendous. He was chubby but he was awed. At one point while I was telling Len and Milly and Lily my story of the night at Barbados Hall he took a jar of redcurrant jelly and forgot his intention to give himself a helping, and then passed into a sort of trance. What I had seen he had seen also.

So uninterested in my story was I that I had to tell it on technique, as one has to play when one is very tired. My hearers were all indignant and I had to force myself to accept graciously their sympathetic explanations, although what I wanted to do was to go upstairs to my bed and lie down on it and sleep until I had to start on my way next morning. I thought of myself as lying down fully dressed, so sensible was I of the need to start early.

'Ah well!' they all said at last, getting up and starting to clear the table. 'People with every opportunity, that's what I can't understand' – 'Well, it takes all sorts to make a world' – 'I wouldn't say that, there's sorts that unmake the world.' Then Lily halted. 'Queenie's not back.'

I looked in terror at Mr Morpurgo. Perhaps Mr Bates was

praying beside Queenie's dead body, which he had offered as a sacrifice to his vengeful God. But first Mr Morpurgo shook his head and then gave me a reassuring nod.

'I'll leave the back door open, then,' said Uncle Len.

'I hope he's not give her the rough side of his preaching tongue,' said Aunt Lily apprehensively. 'Queenie's so sensitive, if someone spoke unkindly to her, it wouldn't be hard to break her heart.'

Again I sought Mr Morpurgo's eyes. But again he shook his head.

When at last I got to bed, I neither slept nor was awake, I was still split in two. Surely I did not sleep, for I could look up at my ceiling and see the cracks on the plaster that drew something like an outline sketch of Paderewski. I could look out at the dark tracery the wisteria round my blindless window drew against the stars, and sometimes I turned on my light, and sometimes I turned it off. But I neither thought nor felt, I was a suspended intelligence conscious of nothing but the persistent ringing in my ears and this sense that something had been settled. It was the law, the law had been established, it would be maintained. When ordinary sleep came to me, that sense of settlement came with me into my dreams, and when I woke, it was to know that disputation was over. I had to get to town as quickly as possible, and I rose at once and washed and dressed, I did not know the hour, for I had left my wrist-watch somewhere during the previous day, I had thrown time away. But the morning had the pearly light, I could hear the vacuum cleaner going in one of the rooms. They would all be about, I would probably not be able to get the potboy to take me over on the ferry and slip away without breakfast. But I would try. I padded softly downstairs, with my bag in my hand, and let myself out into the stableyard, where the potboy would probably be at this moment.

But I found Uncle Len there. He was comforting Oswald, who was shuddering as if he were cold, and wearing a raincoat, though the day was fine and warm. He had not shaved.

'Come on, young fellow my lad,' Uncle Len was saying. 'What is it that's making you look so sickish?'

'It is what my father has done,' said Oswald.

'Has he definitely been caught out doing anything?' asked Uncle Len. The implication of his speech might have distressed a less distracted Oswald, so plain was it that neither Oswald's

223

wounded feelings, nor the allegation that old Mr Bates had shown an unworthy side of his character, worried Uncle Len very much. So long as there was no question of the police being called in he would remain unmoved.

'It's this,' said Oswald, taking an envelope out of his pocket. 'We found it on the mat this morning, and I cannot believe it.'

Uncle Len put out his hand for it.

Aunt Lily pushed past me through the doorway where I was standing. 'Len,' she called shrilly. 'Queenie hasn't been back all night.'

'What goings on,' said Len, looking down on the letter he held in his hand.

'My God, what's Os doing here so early in the morning?' asked Aunt Lily, and her suspicion made her scream. 'I knew it. Your bloody father's preached at her, and the sensitive little darling's made away with herself.'

'Naoh!' jeered Uncle Len. 'She's been a sensible girl and chosen a fate worse than death. Or sort of. Let me finish reading this.'

'I can't understand Nancy not minding,' said Oswald. Almost weeping, he complained, 'It's so undignified, at their age.'

'It's so undignified at any age,' said Uncle Len. 'Listen, dignity's hardly the object of the exercise. I'll just give you the sense of it, and you can read it yourself at your own pace. It seems your sister and Os's pa didn't get to Nancy's last night. He took her to the house of Brother and Sister Clerkenwell and they wrestled in prayer all night, and he won her for the Lord God, and they are going to marry. And so they are going to marry, is how he puts it. Though how the Lord God and their marriage mix in together I don't know, but read it for yourself and work that one out.'

Lily could not take the letter. She supported herself against the doorpost. 'You mean Mr Bates is going to marry Queenie?'

'That's what he says.'

'But are you sure,' stammered Aunt Lily, 'that he realises just how – how high-spirited Queenie's been?'

'Oh, Lil, you are a worrier,' expostulated Uncle Len affectionately. 'Of course he knows all about that. Everybody does. And the matter would have been bound to come out during this all-night prayer-meeting, I would think. Though I've no experience of this kind of night wrestling between a man and a woman. But what's eating you over this, young Os? Here, pull yourself together and take the letter, Lily. Psst. Os. Step over here for a minute. And you come here too.' He drew us towards the opposite corner of the yard and casting an eye over his shoulder at Lil, said, 'Here, Os, if you're worrying about her doing it over again, your pa's safe. She was a lot younger then and this man Phillips was a good chap, but soft, who didn't know how to keep her down. Take it from me, she'll be all right with your pa. They're the same sort really.'

'But it's not right at their age,' said Oswald, obstinately.

'Milly!' shrieked Lily. 'Milly!'

'Why not? You should be glad they have the health and spirits,' said Uncle Len. 'God, you're young, Os.'

'Milly!' Lily shrieked again. 'Milly!'

Milly came through the doorway with a feather duster in her hand. Lily handed her the letter, she read it, said, 'What of it?' and went away again. I had had no idea till then how oppressive her matter-of-fact mind had found Queenie's dramatic quality.

But Lily sat down on a barrel and said to us, 'But I can't like it!'

'Why not?' said Uncle Len.

'Why not?' repeated Lily. 'Well, what's old Mr Bates to give her we couldn't give her here? What's she want to go off with him for? Though it makes her happy.' She left us suddenly.

'I hate this preaching,' said Oswald suddenly, 'when science has proved there isn't a God. My father won't sit down and learn anything. He sits and talks this rot about the Heavenly Hostages. And as for marriage, my mother ought to have been enough for him.'

'Enough's something you can't be when you're dead. Those racehorses I got pictures of, they were all enough for the sport of kings when they were alive, dead they weren't enough for any but the cats to eat. It's a horrid thing, eating,' said Uncle Len, and suddenly lifted up his voice. 'Milly! Breakfast ready?'

'For how many?' Milly replied from the kitchen window.

'Bacon and eggs for four,' said Uncle Len.

'For five,' said Mr Morpurgo from his window on the first floor. He had been leaning out of it for some time.

'Not for me,' said Oswald. 'I couldn't touch a thing.'

'You're squeamish over this wedding, aren't you?' enquired

Uncle Len with clinical interest. 'Try a nice fried egg and some real fat Wiltshire back.'

Oswald shuddered and said, 'I got this taxi waiting. I'll be late for school if I don't hurry.'

'Creeping like a snail unwillingly to school,' said Uncle Len. 'Well, ta ta.'

His hands on his hips, he watched Oswald go out to the taxi, then said to me, beaming maliciously, 'Funny thing how you can turn up anybody that's poorly by mentioning a fried egg. When I was in my first job as a bookie's clerk I had a horrible boss, Hyams was the name. I could get my own back when he woke up with a hangover by saying, innocent as a lamb, "What, not a nice fried egg, Mr Hyams?" Now, I could eat a wolf this minute. I've always been one to make a good breakfast. And so have you, Rose. It's been a great comfort, the amount you and Mary can put away. Come on and show us what you can do.'

As we sat down at the breakfast table we were joined by Mr Morpurgo. 'Lovely smell, frying bacon,' said Uncle Len. 'That's the smell I hope will come through the pearly gates as they swing ajar for me. I haven't no use for a heaven where there wouldn't be grub. Grub. And girls,' he added, smacking Aunt Milly's behind as she put his plate before him and passed on to me.

'Be ashamed of yourself,' she said, mechanically.

'This is no day for shame,' he said, 'it is a marriage day! For Christ's sake bring in Lily. She's weeping over the sink, she always goes running over the sink, I'll be bound, when she's upset.'

'Well, you can't hear her if she is,' said Aunt Milly.

'But I can feel her,' complained Uncle Len. 'Dripping into the sink, doing the taps out of a job. I'm sick of weeping women. Rose was piping her eyes yesterday. I'd like a lot of busty cheerful women such as you might have blowing trumpets on music-hall ceilings, that's what I'd like. Send Lil in, I mean it, Milly. And sit down yourself.'

In a minute Aunt Lily was with us, sniffling. 'I couldn't touch a thing,' she said through her handkerchief.

'Oh, go on, that's what Os said. I wouldn't have had you in the house all these years if you'd been the same sort of bleater as poor old Os. Here, you got some bacon and eggs for her, Milly? Drop your muzzle to that nosebag and don't let me hear

226

another neigh.' Aunt Lily was so like a horse that Mr Morpurgo and I felt this admonition as an indelicacy, but she obeyed without protest. 'That's right,' said Uncle Len, 'and don't you be a silly girl no more. Your sister Queenie wanted something to fill her life, and she's got it.'

'He's an old bastard of a preacher,' said Lily. 'He'll be bringing up you know what against her all the time, she'll slip back.'

'He won't be bringing any you know what against her,' said Uncle Len. 'He won't have time, he'll be doing you know what to her as often as his years permit him.'

'Len, hush yourself!' said Aunt Milly.

'Preachers are against that sort of thing,' wept Aunt Lily.

'You're just simple,' said Uncle Len. 'Many of them become preachers because they are so much for that sort of thing that they get worried. I could tell you. I seen a lot of life in my time. But another time. Anyway, that old Bates, he's keen on it all right. I can tell you.'

'You're being coarse,' said Aunt Milly. 'What Rose and Mr Morpurgo will think of you I don't know, and, anyway, how could you tell if he was keen on it? We haven't seen him except that time by the river and half a dozen times at Nancy's, and he was hollering his head off about the Heavenly Hostages. How can you tell, Mr Clever?'

'I can tell,' said Uncle Len. 'He knows the quality of a bit of skirt. When Oswald told him it was Nancy that was his young lady and not Mary or Rose the old man had a look on his face like a customer who's been served with chicken and gets dark meat when he's wanted white. So'd anybody, a man who cares about women, if it was a question of having Nancy or having Mary or Rose.'

'Nancy's a good girl,' said Aunt Milly.

'Of course she's a good girl,' said Uncle Len. 'We're not talking of that. We're talking of –' He put down his knife and fork, described the female form in the air, and then took them up again.

'Well, if he's just a dirty old man,' said Aunt Lily, 'what's there in Queenie in that?'

'There's a lot to be said for being a dirty old man,' said Uncle Len, 'it's a lot more fun than just being an old man. You've got ways of passing the time, and the time of whoever's with you, and anyway who says it's dirty? Os would and he's always wrong.' He bent enthusiastically to his plate.

'You'll excuse Len,' Aunt Milly said to Mr Morpurgo and me. 'He's upset.'

'I am not upset,' said Uncle Len. 'I'm glad. There was poor Queenie looking more and more like a waterlogged punt every day, and here she's rushed off down the river like a smart motor-launch from one of those Maidenhead houses. Oh, Lily, sit up and be honest. Something's happened to Queenie, and this in itself is a good thing. But you two.' He put down his knife and fork, and stared at Mr Morpurgo and me. 'You two were in it. You knew.'

'No,' I said.

'Maybe you didn't. But Morpurgo there thought there was something. No use saying you didn't, and I know you when you look as if you'd eaten the canary. Tell us what happened.'

'Nothing,' said Mr Morpurgo.

'Must have been something.'

'Well, obviously there was something,' said Mr Morpurgo. 'But it didn't look like very much. She was coming towards our table, and he intercepted her, and after they had talked for a little they went away together.'

'You didn't hear what they said to each other?'

We shook our heads.

'But you said they'd gone off to Nancy's. What made you think that? They didn't. They went to Brother and Sister Clerkenwell. God, ain't that a shame. I'm sorry they didn't get down to it at once.'

'Len!'

'Well, something tells me they didn't. Even when I was a young man and set on it, and Rose isn't a kid any more and anyway she needn't understand me if she doesn't want to, even when I was a young man, I'm saying, and I met a girl I fancied, I wouldn't take her to stay with a couple who called themselves Brother and Sister Clerkenwell, and hope we'd feel any better in the morning.'

Aunt Lily said, 'Yes, it all seems unnatural, doesn't it? But they're old. We're all old.'

'We're not so damned old,' said Uncle Len, 'and Queenie and Mr Bates, in a manner of speaking, aren't old at all. Oh, Lil, stop being silly. They'll give each other an interest. I don't know what he can manage now. It varies from all I hear. But if all he can do is kiss Queenie on Easter Sunday morning, his mind will be going further than that, and so will hers. They'll have an interest.'

The telephone rang, and Lily sprang from her seat, saying, 'It may be Queenie.'

'Poor duck,' said Uncle Len, looking after her as she went out, 'it won't be Queenie. A funny thing, the way, Lil not having been married or anything, she can't understand. Rose here hasn't either, but from what I gather your music tells you everything. But Lil can't understand that male and female created He them. For what it's worth. And anyway it's worth a lot.' He emptied his cup of tea, and lit his pipe, and, nodding over it, left the room, pausing at the door to say, 'Hell it must be, to be the sort of man who feels up to the old rough and tumble with Queenie, who, let's face it, is a terror, and who's got Os for an only son.'

When he had gone Aunt Milly said, 'I've never known Len so coarse.'

Mr Morpurgo answered, 'He was sensible enough.'

'But he doesn't understand how well it works out,' said Milly. 'Nancy would never have got an upstanding chap like Len or old Mr Bates, but she can hope one of the children'll be a throw-back. And Os will never know. But half the things in life people never know. Thank God for that.' And she too left us.

Mr Morpurgo said, 'Rose, I am thinking of your mother. This is her work. She turned none of the family away. She took in Lily, she held out her hand to protect Queenie, she was a mother to Nancy. So they were all still linked. Through Lily Queenie and Nancy came her, through Nancy Queenie has found –' He broke off. 'Let us go into the garden.'

'First I must telephone to London,' I said. 'I must see someone this afternoon. I will go home and take some flowers in, then I must go and have my hair done. I will just have time.'

'How collected you are,' he said. 'Yesterday you could not stop weeping. You wanted never to make any plans again. Now you are as you have always been.'

'No,' I said. 'I must be ill. I have been so many people in the last twenty-four hours, most of them quite idiotic. I still cannot think of anything or remember anything.'

'It would seem to me,' he said, 'that you were thinking quite a lot systematically.'

When I had spoken to Kate and made my hair appointment with Miss White and got a taxi to meet me on the other side of the ferry, I said goodbye to the family and went into the garden, and waited till we saw the taxi drive up on the opposite bank.

'You said that through Nancy Queenie had found something, and then you broke off,' I said. 'Surely you meant to say a husband. Why did you break off? Do you not think they are going to marry?'

'Of course they are going to marry. But I did not want to say that Queenie had found a husband, for that might mean nothing. It might mean that she had found a husband which was as much use to her as' – his hand performed the counter-caress it often gave his face, it traced the path of his self-loathing from feature to feature – 'as many husbands are to many wives.'

'You mean he will be a companion to her.'

'No,' he said. Then added coldly, 'There is no substitute for sex. I would not be glad if she has merely found someone to play two-handed patience with her. When they looked at each other yesterday evening it was like something I have seen in the streets where a man picks up a streetwalker. That is a curious recommendation. But there is no use in any relationship between a man and a woman which is not one note in a scale, the lowest note of which is not just that, the sort of thing that makes a man go out into the street to look for a woman, that makes a woman stand in the night waiting for a man. It is a pity, but it is so. Or is it not a pity? No. Len can bear that it should be so. Oswald Bates cannot bear it. Len is right, of course.'

He had been speaking in a soft Oriental murmur. He came back to his ordinary voice to say, 'There is your taxi.' We strolled down the lawn towards the punt, and he said, murmuring again, 'I was glad I saw their meeting. Now it seems possible I did witness some classic performance of the raffish kind, perhaps a vicious youth drinking champagne from a dancer's slipper, and that will be just that, yet so much more. For of course that meeting we saw was much more than a man and a woman picking each other up for their last possibility of gratification.'

'Yes, but what was it that happened?' I said. 'I could not understand. But it shook me, it is what is shaking me now, why I cannot think.'

'We heard Mr Bates doing for Queenie what your mother would have done for her,' said Mr Morpurgo, 'and what all the rest have failed to do. He took her seriously. That is the great thing one needs in the world. To be taken seriously. In practice one cannot get it from more than one person. How curious it all is. Goodbye, dear Rose. I hope whatever is going on goes well, and I cannot help seeing that something is going on.'

The house in St John's Wood would be full of flowers, sent to me by friends and by people who had heard me play. But it seemed to me necessary that I should buy a great many flowers myself to decorate the house for that afternoon. I stopped the taxi at a florist's a long way from my home, in North Audley Street, because I felt secretive about this purchase, and after some indecision, since, though it was a big shop, none of the flowers seemed quite good enough, I bought a great many gladioli. I spent a ridiculous amount of money, for far more flowers than I could possibly use. If I put them all in vases the place would have looked like the Chelsea Show. But I felt obliged to have tall glasses in the drawing-room, each holding some scarlet gladioli, some crimson, some rose, some orange, some of that kind that are nearly black. But they sold them only by the dozen of separate colours, so I had to buy five dozen. I hoped I would get into the house without Mary or Kate meeting me and questioning me about this imbecile purchase. They were actually hard to fit in the taxi, they were so long. As we drove past Lord's the sight of the white girl praying on the tomb filled me with repulsion; it is not a good statue, she is coarsely made, surely she would not be given what she wanted. Yet there is something beautiful about the act of prayer, it lent her the beauty she did not possess in her own right, perhaps what she desired would come to her. What one does can surely make one more deserving than what one is. I wish I had not travelled to a country where there were laws I did not know, or perhaps no laws at all.

I had no time to turn my key in the lock of the front door. Kate opened it for me. I could hear someone playing in my music-room; whoever it was must have left the soundproof door open, and was not playing at all well. Kate explained that it was Oliver, who had telephoned that morning, and had on hearing that I would be back by half past eleven said that he would come then and not wait for the appointment he had made with me for the afternoon.

'Oh, this has spoiled it all!' I said, throwing my flowers down on the floor. 'I will not have time to put these in the tall glasses in the drawing-room. And I had planned to have my hair done!'

'Here is your brush and comb, I brought them down,' she said. 'Stand by the glass and I will give you a neater head. It is not as if your hair really needs washing.'

'But it does,' I said, 'it does.'

'No, no, you had it washed and set only three days ago,' she said placidly. 'When you said that you had made an appointment with Miss White for this morning I knew you must be in one of your states, though you have no more concerts.'

'But the flowers,' I said.

'I will put them in water for you,' she told me.

'But I wanted only one of each kind in each glass.'

'I could do things even more difficult than that,' said Kate. 'Now let me run a comb round the back of your neck, and you can run along.'

Where the three steps from the passage rose to the music-room I halted. The playing continued, and Kate had gathered up the five paper-shrouded sheaves from the floor and taken them into the housemaid's cupboard where the vases were kept. There was nobody to stop me if I went out of the house. But I went up the first step and stood listening only, I thought, to protect myself by analysing to the full limit of justifiable contempt this obtuse playing. Oliver was pounding out the second movement of Mozart's Piano Concerto in C Minor. The piano had been his second subject when he was at the Athenaeum, but his technique, and he must have had some, I supposed, had perished beneath the deadly influence of com-position, which, except in the case of such rare and inhuman geniuses as Busoni, makes people quite unable to play the piano except in a crude utilitarian sense. A composer sits down at the keyboard and plays as if he were a strong man using a blunt tin-opener. They do not want to hear the music as the composer wants an audience to hear it; they want to exhaust its ideas and inform themselves how those ideas appeared to the composer at the moment of their inception, so that they can separate (as an audience should not be allowed to do) the matter from the manner. They unpick the work instead of sewing it together. It is a thing offensive to the pianists, unless the composer who plays is greater than the composer whose work he is maltreating. I could not think Oliver a greater composer than Mozart, though for an instant I found myself possessed by the insane hope that in some future work he might prove himself to be this. Then I asked myself what I, who played Mozart so well, by comparison with nearly every other pianist, was doing bothering myself with this man who insisted on spending his life composing so much less well than Mozart. I knew also that this was an idiotic kind of arithmetic, and then again that even by its idiotic laws I was wrong. I went up to the second step and stopped again. The difficult thing about the C minor concerto is that it is elegant and light in texture, yet is tragic, it records endurance of the deepest suffering, of the ultimate doubt. It is extremely difficult not to impair one or other of these qualities, which would seem to be incompatible, and would be so in any other composer's work. The problem is presented in its most acute form in the second movement, where what old people call 'a pretty little tune' is the voice of sorrow itself, lamenting a loss which has really happened, which cannot be converted to a profit by looking at it in any different way. I was gritting my teeth at hearing this tune not even allowed to be difficult in its own subtle way, as it was poked out of the keyboard, when Oliver broke off and repeated, with a delicacy which I had not believed within his powers, the first four bars of the movement, in which the tune is first presented in all its prettiness. The third time he played it he achieved a certain colour of tone in the second bar which somehow solved the problem and established it on the level of classical dignity. I had never thought of this effect. Why had I never thought of it? Because I had a lower order of musical intelligence than he had. I might be a better pianist than he was a composer but to be a creative artist with any valid title to the name is a better thing than to be an interpreter. He was much my superior, and I tingled with pleasure. But all this was irrelevant, even had he not been a musician I could not have obeyed my almost irresistible desire to leave the house. I mounted the third step, and Oliver saw me through the open door.

He stopped playing and stood up. I went into the room and we faced each other, trembling.

A look of guilt came over his face and passed. He said exultantly, 'Now I can love again.'

It struck me to the heart that he should put it in those words, but my deepest self said coldly that so long as I had him nothing else mattered. He came towards me and I became rigid with disgust, it seemed certain that I must die when he touched me, but instead, of course, I lived.

233

VIII

IN OUR BED in the villa by the Mediterranean my husband slid
from my body and said, 'How I hate all Wagner. *Tristan and
Isolde* is nothing like it, is it? It is so sharp and clear, and the
Tristan music is like two fat people eating thick soup. Drinking
thick soup,' he corrected himself pedantically, and yawned,
and nuzzled his face against my shoulder, and was asleep. I ran
my arm down his straight back. When I had thought of his face
in the train to Reading, it had seemed to me more right than
nature could make it, it was as if a master craftsman had
worked on it. His body was like that too. I enjoyed everything
about being married, though I could not have endured it with
any other husband but Oliver. I was amazed at lovemaking. It
was so strange to come, when I was nearly middle-aged, on the
knowledge that there was another state of being than any I had
known, and that it was the state normal for humanity, that I
was a minority who did not know it. It was as if I had learned
that there was a sixth continent, which nearly everybody but
me and a few others had visited and in which, now I had come
to it, I felt like a native, or as if there was another art as well
as music and painting and literature, which was not only
preached, but actually practised, by nearly everybody, though
they were silent about their accomplishment. It was fantastic
that nobody should speak of what pervaded life and determined it, yet it was inevitable, for language could not describe
it. I looked across Oliver at the window, which we had opened
after we had put out the light and there was no fear of attracting
mosquitoes. There was the sea, glittering with moonlight, the
dark mountains above it, then the sky dusted with other
earths, which looking at us might not know that our globe was

swathed in this secret web of nakedness that kept it from being naked of people, chilly with lack of love and life, a barren top spinning to no purpose. Their architecture would be as fantastic but would not be the same, because there were not two of anything alike, every person was different, every work of art was different, every act of love was different, every world was different. It was a pity we did not know the end to which this wealth was to be put, but surely if this plenitude existed, and not the nothingness which somehow seemed to be more natural, more what one would have expected (though it is the one state of which the universe had and could have no experience), we might conclude that all would be well. I could believe that this precious intricate creature I held in my arms, who made love and wrote music, would never be destroyed.

I was amazed by the wealth that had suddenly come to me. I ran my hand over him again. It was a pity I had had to give up something to get this. Mary and I were not as we had been. It was a pity that I had learned this on the very same day that Oliver and I had learned we loved each other, for I could never deceive myself into imagining her recoil from my new state as lover to be simply material distance, but the forking of our several paths through our professions. I was alone that evening, for Oliver had telephoned his solicitor to ask him how we could get married as soon as possible, so that we could have the longest time abroad before the concert season began again, and the solicitor was going on his holidays and would not see him except after dinner. So I lay on the sofa in the drawing-room, wondering at the new properties of my body and my soul, and waiting till Mary came home, to see her pass with grace from the old world I had lived in till that day to the new world that had just received me. When she came in I was enraptured by the sight of her, for she had spent all her day shopping and tying up loose ends that could not be left till we returned, and she was not tired or fretted, she was serene as the swans that had glided by me on the dark waters the night before, her silk dress was not crumpled. She could make any transit calmly, even if it were as strange as this. But not a second passed after I spoke before I knew that I had made a vast miscalculation, and that the sum was not to work out so that my books would balance.

She cried out, 'You are going to marry! You are going to marry Oliver,' so that all I could do was to laugh and

235

expostulate, 'Why do you say it like "Gone to be married! gone to swear a peace!"?'

She did not answer me, but stood staring, her parcels at her feet, as my flowers had been. I said, 'But you like Oliver!'

'Yes, of course, but what has that to do with it?'

'Well, a great deal,' I said. 'I like him very much. I like him so much that I love him. It is an extreme that might be reached from that starting-point, don't you think?'

She wanted to agree, but she could not say the words. She shut her eyes, then opened them. 'Look,' she smiled, 'I am shutting my eyes, as I do when the Queen of the Night in *The Magic Flute* is going to take her top F, as I do when we go to a theatre and I know somebody on the stage is going to fire a gun, or when we go to a horse show and they keep on putting the fences higher and higher. I am frightened.'

'So am I,' I said, 'but millions of people, millions and millions of people, almost all people since the world began have got married.'

'Yes,' she said, dropping on her knees and finding a paper bag and taking out a bunch of gentians. 'Look, I found these for you,' she said, laughing and posing the gentians against my hair, 'and, forgive me for bringing up the matter at this moment, but absolutely everybody since the world began has died. There's nothing in that argument. But, oh, darling Rose, how glad I am that you are happy!' Shuddering, she embraced me. 'Rose, Rose, I hope Oliver understands I will kill him if he makes you unhappy. Oh, all of you are getting married, Rosamund, and Nancy, and you!' The disgusted distortion of her mouth made it plain. 'But never me, I will never marry!'

I said, 'And more than me!' and told her about Queenie and Oswald's father.

'Why, it is like the end of *Der Ring der Nibelungen*, with everybody getting burned!' she exclaimed.

It could be conceived, I supposed, that my marriage was the end, a violent end. But I did not like it so. I cried out, 'It will all be just the same as before. I will go on living here, we must buy the little house next door, it has been for sale for so long. Oliver does not like where he is living, and if he uses the house next door for a music-room and a study, we can fit in on my side of the house.'

'No, no,' she protested. 'Oliver is not marrying me. You will not want a sister, a confidante in white linen. I will go away,' she said, almost blithely.

'Go away!' I exclaimed. 'But where?'

'I went to see a woman in a curious house last week,' she said, 'and she is giving it up. It would suit me perfectly. It is a high building that was once part of a waterworks, in Stoke Newington, not really so far, a little further north than this. It is something to do with some waterworks that are not used now. One could practise whenever one liked, and one could be quite alone. I have never been in a place anywhere in London,' she said with a sudden shining exultation, 'where one could be quite so much alone.'

It was as if she was saying to herself, 'Rose is going away to do this wild and unpleasant thing, I will go away to cling more closely to my delicious safety. You can all burn on your nuptial pyres, I will be above you, in the high, cool air.' It was the thirst for pleasure in her eye which made me miserable. Could it be possible that she would have liked to leave me and live alone, rather than be with me, and that she had not mentioned the visit to this tower, which had evidently powerfully impressed her, simply because it had impressed her by reason of the opportunity it would offer her for complete solitude if she lived there alone, and she did not care to speak to me about it lest she betrayed how she would have preferred not to share a home with me. I wondered if she loved me as much as I loved her, and I feared that it would be my lot always to love more than I was loved. I remembered how Oliver had said, 'Now I can love again,' and not simply, in forgetfulness of all but me, 'I love you.' I wished Richard Quin and Rosamund were with me, because they both spared me this anguish, they both loved me as much as I loved them. But how could that be? How had they managed that? How was it that with them this particular situation could not possibly have arisen, that I could never have felt this sense, strong enough to pay a visit to me in the heights of my happiness, that I was slighted? I knew the answer as I asked it. They loved absolutely, as I could not. Richard Quin and Rosamund would have loved any partner so much that they would have accepted a reference to a previous love as a confidence and not a slight. If anyone they loved had said he or she wanted to go away and live alone their minds would have run to the new home, wondering with what gifts they could garnish it. I prayed for Richard Quin to intercede for me with the God it was so hard for us to approach from our special point of view, to make me able to love better, and I said to Mary, 'I must telegraph to Rosamund and ask her to the wedding. I will do it now, for there is not much time. Oliver wants to be married as soon as possible. Help me with it.'

'Soon,' murmured Mary, infinitely troubled, and I thought to myself, 'Oh, you love me, you would choose to go on living with me even though it meant sacrificing the joy of solitude, for the sake of keeping me from this fearful thing, the top F, the gun going off on the stage, the six-foot jump.' She went on to exclaim, 'Yes, let us send a telegram at once. It will be wonderful, when Rosamund comes you will be able to talk to her about marriage, she will perhaps tell you why she married Nestor and left us.'

I cried, 'No, she will never tell us, because the reason can have nothing to do with marriage.' The delight I had already experienced from the touch of Oliver's lips and arms shivered through my veins. 'Oh, no, oh, no, she married him for some noble, unselfish purpose that she could least of all tell a woman who, like me, was marrying simply to be happy.'

'Oh, Rose,' said Mary, in wonder, 'do you really feel like that? I am so glad.'

But obviously she felt as puzzled as if she had returned to the house that evening to find me wearing marigold wreaths and putting out saucers of clarified butter and doing nautch dances in the Hindu style of worship before our gas-stove. It would have been pleasant if she could have understood something of what I was feeling, and it was strange, it disturbed my heart, that she did not understand nearly as well as Kate or Miss Beevor, who were so virginal and so inexperienced. Both of them realised that I was in a state of holy drunkenness in which there was nothing of illusion or folly. They knew I was thinking of Oliver as if he were all summer, all music, all joy, all worth, and teased me about this foolishness, but they knew it was a necessary step towards wisdom, they knew also that I was engaged in an athletic feat involving my whole organism. I do think it probable that Miss Beevor had no clear idea at all of the act of love, and that Kate saw it austerely, as a part of magic, as a kind of rite like curtsying to the new moon, practised by practitioners of another sort of magic than hers, but they understood well just what I had to do to carry myself along to it. It was a matter of anxiety to me that I would have to let my husband see me with no clothes on, for I knew that my face was considered all right and I felt sure Oliver thought it beautiful but I was not sure how my body, which was perhaps too thin and boyish, would please. I felt as if I had suddenly been told that I had not really got my diploma from the Athenaeum School of Music, which I thought I had gained years before, and had to sit for another examination.

I had also to lift myself to a state where I could advance to as extreme a form of spiritual intimacy as I had ever known, challenging in its confusion with the physical, with somebody who I had thought of all my life as a predestined stranger, and my nerves had to push me towards this climactic achievement. Every word of the old-fashioned raillery that came from Kate and Miss Beevor helped to this end, also the old-fashioned fuss they made; for though it was the case that a trousseau was absurd, since fashions now changed so rapidly that it was absurd to get more than a couple of dresses and a suit at one time, and our underclothing now was made not of cambric that soon lost its surface but of silks and satins that survived many washings, nevertheless Kate and Miss Beevor forced the idea of a trousseau on me, and I made new purchases that kept me busy during the few days that elapsed before my marriage. I was not at first to realise that Kate and Miss Beevor, knowing nothing, knew all that was to the point, and at first it appeared possible to me that Cordelia might be a help.

I came down to breakfast the day after I had become engaged and was glad to see that Mary was not there. I had awakened with a sense of danger that passed at once into ecstasy at my happiness, into incredulous wonder that the world could hold such a marvellous experience as was to be mine when I met Oliver for luncheon in Kensington Gardens. But when I looked at Mary's place at the breakfast table I was afraid that she might revive my sense of danger that I might feel disgusted again, that I might flee from my joy. I knew now what my father felt. There was a rightness in winter; it would be fitting if winter came and was not succeeded by spring and lasted for ever; I would have a sort of sanctity if I denied myself to love and continuity. Only I knew from my mother that such sanctity was evil, was too safe, it meant coming to an end instead of working perpetually, as she and Richard Quin were now at work. In this Mary was, suddenly, on my father's side.

I said to Kate, 'This morning I will go and tell Cordelia.'

She answered, busy over the toaster, 'Your Mamma will be pleased at that.'

239

'I am not doing it because I am feeling priggish,' I said. 'I really want to see Cordy.'

'That is what will please your Mamma,' said Kate. 'They say if you love a changeling enough it turns into the real child.'

She meant what she implied as a literal statement of fact. It was a startling idea even in our household.

'She wasn't a changeling,' I said. 'She had the same red hair as Papa's father.'

'They think of everything,' said Kate.

'You are a superstitious old thing,' I said. 'I suppose you'll want to tie me up with all sorts of amulets and charms on my wedding-day. What is it, something old, something new, something borrowed and something blue?'

'That is all nonsense,' said Kate, in a cold, rationalist tone. 'The ring is all that is needed. It does the work of everything.'

It was about half past eleven when I got to Cordelia's house, I knew she would have done her shopping by then. It was not as pretty as her first house, most of the prettiest houses in London are very small. But Alan's father and mother had died, and they were better off, and they had bought a nice Regency house in one of the older squares, and it was still a charming frame for their good looks and their delightful possessions. Since they had money to spare, Cordelia had collected Italian pictures by the minor landscape masters of the late seventeenth and eighteenth centuries, and among her clean furnitures and greens and golds of her chintzes and brocades and the faint neutral stripes of her wallpaper one got glimpses of palaces and temples and fortresses, against rich blue skies, over seas and lakes that looked warm. The foreground and the background of her life were pleasant, and as I went into her house she was standing there, looking as always so very pretty, with her red-gold curls and her fresh complexion and her neat features. She had been the prettiest young woman, she was now prettily entering middle-age. I was ravished by her and by the greeting she gave me. At once she asked me if I would like tea or coffee or perhaps there was a lot of ice cream left from the dinner-party she had given the night before. Yes, that had been very good, we would each have a plate of that. She rang the bell and gave orders to the parlourmaid and then turned aside, murmuring to herself, almost cooing, pleased because she could give me something that was really nice. She really liked giving, she had said to the parlourmaid, 'And mind you finish it in the kitchen, I will not want any at lunch.'

'I am trying to find a letter that would interest you,' she said. 'It was from our ambassador in Belgium, he was so pleased by your concert in Brussels. So nice for you to play at that festival.'

I said to her, 'Cordelia.' But she did not stop or turn her eyes to me, she was kind but never attentive.

'Cordelia,' I said, 'you remember Oliver?'

'Of course,' she said. 'Dear Oliver. So sad about poor Celia. How beautifully she sang.'

I said, 'Oliver has fallen in love with me.'

Her mental distance from me was so great that it took her a moment for my words to reach her. Then she stopped rustling the papers on her desk, and turned to me, with what we called her 'white look'. When she was troubled or baffled her blue-grey eyes seemed to get much lighter, almost white. She breathed deeply as if she had to collect her forces to meet a crisis. 'Oh, Rose, are you quite, quite sure?' she said.

I could not be unkind to her anxiety, so I at once explained, 'He has asked me to marry him. And we are going to be married as soon as possible, in a few days, we hope.'

She still stared, then suddenly nodded. No doubt she recalled to herself how extraordinarily lucky I had always been. 'How wonderful!' she exclaimed, sinking down into a chair. 'How wonderful! I suppose the poor man is very lonely. Alan will be so pleased. We were talking about you only the other night.' Her voice grew serious. It had evidently been a despairing conversation. 'It comes just at the right time. Oh, if only we could find someone for Mary! You met Oliver here, didn't you?'

'No,' I said. 'We met him years and years ago, when we were playing at a private concert.' I could not bring myself to say that it was the day we got our scholarships. One always spared her.

'But the first time you really talked to him was at a party here,' she persisted.

'No,' I said. 'No. He stayed with us in Norfolk, the first summer of the war.'

'But you were quite young then,' she said, frowning slightly. 'I know that you met him at dinner here, just after Celia died.'

'No,' I said. 'No.'

Yet, by the efforts she made to draw my marriage into the

orbit of her marriage, to free it from the worthlessness she thought inherent in anything that appertained to me, I could see that Alan and she meant much the same thing to each other as Oliver and I meant to each other. It was a pity. Mary knew all about me but she could not understand anything about marriage. Cordelia knew all about marriage but she had no contact with me; I was still the odd-looking and eccentric woman whose undeserved success could not last as the years went by, and I was nothing else. No part of me escaped distortion. She was astonished that Oliver would consent to live in our house in St John's Wood. 'It always seemed so. . .' Whatever I might be, our house was beautiful. Yet such power had she over me that I had to assure myself that my house must be lovely, because Mr Morpurgo had so much to do with it, and his taste was known to be exquisite, and because this and that friend of mine delighted in it. But this, of course, was what love between man and woman was for. One's family grew away from one, from the first unity divergencies developed; and at that point one started another relationship at the point of unity. I did not expect my marriage to be perfectly happy, though I was certain it would be so; and I put that certainty down to my intoxicated state. But if I was to be unhappy with Oliver as Mamma was unhappy with Papa that would be better than happiness. But perhaps it would be better to run away. But that was nonsense because I was going to be happy. I spent all day in such argument between extremes though I knew the argument was settled. Though I wanted to run across London to Oliver, even when I knew it would not be convenient, there were times I wanted to fly out of the house so that I would have gone before he entered it, I wished I could be sure this would end totally when I was married to Oliver, and I thought Rosamund might tell me this, even though her marriage was so strange a sort and so obviously inferior to mine.

But Rosamund did not come to my marriage. I got no answer to my invitation until late on the night before my wedding, when I was roused from my sleep by the telephone-bell and took down a long and loving telegram sent from Colombo, saying that she and Nestor were on their way to Australia and would be travelling for three months. Surely, in that Arabian Nights world, they could have broken their journey and chartered a plane to bring them to London and back. A diamond bracelet came from Cartier's. I could not understand.

I had Oliver. I buried my face against his shoulder and he grunted sleepily, and I said, 'It is Rose.' But he did not hear. I had Oliver, and all my dead, Papa and Mamma and Richard Quin, but not my living. Mary was still with me but what had been without a flaw was spoiled; and I had never had Cordelia. And as for Rosamund, perhaps I had never had her either. The next morning I was wakened by Oliver's kisses and I stared into his eyes and said, 'You are all I want, I do not care for Rosamund any more.'

His hands released me. 'Oh, my dear, that sounds sad.'

'Why should it sound sad that I want nobody but you?'

'We want nobody but each other but that does not mean turning people away. Rosamund, that is the girl you told me that you had loved, when we were at Barbados Hall. You have not spoken of her since then. But I could see you loved her a great deal. Not that it is easy for a man to understand about women loving each other.'

I feared a question in his voice. 'Oh, I am not a Lesbian,' I said. 'That has always seemed so queer to me, all homosexuality does, like a song Kate used to sing to us when we were children. Let me see how it went. . . . I can't remember.'

'I hope you can,' said Oliver. 'I gather you were brought up in a very strange way, but it really seems remarkable that your nurse should have sung you a song that has since seemed to you a satisfactory comment on Lesbianism.'

'I remember it now, "He cut his throat with a lump of cheese, and. . ." It went on like that, always the wrong instrument.'

'It seems so to us. You are made to be loved as a woman by a man, but I always knew that, even when I was not free to love anybody else. I used to notice how after you had played a concerto you used to smile at the conductor and the orchestra in a way that made a remote reference to love.'

'Oh, no!' I cried.

'You did indeed. The reference was prim and stately, but it was there. You would not have smiled like that at women anyway. But talk of Rosamund. I can't bear this thing of throwing people away, of turning them from the door, of stopping to care when one has once cared.' His body became harsh and taut in my arms. 'It is too like Jasperl. Tell me about Rosamund. I am on her side.'

'I cannot be bothered,' I said. 'It is so long a story. It goes back so far.'

'Listen,' he said. 'Just at this time, in the early morning, the sea gets up a little and the waves slap the rock.' We were quiet and listened. The windows looked west, and on the sky we saw the dilute reflection of the sunrise. The water lapped and was still and lapped again. I put my hand on his heart and felt the pulse. The two beats delighted me beyond all reason. 'It is so long a story, it goes back so far,' he repeated. 'Rosamund was brought up with you then?'

'Not from the first,' I said. 'She lived with her mother, who was Constance, who was my mother's schoolfriend, and her father, who was my mother's cousin. He was a horrible man. Beautiful and slender and very fair, he looked like somebody living in the eighteen twenties, he might have been a Lake District poet that had been invisible and so never got written about. He put on a horrible Scotch accent, like a Scotch comedian. He played the flute better than anybody I have ever heard.' I paused. I could not tell Oliver how Cousin Jock had stood in the street outside our house in Lovegrove while my mother died. It was strange, I was lying naked in bed with him, but I did not know him well enough for that. 'He was a horrible man,' I said lamely. 'He made quite a lot of money but he made them live in a dreadful street, almost a slum, and they had evil things in their house.'

I remembered Rosamund's studied nobility, that did not flinch when the forces of hell smeared her house with filth: how she had stood unmoved when the curtains were torn down from the windows and trodden into the filth, and dirty water had been thrown over the sheets.

Oliver said, 'What sort of evil things?'

'You know. You know.' I said the word shyly to the stranger. 'A poltergeist.'

'Oh, that. There was just Rosamund and her father and mother in the house? No other children.'

'None.'

'Then I suppose it was she who was working it.'

'Oh, no! Oh, no!' I pulled myself away from him and sat up. 'You must not think that of Rosamund. She would not have done that, and nobody could have done it. It was beyond anybody's power to produce the things I saw.'

'You saw them?'

'Yes. Three huge iron saucepans going round and round a clothes-line high in the air, and a big preserving-pan, done up in newspaper, because it was winter. And when we were picking up some curtains something twitched them out of our hands. And when Mamma and Constance had tea the forks and spoons flew round the room.'

'You saw that?'

'Yes, yes. As I see you now. And Rosamund did not do it.'

'Did it go on for a long time?'

'I don't remember hearing exactly how long it had gone on, I only saw it once. You see, we had been in Scotland and had just come down to live in South London, because Papa was made editor of a local newspaper, and Constance did not ask Mamma to come and see her, because she did not want her to see the poltergeist. But she could not bear not to send us Christmas presents, so then Mamma knew it was all right, and we went over to see them. And the poltergeist was dreadful, it threw a poker through the window at us when we went to the door. And at first Rosamund was out in the garden, and we went out to find her, and we played with some rabbits she had, and a hare.' I stopped then. Really I could not tell him about the hare. Another time, perhaps. 'But we went back into the house, and as soon as we were all four of us in one room it stopped.' I looked timidly at him to see if he understood the wonder of this. I could not describe how the packet of salt on the kitchen mantelpiece that was overturned voided its contents in a thin white trickle which spread out in a fine spray and fell on the hearthstone. I had told Rosamund that I would never speak of that.

'There may be something wonderful in that,' said Oliver.

'What do you mean?' I said.

'Someone who had been practising a fraud may have liked you so much that they could not bear to be anything but honest.'

'It was not that! It was not that at all!' I cried.

'Why do you hate to think it might be that?' he asked. 'It is not a great sin for an imaginative little girl to play at being Puck, and it would be a lovely thing if such a little girl met a playmate who was so good and honest and trusting that she felt it was a shame to take this darling's money.'

'That would be a pretty story,' I said, 'but it was not true. And yet? And yet? Can I have forgotten? I only think I remember those saucepans circling round and round the clothes-line, and being joined by the preserving-pan tied up in newspaper?'

'I think you only think you saw them,' he said, smiling.

'But she seemed so honest. And we knew her very well. You see, after that Cousin Jock was terrible to Constance and Rosamund, and they had to leave him, and then they came to live with us, there was always room in our house. They both sewed beautifully, they did needlework for shops. And then Rosamund became a nurse, she always wanted to be a nurse, she nursed Cordelia when she had a breakdown after she found out that she was no good as a violinist.' I paused. I could not tell this stranger about that either. I hurried on, 'We loved Rosamund so, she was so beautiful and she was so good, she bore things with us and took the sting away.' I paused again. Neither could I tell this stranger about my fortune-telling and my responsibility for Queenie's crime. 'She was Richard Quin's special love. He could not have loved her if there had not been something wonderful about her, could he?'

'I would think that she must have been very good stuff for him to choose her,' said Oliver. 'There was something extraordinary about your brother.' He looked out of the window over the sea to the far mountains, the still rosy sky. 'I can imagine you seeing visions in your nursery, with him about.'

'They both belonged to heaven,' I said, and then was shaken by doubt and anger. 'But did she? Did Rosamund? She was in love with a young doctor when she worked at a hospital, a doctor named Robert Woodburn. I know she was in love with him because of the way she looked when she spoke of him. She need not have spoken of him at all had she not wanted to have his name on her lips. I remember her lying on the lawn, putting a blade of grass between her teeth, wanting just to lie and do nothing, but being forced to tell us about him. But he was poor, and she did not marry him. Then she married this dreadful man Nestor Ganymedios, who is horrible to look at and is not honest and is cruel and squalid and spends money in a way that is like vomiting and is a sort of racial wastepaper-basket. Think what that means. She must be with him as I am here with you. But he is rich, she must have married him for his money. Sometimes I think there must be some other reason, when we saw her after her marriage she persuaded me that she was still good. But if she did this she can never have been good. And why else did she not come to our wedding? At least she can afford to do anything.'

'Here, take my handkerchief, it is bigger.'

'I cannot think why men's handkerchiefs are so much bigger than women's,' I snuffled. 'But, you see, she must be ashamed, her marriage must be wrong, and if it is wrong it must all have been lies, she cannot have been what we thought her,' I cried furiously. 'Looking back, I am not sure now if she ever cared for anything more than eating honeycomb and cream. She even talked of that when she was saying goodbye to Richard Quin.' It came back to me as a chill memory that Richard Quin also had spoken of that honeycomb and cream. Of that too I could not speak to this stranger. I wept even more than I had to, to cover up my reticence.

'My dear, do not cry,' said Oliver, 'you cannot need to cry like this. If this woman meant all this to you and to Richard Quin, she cannot be what you fear. There is just a part of the story which is missing. Did your mother like her? She was a shrewd woman.'

'Yes, Mamma liked her. And, yes, Mamma was never wrong. She looked after Mamma when she was dying. She was very good to her.' I dried my eyes. 'And yet. And yet. It is a little thing, I should not think of it. And yet. It took a very dishonest person to be dishonest with Mamma. Every single word she poured out, every single vehement movement she made, indicated that dishonesty was not what she wanted in her world, and everyone was in her debt, they should have felt obliged to take her terms. But I remember her lying to Mamma, quite unnecessarily. It was when Papa had gone away and left us with very little money. That is a long story too. I will tell you someday. But anyway Mamma was worried in case we thought she might not have kept back some money from my father and Rosamund told her that we were all frightened at being without money, and that I specially had worried because I was not sure if I could be a musician, because there might not be enough money, and I could not see how I was to earn my living if I was not a pianist. But I had felt nothing of the sort. It was a lie, and I wished Rosamund had not made us lie to Mamma. It could have been done some other way.'

'But, Rose, it was not a lie,' said Oliver.

'It was a lie,' I said. 'I had the courage of ignorance.'

'You poor child,' he said. 'Oh, that poor little brute, the infant Rose whom I shall never know! What a lot of things about ourselves that happened before we met we shall never be able to tell each other! Mostly because it is too much of a sweat.' I blushed guiltily. 'But this is something I know about the infant Rose which you do not know. You were frightened to death by your poverty and insecurity. Rose, you have only been married for a little over a fortnight. Twice you have cried out in your sleep that there would never be enough money for the Athenaeum, that you were not good enough to get a scholarship, and that your Papa was gambling away all your money, and you would have to work in a factory or as a servant and people would turn you out and you would starve. And each time I have woken you up and made love to you. Oh, my poor little Rose! But you see your Rosamund was not lying. She told the truth.'

I whispered, 'Don't let me forget this. Remind me of it if I lose faith in her again.'

'I will. Rose, believe me, there is a gap in this story which may be filled in, or may not. But it is there. Now, come and swim. The water will be cold but it will feel so new, and the kingfisher may be flying about where the stream comes out among the red rocks.'

'But she does not want to see us. I cannot get over that.'

'Yes. She evidently does not want to see us. I will not pretend to you that I think there is any reason but her own decision that kept her from coming to our wedding. But for that decision there may be some compelling reason. My dear, there is no use trying to force the locks that are made of mind and soul. Come and swim in this cold morning sea, come and get born again.'

I did not try to reject Rosamund any more. But it was long before I felt in need of her; not, certainly, during the two months of our honeymoon, when all time, all space, was crowded by our love. The earth, the sea, the sun, the sky, and light itself were all our accomplices. We walked on the hill and the hot air tingled with sharp scents of the pines and the herbs underfoot; at noon we sat on the gritty heights of the ruined fortress and looked down on the wide sea, white under the noon, and the horizon was tense as a stretched bow; in the market, cool under a sanctuary tent, walled in by the honey-coloured stone houses, the fish lay silver and rose and dappled on the slabs, the meat was crimson, the vegetables were green and purple and red, the flowers were white and scarlet and blue and gold, the women sat by smirking like the midwives of

248

creation; on the beaches brown bodies were supple, and at last their primary purpose was known to me, but was still a secret. At any hour of the day we swam, our skins encrusted with salt; if I ran my lips along his arm or mine I could taste the sea; there was no hour when it was not good to make love, but when the night fell there was a special harmony between creation and our state. It was so strange that this new ecstatic life ran parallel with the life I knew. There was a piano in the villa, of course we could not have gone there had there not been one, and I practised for my autumn season in a dream, yet competently, perhaps more aware of error than I was before, more confident that in my body I possessed an extraordinary machine. When we went back to London I would take a train and travel to a provincial town and play at a concert and be wholly absorbed in my music, with that absorption which I now saw proved music, and any art, to be a miracle for it is miraculous that man, born with the power to engender for himself an intoxicating excitement, should not have been satisfied with sex and should have set about, he, the created thing, patently not the divine creator, inventing another form of excitement, and should have made what could compete, what could tempt away the attention. But then I took my train back to London and there in our little house I found, still caged and at my command, this curious, resourceful, enveloping, renewing joy, the archetype of pleasure, the primal model. My wonder that there was not nothingness but existence was now infinitely increased, as I walked down the street and looked about me at the houses and the people I was filled with astonishment. Now I knew how extraordinary existence was, how stupendous its contrast with nothingness.

I was right in fearing that I had lost Mary, or at least I had lost some part of what had been between us. She had not gone away for a holiday at all, but had stayed in London and spent all her time furnishing her strange new house, which was indeed the strangest house I ever saw in London, so that she was installed there when Oliver and I returned. She had taken nothing from our house, though I had told her she could have what she liked, except the furniture and pictures which had been in her own room. I felt a chilly disappointment. I thought she had specially liked the clock in our drawing-room. It was as if what had been shared in our common life had had no value for her. I felt again the suspicion that she had been glad when

I told her I was going to marry Oliver, because it gave her an opportunity to flee to her solitude which she preferred to me. When we met it was all right, she still loved me. She said, 'Oh, how happy you are, you look as if you had been printed by a new process that got in all the colours!' It was a surprise to her. I think she thought it possible that I might have decided during my honeymoon that I did not like being married, and made my way home. I think that she was only able to be glad that this had not happened by practising the sort of dichotomy that is often to be seen in the Protestant relatives of Catholic converts who would prefer them to remain in their new faith because it makes them happy, while regarding Catholicism itself with disapproval. This was not altogether pleasing to me, as I imagine the analogous position is not pleasing to Catholic converts; but I was in a worse position than they are, for they at least can explain their position by theological discussion, whereas I could not make the smallest reference to the essential factors which made me happy with Oliver. I could not explain to Mary that when Oliver and I were lovers it was as important as music; and it was nearly as impossible to explain to Cordelia that Oliver and I were of some importance, not, I mean, that we were important musicians, but that we were as important as other human beings are, for the reason that they are human beings. She gave a dinner-party for us on our return, wearing an exhausted expression, as if I had got into difficulties rashly swimming in a rough sea and she had had to go out and rescue me and had used the last drain of energy in dragging me up the beach. Frequently she spoke as if she had made the marriage, though there was not the faintest reason she should think so. She treated Oliver with notably less respect than she had shown before, often turning away from him before he had finished the end of a sentence; he must be not of the worth she had supposed since he had married me. Yet she too loved me, she like Mary was delighted that I was happy, she gave me not one wedding-present but several. She spared nothing to make this dinner-party, as I think she would have described it, brilliant. I am one of the people (and it is proof of the inarticulateness of the human race of which I am complaining that I do not know whether this is a rare or a common condition) to whom getting married had been as important an event as being born. But of my two sisters, who were my only living relatives, one carried in her mind inadequate pictures of a marriage, the

250

other a distorted image of it; and I was unable, for reasons common to all mankind, to correct their misapprehensions. We cannot talk about our loves, we cannot talk about our own souls. It is remarkable that human intercourse is not more painful than it is.

My daily life went smoothly, more smoothly than before. Miss Beevor and Kate were so enchanted to have a man in the house that I felt humiliated when I realised how wrong I had been when I thought I had given them the essentials of a contented life. They had always enjoyed my good clothes, they liked Oliver's even better. There was a greatcoat of his made of vicuña which they specially cherished, joining together to brush it with a carefully chosen brush, soft but firm, wrapped in a thick silk handkerchief, almost as affectionately as if it were a pet animal.

'It is a pity,' said Kate, one day, when I came into her sewing-room and found them tending this coat, 'that your Papa could not have had such clothes! Richard Quin did not care about such things. But they went with your Papa.'

'Oh, your Papa,' sighed Miss Beevor. 'Such a gentleman! But so,' she added kindly, 'is Oliver.'

I understood what it must have meant to my mother, who for all her genius and mystical accomplishment was a simple woman like these, when my father went away and she was deprived of domesticated vital principle, this unpredictable, extravagant, violent thing that was tamed enough to live in a house. Why, that might happen to me. I knew Oliver would never leave me, but he might die. I had my family's knowledge of immortality, but that is never a complete consolation for mortality, and now seemed less so. Oliver and I could not but leave much behind with our flesh.

'Rose, I declare,' said Miss Beevor. She had looked up and seen my face in the glass over the chimneypiece.

'What have you to cry about, Miss Rose?' said Kate.

'It struck me that Oliver might die,' I said.

'Not for a long time, I should say,' said Kate. 'But is it not good that you should have learned to cry for other reasons than that you are angry? They had terrible tempers when they were little,' she told Miss Beevor, 'all but Richard Quin, the blessed lamb.'

'Oh, they were not so bad,' said Miss Beevor. She could look back on our childhood without distress now. Cordelia had long forgiven her, and had her to a meal once every two months.

'No, they were not so bad, but they were not so good,' said Kate, 'and will you tell me, does Mr Oliver like prawns?'

'He says he does. I asked him when you told me to, and he distinctly said he did.'

'But he always leaves them. I think he has mixed them up with something else. With Dublin prawns, perhaps. We will try. Your Papa was like that. He often got names wrong. But your Mamma was very clever at finding out what he meant. You must make an effort, Miss Rose.'

Literature was then delivering a heavy broadside against marriage, which was regarded as so unsatisfactory an institution that a divorce was no longer assumed to be a tragedy. If one knew the people who were getting divorced it usually turned out that there was some sadness attached; either there was some condition that had made for prolonged unhappiness, drunkenness or insane jealousy, or one partner had ceased to love a still loving partner; but the picture that was provoked by the news of a divorce was simply of the sensible cancellation of an arrangement that had appeared irksome. Yet everybody whom I met when I was still so newly married that they took note of my state showed a faith in marriage, gave signs that they thought it not an unreasonable hope that Oliver and I would be happy together for ever. The only exception was Lady Tredinnick. I had sent her a slice of my wedding-cake, and a letter in which I had tried to breach the gulf that had opened between us in spite of the affection Mary and I had always felt for her, because she had tried, vainly but generously, to admit us into the world of fortunate young girls, and because when she had failed, she had so sweetly tried to substitute another kind of gift by showing us her flowers. When she had stood by the daffodils in her Cornish garden she showed a loyalty to beauty that was disarming. She sent me a present, a Chinese vase, which I recognised; it had stood on the chimneypiece in her library in the Cornish home, and she had told me that it had been brought from Siam by one of her husband's ancestors who had gone to the East with Samuel White in the seventeenth century. It was not a possession I would have expected her to let pass out of the family, and I could not doubt her continued affection for me, so I wrote to her and asked her to come and see us on our return from the South, but she made the excuse that she was still in Cornwall. Then one day, I was walking along the Brompton Road, on the side where trees grow and there is a sort of ledge along the pavement, I saw her some yards ahead of me. She looked an old woman not by reason of any signs of physical weakness; a wide black felt hat was crushed down on her head, forcing a knot of iron-grey hair which was disordered down on the collar of her long and shapeless coat. She was walking along very slowly, looking into the windows of the antique-shops which are so numerous in that street, and I was reminded of the evening at the party where Mary and I had first realised that our old friend was degenerated into awkward oddity, because she was so rude to an inoffensive young man. She had then stared at a Poussin and not known what it was till we spoke of it; she could not be observing anything of the objects on which she was setting her eyes, for she was spending as long on those that were trumpery as those that were precious, and it must have been that she was simply using them as places on which to repose her discouraged sight, as a lame man might support himself on posts set along the road without feeling any interest in those posts for their own sake. I spoke to her and, as she did not hear, touched her gently on the shoulder, and she wheeled about, her upper lip raised from her teeth; and a long moment passed when she stared at me and made sure who I was. The bones of her face were taking control of her ageing flesh; her nose was now very Roman, and the bridge shone white and her greying brows had settled in a fierce line, so that her eyes appeared to have no other expression but impatience and command. She looked not unlike the later pictures of the Duke of Wellington. 'Why, it is Rose!' she exclaimed, and then said with a nervous laugh, 'I cannot think who I thought it might be.' I told her how much I had hoped she would dine with us, and she said, 'Ah, yes, you married Oliver. You will be very happy. No doubt,' she repeated, without a shade of geniality, even with some rage, 'you will be very happy.' We walked alongside for a little while, trying to talk and then I went into a shop, so sure was I that if I went any further with her she would take the too plain path of evasion and turn into Brompton Oratory, though I knew she was not a Catholic. I was so disturbed I told nobody of this. But a few days later Mary met her and had the same impression of angry degeneration.

But this was the one note of hostility that my marriage evoked. I did not go so often to the Dog and Duck, for Oliver had more friends than I had had, and we had to visit them and be visited; but Len and Milly and Lily were so contented with my marriage that they could take all its consequences, even if they included less of my company. The first time I went down after our return from the South they found their own ways of telling me that. Uncle Len said to me, as he washed some glasses and I dried them, 'You're better off now, Rose. It's more natural to be married, no matter who you are. And you were always the natural one of you three girls. From a child up. But you'll have to fall in with this Oliver's ways, and if they aren't ours, well, we heard you take your vows at that church up your way, and if keeping them means we don't see so much of you, there'll be no hard feelings.' Milly, sitting in front of her dressing-table, said, 'In the long run it's worth it,' and ran a comb through her silver hair so that it rose like a coronet, and added, 'Come down when you can, but your young man may have his ties and prefer them and you must respect them. When I married Len I threw a lot overboard that had belonged to the old days.' Her comb primly lifted her hair higher still to the likeness of a crown, and I saw that she had nourished through the years the vision of a picturesque alternative career which she had sacrificed for the sake of an elevation that still seemed to her miraculous, and she considered this the mark of a creditable marriage. Aunt Lily, planting peach-stones in a flower-bed under the bar window, as she always did every autumn, never with any success, was more wistful.

'Queenie's very happy with Mr Bates, Fred I should call him, though it will never come natural if I live to be a hundred,' she told me. 'She goes to all his services, and she's got her own job there, she helps with the hymn-singing.'

'I did not know she sang,' I said.

'Oh, yes, she's got a fine contralto, a mezzo-soprano, whatever you need to sing Carmen, but she wasn't one just to sing when there was no purpose to be served by it.' It was true, there was an economy about Queenie. 'When we were young she would always sing a tune if there was a jollification, then afterwards she let her voice be. But now she's singing a lot. Funny, your music brought you and Oliver together, and Queenie's singing's helping her with Fred, but I played the piano not so badly, not like you, still I could always get through the Lancers, yet it didn't bring me anything. Oh dear, I try not to feel bitter. I know it says in the Bible that one shall be taken and one shall be left, but there's such a lot been taken, there's

254

Queenie, twice over, and Milly, and your sister Cordelia, and then Nancy, and now you, and there's only Mary and me left, and Mary might go any time, and there'll be only me. I don't really mind, there's lots of ways for me to share in your lives, but sometimes I worry, it's as if there must have been something the matter with me, as if I must have been plain. But I don't think I was. There was someone, you know, but he never wrote a line after Queenie's trouble started. And I am bound to say he'd never been what you'd call assiduous. Just another bastard, I suppose. Excuse me, dearie, I suppose I can use that word now you're a married woman. Let's face it, I've been left. Well, it's this way, and the way you've been taken means that you can't come down so often, there's no fighting against it. I would far rather lose you,' she said incomprehensibly, 'than really lose you.'

But their obvious fear that Oliver would feel unfriendly to them because he came of a different class was without foundation, and it would have been difficult to explain to them without offending them that, as he was composing a new symphony, he was not clearly aware of anything about them. They were amiable coloured shadows, creatures which lived for him only because I loved them and would have disappeared if I had tired of them, and Uncle Len became real to him only because of that weekly paper devoted to puzzles. Often Oliver and Mr Morpurgo and Uncle Len used to spend happy hours on a weekday, particularly at tea-time, eating sliced buns and drinking strong Indian tea by the fire working out 'What then was the chance of X being dealt an ace out of the third pack?' and Len would ask the others, 'You with all your education, don't you follow what's going on?' and they would shake their heads. 'Funny, that!' he once exclaimed. 'I'd give my ears to have had the schooling so that I could understand what they mean when they say that modern physics shows us a universe our five senses can't picture. That mean anything to you? Sometimes I think I get it. Sometimes I know I don't.' Mr Morpurgo and Oliver shook their heads. 'Could you write music that made sense but nobody could hear?' Len asked Oliver.

He was startled by the question. 'Yes. Of course I could. I could write music that made a rhythm out of superimposed and competing rhythms which would give me enormous satisfaction to imagine but which no instruments could convey to any listener's ear. But many composers have written music which, at the time they wrote it, nobody could hear because the instruments of their time could not reproduce it.'

'So music's always catching up on itself,' Len reflected, 'and maybe we'll learn to think so that we can get a picture of this new universe. No, I don't think that's what they mean. I think they mean we won't never be able to see what it's really like, it'd need more than our five senses.'

'There is something which may be relevant,' said Mr Morpurgo. 'I have noticed as I have gone through life that the more people know the more they become incomprehensible to those who know less. People who are very good or very clever, I put it that way though of course to be good is to be clever in a certain way, people who are very good or very clever always seem to stupid people to be acting irrationally. Very often we call such people eccentric, off the centre when, since they know more of the whole than the rest of us, they are probably better able to judge where the centre is. There is always mystery above us. The appearance of mystery in the universe is therefore nothing new. It is a constant condition of our lives.'

'I do not know why Christ got Himself crucified,' said Oliver, who had fallen to scribbling a staff and some notes on an envelope.

'You do not, and you are a Christian,' said Mr Morpurgo, 'and I do not, and I am a Jew. But we may count ourselves happy, if we observe the argumentative despair of the Moslem peoples, whose saviour did nothing which the least of them cannot understand.'

'I'd like to understand everything,' said Len. 'It seems more natural. Give me old Ptolemy. There is a nice system for you, a downstairs and an upper stairs, a floor and a ceiling.'

'You are right, it would be happier if it were so,' said Mr Morpurgo. 'The human race is not a beautiful spectacle if it is a pyramid with the top wrapped in mist and the base sunk in mud. But we must have faith.'

Oliver was lost in his music, Uncle Len's eye had gone back to the puzzle magazine, Mr Morpurgo leaned over to re-read the puzzle. Aunt Milly brought in hot water and filled up the tea-pot.

'Why don't we have tea like this at home, Rose?' asked Oliver.

'This illustrates what I was saying a minute ago,' said Mr Morpurgo. 'Rose knows that no palate enjoys the same tea over a long period of time. You have excellent China tea at home. You enjoy this Indian tea because it is a change, and enjoy your own tea more when you get back to it. The children learned many such things from their mother. But for a moment you wrongly suspected her of negligence, of not getting you the best tea, for the reason that you know much less about tea than she does.'

Nobody was listening to him but Milly and me. The puzzle was never solved. Oliver lost the envelope he had scribbled his notes on. Such are the hours which refresh the soul, which stoke the furnace for performance. There were such hours for me, though not for Oliver, under Nancy's roof also. I rarely took him there because I could see that her quality was not apparent to him. He could sympathise with my love for Lily, partly because he saw her as the *ideal* Papagena in *The Magic Flute*, partly because I had told him how she had loathed her sister's crime but had not let her loathing diminish her love, how she was so generous that, though she had come into our house as a refugee from misfortune, we were now all her debtors. But he could see nothing in Nancy but a dull, prettyish, provincial housewife, and I could find no words to express the feminine mystery in which her value lay. There was not a grain of glory in her house. It was a house like millions of others, and she did not move an inch from the routine followed by the millions of women who inhabited such houses. It was not in her power to do so, she had not a ranging fancy, and it would have puzzled Oswald. She should not have felt happy in this little world, for she knew that the belief in stability which was its foundation was unfounded. A father could be murdered, a mother could be a murderer; a brother could desert, an uncle could nearly kill by his gross kindness. She had missed not the least overtone of the discord in which her normal destiny had died. But she had transmitted her cynicism into something so different that it expressed itself in that faint smile which was always so delicious to me, which was sharp and yet sweet, like the taste of tart fruit lightly sugared, and she made every day pretty with trivial things, with care for her baby son, with chatter to her little Welsh servant, with visits to the shops to exercise small prudences and insipid preferences, to do nothing guilty, to make improvements what would otherwise have been not quite so good, till the sum, as I one day learned, was far vaster than

257

the little world in which the accountancy was carried on. I went
into her house one afternoon while she was still resting, and
she called me up to her room, and I stood at the end of the bed
while she rubbed her eyes and explained that she felt better for
her sleep, that she had really been tired, Richard Adam had
kept her awake nearly all night, and blew a kiss to me, and told
me not to go away, she was still sleepy, but she would have to
get up soon to take Richard Adam from Bronwyn. She closed
her eyes again for a moment, and as she lay there, with her
head thrown back on the pillow against her spread hair, her
long and very white throat bare, her faint, teasing smile on her
lips, I thought that she too should have known what it was to
be desired again and again by someone better than herself, and
it seemed a shame that it was only by Oswald who shared that
bed with her. I wished that I knew as well as I knew her some
woman who was really happily married, so that I could ask her,
'Are you, too, frightened by the thought that your husband may
die?' But Nancy, before she rose, asked me that very question.

Everything went so well that it was as if I had abolished
misfortune by my marriage; for surely Mary would fall in love
too and marry and would understand. But one day in the
second winter of our marriage Oliver and I went to Bournemouth; I had an afternoon concert at the Winter Gardens, and
Oliver was stuck in his work so he came too. It is a frightening
place. Those fir trees have so much an air of having the last
word. The houses have won a victory over the woods, there is
not an inch of them that is not now town; but in the gardens the
black branches remind the people in the houses of the hearse.
But we were not frightened. I had a new crimson coat with a
long collar of black moleskin, which delighted Oliver to the
point of foolishness; he seemed to think I had designed it and
made it as well as bought it. My rehearsal went well; my
performance went well; it was pleasant with the special
pleasantness that has no particular cause. In the train going
home, under a plaid rug that he had bought as a young man
and thought as a certain prescription for warmth, not having
noticed that it had worn thin during the years, we dozed
together in a warm adhesion. But when we got back to our
home there was a light in the drawing-room windows, I
thought it might be Avis Jenkinson; sometimes when she got in
a great state she would suddenly come to see us; and Mary was
waiting for us.

She smiled over my head at Oliver and said, 'I am pretending that I have come to save Rose having a shock when she reads this thing in the morning papers, but I have come because I cannot sit alone and think about it in my tower. It is Lady Tredinnick.'

'Oh, she is dead?' I whispered.

'Late this afternoon she climbed up to the roof of her house and threw herself out of the window. Her body caught in a tree. They could not get to it. They had to call the Fire Brigade. But she was dead. She had broken her neck.'

'How did you hear?' I asked, then turned and explained to Oliver, 'She took us to our first dance. It was horrible but she was nice. She was so nice.'

'I have a pupil who lives next door to the Tredinnicks, she rang up and told me that she could not come for her lesson, she was upset by the dreadful thing that had happened.'

'At this first dance she told me about a wonderful white orchid that her husband had seen growing on a tree,' I told him. 'They could not get to it.'

'Does anybody know why she did it?' asked Oliver.

'She had been getting more and more strange,' I said.

'No,' said Mary. 'We had missed the point. We had simply not seen what was the matter with her. She had not been getting more and more strange. Her world had been doing that, not she. Which of her sons was Austell?'

'The one in the Treasury,' I said.

'He was brought up in the West London police court this morning,' said Mary. 'Did you not buy an evening paper? It is in all of them. He had been found with a soldier in a square somewhere near Knightsbridge.'

'Oh, God! oh, God!' I said. 'So that was what she was afraid of.'

'Yes. It seems so obvious now. I cannot think how we did not see it.'

'But why should he do that?' I marvelled. 'Austell did not live with her. He had a little house in Westminster, she took me there once, a very pretty house with very good panelling and a vine in the garden. Why did he not take anybody he liked to his own house?'

'You do not understand,' said Oliver. 'My God, it makes one sweat to think that it is mere chance one is not born like that. There are different kinds, of course, Lionel de Raisse would not do this. But this kind must have a stranger, and must run the risk of being caught. Caught, what a hideous word! And what a hideous thing! Think of being compelled by desire as intense as anything we know, to go with some snotty boy into the streets at night; and mating like an alley cat, like a stray dog, with the hope, the fear, that you find yourself under the beam of a policeman's torch, and everything else in the world stripped from one, the light casting complete and eternal bankruptcy.'

'Is that what some people want?' said Mary. I had an uneasy feeling she thought it hardly stranger than what Oliver and I wanted.

'It is in a way quite rich,' said Oliver. 'There's the perverse joy of rejecting all the delicacy of life, the little house in Westminster, the panelled walls, the vine, the Guardi and the Gainsborough drawing, the soft-voiced friends, for a coarse boy and the open street. There's the joy of forcing the world to punish one when it meant one no harm, there's the joy, of course, of getting one's poor little bastard of a partner into trouble too, of taking something so much lower than oneself that it would seem impossible to protect it, and railroading it into the police court and the cells. I have often wondered how it is that Jasperl has never tried this form of pleasure.'

'My love, my love,' I said, 'you need not follow that damned soul into sins he has not yet committed.'

'I am hungry,' said Mary. 'I have had no dinner. There is a very good cold supper waiting for you, I am going to share it. I asked Kate to put out some of that Pontet-Canet Oliver likes.'

On the dining-room table there was a bowl of cyclamens, great white ones like poised butterflies.

'It is foolish, but one thinks that people who love flowers and are clever at growing them should be rewarded by happiness,' said Mary.

'Or even having flowers in the house. So odd to turn one's back on all the things on this table, the flowers, the silver, the glass, the wine, the food,' said Oliver. 'But people do it, both men and women, they choose damnation.'

'I see it now,' said Mary. 'Lady Tredinnick thought we were pretty, she was puzzled by her son's indifference to women, she asked us to her house because she hoped her sons would like us. But of course they did not like us at all. Looking back, I see all of them were like that.'

'I wonder when she began to guess,' I said.

'Some time ago. You remember how oddly she behaved at that party when she was rude to that young man who said he was a friend of one of her sons.'

'She had lived a long time in a state of bewilderment and then for a long time in a state of horror and fear,' said Oliver, 'and at the end the blow fell. What did he get?'

'He was remanded for three weeks,' said Mary.

We ate and drank. I got up and filled Oliver's glass and he stroked my head and said to Mary, 'Odd that two sisters should both have such lovely hair, of quite different kinds. Rose's so soft and curly, yours so smooth.'

'But Cordelia has the prettiest hair of all of us,' said Mary.

I wondered why she needed to think of that stranger, when we were all together, in such a private grief, and finding such private consolation; for while my heart ached for Lady Tredinnick, caught for ever, in my mind, up in her tree like a great black bird, it comforted me to note that Oliver's glass was empty and to fill it with the wine he liked, to feel his hand caress my head, to see him treat Mary as if she were his sister too, and it was a legitimate comfort; Lady Tredinnick in her tree would have approved the way we were spending the night of her death. But what Cordelia did was neither here nor there.

'Rose played so well this afternoon,' Oliver told Mary, setting down his glass.

'What, were you there?' I asked.

'Yes, I started out to obey you and go for a walk on the cliffs, but I turned back and stood at the back of the hall. And it was superb.'

'You were possibly the only person in the hall who deserved to hear her,' said Mary.

'Why have you such a down on audiences?' I asked. She gave a dark look into the distance as if she saw something that she feared, and I gave her a tender shake, filled her glass and then put the decanter down and went back to her and said, as I had said to her a million times, 'Don't be such an ass.'

Oliver said suddenly, 'I wonder what the poor chap is doing. She should not have done it, you know. It is too hard on him. He loses his job and many of his friends and becomes a sort of lewd joke, and he has this as well. She had hardly the right to do it.'

'That is what is so unbearably horrible,' said Mary. 'This is

261

utter defeat. Everything she did was right, she never can have needed to think out the moral aspect of any act, her taste settled everything before it reached that level. Now at the end she has done this thing which is cruelly wrong.'

'No, you do not understand,' I said. 'She thought her son might try to kill himself, and she went first to show the way. Can't you see her, going up flight after flight of stairs, and going out on the roof, and stepping into space, as she would have gone into battle if she had been a soldier? There was only a limited number of actions one could expect from her. This is the only way she could have committed suicide. She could not have run up those stairs and thrown herself out of the window in an effort to reach forgetfulness, it was not in her character, she could not have done it any more than she could have played my programme at Bournemouth this afternoon. So she did not see herself as torturing her son, she saw herself simply as leading her son out of disgrace.'

'Yes,' said Mary. 'You are right. That is what she must have wanted.'

'But do you think her son will do it?' asked Oliver.

'No,' said Mary. 'It does not go with that little house in Westminster.'

'Then what she did is still wrong,' said Oliver.

'Yes,' said I, 'but it is better to think of her as being wrong in her way of being wrong; and it is a nobler way of wrongness than the one we first thought of.'

'Where she went wrong is in not understanding that what her son did seemed entirely natural to him', said Oliver. 'It will seem to him no more reasonable for his mother to require him to jump off a roof because he had been charged with sodomy at a police court than it would seem reasonable to any of us if somebody came into this room and told us we must jump off a roof because we are musicians and have composed and performed. It seems natural for him that he should mate with his own sex. It seems natural for him that he should mate in such a way that he lands in the police court. Why should he kill himself? He may be weeping at this moment but he will be feeling that something has been accomplished, he has obeyed a summons to doom.'

'She was more wrong than that,' said Mary. 'For where did the confusion arise? In her. Every day she grew less like a woman. It was no wonder if her sons were part men and part women. She had no right to blame them.'

262

'Again, it was like music,' I said. 'Like Mamma being a pianist and Mary and I having inherited part of her gifts.'

It hurt me that I saw from a twist of Oliver's eyebrow that he suspected me of exaggerating my mother's greatness as a pianist out of my love for her, that he thought it improbable that she had played better than we did. Yet her superiority was what had made us. That is the great handicap of sexual love, that lovers can share everything except what explains the past, of which their enjoyment is a part.

'We should have seen all this before,' said Mary, 'and we could have saved the poor old dear.'

'But how?' asked Oliver. 'How could you two save a woman who has sodomite sons and is shocked by them?'

Mary and I looked at each other across the table. 'Oh, we do not know how,' I said, 'that is the point. We have not the least idea.'

'But Rosamund would have known,' said Mary.

'Your Rosamund might have known, but what could she have said to the desperate old lady?'

'What she would have said neither Rose nor I know,' said Mary, 'but it was her talent to put an end to desperation.'

'Oh, Oliver, it is true,' I said.

'All you have told me up till now is true,' he said.

'And mother played better than we do,' I said.

'She played in a sense better than anyone I have ever heard,' said Mary.

'Was it really so?' asked Oliver, and shook his head, not in denial but in wonder.

His glass was empty, his plate was bare. I filled his glass again, I gave him another slice of cold lamb. Presently he put down his knife and fork and asked diffidently, 'Could your Rosamund have helped me with Jasperl, do you suppose?'

Mary looked away, seeing that we spoke of a secret. I answered, 'You do not need much help. You have done marvels. But, yes, Rosamund could have helped you.'

When he had eaten the lamb he passed his napkin over his lips, looked down on the circle of white flowers on the table, and sighed. 'Your Rosamund did what we three could not. She had, I imagine, moral genius. We forget that there is such a thing, but of course that is what the saints had. And it is absurd for us to doubt that the saints really existed, as it would be for the tone deaf to doubt that there are great composers. None of

263

us three can compete in that field. We are musicians. But we care about people, that means we care about morality, which I suppose is the art by which people are kept from harm. We could use the services of a moral genius now. But we want them only to work on the other kind of genius. The kind that go too near the crater's edge because they have the Plutonic fire in them and they want to leap into the volcano and be united with the source of their being. Lady Tredinnick was pushed out to the frontiers of the desert, into the confusion of the jungle, on to the extremes of courage. Jasperl dashes himself against the frontiers of music. We would like to be able to stop them from this self-arson, and with Lady Tredinnick you have failed, and with Jasperl I am failing. But such people are exceptional. We do not come across them often. That means we rarely have need of a miracle-worker. For our own plain business we can get on by ourselves. Mary, let me peel you a peach.'

'Thank you,' she said.

But soon he laid down the silver knife. 'I can see the tears shining on the cheeks of both of you. How sensible of you not to wipe them away. And how beautiful you both look. It must have been bitter for Lady Tredinnick to want wives for her sons, who were lovely like you, and could love like you, where she had no daughters-in-law except unknown Guardsmen grappling in the night.'

IX

SINCE THE CRASH in America Mary and I were not offered
nearly such good tours, and our agents told us we need not go;
but we could not keep away, and we felt a longing to see the
autumn foliage again, and to be with our friends again. They
were so friendly and they were so violently engaged in life;
being with them was like getting on a toboggan behind somebody one liked, putting one's arms round them, and dashing
off downhill over the spurting snow. I was not sorry that I had
gone, though it had meant leaving Oliver for nearly three
months, and Mary liked it, because she liked to know things.
The aim of her playing was always intellectual certainty. We
had not been able to understand what had happened in America
in 1929 before we went there. We knew it to be rich, by knowledge planted in our mind in our childhood by the little facts
that can never be rooted up. Papa had spent a year in a mining
camp on the Sierras when he was young; the American
heiresses whom King Edward liked so much brought dowries
large enough to restore the best estates that ruined peers could
bring them; a poor Scottish boy called Andrew Carnegie went
to America and worked in a mill and made so many millions
that he had given Lovegrove the library where we got out
books and had set up a trust which enabled any Scottish boy or
girl to go to a university, we would have had to apply to it if we
were no good at music. There were Americans who were poor
and oppressed, we knew that from Upton Sinclair's *The Jungle*.
But this was because greed made the manufacturers conspire
on helpless immigrants and trap them into working for low
wages. America was rich, naturally and unalterably as green is
green and the sea is salt; and we proved that this was true when

we crossed the Atlantic and found that the towers of New York were an Aladdin's cave growing upwards, that there and in the continent beyond Mary and I could get all we wanted, of money and enjoyment and praise. There was nothing criminal in this wealth, for those Americans who were poor would soon be rich. Providence was emptying a vial of prosperity over the United States and presently the generous flow would cover all its surface. We believed the Americans when they told us this. The United States is the child of Great Britain, and no parents wish to think that their children are not to be eternally happy. Also it seemed a shame, if people took the trouble to sail six thousand miles over the ocean and face the hardships of emigration, in order to found a society better than the one they had left, that they should not get what they wanted. It would have been as if, after all our practising, we had not been able to play any better than other people.

When it was said that the United States was poor, we thought at first that it might conceivably be poorer than it had been. But we were disconcerted because there were far fewer liners crossing the Atlantic. In earlier years we had never had to worry about catching any particular boat, there was always another one belonging to a different line leaving a day or two later. But now there were few sailings a week. On the boat the American passengers told us stories of ruin, but with an upward, hopeful inflection that made them hard to consider: it was as if we were trying to look into the eyes of someone who wore brightly polished spectacles. We were doubtful, until we had landed, and taken the night train to a town in New England, where there was a college for women; and we had the intention of playing on our tours some sonatas by a young American composer called Arthur Todd who was head of the music faculty there. The professor and his wife, who was named Abigail, met us at the station and drove us to their house; he was long and sandy and spectacled, with such beautiful hands that one wished he would not drive a car, and she was nice but unwise, she kept on saying that she always had had faith in her husband, with an emphasis suggesting that this had often been a considerable feat. But she was, like so many American women, exquisitely domesticated. They lived in a small white frame house, in a street of such houses, that were old and graceful, with the sweet air of Georgian architecture copied by country craftsmen from pictures in books, their unhedged lawns set trim and swept in spite of the flaming leaves that were falling from the trees that shadowed the sidewalks. Inside it recalled the illustrations in children's books that show the homes of the imaginary animals that wear clothes; there were the same clean colours, highly polished furniture, and censored contentment. There were windows on both sides of the sitting-room, so to take the glare out of the light Mrs Todd had put thin shelves across the windows that looked on to the street, and she had put on them a collection of coloured glass. It was an idea that we were to see everywhere we went that year, and for that matter most of the houses in that street would be furnished exactly in the same way; but it was a good idea, and there was no country we ever visited where so many houses were so pleasant to see. Mrs Todd made us some coffee, and gave us coffee-cake that she had baked before she went out, and then we rose to go upstairs and have baths and change before we played to her husband. As we left the room Mary turned to have a last look at the red and blue glass, and cried out. She had seen something through the clear panes between the shelves. She ran out of the room and out of the house, and when we followed her we found her standing where the lawn met the sidewalk. A neatly dressed man was lying on the ground, with his head on the grass and his feet on the sidewalk: this was better than the other way round, and he looked so much as if he were the sort of person who would be careful to make such sensible arrangements that it seemed odd that he should have done anything so irregular as to fall down in the street. If he had felt ill, one would have thought, he would have stayed at home. There was an earthy pattern about him such as we had never seen before. The professor sighed, eased his cuffs round his wrists, put out his beautiful hands, and lifted up the man and carried him into the house. As we followed him Mrs Todd told us that he had been a clerk, she called it 'clurk' and on her lips the word meant a shop assistant, in a small old-fashioned store which had closed down some months ago, and he had probably been on his way to sweep up leaves for a widow who lived down the street, and had been one of his customers. But everyone was out for jobs like that, there were not many to be had. She guessed the poor man was starving. They put him on a sofa and consciousness came back to him. He cried out in misery because he was not wearing spectacles. He said that he would never get another job if he

267

had lost his spectacles. The Todds made to keep him on the sofa while we went and found the spectacles, which were not broken. Mrs Todd had not yet got him to drink a cup of coffee, and had thought that he was refusing it because he was worried about his spectacles, but even when we had brought them to him, he would not drink. Arthur Todd was from Iowa and he spoke with the tender reverberating Middle Western accent. Gently he urged the man to drink; and the clerk finally admitted, sulky with shame, that he had not eaten for twenty-four hours. His wife and children had gone to stay with his people in Maine, and they were poor enough: he had had to give his wife the greater part of their savings, hoping he would get along, but it hadn't worked out. He had been going along to earn his dollar from Mrs Kirby and had thought he would last out and eat afterwards but, he repeated, it hadn't worked out. Well, would they mind calling a doctor, because he had read once in an article in the *Literary Digest* that when people hadn't eaten for a long time they had to be mighty careful what they took when they started eating again.

We had till then thought of starving people as slum-dwellers, or peasants in a blighted land, who would claw at food when it was offered them. A starving man so thoroughly geared to a complicated society that he dared not relieve his hunger till he had consulted a doctor struck on my understanding as strangely as atonal music strikes on an untrained ear. We were to be more disconcerted after he had gone, when we asked the Todds how much unemployment benefit the man would be getting, and we learned that he would get none. Mrs Todd told us of neighbourhood projects to help the unemployed, and again what we heard struck us as strange, though not with the strangeness of novelty, but of the obsolete. This was Victorian charity of the soup-kitchen sort, which in England had long been rejected, because it offended against the idea of equality, which one had thought was specially dear to the Americans. The poor should not be put in the position of dependants on the rich; the state could not exist without their work, and therefore the state should keep them if by some accident it had for a time no work for them to do. Mary and I rarely thought about such things, but we suddenly realised that that was what we had been thinking about then. It was all right when we got to the piano, for after we played the sonatas Arthur Todd eased his cuffs round his beautiful hands, as he had done before he lifted the starving man, and lifted a new meaning out of the sonatas for us. But when we were alone again there came to us a frightened sense of America as an artificial society with insufficient artifice; and that had always to be succeeded by the admission that up till then America had certainly had all the artifice it needed. This was not a thoughtless, not a cruel country. It had been visited by an unpredictable event which had afflicted on it wounds of a sort it had not known before, and it had not yet improvised the bandage and the tourniquet.

Yes, it was like that, and the innocence was even more elemental. And it was hard during our tour to keep our mind on our music, when we were faced with this situation, which was extreme. It could even be stated thus: two people had known each other for a long time and had a friendship based on what seemed a common culture. They could have gone to Venice together and never been surprised by what the other one wanted to see, and between them would have seen everything. But suddenly one received by an accident a deep cut in his body, and cried out, not in amazement because he had been wounded, but because blood was issuing from his body. Until then it appeared he had had no idea that blood flowed under his skin, it was still true that he had known all about the churches of Venice, that he had been the most agreeable of companions; and it even turned out that he knew all about X-rays.

On our last night in New York, we went to a party of the kind that Americans give better than any other people in the world, a small party for people who are ordinarily asked to big parties. There were three pianists in the room, but, as was right, at the piano there was someone who could hardly play at all, who just bent over the keyboard as if it were a syrup-tin and spooned out the sweetness then faintly spiced with jazz of musical-comedy tunes. There was an actress who wore a white dress with a circle cut in it just above her navel so that her skin could be seen, which looked very pink. Against the white, it was as if she had dropped a slice of ham on her lap; but it showed good feeling and willingness to think out new ways of pleasing. There were playwrights of the sort common in New York at that time, melancholy men, usually Jewish, who built intricate plays which were more profoundly funny than they had any right to be, considering that they were written without resort to the creation of character, solely by piling up situations; it was as if a Chinese puzzle should turn out to be satirical.

269

There were some millionaires and their wives who were felt to have thrown off their guilt by consenting to know people like us. Americans had a strange sense of guilt about possessing things, although possession was imposed on them by their climate. None of them were politicians, that was what made American cities different from London, where one meets at parties what seems far more than the six hundred and twenty-six Members of Parliament than actually exist. But these people spoke always of general ruin, which had not touched them yet but must, of this paralysis, spread further. They spoke too of prescriptions to end it, and showed themselves naked and newborn in their innocence, as unaware that blood ran in their bodies as they were of bandages and tourniquets.

'They are like us when Papa went away,' said Mary, as we drove home. 'Do you remember how we talked about going into factories, we did not know which, and making enough to keep the house going?'

'They are like us in other ways,' I said. 'They speak of the stock market as something that has an independent existence and sometimes gave them lots of money. It was their father, they are like us, they are gambled children.'

The car stopped. We were staying at a hotel by Washington Square, and had to go right up Fifth Avenue, and the traffic lights worked all night, though in the early hours of the morning there are hardly any cars on the street at all. The red light burns; and you sit still in your car, the canyon of the avenue rising black before you, the white lights at its base announcing distance that is just distance. One stops every few blocks for a long time. The halts come to seem discipline imposed by the time, like the night itself, and one sits and waits for the sign, the order, which will come at some point in the rite.

'Everything is changing,' I said, as the car sped on. 'Do you suppose that all the disasters and wars that he foresaw are going to happen?'

'It might be so,' said Mary. 'I never was sure that the last war showed he was a prophet, but that is only because I always thought that if his prophecies came true everybody involved in them would be dressed like the actors in a Shakespearian play, and move and speak like that.'

'I thought that too,' I said. 'How happy those days were. Wars and disasters, we knew no parallel to them. In our days they belonged to the past, like Shakespeare.'

'So I feel that if the war had been one of the wars that Papa foretold Richard Quin would have worn doublet and hose when he went out to be killed.'

'And been followed by a circle of limelight,' I said, 'and spoken his farewells in blank verse.'

The memory of him suddenly grew strong. He stood tall between the houses, he was the distance at the end of the avenue.

We halted at another traffic light. 'Do you think they are really finished, that it is all going to break up?'

'I don't really,' said Mary. 'We have only Shakespeare to go by, and according to him they have a long way to go, their end is not in this play. What they say never sounds like the things his people say when their story has gone wrong for good. You know, like Desdemona when Othello has gone out after he has been cursing her as a strumpet, and Emilia asks her how she does, and she answers, "Faith, half asleep," and you know it is all over with her, there is no hope.'

'Or like Richard the Second when he says to his queen, "I am sworn brother, sweet, to grim Necessity,"' I said.

'Still, had we not better see if we have any money?'

'I never thought of that,' I said. 'Would you mind being poor again?'

'Well, we could sit and eat boiled eggs among our loot comfortably enough, provided we could pay the rates,' said Mary. 'But sometimes I remember how frightened Cordelia was of poverty, and I get frightened too.'

'We must ask Mr Morpurgo how much money we have,' I said.

'Wouldn't Oliver know?'

'Not a bit,' I said.

On that Mary made no audible comment, and I was annoyed. Her silence was asking, 'Was there no sense at all, then, in her getting married?'

I sent a cable the next morning and asked Oliver to get Mr Morpurgo to dine with us the second night after Mary and I got home. Then later in the day we sailed on the *Olympic*, and slept and read, and lunched on deck, rolled up in rugs with hot-water bottles, while the boat straddled the black-green walls of water, and dined in bed and read each other passages we liked out of our books. It perturbed me a little that our tastes were dividing. I could still read anything. Mary was rejecting more and more, she went back all the time to Wordsworth's *Excursion* and Paul Valéry's *La Jeune Parque*. I did not like it that we ceased

271

to be nearly identical. I was even a little sad when Oliver met us at Southampton and first kissed Mary and let her go on, and then took me in his arms, and told me, by the private centre of his public kiss, how much he had missed making love to me. As my mouth gave him my secret answer my eyes were on Mary as she moved forwards under the ugly lights of the Customs-sheds, in a black coat straight as a pillar with a round white fur collar, and a round white fur hat on her shining black hair. She was still like a girl; though we were passing into middle-age, she walked lightly and was alone. I longed to be with her, though I rejoiced at being in Oliver's arms. But then he drew back and looked at me a little sadly, and I knew that something horrid had happened while we were away.

He told us in the train. Miss Beevor had died in her sleep a week ago. She had had no suffering at all, and Cordelia had had tea with her the day before. 'It was all right,' he said, with surprised eyes, and Kate told us too without surprise, 'It was all right.' She took us into Miss Beevor's bedroom, which smelt of lavender and was very cold, and opened the chest of drawers and showed us parcels wrapped in tissue paper. 'Nothing was untimely about it,' she said, 'she left all her Christmas presents ready. And though that is a new cemetery up in North London, there are some fine trees. I would not take the first plot they offered us, oh, no, I winked at Mr Oliver and we went off without the man, and I found her a good place, better than I could have hoped for, close by a yew.'

'Is that good, near a yew?' I asked.

'Tchk, tchk!' she said, pained at the thought of all she had been unable to teach us. 'Yes, indeed, a yew is best.' She looked round the room and said, as if repeating a promise, 'I will leave it as it is, of course, for the full month.' We waved our hands at the emptiness about us and smiled and tiptoed out, and Kate shut the door softly, to suit a phantom's senses. As she went along the passage before us her skirts flapped desolately round her long legs, as if virtue had gone out of her starched petticoats. I asked her if she would like us to find another old person for her to look after, and she halted and gave me a queer glance as if I had failed to notice something under my nose. She thanked us for being so thoughtful, but no, that was not needed. The light in the passage shone strongly down on her tallness. If she had had a pigtail caught at the back of her neck with a black bow she might have been one of Nelson's sailors: her eyes looked past us at a far horizon, and her great hands were clenched, ready for the next chore. For her we were already at sea, on a new voyage. It was most likely that she was right.

'Any news from Miss Rosamund?' I asked. But there was none.

The next night Mr Morpurgo arrived with a briefcase full of files that would tell us how much money we had. Mary and I were waiting for him, one on each side of the fireplace, wearing dresses we had bought at Benoit Teller's, of pleated georgette, a material hardly ever seen now, like chiffon but warmer. It was the same dress in two different colours: hers was lime green, mine was in emerald. Mr Morpurgo liked them and put his arms round our waists and stretched his neck in an attempt to get rid of his rich Oriental chins and pouted at himself in the looking-glass over the chimneypiece, and complained, 'Now, me, I look older.' We laughed and kissed him but I had noted that the time had come when people told Mary and me that we were not looking any older. We had reached the middle term. The pattern of our lives was determined, we had only to work out the other half and make it symmetrical. To confirm this thought, which was not sad but solemn, I looked at our reflections, and it struck me that Mary looked much younger than I did, younger by far more years than she was my elder. I felt no envy but concern, as if I had recognised in her the first signs of a sickness.

'It is so pleasant that you are here,' Mr Morpurgo said to her. 'It is like old times.'

'Before I broke up the happy home,' said Oliver, from behind us, busy with the sherry.

'It is better than before,' said Mary, smiling, 'we are both guests, you will drive me home, and we shall say what was wrong with the dinner.'

'What was wrong with the room,' said Mr Morpurgo, looking round him tenderly.

'What was wrong with the host and hostess!'

'Alas,' sighed Mr Morpurgo, with his luxurious Jewish sadness, 'all is so right here, in the midst of – ' His voice died away.

'What exactly is happening?' asked Oliver, giving him his sherry.

'Ah, what do you think is happening?' sighed Mr Morpurgo.

'I don't know,' said Oliver. 'I'm still on the last movement of this symphony.'

'Well, what do you two girls think is happening?'

273

'People in America fall down and faint because they are starving and there is no unemployment benefit,' I said.

Mr Morpurgo wondered, 'Surely people are meant to know what is happening to them. Surely their consciousness should cover that area. Yet I do not know why it should. The clerks in my firm understand very little of our transactions. I class you with the clerks, they like you are specialists. It is only those of us who cannot specialise who get to the top in my business.' The parlourmaid told us that dinner was served and he grumbled along the passage behind us. 'It is terrible to think what would have happened if I had been a good book-keeper, but I was good for nothing at any process of banking. I served as apprentice in several offices and each of them reported that I was useless. I could not keep my mind on the ledgers, I covered them with blots while I reflected on what I had heard at the opera, seen at the museums, the bookshops, the botanical gardens. However, by large vague thoughts about man and the universe, I came to understand the large vague business that is banking.' I had ordered his favourite soup, cream of chicken à la Célestine, a curious soup with almonds in it, which in our house was faintly dusted with nutmeg. The chicken was put through a hair sieve with some boiled rice, it was a little less gritty than the ordinary bisque. He enjoyed the texture, he pressed his spoon down on the plate to make sure it was so, before he started eating it. 'My uncle detested this when I returned to England, he saw to it that in the course of time I became partner on terms which had consequences which did not appear at a first reading and gave me considerably more power than his own son, whose ledgers never showed a blot. You never heard of my cousin, did you?'

'No,' we answered.

'No,' he agreed blandly and finished the bland soup. 'He is much perturbed by the situation,' he told Oliver's back, as Oliver carved the young turkey.

'And you are not,' said Oliver.

'Yes, I am,' said Mr Morpurgo. 'All through the ages my uncle would have been doing a very sensible thing to choose me rather than my cousin as head of his firm, but at the moment neither he nor myself understands what we are to do if the world is not to go bankrupt.'

'Look, we have brought some wild rice to go with the turkey,' said Mary.

'Good girls, good girls,' said Mr Morpurgo. 'It is the one luxury I envy the Americans. Their terrapin they can keep, it is like some object removed surgically from nature, it is no exchange for grouse. If the world is not to go bankrupt, I was saying.'

'Why should it go bankrupt?' said Oliver. He was the only one free to go on with the serious talk; I was taking the claret from the chimneypiece, Mary was making the salad dressing.

'Because there are too many people in it,' said Mr Morpurgo. 'Too many people. The banking rot set in in Vienna, with the Boden Credit-Anstalt. That is a stupid situation. The Austro-Hungarian Empire fell, because there were too many people. It went very well when the population was small. The Austrians were able to rule Hungarians and Czechs and Croats and Slovaks when there were only the three hieratic cities, Vienna and Budapest and Prague, and outside only squires and peasants and the kind of little people that live in small towns. But then there were many more people, and there were many big towns, and they asked questions, as people do in big towns, and they all asked why they should be governed by the Austrians, and there was no answer, so the Empire dissolved. But Vienna remained, the huge institutions of Vienna remained, with no power behind them. The Viennese banks remained. But banking is power, banks without a nation behind them are a dream, they end, they play politics, they gamble, they crash.'

'Have you everything?' said Oliver, sitting down at the table.

'Yes, I have everything, and everything is perfect,' said Mr Morpurgo. 'Here I eat much better than at home. My daughter Zoe keeps house for me since her divorce, she engages chefs that give me palace food, things that lie in state in aspic, and taste of nothing.'

'But why should America have a crash because Vienna did?' said Mary.

'Because the American structure was ready to fall before a breath of wind,' said Mr Morpurgo. 'That too is a matter of there being too many people. A stock exchange is only a valid institution if the community which buys stocks and shares is compact enough to know the value of the commercial and industrial institutions behind those stocks and shares, and the professionals who sell stocks and shares know that their customers have this knowledge. Otherwise the buyers will pay prices which are simply fairy tales told in an abbreviated form. But, my children, there is only one thing wrong with this evening.'

'Oh, you do not like the wine,' I said. 'Mary thought you might think it a little past its best, but Oliver and I think it is at its perfection.'

'No, the wine is delicious, though it is on the edge, Mary is wrong today but she will be right tomorrow. It is not anything of what I am eating or drinking that worries me. It is what you are wearing.'

Mary and I cried out in distress. 'Oh, we thought the dresses were so pretty.'

'Yes, they are pretty, but there is something wrong. Oliver, can you not see that there is something wrong?'

Oliver stared but shook his head.

'What, you married Rose, and you cannot see what is wrong? That I find extraordinary. Call Kate, and see if she had noticed anything.'

When Kate came and heard what was wanted of her, she clicked with her tongue and smiled rebuke at Mr Morpurgo. 'I would have brought it home to them in time,' she said, 'but this first time I did think they might be allowed to have it their way. You might at least have let them have their dinner out!'

'But what is it?' we cried. 'Tell us, you must tell us.'

'Why, you each are wearing the dress that would suit the other better,' said Mr Morpurgo. 'Oliver, do you really not see that? Kate, you saw it at once.'

'Yes, indeed,' said Kate, 'but their Mamma noticed that, they often favoured what suited the other, it was as if they were so close together that they mistook each other.'

'But what is wrong?' asked all three of us.

'Why, Mary should be wearing the emerald dress, it would look well with her black hair and her white skin, the lime green looks vague on her,' said Mr Morpurgo.

'And the lime green would look beautiful on Miss Rose,' said Kate. 'It would go so well with the brown in her hair.'

'Why, that is true!' Oliver exclaimed.

'We are mortified, for like all women we think we have perfect taste,' said Mary.

'But what asses we were!' I cried. 'Shall we go up now and change?'

'You were always the one to rush at things, Miss Rose,' said Kate. 'Look how Miss Mary is going on quietly with her dinner.'

'The question is, what is there to follow?' said Mr Morpurgo.

'A ginger ice,' Kate told him.

'That can wait,' said Mr Morpurgo. 'They can change at the end of this course. I would like to see them as they should be, it will be worthwhile.'

Oliver's brow clouded and I said, with some coldness, 'It will not take a minute.' Celia must have moved very slowly, for Oliver was always expecting me to take twice as long as I needed for the simplest actions. He never went on to the next stage and said to me, 'Rose, how quick you are.'

'But wouldn't you,' he asked Mr Morpurgo, still not on the level of intelligence where I would have wished him, 'rather get on with dinner?'

'No, not at all,' said Mr Morpurgo. 'Even such a minute adjustment takes us a stage nearer the ideal universe.' Between mouthfuls, sometimes pausing to inhale the bouquet of the claret, he told us that the distress of America might be considered relevant to the question of whether we three ought to be aware of what was happening to us or not, for that distress did not proceed from the material conditions in America, but from the failure of Americans to form an accurate estimate of these material conditions. 'America,' he said, 'has just as many acres of wheat, just as many cattle and hogs and just as many mines and quarries and sources of hydro-electric power as she had before the crash. The present American misery was of the same sort that in the past has usually been caused by an actual failure of crops or plague among beasts or men; it is caused by the tendency of Americans to over-estimate the dividend that can be yielded by this capital. Alas,' he breathed, and laid down his knife and fork. 'Alas, that the dream is over, that slice of turkey, that wild rice, that cranberry sauce, cannot be eaten all over again. Now go and change your dresses.'

'Then you are not really worried over the situation?' Oliver asked him, rising to open the door for us.

'I wonder why you should think that?' said Mr Morpurgo.

I did not let Mary go out of the room, I was anxious for her to hear what I had to say. 'Oliver thinks,' I told Mr Morpurgo, 'that because you liked the turkey and the claret and are making a fuss about our dresses that you cannot be worried. Stupid,' I told Oliver, 'it is when he feels things are all wrong that he likes to get what he can right. He is like you in that. He grows all these flowers in his gardens because so much of the rest of the world is a slag-heap.'

Oliver looked down at me with a faint smile, hoping I was

right, but not sure. He was always making mistakes about other men because he believed that they were male in some forthright and uncompromising way that he was not, in a way, that was, indeed, not discernible in any man we knew. He expected that a banker who had made a great fortune in the City would respond to a financial crisis by becoming inflexible and thinking and talking of nothing but figures, and presently arriving by logical steps at a conclusion which averted that threat. Yet he knew that such concentration is by instinct practised only on technical problems, that the act of composition flows through the whole day, in and out of consciousness, which it often permits to occupy itself with other matters; and surely he must know that our practical brothers, when they were as great as Mr Morpurgo, knew such a merging of the essential and inessential, only to be ended when the tug of the moon brought the sea back to its bed. But in the straightness of Mary's back, as she went out of the room and up the stairs before me, I could see that she was ascribing Oliver's misapprehensions to superficiality, that she was wondering, as I knew she had wondered many times before, why I should have married him. I would have liked to cry out to her that she was being unjust to Oliver because she disapproved of marriage so deeply that she must pick a hole in any husband that spoiled whom she loved, but we were in the middle term of life, it no longer seemed necessary to discuss fundamentals, we might perhaps get on with as much of them as we had worked out already. But in the bedroom when we stepped from our coloured dresses her body in her white slip was so stern in its slimness that it seemed to be declaring a law, and I wanted to dispute her judicial power, and to tell her that Oliver knew all we both knew, that he was not literal, that he was aware that the intellect has not anatomised the universe, that the soul and the body recognise connections not yet systematised. But the instance of his awareness which came to my mind, a dent in the pillow on our bed recalled it to me, was not for telling; when he received a letter from Jasperl, or worse still one of those letters that were sometimes written to him about Jasperl, and the nature of evil was made clear to him by some gross example of destruction, he found great pleasure in making love to me, he came to me for refuge but he ended by giving me reassurance, and of that great pleasure the core was his joy in a blue vein that crossed my left breast. I was separate from my sister indeed. I was gentle to her and slipped

278

her dress, that had been mine, over her head with a caress, because I had deserted her, and she was as gentle to me, with kindness that brought tears to my eyes because it came from her delusion that Oliver was a fool, she had deserted me. Who should I think of but Rosamund, who, when she had been with us, had welded everyone? Yet I could not think of her for long. Since I had known love the profanation of love that she must know forbade my mind to rest on her in happiness, even in longing.

'It is strange that we wear the same size of dress,' I said, as we smoothed ourselves and combed our hair, 'you look so much slimmer.'

'You are round, and I am flat,' said Mary.

'Nonsense,' I said. 'You could never pass yourself off as anything but a mammal.'

'Yes, but I seem to have thought of it just at the last moment, you give indication of it long before you get to the point.'

'You're getting near the sort of thing Cordelia might say!'

'Oh, no! Oh, no!' She really minded me saying that. She had always been more afraid of Cordelia than I was.

'Silly, I didn't mean it, if I had meant it I wouldn't have said it. Come on. I told him we would only be a minute.'

'Yes, yes.' I hurried so that my husband should see I moved more swiftly than Celia, she hurried to save me from losing face before a stranger.

Kate had come into the dining-room and Oliver was asking her nervously whether the ice would not melt, and she was telling him that Mr Morpurgo liked his ice half melted, and would not be sorry if we were another ten minutes upstairs. She had known that there was less need to help Mary and me to change than to reassure Oliver, always hounded by fear when Mr Morpurgo was our guest. It was again this belief of his in the inflexibility of the successful man, who would keep to a timetable, who would accept standards, who would want to eat an ice as soon as it was brought into the dining-room, who would feel obliged to eat it hard because cooks always freeze ices till they are hard. Oliver, who would put his nose against the window to watch a bird while the soup was cooling, he who liked things never to be so hot nor so cold as when they were served, believed that he had these brothers born without caprice. It is something, I believe, that is instilled into boys at public schools, they are sent to boarding-schools so that they do not see in adolescence (which is the most critical time of life) how unstable and whimsical men are and grow discouraged by seeing what they must become; and so they never have any opportunity to see what men are like until they are men themselves, and therefore unwilling to admit their own defects. Absurd, absurd! I could not help laughing, and Mr Morpurgo rebuked me.

'Rose, no mannequin should laugh. You never free yourself from your relationship except at the piano. Mary is right, she is there in her dress, apart as a star. And now, Oliver, you see that Kate and I are right.'

Oliver saw. His eyes rested on Mary with the total admiration he would have bestowed on an object in a museum, they passed to me with the readiness to find fault that he would have shown towards his own image in a mirror. But he found little fault. Smiling he said, 'Of course, if one had never seen them but simply listened to their gramophone records, one would have known the emerald for Mary, the lime green for Rose.'

'They have everything,' said Mr Morpurgo, 'except the preternatural brilliance of eye their mother had. But that would not have been appropriate in their faces.'

'Every one in the family is different,' said Kate. 'No two alike. These two are not like their mother, nor their father neither, nor is Miss Cordelia.'

'Nor was Richard Quin,' said Mary.

'They are archetypes,' said Mr Morpurgo. 'Now let us have the ice. Ices should not be such that polar bears should be able to live on them, huskies to draw sledges over them, but they should still recall the arctic. They are archetypes, all of the family into which you have married, being universal they have also to represent the universal quality of uniqueness. Each is different, because each child that is born is different. You are right, just right to serve Monbazillac with this ice.' He lifted up his voice and cried sometimes through the spicy ice, sometimes through the perfumed wine, ' "The streams of the earth shall be turned into pitch, and the ground thereof into brimstone, and the land thereof shall become burning pitch. Night and day it shall not be quenched, the smoke shall go up for ever. From generation to generation it shall be waste. None shall pass through it for ever and ever. The cormorant and bittern shall possess it, and the ibis and the raven shall dwell in it; and a line shall be stretched out upon it to bring it to nothing, and a plummet into desolation." '

For the savoury we had tiny little cheese soufflés, one for each of us. 'What horrible noises I shall make in my stomach as I go home. When one is old one is Lear but the blasted heath is outside one. Words, words,' he said, 'one can do anything with words. "And thorns and nettles shall grow up in its houses, and the thistle in the fortresses thereof, and it shall be the habitation of dragons and the pastures of ostriches." Isaiah could make one believe anything. "And demons and monsters shall meet, and the hairy ones shall cry out one to another. There hath the screech owl lain down and found rest for herself." But it is nonsense. But we may take it. Isaiah takes it all back in the next chapter. I suspect him of being a disagreeable man. There is no zest in his destruction of salvation. This prodigality which your wife and her sister proclaim in their uniqueness would send in creatures that shall kill the thorns and nettles and by the excess of flowers that spring up under their tread, that shall pension off dragons, bridle the ostriches, teach demons and monsters to play various instruments, persuade the hairy ones to sing melodiously, and convert the screech owls to an audience and charge them a stiff price for admission. No brandy, thank you, but a Benedictine. I am an Edwardian and we were great drinkers of Benedictine. "A line shall be stretched out upon it to bring it to nothing, and a plummet into desolation." Oh, it shall not be so.'

'But the world will come to an end some day,' I said.

'Not like that,' said Mr Morpurgo.

'Oh, the actual end of the world will not be like that, I know,' I agreed. 'It will be splendid. But first there will be the thorns and the nettles and the thistles, and the hairy ones will cry out to one another. That cannot be avoided.'

'Mad grasses,' said Mary, 'how good that tough way of saying weeds is. But one can stay indoors, and against the hairy ones one must stop one's ears.'

'No, one must listen to what they are saying,' said Oliver. 'They conspire against us. They would about this Judgment Day to which my dear wife seems to be looking forward with such anticipation.'

'Surely it must come whatever the dragons and the demons and the monsters do,' said Mary. 'Anyway I mean to shut my windows. And, Morpy, please have we any money?'

'It is all in that brief-case I left in the hall,' said Mr Morpurgo.

'But can't you tell us now?' I asked.

'Oh, darling, I don't expect it is as simple as all that,' said Oliver, again obsessed by his idea of this other maleness, which by being inflexible and insisting on timetables and acceptance of standards created a complicated universe about itself.

'No, there is no reason why I shoud not tell them now,' said Mr Morpurgo, he was always willing to betray his own sex to women, it was his pasha-like nature. 'Putting the little I know about your affairs, Oliver, together with my complete knowledge of Rose's affairs, I think this household is on a sound basis, and I am sure that Mary has no reason to be anxious. I invested the money their mother got from the family pictures very fortunately, and I have been as lucky in investing their savings. I wish Rose would save a little more.'

'I do not waste money,' I objected.

'Nobody really does that,' he conceded. 'It is very hard to imagine an action that falls into that category except lighting one's cigarette with a five-pound note. It is almost impossible to spend money without getting something for it. Even if it gives one only a momentary satisfaction that is something for which only a miser would be unwilling to spend money. Nevertheless, the fact that you have never really gone without anything you wanted since you were a grown woman might, if you considered it carefully, have some effect on your conduct. And remember, dear Rose, that you and Oliver have a more expensive household to keep up than Mary who is, now that she lives in her water-tower, in the position where I would like Rose to be. If Mary were unable to give another concert she would be able to go on living exactly as she does now, on her income from her investments, and even still save a little, to make her income larger in the case of a rise in prices. Rose could not do that. She will have to save quite a bit more in the next two years than she has been saving before she is in the same position.'

'But this is extraordinary,' said Oliver. 'You must have had great difficulties in doing this for them, sir. For they're both horribly careless about money.'

'Horribly careless,' said Mr Morpurgo, 'and horribly lucky. I really should make no effort to control them in the actual handling of the money, apart from suggesting that they do not spend it like drunken sailors. But the idiot whom you married left ten thousand dollars in a San Francisco bank; she forgot about it for two years, she then remembered it suddenly in the

282

worst period of the depression and got the banker to buy some stock for her at bargain prices. I think in ten years that stock will be worth a small fortune in itself. If she had invested the money at once, as I have taught her, she would have made not a fraction of it. Oh, leave them alone, it's really safer.'

AFTERWORD

by

Victoria Glendinning

There will be no sequel to *Cousin Rosamund*. It represents unfinished business.

Rebecca West left the continuation of her novel *The Fountain Overflows* in a typescript dating probably from the late 1950s, and part of it was published the year after her death as *This Real Night*. The remainder constitutes about two-thirds of this third volume of the saga of the Aubrey family. After her death her secretary, the novelist Diana Stainforth, found manuscript notebooks which advanced the story beyond the point where the typescript ended, and at the request of the author's executors she typed up and added on all this material; the break comes, imperceptibly, in the middle of the visit to Barbados Hall. Rebecca West always revised her work considerably before producing a definitive typescript, and presumably would have done the same for the last third of *Cousin Rosamund* had she been willing and able to see her great project through. Nevertheless there is such fierceness and freshness in the drafted later section that one cannot regret what she might have considered as its lack of polish. In the account of Rose's marriage to Oliver we have, in addition, the only explicit writing about sexual pleasure in the whole of Rebecca West's published work to date.

When in 1956 she sent *The Fountain Overflows* to her publishers, she said that she thought the total work would make four full-length novels. The next two were finished, she said, 'except for the final revision'. She hoped to reach the end of the whole sequence by the end of that year.

The end was never written, though she went on adding to the manuscript for another decade. She wrote to a friend, 'I think some of what I'm doing is nearly beyond me, though I thought of it, which isn't fair.' She had however written out a long synopsis of 'Cousin Rosamund – a Saga of the Century'. By far the fullest account is given, in this synopsis, of the material she had already used in *The Fountain Overflows*; and it might be helpful here for readers who have come to *Cousin Rosamund* without having read *Fountain*, or not for a long time:

Piers Aubrey is the disgraced son of an Irish landowning family, who is a reincarnation of Edmund Burke, for all intents and purposes. He is a political thinker of a Conservative type, and a very vigorous political pamphleteer; and he is hopelessly given to gambling on the Stock Exchange and to borrowing from all his friends and admirers. He has married a Scottish woman pianist of great talent, named Clare Keith, and has lived with her for some years in South Africa, during which time they have four children, Cordelia, Mary, Rose (who tells the story) and the one son, Richard Quin. Piers loses his post in South Africa, again and again, and comes to Scotland as the editor of an Edinburgh paper, and he loses that post too. When *The Fountain Overflows* begins Clare Aubrey takes her family, who are still small children, to a farmhouse on the Pentland Hills, outside Edinburgh, while her husband goes off to find a house in Lovegrove, a suburb of South London, where he has been given a job as editor of the local paper by Mr Morpurgo, a wealthy Jew who has a great admiration for him but who refuses to see him any more because of various unfortunate incidents. Aubrey sends his wife no news of what he is doing, and drifts off to Manchester on some financial adventure which comes to nothing. Clare finds when she goes to Edinburgh to arrange for the removal of her furniture to Lovegrove that Piers has sold all of it that is of any value (which was her property) in order to pay some of his debts.

Clare and her children start off for Lovegrove knowing nothing except that a house has been taken for them. They find that Piers has persuaded his cousin Ralph to lease him a house he owns in Lovegrove, at which Piers had spent part of his childhood. As Clare and the children go into the house they find Piers there, scraping at the wall-paper over the chimneypiece in the drawing-room. He explains there was a painted panel there but leaves it as it was, and takes the children round the house and the stables and tells them of his childhood. There then develops the story of the conflict between the husband and wife. He represents the pessimism of the nineteenth century, and its sense of doom; she represents the artist who continues to function in any time or climate. She has realised that two of the children, Mary and Rose, are pianists of great talent and she teaches them her art, while at the same time keeping the home together against innumerable threats. It is unfortunate that the eldest girl, Cordelia, has no musical talent but insists on playing the violin and believes herself a genius; and she excites a wild passion in the heart of an elderly schoolmistress, Miss Beevor, who falls in love with her and thinks she is a genius, and insists on running her as an infant prodigy to the infinite distress of Clare and of Mary and Rose.

Clare has a cousin called Jock, who is an artist gone bad: a poet and a flautist, and also a successful business man. He has married a school-friend of Clare's, named Constance, and they have a daughter, a beautiful, apparently rather stupid little girl, with a stammer. Constance does not ask Clare to come to her house when she comes to London, though she lives not far from Lovegrove. Clare and Rose visit Constance one day uninvited, and find that her house is in the possession of a poltergeist. Nobody is ever quite sure whether this is a genuine manifestation of evil spirits, or whether Jock (who is a sort of Scottish Huysmans) is having a macabre joke with his family, as he dabbles in spiritualism and particularly rejoices in spurious mediums. But Constance and Rosamund behave with great stoicism. All the Aubrey family become devoted to Rosamund but her special friend is Richard Quin, the little boy, who is some years younger than she is.

The truth is that both Rosamund and Richard Quin have before them tragic destinies, and are dimly aware of them. Rosamund is going to die in Belsen, by her own choice, refusing to avoid a fate she foresees because she fulfils a divine purpose by her martyrdom. Richard Quin is going to be killed long before her, in the First World War, and his death is going to serve a peculiar purpose. There is no vulgar fortune-telling about this, they have a certain prophetic sense. Both are strongly sensuous, happy natures, and their martyrdom is hard for them to contemplate.

Rose goes to a children's party given by a school-fellow, Nancy Phillips, and becomes curiously involved with the family. Nancy's mother is a former barmaid, who has married a foolish business-man with some money and she has to live with her sister, Lily, a good-hearted simpleton. Later it breaks on the suburb that Mrs Phillips has poisoned her husband. Piers and Clare at once take in Nancy and Lily. The murderess is condemned to death, but there is an irregularity in her trial, of which Piers takes a very characteristic advantage, and gets her reprieved. Nancy is removed by her relatives, and the Aubreys do not see her again for years; but Lily, who goes as barmaid to a Thameside inn kept by her old friend, Milly, and her bookmaker husband, Len, remains a close friend of theirs.

Piers is becoming more and more pessimistic; and he falls into disrepute as a lunatic, because he foresees the rise of Fascism and the two World Wars. He sinks into melancholia, and after one last bout of gambling which leaves his family nothing, he leaves the house one night. The wall-paper over the chimneypiece, which he was scraping with a knife when they first came into the house, is now torn away and a cupboard is disclosed. Inside is string and paper which suggests that there was a cache of valuable jewellery belonging to the members of his family who previously occupied this house. The Aubrey children and their mother are broken-hearted by the loss of their father, and they go off to spend the day in Kew Gardens. In a hothouse where they have gone to look at an especially beautiful creeper, Clare confesses to her children that after all they are not destitute. In their bedrooms there have always hung what are supposed to be three copies of family portraits of three beautiful women, one by Gainsborough, one by Lawrence, the third by a minor artist. These pictures are in fact originals. They were left to Clare by a member of the Aubrey family who realised her plight as a gambler's wife. She has always pretended to Piers they were copies because she feared that he would sell them, and she felt that she must keep them as a guarantee of her children's safety if in the end he should desert her. But she is wretched, for she loves Piers so much that she cannot help reproaching herself for not giving them to him.

The children assure her that they cannot blame her, but they are obviously interested parties; and the situation is not solved until Rosamund, who is by now just waiting to go into a children's hospital as a nurse, tells Clare how desperately frightened all the children are by their state of insecurity. This is in fact the truth, but the children do not know it. They then go on to face life without their father, but with the money derived from the sale of the family pictures. Now Clare takes Rose and Mary to a famous piano-teacher in London, who thinks well of them and prepares them to take scholarships at two London Schools of Music. Cordelia, still obstinately playing the violin, insists, with Miss Beevor's connivance, in going to play to a famous violin-teacher. He tells her brutally that she is a bad violinist and she goes back to the house in Lovegrove and makes an attempt at suicide. When her mother and her sisters and brother break into her bedroom to save her she says, 'But how am I to get away from you all if I do not become a famous violinist?'

Her sisters are deeply hurt. But the mother explains to them that whereas they have not minded poverty and social ostracism their eldest sister has hated her situation, she has not enjoyed a moment of the childhood that has struck them as exciting. Rosamund and Clare together treat Cordelia as an invalid, and Rosamund turns her mind to feminine things, with an art that is wholly concealed. Rosamund has the ruthlessness and cunning that have been remarked in any saints. Meanwhile Rose and Mary go on and get their scholarships, and have their first professional engagement. On that occasion Rose takes fright, she suddenly feels that she will never play so well as her mother, that she is an inferior human being to her father and mother. She wants to take to her heels and run away. But she is carried on into the concert room, 'perhaps by the strong flood of which she was a part'.

There *The Fountain Overflows* ends. Rebecca West had relatively little to say in her synopsis about the next section:

> The subsequent volumes show Mary and Rose becoming famous pianists, Rosamund becoming a nurse, Cordelia making a conventional marriage, and Richard Quin, after a promising youth, becoming an officer in the First World War and being killed. Shortly afterwards Clare [their mother] dies. Mr Morpurgo has meanwhile become a close friend of the family and proves to be a lonely and doubtful man, distressed by the flight of his family from their Jewish origins. Mary and Rose and he rely more and more on the companionship they found in the Thameside inn, where Lily is a barmaid, for Len proves to be a remarkable person, a natural scientist.

She may not have envisaged the complexities into which these developments would lead her, for this briefly summarised material became a whole book – published in 1984 as *This Real Night*.

Now we come to the part of the synopsis that deals, also rather briefly, with what has become *Cousin Rosamund*:

> Nancy leaves the uncle and aunt who have looked after her and comes back to Lily, and at the Thameside inn she meets a young science master and marries him, and has children. Suddenly all these people are distressed because Rosamund makes what seems a horribly mercenary marriage with a Lavantine financier of dubious morals. This is a great grief to Mary and to Rose, because Rosamund was all that their art did not give them – she was, in fact, religion. She fades entirely out of their lives. She lives in Germany, and when Hitler comes to power they think she and her husband are bound to leave the country. But they stay there, and Rose and Mary mourn her as one totally lost to them. Perpetually they feel the lack of what she gave them. Rose marries a composer, who nearly gives her what Rosamund gave her, but not quite. Mary shocks her very much by retiring and playing simply for her own pleasure as soon as she has enough money – this seems to her an

offence against art, she feels her sister would not have done this if Rosamund had still been with them, and if she had been what they thought her.

Cousin Rosamund, as published, stops just short of Mary's decision to abandon her career as a concert pianist; this last scene was rather sketchily drafted in manuscript, and Rebecca West's publishers decided not to include it. But Mary's withdrawal from painful human contacts and the public gaze is crucial to the novel, in the light of what happens to Rose.

Like its predecessors, *Cousin Rosamund* is richly documented in period detail, and lyrical in its evocation of the Thames riverscape (the stretch between Cookham and Maidenhead) which, at the Dog and Duck, represents a haven of security for the girls. There are unforgettably theatrical set-pieces in this novel too, such as the party in the gardens at Carlton House Terrace – a morality play under spotlights – and the pillaged dinner-table in the Parrot Room at Barbados Hall. The corruption of wealth is a constant theme in this book.

But the real subject of *Cousin Rosamund* is marriage, and the resolution of Rose's problems about sex – which include the ambiguity of her own sexuality, and that of others. Homosexuals, who teem in this book, confuse the issue for her; Lady Tredinnick, unhappy about her own sons' inversion, looks like 'a man dressed up as a woman'; Rose herself may be 'too male' to perform a delicate piano work. She and Mary love no living persons so much as they love each other and Rosamund – but Rosamund, the 'moral genius' whom they rely on to mediate between themselves and the universe, bewilders them by her incomprehensible marriage to a millionaire vulgarian.

Rose and Mary find it impossible to love anyone who does not belong to the magic circle of their irrecoverable childhood. Their secret Christmas together in the Chicago hotel is like a return to that lost time, a luxurious regression. 'We are by nature children.' Yet everyone is getting married. Cordelia is safe with Alan. Nancy marries her Oswald, and even Rose has to acknowledge the 'holiness' of their contented mediocrity. Queenie, the gaunt murderess, is redeemed, astonishingly, by the passion of fanatical Mr Bates. Rose understands the power of love – 'the choice that is made by something deep down in one which will not be satisfied by anything else' – but neither she nor Mary will consider it in relation to themselves.

Rose seems on the edge of breakdown throughout much of *Cousin Rosamund*. In Nancy's marital bedroom she feels frighteningly alienated, almost suicidal. She feels personally responsible for Queenie's crime, as if she were infected with the 'darkness' that she connects with her aberrant father. The darkness threatens to overtake her; her crisis comes in chapter seven, where she finds herself 'loathing' Oliver's masculinity, imagining the 'pollution' of sex with violent disgust, and breaking down completely with Mr Morpurgo at the Dog and Duck. In her conflicted state she longs to do what Mary, less vital than she, will in fact do – abandon her career, withdraw from the world into childhood memories, small nursery sensualities, and the safe company of the few who knew her as a child.

But 'there is no substitute for sex', as Mr Morpurgo says. Rose, after her collapse, recovers and allows herself to love Oliver. The resolution of her crisis is conveyed with brilliant poetic economy, in a single sentence:

> He came towards me and I became rigid with disgust, it seemed certain that I must die when he touched me, but instead, of course, I lived.

Rose finds herself ecstatically fulfilled by sexual love. One could wish that Rebecca West, who often wrote sharply about the ways in which men and women fail one another, had written more frequently about happy physical love, since she does it with unusual grace and candour. But there is a price to pay for everything; Rose's new life separates her a little from her old alliances. 'I could not explain to Mary that when Oliver and I were lovers it was as important as music.'

We have left them at the end of *Cousin Rosamund* on the threshold of middle age. It is 1929, the year of the economic crash, and the western world will soon be overtaken by the darkness of the coming war. Rebecca West wrote no more of her novel sequence. Having 'settled' most of her surviving characters in their maturity, and having personal and professional problems of her own, she perhaps could not face the great unsettling that her conception of their destinies required. The last line of *Cousin Rosamund*, as published here, maybe sums it up: 'Oh, leave them alone, it's really safer.'

There was a technical difficulty, too. The story, as outlined in the synopsis, is not picked up until after the Second World War. If she filled in the years between 1929 and 1945, the problem of length might have become overwhelming. In the final book she was planning to draw on her experiences of the Nuremberg war tribunals, which she had reported in her capacity as a journalist. This is the synopsis of that last, unwritten volume:

The Second World War breaks out. At the end of the war Mary and Rose are called to Germany because an Englishman has been arrested, who has been engaged in treasonable activities during the war and has before that been living as a criminal in Berlin, and who claims to be Richard Quin, saying he had deserted in the First World War. Cordelia, who never trusted her brother, has identified this man as Richard Quin. But Mary and Rose know that he is not; and they have a long conversation with him in which he turns out to be a brother-officer of Richard Quin, who had a slight resemblance to him, and who had been kindly treated by him. In that conversation he puts the case for being evil. They leave him, and are distressed to find that the Intelligence Officers take Cordelia's word and not theirs, and that this scoundrel will go down in the records as their brother. In a state of great distress they go on their way through Germany, and stop near Nuremberg to make an official visit, and are taken to the Nuremberg trial. From the evidence given by a witness they realise that Rosamund is a woman who died in Belsen Camp, and as they look back through the past they realise that all she did was planned to the one moment described by the witness, when she appears as doing a deed of unique mercy. They also perceive that Richard Quin's last days and death were designed to be an answer to the arguments for evil which were put forward by the fraudulent officer, and that he and the fraudulent officer are engaged in a contest which is being carried on still, though their brother is dead, and that their brother will win, and that the staining of his name is of no consequence to him.

The impostor is, of course, Gerald de Bourne Conway, the young man Rose and Mary met with Richard Quin at the beginning of the war in *This Real Night*.

In an important last paragraph, Rebecca West spelled out what the work as a whole meant, for her:

The point is that Mary and Rose represent all that can be got out of art, all that art can do: which is not everything. There is something else, the work of the spirit, which was done by Rosamund and Richard Quin. But because they moved on a higher plane than Mary and Rose, Mary and Rose could not understand what they were doing, as Cordelia could not understand what Mary and Rose were doing. There is also a sense throughout the book that what Rosamund and Richard Quin did was the more visible, the more essential to Mary and Rose, because the world was passing through a phase of disintegration.

The strength of her conception, and of its partial realisation, is its prodigious combination of narrative detail, psychological insight, social documentary, humour, and realisation of character (Queenie, Lily, Len, Miss Beevor or Nestor would stand up well against Dickens's more eccentric creations). She was prepared to take on board both the world of the senses and 'the work of the spirit'. The moral tone is given by the controlling myths of all Rebecca West's life and work: the strange necessity of art, and art's limitations; and the struggle of light against darkness, good against evil – exemplified here by social injustice and war, and confronted, in microcosm, within families and within the conflicted minds of individuals. The abiding vision is of hope through love. Rebecca West's unfinished novel sequence would have constituted her most public and her most intimate personal statement. Perhaps that's the real reason why she could not complete it.

Fic Cat